The Dedalus
Book of Russian
Decadence

Perversity, Despair and Collapse

Edited by Kirsten Lodge
Poetry translated by Kirsten Lodge
Prose translated by Margo Shohl Rosen
with Grigory Dashevsky

Dedalus

LOTTERY FUNDED

Published in the UK by Dedalus Ltd
24–26, St Judith's Lane, Sawtry, Cambs, PE28 5XE
email: info@dedalusbooks.com
www.dedalusbooks.com

ISBN 978 1 903517 60 4

Dedalus is distributed in the USA by SCB Distributors,
15608 South New Century Drive, Gardena, CA 90248
email: info@scbdistributors.com
www.scbdistributors.com

Dedalus is distributed in Australia by Peribo Pty Ltd.
58, Beaumont Road, Mount Kuring-gai, N.S.W. 2080
email: info@peribo.com.au

Dedalus is distributed in Canada by Disticor Direct-Book Division
695, Westney Road South, Suite 14, Ajax, Ontario, LI6 6M9
www.disticordirect.com

First published by Dedalus in 2007

Printed in Finland by WS Bookwell
Typeset by RefineCatch Limited, Bungay, Suffolk

ABOUT THE EDITOR

Kirsten Lodge (Ph.D., Columbia University) is currently working on a book on decadence in central and eastern Europe. Her collection of Czech decadent poetry in English, *Solitude, Vanity, Night*, is forthcoming. She is also the author of *Translating the Early Poetry of Velimir Khlebnikov*.

ABOUT THE TRANSLATORS

Margo Shohl Rosen has published her translations of Russian literature in *The London Review of Books, American Poetry Review*, and most recently, *Lions and Acrobats: Selected Poems of Anatoly Naiman*.

Grigory Dashevsky, a professor of Latin at Moscow University, is a poet and a translator from English, French and German. His translations into Russian include Fr. Yates's *Giordano Bruno and the Hermetic Tradition*, Z. Bauman's *Freedom* (both from English) and Hannah Arendt's *Men in Dark Times* (from English and German).

DISCLAIMER

Despite the best endeavours of the editors, it has not been possible to contact the rights holders of the texts in copyright. The editors would be grateful, therefore, if the rights holders could contact Dedalus.

Contents

This collection is dedicated to Oliver Lodge.

Acknowledgements

I wish to express my gratitude to Ilya Vinitsky, who introduced me to Oliver Ready in 2004, thus initiating the chain of events that led to the publication of this anthology. I am thankful to Oliver for putting me in touch with Eric Lane at Dedalus Books, and to Eric for his enthusiastic support of the project from its inception. Thanks also to B. Tench Coxe for his suggestions for both the poetry and prose translations, and Grigory Dashevsky for carefully checking the translations of the poems against the originals and offering his comments. The translators are deeply indebted to Simon North for diligently combing all of the texts for Americanisms, Emily Mitchell for her assistance with colloquial British English in "Moon Ants" and "The Sting of Death," and Craig Beaumont for acting as our consultant on British English. We also wish to acknowledge Frank Miller's aid in rendering torture instrument vocabulary into English. Of course, we are fully responsible for any remaining deficiencies in the collection.

Kirsten Lodge

Introduction

The depravity and despair of decadence that burgeoned in France in the latter half of the nineteenth century had gripped all of Europe, including Russia, by the century's close. Originating in the superbly refined and subtly perverse poetry of Charles Baudelaire, Stéphane Mallarmé and Paul Verlaine and finding its quintessential expression in Gustave Moreau's sensual paintings of Salomé dancing for the lecherous King Herod, decadence gained widespread popularity in France in 1884 after the publication of Joris-Karl Huysmans's novel *Against Nature*. *Against Nature*, which became known as "the breviary of the decadence," gives expression to the movement's fundamental tenets: that modern-day civilisation is in decline, that reality as it exists is contemptible, and that the decadent hero, who is neurotic and sexually deviant, must create an alternative world for himself alone. Des Esseintes, the main character of *Against Nature*, retreats to a house outside of Paris, where he has his surroundings constructed in accordance with his whims. The cabin of a ship, for instance, is built within his dining room, and he spends hours sitting inside it, watching mechanical fish swimming in an aquarium placed between the porthole of the cabin and the dining room window, so that the water subtly changes hue with the varying sunlight. He can thus pretend to be travelling and enjoying nature without having to deal with the annoyances and ugliness of reality. This image of pseudo-sailing exemplifies the decadent cult of the artificial: artifice for the decadents is superior to nature.

At the turn of the century decadence flourished in the work of Russian writers of various schools: hence this anthology groups Leonid Andreyev, who frequented Maxim Gorky's

Realist circle, and Alexander Kondratiev, who did not consider himself part of any school, with the other writers included here, who identified themselves primarily as Symbolists. Symbolism derived from the same French models as decadence, but it emphasised different thematic and stylistic concerns, evoking the poet's inner world or a mystical world beyond our own through suggestion and the use of poetic symbols. More ambitious than their French counterparts, many of the Russian Symbolists hoped to transfigure the fallen world, which they found execrable, either by the power of their own creative will or with divine aid. However, their mood would vacillate from yearning for a miracle to black despair, and this is when they would enter into the decadent mode. In this collection, this sense of hopelessness after faith in an imminent miracle is most evident in the poetry of Zinaida Gippius and Alexander Blok. If the world could not be transformed, the alternative was to withdraw from it. For the decadents there were several ways to escape from deplorable life: these included the creation of art or an artificial environment, sexual deviation, madness and suicide. The authors included in this collection dramatise these various alternatives.

A powerful will is necessary to create an ideal environment, and the decadents' worship of the will is related to their stance of extreme individualism. In the late nineteenth and early twentieth century, it was widely believed that European civilisation was in decline, or "decadence": that is, society was becoming increasingly fragmented. It was no longer unified by higher values, such as religion. Individuals were becoming increasingly isolated in an age of declining morals. Many deplored this fact, while others upheld individualism as a positive principle. Commentators frequently compared their age to the final days of the Roman Empire and predicted imminent collapse. Decadents also looked back to the Roman Empire for inspiration and found it not only in images of decay and decline, but also in the dramatic personalities of the cruel Roman emperors, whose every whim became reality. They became prototypes of glorified egoism, with their unbridled cruelty, perverse pleasures and excessive indulgences. Decadents often took individualism to the extreme of solipsism. Valery Briusov is a case in point. He believed that the individual could truly know nothing outside of himself—his own thoughts, feelings and desires. For Briusov it is even impossible to be certain that the outside world actually exists. The confusion of dream or fantasy and reality is thus central to many of his stories, including "Now That I'm Awake . . ." (1902).

In this dramatic tale of demonic savagery, egoism merges with sadism as the narrator gives full reign to his cruel fantasies—at least within an environment he believes to exist only in his imagination. He asserts that he has always preferred dreams to reality, and boasts that he has learnt to control his dreams. Above all, he likes to torture people in his dream world, never relinquishing control of the narrative of agony. However, the line between dream and reality becomes blurred: this is the diary of a psychopath.

"Art" and madness are likewise closely linked in Fyodor Sologub's first published short story, "Light and Shadows" (1894). In Sologub's story, young Volodya discovers art as a means to escape from the monotonous reality of school and the useless lessons he is forced to learn. After finding a booklet giving directions on how to make shadow figures on a blank wall, Volodya soon masters the examples provided and begins to create his own, more complex figures. He is driven to indulge in these creations at the expense of his schoolwork and even his health. Like a writer, he invents narratives, personalities and feelings for his figures. Soon, however, they take on their own, independent reality. He senses their unbearable sadness, and he is overwhelmed. Volodya's obsession is contagious: his mother, too, begins to make shadow figures secretly in her room, and shadows soon start to pursue her as well.

Sologub is more optimistic about the power of art and the artist's will in some of his poems. In "My tedious lamp is alight . . ." (1898), for instance, he prays for inspiration to create the perfect work, which will grant him immortality.

The artist, he implies, has the potential to become a deity, and the creative will can work miracles. In "For me alone my living dream . . ." (1895), he imagines the sadomasochistic world of his dreams, established by force of will, and full of revelry, sex and whipping. The artist's will is omnipotent, capable of transfiguring reality—or at least creating a second world within the realm of literature.

Of the various escape routes from reality, suicide is by far the most popular in these works by writers of a decadent bent. "O death! I am yours," Sologub exclaims in a well-known early poem, rejecting life as unjust and disdainful. In his story "The Sting of Death" (1903), two friends nurture an ever-growing attraction to death, which one boy depicts as a comforting, faithful and beautiful lover. The poetic register of his description contrasts sharply with the colloquial language of the rest of the story. In "The Poisoned Garden" (1908), seductive death is personified as a *femme fatale*. The Beautiful Lady of this stylised tale is herself like the poisonous, carefully cultivated flowers of her garden, flowers that recall Des Esseintes's attraction to horticulture and predilection for real flowers that appear to be artificial. This story demonstrates that Sologub shared with Oscar Wilde the decadent attraction to fairy tales as a genre divorced from reality. Within the fairy tale the writer is free to polish an artificial, archaic style and to use motifs and characters symbolically, without locating them within a specific historical context. The result is a stylistic gem sparkling with Beauty, Love and Death. At the same time Sologub's story, published shortly after Russia's failed revolution of 1905–07, is clearly concerned with class conflict. It is a rare example of a fairy tale mingled with Marxism, in which the main characters are revolutionary activists, each in their own way.

Charlotte of Zinaida Gippius's "The Living and the Dead (Among the Dead)" (1897) is repelled by the physicality of life. She is disgusted by the sickliness of her brother-in-law and nephew, and above all by the prospect of marrying a butcher. She is nauseated by the bloody carcasses, flesh and bits of bone that fill the butcher shop where her fiancé indifferently slices meat with a butcher knife. She prefers to spend time alone in her room, where she observes the cemetery through blue stained glass that softens everything she sees. The delicate blue glass, which she associates with the cemetery and death, contrasts with the red and yellow glass in her father's dining room—colours associated with the butcher shop. Fleeing the earthly world she despises, she dreams of the "light-blue world" of death, filled with peace and love.

Death is not always conceived in such mystical terms in Gippius's work. The narrator of her "Moon Ants" (1910) strives to comprehend suicide, only to conclude that it is impossible to predict or understand. People may attempt suicide for the most insignificant reasons, and they may not even know why they have decided to kill themselves. The narrator of "Moon Ants" is astounded at how many people have been killing themselves recently, and he is obsessed with the phenomenon, which he traces back to the failed revolution. Had life in Russia at the turn of the twentieth century become so harsh and hopeless that it unleashed an epidemic of suicide? The narrator of "Moon Ants" offers an alternative explanation: people have become weaker—so weak, in fact, that they kill themselves at the slightest provocation. Like the moon ants in H. G. Wells's novel *The First Men in the Moon*, they crumple up and die the moment they are touched.

It was widely believed at this time that humanity was degenerating. The theory of degeneration was a logical extension of Darwinism, which argued that evolution takes place in a natural environment. Proponents of degeneration theory such as Cesare Lombroso and Max Nordau reasoned that mankind was completely estranged from nature in modern society, and therefore removed from the life-threatening factors necessary for evolution by natural selection to take place. The comforts of urban life, they argued, were causing regression to earlier stages of development. Mankind was becoming weaker, sicklier and more prone to nervous ailments of all kinds. Nordau's *Degeneration* (1892), published simultaneously in two Russian translations in 1894, became one of Europe's bestsellers, fuelling popular fears with its warning of an epidemic of degeneration. The narrator of "Moon Ants" expresses similar qualms, imagining a plague of weakness and suicide to which he himself may fall prey. Many other stories in this anthology are also accounts of contagion leading to death. The contagion may involve the spread of ideas, as in "The Sting of Death," or of disease, as in Leonid Andreyev's "In the Fog" (1902). In addition, it was believed that asymmetrical facial features were symptomatic of degeneration, that it was hereditary and that artists were particularly degenerate; thus the irregular features Volodya and his mother share in "Light and Shadows" should be understood within the context of the European obsession with degeneration.

Andreyev treats the issues of lust and prostitution, which were considered to be symptomatic of degeneration, in the stories "In the Fog" and "The Abyss" (1902). In "In the Fog," Pavel's father, who, the author tells us, represents the prevailing views of his time, expresses his fear of "civilisation's darker side." He warns his son against phenomena typically associated with degeneration, including alcoholism and, above all, debauchery, which causes venereal diseases that lead to debility, insanity and death. Pavel, however, feels he has already been corrupted. His "filthiness" permeates his entire being like the yellow fog outside, and he can escape neither one. Like his sense of being corrupted, his view of women is also typically decadent: he is attracted to them, but at the same time overwhelmingly disgusted and horrified by them, and he believes them all to be hateful, vulgar and deceitful. His misogyny is reflected in the fact that he completely forgets women—whether his mother or a prostitute—the instant he turns away from them.

In "The Abyss," Andreyev shows what may happen when the veil of culture is suddenly lifted. A young couple on a walk, Nemovetsky and Zina, speak romantically of pure love and eternity until they are caught at dusk in a field among prostitutes and drunken men. An unfortunate incident entirely changes Nemovetsky's perception of the young woman, and he falls into the "abyss" of irrational, bestial instinct. Like "In the Fog," this story sparked controversy upon its publication; Andreyev's explicit treatment of the themes of prostitution, venereal disease and rape were considered scandalous by some critics, while others defended him for bringing to light moral problems that society must address. When Lev Tolstoy's wife berated Andreyev for depicting the most abject human degradation and slandering humanity in "The Abyss" rather than praising the miracle of God's world, Andreyev responded that civility is deceptive, and beneath it lies a beast straining to devour itself and every living thing around it the moment it breaks out of its chains. It is impossible, he wrote, to "slander" a humanity that has on its conscience such heinous crimes as those committed during recent imperialist wars. Several years later, Andreyev vividly portrayed the cruelty and madness of war in his novella *The Red Laugh*, inspired by the shocking bloodshed of the Russo-Japanese War of 1904–5.

In "The Story of Sergey Petrovich" (1900), Andreyev applies his skill in describing a character's psychological vacillations to an ordinary man who happens to have read some of Friedrich Nietzsche's *Thus Spake Zarathustra*. We have heard a lot about men who read Nietzsche and think they are supermen, but what about those who realise they are part of the herd? As Andreyev wrote in his diary about the story, Nietzsche teaches Sergey Petrovich to rebel against injustice—against nature and humanity.

Some of the writers featured in this collection had some hope for the future, though not necessarily for themselves. They sensed the imminent collapse of the culture they represented. In his programmatic 1894 poem "Children of Night," Dmitry Merezhkovsky, speaking for the generation writing at the turn of the century, proclaims that there is hope—but not for us. This generation will perish beneath the first rays of the sun that will shine for the new era that will replace it. Similarly, in the classic poem "The Coming Huns" (1905), Briusov's lyrical "I" welcomes the "barbarians" that are destined to destroy contemporary civilisation just as they had once razed Rome. The belief that history was cyclical was prevalent at the time: civilisations, it was believed, are born and age like human beings, only to die and be replaced by healthy fledgling societies. Contemporaneous civilisation awaited its "barbarians" with mixed feelings, as they represented both its death and the panacea for its "sickness." The speaker of Briusov's poem is resigned to his fate, prepared to collect the fragments of high culture and attempt to preserve them for future generations, retreating with them to caves like the early Christians. Briusov composed this poem at a critical juncture in Russian history, during the Russo-Japanese War of 1904–5 and the failed 1905 Revolution. After Russia's catastrophic defeat at the Battle of Tsushima in May 1905, in his correspondence Briusov likened the Japanese to the barbarians who brought down Rome, and this may be one reason the barbarians in this poem come from the East (the phrase "over Pamirs as yet unexplored" refers to the steppes between Mongolia and southern Russia). Another reason for their eastern origin is that the Mongols who ravaged Rus' in the thirteenth century had also invaded from the East. In the 1903 essay "The Triumph of Socialism," Briusov compared the revolutionary masses to barbarians as well; this is thus another significant subtext of "The Coming Huns."

In "The Last Martyrs" (1906), Briusov sets the victory of the revolutionaries, whom one of the characters explicitly calls "barbarians," in the future. In this story there is a clear division between the representatives of high culture and the "barbarian" revolutionaries. The narrator belongs to a sect that worships mysterious "Symbols," a detail that suggests the group is modelled on the Symbolist movement. Briusov's over-the-top description of their final orgiastic rites in the face of death, however, may be read as a parody of certain Symbolists' views, particularly those of Vyacheslav Ivanov, with his ideal of mystical communion through Dionysian celebration. The sectarians, like typical decadents, are highly sensitive, refined individuals who have dedicated their lives to luxury and the cultivation of their souls. In one character's words, they are "the hothouse flowers of humanity." In the view of the emissary of the revolutionaries, however, they are mere degenerates, and as such they must be mercilessly cut out of the body of society. The emissary thus reiterates Nordau's proposed solution to the problem of degeneration: the extermination of all those who are infected and thus weaken society. With great prescience Briusov condenses the cruel rhetoric of power against those it deems undesirable, a rhetoric strikingly similar to that of later Soviet and Nazi campaigns against those they labelled "degenerate."

Is it to this sort of violence that Briusov is referring when, in "The Republic of the Southern Cross" (1905), he mentions that the government takes "decisive measures in a timely fashion" to prevent the spread of the epidemic outside of the capital city? Indeed, such is the solution that Whiting and his followers attempt to implement in Star City. In any case, "The Republic of the Southern Cross" warns us that the advance of civilisation, even if it does not lead to its collapse at the hands of barbarians, may lead to barbarism nonetheless. Star City's overemphasis on reason, order and regulation, combined with its luxury and debauchery, contributes to the outbreak of a disease called "contradiction." The government's attempt to place total control over the population leads to the eruption of the repressed irrational, and in the end people are dancing around bonfires like cavemen, indulging in orgies and at each other's throats. This breakdown of order is reflected in a disintegration of style from an objective, distanced language typical of newspaper reporting throughout most of the work, to a more emotional and literary style in the description of the loss of the last vestiges of morality and law. Like Andreyev in "The Abyss," Briusov depicts the brute instincts of humanity lurking beneath the veneer of culture.

Alexander Kondratiev tells very different tales of aggression and rape. Unlike Briusov and Andreyev, he treats violation not as an act of brutality, but as a natural part of the mythical pagan world of gods and goddesses, who behave like satyrs and nymphs. His tales are comparable to the decadent writings of the French author Pierre Louÿs, whose novel *Aphrodite* was a bestseller in 1896, and whose work Kondratiev translated into Russian. Both Kondratiev and Louÿs are remarkable for their playful depictions of the sensuality of the ancient world. The decadents were attracted to the pagan gods because they associated them with the body and sensuality, free and naïve before Christianity fettered the passions. Just as Sologub's story "The Poisoned Garden" offers the reader a retreat from reality into the fantastic and beautiful world of the fairy tale, Kondratiev's myths draw the reader into a finely crafted and subtly perverse created world.

The stories and poems included here will give the reader an overview of decadence in Russian literature at the turn of the twentieth century, with its prominent themes of perversity, despair and collapse. Despairing of the state of society, wavering in their hope for a miracle, the Russian decadents had a vague presentiment of impending perdition. They expressed their sense of futility in stories of madness and suicide, and they took egoism to extremes in fantasies of sexual aberration. They found solace in art, which they worshipped as a cult, and they had a particular predilection for highly stylised, timeless genres such as the fairy tale and myth. The importance of Russian decadence has been underestimated, and it is hoped that this anthology, which includes many works never before translated into English, will bring it the recognition it deserves.

The Last Martyrs

Valery Briusov

An Undelivered Letter,
Consigned to Flames by the Executioner

Preface

This letter was written to me by my unfortunate friend,
Alexander Athanatos, several days after his miraculous rescue,
in response to my insistent urging that he should describe the
astounding scenes of which he was the sole surviving witness.
The letter was seized by agents of the Provisional Govern-
ment and destroyed as subversive and immoral. Only after my
friend's tragic death, when his remaining belongings were
delivered to me, did I find among his papers a draft of this
account, and still later I learnt what had happened to the letter
itself.

I believe that this faithful and—as far as I can judge—
dispassionate narrative of one of the most distinctive events of
the beginning of that momentous historical movement now
called by its adherents the "World Revolution" ought not to
be consigned to oblivion. Of course, Alexander's notes cast
light on just a small fraction of what happened in the capital
city on the memorable day of the uprising, but nonetheless,
for future historians they will remain the only available source
of certain facts. I believe that awareness of this circumstance
compelled the author to weigh his words with special care
and, despite his rather florid style, to remain within the
bounds of strict historical accuracy.

In conclusion, I cannot but express my gratitude to the
country that gave me refuge and my joy that there exists a
place on earth where freedom of the printed word has been

preserved, and where it is possible to boldly proclaim one's opinions without being obliged to extol the Provisional Revolutionary Governments.

I

You know that I, like so many others, was completely unprepared for the outbreak of revolution. True, there had been vague rumours that a general uprising was planned for New Year's Day, but the recent anxious years had taught us not to believe too much in such threats.

The events of that night took me completely by surprise. I wasn't planning to celebrate the New Year, and was peacefully at work in my room. Suddenly the electricity went off. By the time I got a candle lit, I could hear the wooden crackle of gunfire outside the window. We were all familiar with those sounds by then, and there was no mistaking it.

I got dressed and went out.

In the pitch darkness of the winter night I more divined than saw a heaving crowd of people on the street. The air was one continuous din of movement and voices. The nearby gunfire had not abated, and it seemed to me that bullets were hitting the wall just above my head. After each volley, joy at having escaped death flooded my heart.

But my desire to see for myself what was transpiring was greater than my fear. I hovered in the doorway of my building with a clutch of other dumbfounded spectators like myself. We exchanged terse questions. Suddenly, like a flood from a breached dam, a mass of people swept towards us, bowling along in panic-stricken horror with shouts and cries. I had no choice but to be swept along with them, or else be trampled.

I saw myself on Glory Square. The town hall was burning, and the light of its flames illuminated the surrounding area. It reminded me of a line from Virgil: *dant clara incendia lucem.*[1]

---

[1] Bright fires are giving light.

You know how big that square is. And now it was so full of people that one could hardly move. I think there must have been several hundreds of thousands of people there. Their faces, lit up by the flickering red flames, were strange, unrecognisable.

I asked many people what had happened. It was amusing to hear all the contradictory and absurd answers. One man said that the workers were slaughtering the wealthy. Another, that the government was exterminating all the poor to put an end to the revolutionary movement. A third, that all the buildings had been mined and were being blown up one by one. A fourth tried to convince me that this wasn't a revolution at all, but that there had been a terrible earthquake.

It was just then, when a good one quarter of the city's population was gathered on the square in front of that flaming building, talking, exclaiming and fretting, that the terrible event you read about in the paper took place. We heard the hollow rumble of a gun volley, a fiery line cut through the darkness, and a shell crashed down into the thick of the crowd. Wails rose above every other noise, immediately deafening, like a physical blow. But just at that moment a second shell exploded. Then another, another, and another . . .

A panicked ministry had ordered the commander of the Central Fortress to shoot into any crowds that gathered.

Once again the senseless stampeding began. Amidst the careering shrapnel of grenades, under the threatening rumble of gunfire pierced by the heart-rending cries of the wounded, people were rushing madly among the stone walls, trampling the fallen, beating anyone in their way with their fists, scrambling up onto windowsills, onto lamp-posts, again falling down and in their frenzy sinking their teeth into the legs of whoever was nearby. It was horror and chaos, a maddening hell. How it was that I finally ended up on Northern Boulevard, I don't know.

Here I met with a detachment of revolutionaries.

There weren't all that many of them, about three hundred,

not more, but they were an organised army within the tumultuous crowd. They were able to recognise one another by the red armbands they wore. Their measured movement put a stop to the flow of people. The mad flight ceased, and the crowd quietened down.

In the light of pitch torches that made the surroundings look strange and archaic, a man climbed onto the base of the statue of the North and signalled that he wanted to speak. I was standing rather far away, pressed up against a tree, and could catch only the general sense of his speech. The individual words died away before reaching me.

The speaker called for calm. He announced that the normal flow of life would not be disturbed and that no citizen was in any kind of danger. That what was occurring in the capital was occurring at that hour throughout the country: everywhere power was temporarily in the hands of militia units. That only a small number of people were to be executed—all who belonged to the overthrown government, "equally hateful to all of us," and that those people had already been sentenced by the Secret Tribunal.

In conclusion, the orator said something about the day that had been awaited for thousands of years and about the freedom of the people having finally been won.

In general the speech was of the most ordinary kind. I thought the crowd was going to throw that windbag to the ground, drive him away like a buffoon making jokes in a moment of danger. But instead I heard vehement shouts of approval from all around. The people, who a moment before had been wavering, confused and timid, were suddenly transformed into a whole army of irrational and self-sacrificing insurgents. They lifted the speaker onto their shoulders and began to sing a revolutionary hymn.

Then I suddenly felt I needed to be not in this crowd, but with people who thought as I did, with my closest friends. The image of the Temple arose in my heart, and I realised that the place of every believer that night was close to those Symbols our generation had made sacred.

I ran off down the boulevard as quickly as I could through

the moving crowd. Everywhere militiamen, preferring not to turn the electricity back on for the present, were lighting torches. Patrols went by, establishing order. Here and there I saw little rallies like the one at which I had been present.

Occasional volleys stuttered somewhere in the distance.

I turned onto dark Court Avenue, and finding my way among the labyrinth of old streets almost by intuition, arrived at the entrance to our Temple.

The doors were locked. The area was deserted.

I gave the pre-arranged knock on the door, and I was let in.

II

The stairs were weakly lit by a lamp.

Like shades in one of the circles of Dante's *Inferno*, people clustered and moved slowly up and down. The semi-dark made people speak in half-whispers. And beneath the low murmur of voices the presence of something terrifying could be felt.

I made out some familiar faces—Hero was there, and Irina, and Adamantius, and Dimitrius, and Lycius—everyone was there. We exchanged greetings. I asked Adamantius, "What do you think of all this?"

He answered, "I think it is an ultimatum. It is, finally, the collapse of that new world, which, counting from the Middle Ages, has existed now for three millennia. It is an era of new life, which will unify our entire epoch into a single whole with the Russo-Japanese War and Charlemagne's campaigns against the Saxons. But we, all of us who are caught between the two worlds, will be ground into dust on those gigantic millstones."

I went upstairs. The barely illuminated temple sanctuary seemed more enormous than ever. The far corners melted away into infinity. The Symbols of our service loomed mysteriously and eerily out of the murk.

Groups of people were scattered here and there in the

half-light. From somewhere came the sounds of women hysterically sobbing.

Someone called me. It was Anastasia. She was sitting on the floor. I sat down next to her. She took my hands, and she who had always been so reserved, even in the hours of our saturnalia, fell sobbing upon my neck, and said, "And so, all is finished, all of life, all possibility of living! Generations, dozens of generations have gone into the cultivation of my soul. Only amidst luxury am I able to breathe. I have to have wings, I can't crawl. I have to be above other people, I suffocate when there are people around me. My whole life is in those delicate, refined emotions that are possible only in the heights. We are the hothouse flowers of humanity; exposed to wind and dust, we'll perish. I don't want it, I don't want your freedom, your equality! I'd rather be your perfidious slave than a comrade in your brotherhood!"

She sobbed and made vague threats, clenching her little fists. I tried to soothe her, saying that it was too early yet to despair, that it was irrational to trust a first impression. The revolutionaries, naturally, were exaggerating their victory. Perhaps tomorrow the government would gather its forces and overthrow them. Perhaps the revolt had not succeeded in the provinces . . . But Anastasia wouldn't listen to me.

Suddenly there was a general stir. Many people stood up, others raised their heads. There was a gleam of light, and Theodosius appeared before the altar.

Two deaconesses in white surplices carried tall lamps before him, as always. He wore a snow-white tunic, with his long locks of dark hair flowing loose, and a calm, severe expression.

He took his place at the pulpit, raised his arms in blessing, and began to speak. His voice penetrated like wine to the depths of our souls.

"Sisters and brothers!" he said. "Behold the breaking of a joyous day for us! Our faith cannot die, for it is the eternal truth of being, and our approaching executioners themselves harbour its truth in their very essence. Our faith is the last

24

Mystery of the world, to whom all bow equally through all centuries and on all planets. But now the time has come for us to confess our faith before the ages and all eternity. It is given to us to take the communion of the supreme passion, the final communion before death. Remember how many times we whipped our bodies in a frenzy of sensuality, and how the pain doubled the pleasure of receiving communion. The death-blow will triple our ecstasy; it will magnify it ten times over. The death-blow will throw wide the gates of rapture, such rapture as you have never experienced, and it will dazzle you beyond anything you have ever known. Sisters! Brothers! The moment of our last union will penetrate our entire essence like a bolt of lightning, and our last breath will be a cry of untold happiness. O, last of the faithful, last martyrs for faith, I see it, I see crowns of glory upon your heads!"

I am certain that there was a hypnotic force in Theodosius's voice and gaze. Swayed by his influence, everyone in the sanctuary seemed transfigured. I saw ecstatic faces. I heard heroic exclamations.

Theodosius commanded us to sing our hymn. Someone sat down at the organ. The air rippled. The melody filled up the dark expanse, poured down among us, bound us all together in its irresistible net into one many-visaged being. Our great poet's verses burst forth instinctively from our lips, as the ocean instinctively roars in response to the call of the wind. We were the singing strings of a great orchestra; we were the voices of a single organ, glorifying the eternal Mystery and the creative Passion.

III

Somewhat later I was summoned to the Council of Acolytes. We gathered by candlelight in the usual Council meeting room. The divine frescoes on the walls were barely discernible. Theodosius presided over the meeting.

He summarised all that was known about the progress of the uprising. Our situation was hopeless. The entire army had gone over to the revolutionaries. All generals and senior officers had already been arrested and executed. The Central Fortress had been taken by storm. All government buildings—the palace, the parliament and the police stations—were occupied by the militia. News from the provinces confirmed the rebels' victory in every other city as well.

The question was posed: what should be done? The majority was for surrendering and giving in to the overwhelming force of the revolution.

Theodosius heard out these opinions in silence. Then he took a paper from a casket and invited us to examine it. It was one of Central Militia Headquarters' proscription lists. In it were named all the acolytes serving in the Council, myself among them. We had all been sentenced to death by the Secret Tribunal.

A bewildered silence fell. Theodosius said, "Brothers! Let us not lead our lesser brothers and sisters into temptation. If we allow all our faithful to know of this list, many will be troubled by doubt. They will wish to buy their own lives through betrayal and apostasy. By keeping it secret, we will give them the great honour of sealing the purity of their faith with a heroic death. Let us allow them to join together with us in our thrice-blessed fate."

Someone tried to protest, but weakly. Theodosius calmly put the paper with the names up to a candle and burnt it. We watched as the small scroll turned slowly to ashes.

Just then a deaconess knocked at the door. A representative from the militia's headquarters wished to speak with us.

In came a man, young, confident and self-assured. In the name of the Provisional Government he demanded that we disperse to our homes. The Special Committee, he said, was to examine the statutes of our religious union and determine whether it was a threat to public life.

We knew that these words were a trick—that we had already been sentenced. For a few moments all were silent. I remember the two speeches that followed—Theodosius's and the emissary's—by heart. In these two short speeches, two worldviews found full expression.

Here is what Theodosius said:

"The new government speaks its deceitful words to us in vain. We already know that everyone who is present here has been sentenced by the Secret Tribunal to execution. We know that you have already judged our sacred faith an immoral sect. But we do not accept your power and your court. We live on heights of consciousness such as you have never achieved, and therefore it is not for you to judge us. If you are even but a little familiar with the cultural life of your homeland, take another look at those gathered here. What do you see? You see the flower of our time—your poets, your artists, your thinkers. We are your mouthpiece, we are the voice of the wordless, eternally silent whole that is the sum of individuals like yourselves. You are darkness; we are the light born from it. You are the possibility of life; we are life itself. You are the soil that is necessary and right only because we, the stems and blossoms, grow from it. You call upon us to disperse to our homes and wait for your proclamations. We demand that you carry us to the palace in your arms and, kneeling before us, await our commands."

You know Theodosius. You know all his shortcomings: his hypocrisy and pusillanimity, his petty vanity. But at that moment, as he gave the last sermon of his life, he was truly great and splendid. He seemed a biblical prophet, speaking to the rebellious people, or an apostle during the first days of Christianity, somewhere in the bowels of the Coliseum, amidst a crowd of martyrs about to be led out to the arena to be torn apart by wild beasts.

And here is how the herald answered Theodosius:

"So much the better, if you know your fate. The experience of millennia has shown us that there is no place in the new life for ancient souls. They are a lifeless force that has always destroyed all of our victories up until the present day. On this day of the world's great transformation we are resolved to make the necessary sacrifices. We will cut out of our body all the dead, all those unfit to be born anew, with the same suffering, but also with the same pitilessness with which one cuts off an infected limb. Why do you lavish praise on

27

yourselves for being poets and thinkers! We have enough strength to give rise to a whole new generation of sages and artists, the like of which the earth has never seen, the like of which you cannot even begin to fathom. He who is afraid of loss has not the strength to create. We are a creative force. We have no need of anything old. We renounce all heritage, because we ourselves will forge our treasure. You are the past, we are the future, and the present is the sword we hold in our hands!"

The room buzzed. Everyone was talking at once. I, too, could not resist shouting, "Yes! You are barbarians without any predecessors. You despise the culture of the ages because you don't understand it. You boast of the future because you are spiritually impoverished. You are the shot that brazenly shatters the marble of antiquity!"

Finally, the emissary from the militia's headquarters said in an official tone, "In the name of the Provisional Government I give you until today at noon. By that time you must open the gates of your temple and surrender into our hands. By doing this you will save hundreds of people from a senseless death—people you have lured here through trickery and temptation. That is all."

"And if we don't submit?" asked Lycius.

"We will destroy this building to its very foundations with our weapons, and you will all be buried beneath the rubble."

The emissary went out.

"Destroy the temple!" repeated Lycius. "Our temple, the best of Leander's architectural creations! With its statues and paintings by the greatest masters! With our entire library, the fifth greatest in the world!"

"My friend," replied Adamantius, "for them our art is no more than archaeology. For them it is not all that important whether their museums will hold a dozen superfluous antiquities or not."

Someone expressed regret that we had let the emissary go alive. Theodosius reined in the speaker.

"We are here," he said, "in order to spill our own blood, not that of others. We are here for the heroic deed of faith, not for murder. Let us not mar the crimson purity of our martyrdom with the black wings of wickedness and revenge."

IV

The rays of the dawning winter's day shone weakly through the heavy curtains.

Our temple was magnificently illuminated by the light of all our candles. I had never seen such a festival of lights. There were perhaps several thousand flames.

Theodosius commanded us to celebrate the liturgy.

Never before had he been so majestic. Never had the voice of the chorus sounded so solemn. Never had Hero's naked beauty been so blindingly dazzling.

The censers' intoxicating smoke caressed our faces with wispy, cloud-like fingers. The great rituals were performed in a dark-blue, transparent haze of incense before the Symbol. Naked youths, according to their rank, removed the veil from the holy of holies. The invisible choir of deaconesses glorified the Occult Mystery.

The fragrant, searingly sweet wine, only barely inebriating, aroused trembling throughout the body, and agitation in the soul. The awareness that this moment was unique, never to be repeated, was inspiring.

And now Hero, in golden sandals, with a single gold serpentine belt about her waist instead of clothing, went forth with twelve sisters garbed likewise, and their silent circle dance wended along the length of the temple. And the magical sounds of the organ and the harmonic, mysterious singing captivated all as she passed, riveting our gaze to her smooth undulations.

Imperceptibly, insensibly, instinctively we were all drawn into the silent circle dance after them. And this circling was more intoxicating than wine, and the movement was more enrapturing than caresses, and the celebration of the service was loftier than any prayer. The rhythm of the music grew faster, and faster grew the rhythm of the dance, and with

29

outstretched arms we sped onward, in a circle, after her, after the unique and divine Hero. And now we were carried away with exaltation, we panted and gasped for breath, inflamed with a mysterious fire, and now we trembled through and through in the shadow of the godhead.

Then Theodosius's voice was heard: "Come, all you faithful, to make the sacrifice."

Everyone stopped, froze where they were, motionless. Hero, once again standing near the altar, ascended the steps. Theodosius gestured for a youth, whom I had not noticed until then, to approach. Blushing, the boy threw aside his clothing and stood by Hero, naked as a god, youthful as Ganymede, fair as Balder.

The gates opened up and swallowed the couple. The curtain closed.

On our knees, we began to sing the hymn.

And Theodosius spoke thus to us: "It is done."

He lifted the chalice and blessed us.

Ecstatic sounds gushed from the organ and we could no longer restrain our passion. And we fell on one another, and in the sudden dusk of smoky incense lips sought lips, arms sought arms, and bodies other bodies. There was intimacy, intertwining, unity; there were shouts and groans; there was pain and ecstasy. There was the intoxication of a thousand-visaged passion, when you see around you every image, every form, every possibility of celebration, all the contortions of women's, men's and children's bodies, and every possible distortion of faces transfigured with frenzied rapture.

Never, never again have I or has anyone else experienced such passion, such insatiable desire, as we flung ourselves with abandon from body to body, into double, triple and multiple embraces. And we had no need of the flagellants, who on that day were, like everyone else, seized with the ecstasy of passion.

Suddenly, apparently in response to some sign, the heavy curtains that had been covering the windows parted, and the whole interior of the temple was opened to the view of those outside it: everything, including the image of the Symbol, the mysterious frescoes on the walls and the people scattered around in strange combinations on the soft rugs.

The sounds of enraged shouting reached us from outside.

Immediately the first ringing shot pierced the mirrored glass. After the first came more. Bullets whistled by and bored into the walls. The militiamen hadn't been able to bear the spectacle revealed before their eyes, and could no longer wait for the appointed hour.

But it was as if no one heard the shots. The organ, beneath unseen hands, continued its seductive song. The aroma of incense undulated in the agitated air. And in the clear light of day, as earlier by the light of sacred candles, the passionate celebration continued unabated.

And now Hero, before any of us, suddenly staggered where she stood in the gates of the altar and, lips distorted in pain, fell down. Here and there people paused; a second, and a third, and yet another body sank down, as if in final, utter exhaustion.

A terrible slaughter began. Bullets fell among us like rain, as if gigantic hands were throwing them down upon us by the fistful. But none of the faithful wanted to run or voluntarily disengage from their embraces. Everyone, everyone—even the worthless, even those of little faith, became heroes, became martyrs, became saints. The horror of death was banished from our souls, as if by a magic word. We sealed the truth of our faith with our blood.

Some of us fell, slain. Others, near the fallen bodies, clung ever closer to one another, breast to breast. The dying were still struggling to complete the caress they had begun with a final frenzied kiss. Weakening hands were outstretched in languorous passion. In the pile of writhing bodies it was impossible to tell who was caressing, who dying. Amidst the shouts and cries it was impossible to distinguish passionate gasps from the moans of the dying.

Someone's lips were still pressing against mine, and I felt the pain of an ecstatic bite that might have been a paroxysm of death agony. In my arms I still held someone's body, grown cold from rapture or death. Then a heavy blow to the head felled me as well to the heap of bodies, to my brothers and sisters.

The last thing I saw was the image of our Symbol. The last thing I heard was Theodosius's cry, echoing a thousand times not beneath the temple vaults, but in my own soul's endless passages, now flooding with darkness:

"Into your hands I commend my spirit!"

Oh, cover your pale legs!

Valery Briusov, 1895

Presentiment

My love is like a sultry Javan noon
Drenched in noxious scents, as in a dream,
Where lizards laze with heavy lids
And boas coil round the trees.

And you entered the inexorable garden—
For respite, or for sweet delight?
Flowers tremble, grasses pant,
Everything intoxicates and blights.

Let's go — I'm here — we'll luxuriate,
Weave orchid wreaths, play, embrace,
Our bodies clinging like a pair of greedy snakes!

The day will fade. Your eyes will close.
That will be death. And I will entwine
Your immobile form in a shroud of vines.

Valery Briusov, 1894

Messalina

Burning with desire, in Rome
I did not find passion,
So I summoned slaves from the Danube lands,
I summoned wild Dacians.

To my chambers, one by one,
My eunuch led all three,
But his efforts were in vain,
They could not satisfy me!

I felt cramped in my bed,
So I wandered around the palace,
And I came upon an unknown room,
Where your bed stands.

Your robes on the floor,
You slept, perfectly limber,
All downy, tenderly naked,
Like coral, and flax, and pearls.

My boy, my boy! Be brave!
In the silence of the night we are alone:
Nestle your compliant body against me,
Press your loins close!

There is passion as yet untapped
In your perplexity . . .
Let me fall upon your breast,
All will be revealed in ecstasy . . .

Quiet, quiet! Soon, soon!
Our executioner is near!
Oh, no more strength to feel or see . . .
My boy, my boy, let me dry your tears . . .

Valery Briusov, 1903

Now That I'm Awake . . .

Valery Briusov

The Diary of a Psychopath

Of course, ever since I was a child people have thought me perverted. Of course, I have always been assured that no one shared my feelings. And I got used to lying, used to giving hackneyed speeches about compassion and love, about the happiness of loving others. But deep in the recesses of my heart I was convinced—and I remain convinced even now—that man is criminal by nature. It seems to me that among all the sensations that are called "pleasures," there is only one worthy of such a name—the one that overcomes a man as he contemplates another's sufferings. It is my belief that man in his primitive state can lust for just one thing—the pleasure of causing pain to others. Our culture has reined in this natural drive. Centuries of servitude have inculcated in the human heart the belief that it is hard to bear another's torments. And now people weep quite sincerely over others and sympathise with them. However, this is but a mirage and a sensory illusion.

One can make a certain mixture of water and spirits such that within it olive oil will balance wherever it happens to be positioned, neither floating to the top nor sinking down. In other words, gravity will cease to act upon it. Physics text-books tell us that then, obeying only the force inherent in its own particles, the oil will form a ball. Similarly, there are moments when the human soul is freed from the force of its gravity, from all the fetters imposed upon it by heredity and upbringing, from all the external influences that ordinarily condition our will: from fear of judgment, from the dread of public opinion, and so forth. In these moments our desires and

37

deeds submit only to the primitive, natural inclinations of our own being.

These are not the hours of normal sleep, when our daytime consciousness, even if somewhat dimmed, still continues to maintain authority over our sleeping "I"; nor are they days of insanity, of madness: these are times when other, even more despotic influences take the place of ordinary ones. These are moments of that peculiar state when our body rests in sleep, and knowing this, thought secretly alerts our spirit as it wanders in the world of reverie, "You are free!" Having grasped that our deeds will exist only for our own selves, that they will remain undiscovered by all the world, we voluntarily give ourselves over to the original impulses issuing from the dark depths of our own will. At such moments, at least in my case, never once has the desire arisen to do any kind of good deed. On the contrary, knowing that I would remain completely and utterly unpunished, I have always made haste to do something wild, vicious and sinful.

I have always considered—and continue to believe—that sleep is as legitimate a state as waking. What is reality? It is our impressions, our feelings, our desires, nothing more. All of this is present in sleep as well. Sleep fills the soul just as much as reality does, it agitates us just as much, or makes us happy or sad. Deeds done by us in dreams leave just as deep an impression on our spiritual being as those done in a waking state. In the end, the only substantial difference between reality and dreams is that for each individual person his dream-life is his own and apart, while reality is the same for everybody, or at least is considered to be the same . . . From which we can conclude that for each particular person dreams are a second reality. Which of the two realities is preferred—dreams or waking life—depends on one's inclination.

Since childhood I have liked dreams better than reality. Not only did I not think time spent sleeping wasted, but quite the contrary—I always begrudged the time waking life took away from sleeping. But of course in sleep I always sought life, that is to say, dreams. Even as a boy I considered a night without dreams a severe deprivation. If I happened to wake up without remembering my dream I felt miserable. I would rack my brain all day, at home and in school, until I found a fragment of the forgotten images in some dark recess of memory, and then suddenly my renewed efforts would bring forth that recent dream life in all its vividness. Greedily I would delve into that resurrected world and recall to memory all its tiniest details. By training my memory in this way, I became skilled enough never to forget a single one of my dreams. I always waited eagerly for night and sleep as for a rendezvous with a lover.

I especially loved nightmares for the astoundingly strong impressions they made. I developed in myself an ability to provoke them artificially. All I had to do was fall asleep with my head positioned lower than my body, and almost instantly the nightmare would clutch me in its sweetly agonising claws. I would wake up from an inexpressible torpor, gasping, but hardly had I taken a breath of fresh air before I rushed to fall back in, into the black pit, into the quaking and horror. Monstrous faces appeared all around from the murk, and monkey-like devils went to war against each other, suddenly falling upon me with horrible cries, knocking me down and smothering me; my temples throbbed, it was painful and terrifying, but so unspeakable that I was happy.

But even more I loved, from early on, those states in sleep when you know you are sleeping. It was then, too, that I grasped what great freedom of spirit these states yield. These I could not summon at will. While dreaming, I would feel something like an electric shock and immediately find that the world was now in my power. I would walk along the roads of dreams, their castles and valleys, wherever I wanted. By exerting my will I was able to see myself in whatever situation I liked, and could bring into my sleep-state anyone I had ever fantasised about. In my earliest childhood I used these moments to play jokes on people, indulging in all kinds of pranks. But with the passing years I went on to other, more esoteric joys: I raped women, committed murder and became a torturer. And only then did I realise that ecstasy and rapture are more than empty words.

The years passed and the days of being a student and a subordinate were now over. I was on my own, with no family, and with means enough that I was not obliged to work in order to secure my right to breathe. I now had the chance to give myself over completely to my happiness. I spent the better part of the day in sleep and somnolence. I used various narcotics: not for the pleasures they promised, but in order to make my sleep longer and deeper. Experience and habit allowed me to revel in the most unfettered of freedoms, a freedom man dares only to dream of. Gradually my night-time consciousness in these dreams became similar in strength and clarity to my waking consciousness and, perhaps, even began to supersede it. I was able both to live inside my reveries and to contemplate that life from without. It was as if I observed my spirit committing this or that act in my dream, and I had control over it while at the same time I experienced everything it felt with a full measure of passion.

I created for myself the best possible environment for my dreaming. It was an expansive hall somewhere deep underground, lit by the red flame of two enormous furnaces. The walls, apparently, were of iron; the floor, of stone. It had all the usual instruments of torture: a rack, a stake, spiked chairs, contrivances for stretching muscles and for disembowelment, knives, tongs, lashes, saws, red-hot pokers and rakes. Whenever good fortune gave me my freedom, I almost always headed straight off for my secret hideaway. By channelling the intensified energy of my desire, I brought whomever I wanted into this underground refuge, sometimes people I knew, but more often those born in my imagination, usually adolescent girls and boys, pregnant women, or children. I indulged myself with them like the most powerful despot on earth.

With the passage of time I grew to have favourite types of victims. I knew them by name. Some enticed me with the beauty of their bodies, others by the courage with which they bore the greatest of tortures, the contempt they had for all my sophisticated devices; and yet a third group lured me, on the contrary, by their very weakness, their lack of will, their moans and vain pleas. Sometimes—indeed, quite often,

I would compel victims I had already tortured to death to be resurrected so that I could take pleasure yet again in their excruciating demise. At first I was alone as both torturer and witness. Then I created for myself a band of disfigured dwarves for helpers. Their number grew according to my desire. They would hand me the instruments of torture, and they carried out my orders, guffawing and grimacing. In their midst I celebrated my orgies of blood and fire, shouts and curses.

No doubt I would have remained bizarre, solitary and happy. But the few friends I had, judging that I was ill and close to going mad, decided to save me. Almost by force they compelled me to go out, to attend theatre performances and to socialise. I suspect that they purposely set about presenting a certain girl to me in the most attractive possible light, and she later became my wife. But in fact, a man could hardly be found who would not consider her worthy of worship. All feminine and human charms united in this one woman whom I came to love, whom I so often called my own and whom I will never cease to mourn every day for the rest of my life. And to her they depicted me as an unfortunate wretch, a miserable man who needed saving. She was curious at first, and quickly became most fully and selflessly devoted.

For a long time I couldn't even entertain the thought of marriage. No matter how powerful this feeling that for the first time in my life enslaved my soul, still I was horrified at the idea of losing my solitude, the solitude that permitted me to indulge freely in my dreams. Nonetheless, the proper life to which I was being constrained gradually obscured my consciousness. I sincerely believed that it was possible for my soul to undergo some sort of transformation, that it could disavow its secret, inadmissible truth. On my wedding day my friends congratulated me as if I had emerged from the grave into daylight. After our honeymoon my wife and I got settled in our new, bright and happy home. I convinced myself that I was interested in world events and the local news; I read the newspapers and kept up my friendships. I relearnt how to keep awake during the day. At night, after the frenzied caresses of two lovers, the sleep that came to me was usually dead and flat, without distant horizons, without visions. In my brief moment of blindness I was ready to rejoice in my recovery, my resurrection from madness into normal daily life.

But of course the desire for other raptures never—oh, never!—completely died away inside. It was only muted by all too palpable reality. And in the honeymoon days of the first month of marriage, somewhere in the secret recesses of my soul I felt an unquenchable thirst for impressions that were more dazzling, and more devastating.

With the passing of each new week this thirst tormented me more and more importunately. And along with it another importunate desire began to grow, one I was hesitant to acknowledge even to myself: the desire to bring her, my wife, whom I loved, to my night-time feast and to see her face distorted from the tortures inflicted on her body. I struggled, for a long time I struggled, trying to maintain my sobriety. I would try to convince myself, using all the arguments reason could produce, but I myself did not believe them. I sought diversions and did not let myself remain alone, but in vain— the temptation was inside me and there was no escape.

And finally I gave in. I pretended I had undertaken a substantial project on the history of religion. I put wide couches in my library and began to shut myself up there for the night. Somewhat later I began to spend whole days there as well. I kept my secret from my wife every way I could; I shuddered to think she might penetrate the secret I guarded so jealously. She was as dear to me as she had been before. Her caresses delighted me no less than in the first days of our life together. But I was drawn by a more powerful passion. I couldn't explain my behaviour to her. I even preferred her to think that I had ceased to love her and was avoiding relations with her. And in fact she did think so, and became downcast and weary. I saw how pale and weak she was getting—that sorrow would soon take her to the grave. But if, giving in to impulse, I uttered some banalities about love, she would revive, though only momentarily: she was unable to believe me, because my words and my deeds seemed so contradictory.

But although I now spent almost entire days and nights in sleep, as I had before, giving myself over to my dreams even more wholeheartedly than I had prior to my marriage, I had somehow lost my former ability to find my full freedom. For entire weeks I remained on my couches, waking up only to fortify myself a little with wine or bouillon, or to take another dose of sedatives, but the longed-for moment never came. I would experience the sweet torments of a nightmare, its magnificence and mercilessness, I could recollect and string together rows of various dreams, some quite logical and terrifying precisely because of that triumphant logic, some wildly incomprehensible, ravishing and splendid in the madness of their combinations—but my consciousness remained clouded by a sort of pall. I didn't possess the power to control my dreams; I was compelled to hear and observe what was being conveyed to me from somewhere outside, by someone else.

I resorted to every method and means I knew: I deliberately cut off my circulation, I tried hypnotising myself, I used morphine and hashish and every other sleep-inducing drug, but they yielded only their own particular charms. After the agitation provoked by the demon of India poppy, the sweetest exhaustion would set in, the feeble rocking of a sleepy ship on a boundless ocean constantly generating new visions from its waves. . .but those images would not obey my adjurations. Awake again, I would recall with fury the long series of pictures that had unfolded before me, tempting and alluring, but prompted not by my caprice and disappearing not by my will. I would become exhausted from rage and desire, but I remained impotent.

As I recall, more than six months passed between the time I first resolved to return to the interrupted rapture of my visions and the day when my most cherished happiness was restored to me. In my sleep I suddenly felt that electric shock I knew so well and immediately found that I was again free— that I was asleep, but I had the power to control my dream; I could do whatever I might desire, and it would all remain just a dream! A wave of untold rapture flooded my soul. I couldn't resist the old temptation: my first step was to look for my wife right away. But I didn't wish for my underground hideaway. I preferred to be in the environment to which she had grown accustomed and which she herself had arranged. This was a more exquisite pleasure. And just at that moment, in the alternate consciousness of dreams, I saw myself standing at the doors of my library.

"Let's go," I said to the spectre of myself. "Let's go, *she* is sleeping now, and take along a slender dagger, the one with the carved ivory handle."

Obeying, I set off on the familiar way through unlit rooms. It seemed to me that I was not walking, moving my legs, but flying, as always happens in dreams. As I went through one room I saw through the windows the roofs of the city and I thought, "All this is in my power." The night was moonless, but the sky glittered with stars. My dwarves eagerly started to crawl out from under the sofas, but I made the sign for them to disappear. I silently pushed the door ajar. The icon lamp lit the room well enough. I stepped over to the bed where my wife was sleeping. She seemed so helpless lying there, so small and thin; her hair, plaited for the night in two braids, hung over the bed. Next to the pillow lay a handkerchief: she had been crying as she went to bed, and had cried herself to sleep again waiting for me. A kind of sorrowful feeling clutched my heart. In that moment I was ready to believe in compassion. A fleeting desire to fall upon my knees before her bed and kiss her chilled legs came over me. But just then I reminded myself that this was all a dream.

An astonishingly strange feeling came over me. I could, finally, realise my secret fantasy, do everything I wanted with this woman. And all of it would remain known only to me alone. And in reality I could cover her with ecstatic caresses, comfort her, love and pamper her. . . Bent down over my wife's body, I squeezed her throat with my strong hand, so she couldn't cry out. She woke up immediately, opened her eyes and thrashed about with all her might under my hand. But I had her pressed tightly to the bed. She flailed all around, trying to push me away, trying to get some words out, looking at me with panic-stricken eyes. For some moments I looked into the dark blue depths of those eyes, and I was filled with untold excitement. Then suddenly I stabbed this woman in the side with my dagger, underneath the blanket.

I saw her whole body shudder; she reached out, still unable to scream, but her eyes filled with tears of pain and despair, and tears ran down her cheeks. And warmish, sticky blood dripped down the hand that held the dagger. I stabbed her slowly at first, then I tore off the blanket and stabbed her naked body as she fitfully tried to cover herself, to stand, to crawl. Oh, how sweet and horrible to cut up the supple curves of her body, and to completely entwine it—her beautiful, tender, beloved body—with scarlet ribbons of wounds and blood! Finally, seizing my wife by the head, I plunged the dagger into her neck, through it, behind her carotid artery, then gathered up all my strength and cut her throat. Blood gurgled up as the dying woman attempted to breathe; her hand vaguely grasped or brushed at something. And then she remained motionless.

Then such a staggering despair enveloped my soul that I urgently struggled to wake up that instant, and I couldn't. I exerted all my willpower, expecting that the walls of the bedroom would suddenly disintegrate, recede and melt away, that I would see myself on my couch in the library. But the nightmare didn't pass. My wife's body, bloody and disfigured, lay before me on the bed, covered in blood. And people with candles were already crowding the doorway, people who, hearing the sounds of a struggle, had rushed over, and their faces were distorted with horror. They didn't say a word, but all of them looked at me, and I saw them.

It was then that I realised that what had happened this time had not been a dream.

For me alone my living dream
Will raise a marvellous kingdom,
Where ecstasy and suffering
Miraculously will mingle.
I'll adorn my court
with unclad beauty
And I'll sate my gaze
With pages' nudity.
The radiant beauty
Of naked girls
And my own nude body
Will fill my world.
There will be dancing,
Laughter and wine,
And my bedroom door
Will be open wide.
And when I get tired
Of dancing and fun,
I'll order the clumsy
To be tied up,
And I will command
The handsome pages
And trembling girls
Be ruthlessly flayed.
Sweeter than music
Will be their cries—
Piercing, resonant,
Discordant and wild.
Then, immersing myself
In voluptuous pain,

I'll order that I
Should be brutally flayed.
The relentless pain
Will delight and thrill
In the merging of cruel
And unbridled wills.

Fyodor Sologub, 1895

The Slave

I am a slave, and I was the humble slave
Of the most beautiful queen of all.
Before her dark and fiery gaze
I would wordlessly fall to the floor.

I would kiss the traces of her sandals
On the moist morning sand.
When the queen went down to the river,
I was intoxicated by fantasy.

And once from the dust I lifted my gaze,
Passionate and pining,
And it slipped up to the beauty's face,
And briefly burned her eyes . . .

She winced with rage:
Torture the defiler of the sacred!
And she left, as slave girls,
Encircling her, sang praises.

And that very night I was chained
Like a dog to the bed of the queen.
And I trembled all over, enchanted,
Awaiting unknown dreams.

As a priestess enters a temple,
She came into the chamber,
So beautiful and sinless,
That it made my eyes ache.

And her vestments dropped,
Down to the fabric on her bosom . . .
And in terror I closed my eyes . . .
But a voice whispered: Look!

And a youth slipped towards the bed.
Submissively, she waited . . .
The wicks in the lamps hissed,
And silence and darkness flooded the chamber.

And I witnessed night-time magic—
It was like a delirium!
Their shudders and their moans,
Everything the bed secretly conceals.

In the morning I saw them—next to me!
Still trembling in dream after dream!
And, chained to their bed like a dog,
Into the day I stared at the scene.

Now I've been sent to the quarry,
Wiping blood away, I crush granite.
But I remember that night! I remember!
If only I could live it all again!

Valery Briusov, 1901

Because she hadn't studied hard,
Heloise was flogged by Abelard
With birch rods, many times.
Her uncle heard the dear girl's wails,
A wrathful voice, the cruel flail,
And rubbed his hands, satisfied.

"Eloise knows quite a bit,
But still her teacher must be strict,
And put her in her place.
The girl is clever for her age,
Far wiser even than many a sage,
But the paths to knowledge are fraught with pain."

Stupid canon! He does not see
That the naughty girl is pleased
To be lying across her sweetheart's knees,
Relishing his thrilling clouts
And expressing in sweet shouts
Her exquisite agonies.

The canon will never understand:
Abelard is so roused by his reprimand,
And so dear is the flesh thus mortified,
That not with hoarse anger, but with love
The thrashing washes the girl with blood,
And their diversion is sanctified.

And, surrounded by joyous cherubim,
A winged god smiles down at them,

At the struggling, shapely legs,
At the flashing, naked heels,
At the fiery, scarlet weals,
At the body where roses blaze.

Fyodor Sologub, 1910

The Republic of the Southern Cross

Valery Briusov

A Special Edition Feature in *The Northern European Evening Bulletin*

Quite a number of accounts of the terrible catastrophe that has befallen the Republic of the Southern Cross have recently appeared. They are strikingly contradictory and relate not a few obviously fanciful and incredible events. The compilers of these accounts have evidently relied too heavily on the testimony of the rescued inhabitants of Star City—who, as is well known, *were all stricken with a mental disorder.* This is why we consider it beneficial and timely to bring together here all the *reliable* information currently available to us on the tragedy that has been played out at the South Pole.

The Republic of the Southern Cross was founded forty years ago by a trust of steel mills located in the southern polar regions. In a directive dispatched to all the governments of the entire planet, the new state laid claim to all domains, both continental and insular, that lay within the boundaries of the Antarctic circle, as well as any parts of those lands falling outside of those boundaries. It declared its readiness to purchase these lands from states considering them to be under their protectorate. The new republic's claims met with no objections from the world's fifteen great powers. Disputes over certain islands that lay completely outside the Antarctic Circle, but abutted on the southern polar regions, required separate treaties. Once the various formalities were completed, the Republic of the Southern Cross was admitted into the family of world states and her representatives were officially recognised by their governments.

The principal city of the Republic, Star City, was situated

directly on the South Pole. On that imagined spot through which the earth's axis passes and all the meridians come together stood the Town Hall, and the tip of its spire, high above the roofs of the city, pointed towards the celestial nadir. The city's streets fanned out along the meridians from the Town Hall, and the meridian streets were intersected by others laid out in concentric circles. The height of all structures and the façades of all buildings were the same. The walls had no windows, as the buildings were illuminated from within by electricity. Electricity lit the streets as well. Because of the severe climate, a lightproof roof was built over the city, with powerful ventilators for constant air exchange. These parts of the planet know only one six-month-long day and one six-month-long night, but the streets of Star City were constantly flooded with bright, even light. Similarly, at all times of the year the outside temperature was artificially kept at precisely the same level.

According to the last census, the number of people living in Star City had reached 2,500,000. The rest of the Republic's population, numbered at 50,000,000, was concentrated around ports and factories. Millions of people were concentrated at these points as well, which all looked very much like Star City. Thanks to the sophisticated application of electrical power, the entrances to local harbours remained open all year round. Suspended electric railways linked the populated areas of the Republic, transporting tens of thousands of people and millions of tons of wares from one city to another every day. As for the country's interior, it remained uninhabited. A traveller looking out of the window of his train would see only monotonous wilderness, totally white in the winter and smattered with scant grass during the three months of summer. All wild animals had long been exterminated, and there was nothing a person could live on there. All the more striking, then, was the intense life of the port cities and factory centres. To give an idea of what that life was like, it is sufficient to say that in recent years approximately *seven tenths* of all metal extracted from the earth was processed by the state factories of the Republic.

53

To all outward appearances, the Constitution of the Republic seemed to be the realisation of the most extreme form of democracy. The only citizens enjoying full rights were those who worked in the metallurgical factories, comprising approximately 60% of the population. These factories belonged to the State. Factory workers were not only granted every conceivable convenience; they even enjoyed luxury. Aside from splendid rooms and exquisite meals, they had at their disposal a wide variety of cultural institutions and entertainments: libraries, museums, theatres, concerts, gymnasiums for every conceivable type of sport, and so on. The number of working hours in a day was utterly insignificant. The upbringing and education of children, medical and juridical assistance, and the celebration of various cults' religious services were all provided for by the State. Generously afforded the satisfaction of every need, want and even whim, workers in state factories received no wages; but the families of citizens serving in a factory for 20 years, as well as those who died or were disabled during their working years, received a rich lifetime pension under the condition that they never quit the Republic. Representatives from among these same workers were chosen by popular vote to the Legislature of the Republic, which handled all questions of political life in the country, but without the right to alter its fundamental laws.

However, this democratic façade disguised the purely autocratic tyranny of the former trust's founding members. While allowing others to be delegates in the Legislature, they invariably put their own candidates in charge of the factories. The country's economic life was concentrated in the hands of the Council of these factory directors. They received all orders and divided them among the factories; they acquired the materials and machines for work; they managed all the factories. Huge sums of money—billions—passed through their hands. The Legislature did nothing more than confirm the operational income and expense figures presented to it, although the balance of these figures far exceeded the entire budget of the Republic. The influence of the Council of Directors in international relations was enormous. Its decisions could bankrupt entire countries. The prices it set determined the salaries of millions of the working masses all over the world. At the same time—although indirectly—the Council's influence on the Republic's internal affairs was always decisive. The Legislature, in essence, was merely the humble executor of the will of the Council.

To keep power in its own hands, the Council was obliged to mercilessly control every aspect of life within its borders. For all its seeming freedom, civic life was regulated down to the most insignificant details. Buildings in every city of the Republic were constructed according to one and the same plan, determined by law. The appointments of all rooms assigned to workers, for all their luxury, were strictly uniform. Everyone got the same food at exactly the same hours. A dress distributed from state warehouses was invariably—over the course of decades—of the same cut. After a certain hour, at a signal raised from the Town Hall, it was forbidden to leave one's house. The country's entire publishing industry was subordinate to a keen-eyed censor. Articles critical of the Council's dictatorship were not permitted. But even so, the entire country was so convinced of this dictatorship's benefi-cence that the typesetters themselves refused to set lines crit-ical of the Council. The factories were full of the Council's agents. At the least sign of dissatisfaction with the Council the agents, at hurriedly called meetings, quickly dissuaded the doubters with passionate speeches. Of course the overwhelm-ing proof was that the life of workers in the Republic was an object of envy to the entire world. It has been claimed that in certain cases of persistent agitation, the Council did not dis-dain assassination. In any case, throughout the Republic's entire existence not a single director hostile to the founding trustees was ever chosen by general election.

The population of Star City was made up mostly of work-ers serving out their term. These were, so to say, state rentiers. The facilities provided to them by the state allowed them to live well. Therefore it is not surprising that Star City was considered one of the world's most exciting cities. It was a goldmine for various entrepreneurs. The world's renowned brought their talents to this place. Here were the best operas, best concerts and best art exhibitions, and the most informative newspapers were published here. Star City's shops were amazing in their rich variety of goods, and the restaurants' luxury and fine service were astounding; clubs and taverns enticed one with every form of debauchery invented by the ancient and modern world. However, life in Star City continued to be strictly regulated by the government. True, the furnishings of flats and styles of dress were not constrained, but the prohibition against going outside after curfew remained in force, strict censorship was preserved, and the Council maintained an extensive network of spies. Order was officially kept by the national guard, but it was backed by the secret police of the omniscient Council.

This was, in its broadest outlines, how life was ordered in the Republic of the Southern Cross and its capital. The job of future historians will be to determine to what extent this order influenced the appearance and spread of the fateful epidemic that led to the destruction of Star City, and perhaps even to the entire fledgling state.

The first cases of "contradiction" were noted in the Republic as much as 20 years ago. At that time the disease was sporadic and incidental in nature. However, local psychiatrists and neuropathologists found it interesting and described it in great detail; at an international medical congress in Lhassa at that time, several papers were devoted to it. As time went on, people more or less forgot about it, although there was never a shortage of infected patients in the psychiatric wards of Star City. The disease got its name from the way its victims constantly contradict their own desires, wanting one thing, but saying and doing another (the scientific name for the disease is *mania contradicens*). It usually begins with rather weakly presenting symptoms, primarily in the form of a peculiar aphasia. An infected person says "no" instead of "yes"; wanting to say some tender words, he instead showers his addressee with invective, and so on. In the majority of cases, the patient begins to contradict himself in his actions as well: intending to

56

go to the left, he turns right; thinking he will raise his hat so he can see better, he pulls it down over his eyes, and so on. As the disease develops, these "contradictions" begin to fill the entire physical and mental life of the patient—manifesting, of course, in infinite variety according to the particularities of each individual. Generally, the patient's speech becomes incomprehensible, and his actions absurd. The bodily functions, too, become disordered. Aware of the foolishness of his behaviour, the patient becomes extremely agitated, sometimes to the point of frenzy. A great many of them commit suicide, sometimes in a fit of madness, sometimes, on the contrary, in a lucid moment. Others die of cerebral haemorrhage. The disease is almost always fatal; cases of recovery are extremely rare.

Mania contradicens took on epidemic proportions in Star City in the middle months of the current year. Until that time the number of people suffering from "contradiction" never exceeded 2% of the total of all cases of illness. But that proportion suddenly rose in May of this year (an autumn month in the Republic) to 25% and continued to grow in succeeding months, while the absolute number of infections was rising just as quickly. By mid-June approximately 2% of the *entire population*—that is, approximately 50,000 people— were officially diagnosed with "contradiction." We have no statistics for after this period. The hospitals were overflowing. The contingent of doctors soon proved inadequate. Moreover, the doctors themselves, as well as their medical staff, began to fall victim to the disease. Quite soon the afflicted had no one to turn to for medical help, and an exact tally of cases became impossible. However, all eyewitness accounts agree that by July not a single healthy family was to be met with. Meanwhile, the number of healthy people was diminishing steadily, since a massive emigration from the city had started, as from a plague-stricken area, and the number of infected was escalating. Those who insist that by August *everyone* remaining in Star City was stricken with the psychological disorder are probably not far from the truth.

One can trace the first manifestations of the epidemic in the local newspapers, which noted them in the rapidly lengthening column headed *Mania contradicens*. Since it is very difficult to diagnose the disease in its first stages, the chronicle of the first days of the epidemic is full of comical episodes. A conductor on the metro, stricken with the illness, paid passengers instead of taking their money. A street constable, whose job was to regulate the flow of traffic, spent an entire day snarling it. A man visiting the museum took down all the pictures and rehung them facing the wall as he made his way through the galleries. A newspaper corrected by a stricken copy-editor was found to be full of ridiculous absurdities. At a concert an infected violinist suddenly wrecked an orchestral performance with horrible dissonances, and so on. A long list of such instances provided fodder for the wit of local satirists. But several instances of another type altogether put a stop to the flow of jokes. The first was when a doctor infected with "contradiction" prescribed an unquestionably lethal medication to a little girl, who subsequently died. For about three days the papers were full of this event. Then two nannies at the city kindergarten slit the throats of forty-one children in a fit of "contradiction." This news shook the whole city. And then, on that very same day, in the evening, two men with the disease rolled a machine gun out of the building that housed the city police and sprayed the peacefully passing crowd with a hail of bullets. There were as many as five hundred dead and wounded.

After this there was a public outcry in all the papers and throughout the community, demanding that something must be done immediately to curb the epidemic. A special session of the conjoined City Council and Legislature resolved to call in doctors from other cities and countries immediately, to expand the capacity of existing hospitals, to open new ones and to establish wards everywhere for the isolation of "contradiction" patients; to print and disseminate 500,000 copies of a brochure on the new disease describing its symptoms and treatments; to provide for doctors and their assistants to be on special duty on every street; to make rounds of private homes to render first aid; and so on. It was also decided to run daily trains exclusively for the ill on every route, since the doctors considered a change of scenery the best treatment for the disease. Similar measures were undertaken at the same time by various private associations, unions and clubs. A special "Society for Combating the Epidemic" was even organised, the members of which soon proved themselves truly self-sacrificing. But despite the fact that these and similar measures were carried out with untiring energy, the epidemic did not subside, but gained momentum with each passing day, striking young and old alike, men and women, people at work and those on holiday, the temperate and the dissolute. And soon the entire community was in the grip of an insuperable, elemental horror in the face of unprecedented disaster.

People began to flee Star City. Certain significant persons left first, including dignitaries, directors, members of the Legislature and the City Council, who hurriedly sent their families away to southern cities in Australia and Patagonia. After them straggled those who had got caught in the city accidentally—foreigners who had willingly come to see "the most exciting city in the southern hemisphere," artists of every profession, shrewd businessmen of various sorts, women of easy virtue. Then, as the epidemic made fresh progress, the merchants, too, abandoned the city. They hurriedly sold off their wares or left their shops to the mercy of fate. With these fled bankers, owners of theatres and restaurants, and news-paper and book publishers. Finally it came down to the ordin-ary, local residents. Former workers were forbidden by law to leave the Republic without special permission from the gov-ernment, under threat of losing their pension. But people paid no heed to this threat as they tried to save their very lives. And they began to desert. The city's civil servants fled, the officers of the people's police fled, nurses fled from the hospitals, and so did the chemists and doctors. The urge to flee itself became a mania. Everyone fled who possibly could.

The electric train stations were mobbed by huge crowds. Train tickets were purchased for huge sums or obtained by force. People spent entire fortunes for seats on piloted balloons that could not ascend with more than ten pas-sengers . . . Just as a train was departing, more people would force their way into the carriages and refuse to give up their hard-won places. Crowds stopped hospital trains, dragged the patients out of their carriages, took their places on the berths and forced the driver to continue on. By the end of May, the entire rolling stock of the Republic's railways ran only on the routes between the capital and the ports. Trains coming from Star City were packed; passengers stood in every passageway, and even dared to stand outside, although the modern electric trains went at such high speeds that this put them in danger of suffocation. Steamship companies from Australia, South America and South Africa made money hand over fist transporting emigrants from the Republic to other countries. Two southern companies specialising in balloon travel made equally enormous fortunes, managing to make ten or so trips to evacuate the last billionaires remaining in Star City. Trains travelling towards Star City, on the contrary, were all but empty. Not for any price could a person be found who was willing to work in Star City; only the occasional eccentric tourists—thrill-seekers—would go to the plagued city. It has been calculated that from the beginning of the emigration to June 22nd, when the trains ceased to run properly, one and a half million people—that is, almost two thirds of the population—left Star City via the six railway lines.

Chairman of the City Council Horace de Ville earned everlasting fame at this time for his resourcefulness, strength of will and courage. On June 5th, a special session of the City Council, in accordance with the decisions of the Legislature and the Council of Directors, granted de Ville the title of Commander-in-Chief and dictatorial power over the city, placing city funds, the national guard and the city works at his disposal. Government institutions and archives were thereupon moved without delay from Star City to North Port. The name of Horace de Ville should be written in gold letters alongside the noblest names in humanity. For a month and a half he fought against growing anarchy in the city. He managed to gather about him a group of equally self-sacrificing assistants. For some time he was able to maintain discipline and obedience among the national guard and municipal workers, who were gripped by terror at the scope of the disaster and steadily decimated by the epidemic. Hundreds of thousands owe Horace de Ville their lives, since it was due to his energy and good management that they managed to escape. He eased the final days of thousands more by making it possible for them to die peacefully in hospital instead of beneath the blows of a maddened mob. Finally, de Ville preserved for mankind a chronicle—there is no better word for the brief, but informative and precise telegrams he sent daily, and sometimes even several times a day, to the Republic's provisional government at North Port—of the entire catastrophe.

De Ville's first task in the capacity of city Commander-in-Chief was to try to calm the anxious population. Manifestos were issued, pointing out that the mental infection was transmitted most easily to people who were agitated, and appealing to healthy, stable people to exert influence on those who were weak and highly-strung. In addition, de Ville established relations with the Society for Combating the Epidemic and gave its members jurisdiction over all public places, theatres, assembly halls, squares and streets. In those days hardly an hour went by without the discovery of more cases of illness. First here, then there, the behaviour of individuals or whole groups of people would clearly demonstrate their madness. For the most part the stricken, aware of their condition, would immediately try to get help. But under the influence of a disordered mind, they would express this desire through some kind of hostile action against whoever was nearby. They might want to hurry home or to a clinic, but instead they fled in panic to the city's outskirts. It might occur to them to ask someone for help, but instead they would seize random passers-by by the throat and choke them or give them a beating, sometimes even wounding them with a knife or stick. Because of this, the appearance of a person infected with "contradiction" would cause crowds to flee en masse. It was at such times that the members of the Society would come to their aid. Some of them took the ill in hand, calmed them and directed them to the nearest hospital; others tried to reassure the crowd that there was no danger whatsoever, that it was just a new misfortune that everyone had to contend with, using whatever strength they had.

At theatres and meetings cases of sudden illness very often led to tragic consequences. At the opera several hundred in the audience were seized by mass insanity, and instead of expressing their delight by applauding the singers, they rushed the stage and showered them with blows. At the Drama Theatre a suddenly stricken actor who was supposed to portray a suicide fired several shots into the audience. Of course the revolver was not loaded, but the nervous tension generated by the incident caused the illness already latent in many of the spectators to surface. In the subsequent confusion, during which the understandable panic was aggravated by the "contradictory" behaviour of madmen, several dozens were killed. But the most horrifying event of all took place at the Fireworks Theatre. In a fit of illness, a unit of city police, there to enforce fire safety rules, set fire to the stage and the veils screening the illumination effects. No fewer than 200 people perished in the fire and the ensuing panic. After this happened, Horace de Ville ordered the termination of all theatrical and musical performances in the city.

Residents were faced with an enormous threat from robbers and thieves, for whom the general disorganisation provided vast opportunity. It is alleged that some of these came to Star City from abroad during that time. Some pretended to be mad in order to escape punishment. Others did not even consider it necessary to conceal their open theft with pretence. Gangs of bandits brazenly entered abandoned shops and carried off the more valuable items, broke into private flats and demanded gold, stopped people in the street and took their valuables, watches, rings and bracelets. Violence of every type soon joined company with the thieving, especially violent attacks on women. The city's Commander-in-Chief sent out entire units of policemen after the criminals, but the criminals were so bold as to meet them in open battle. There were frightening cases in which "contradiction" suddenly broke out among either the criminals or the police, and the stricken turned their weapons on their own companions. At first the

Commander-in-Chief exiled arrested thieves from the city. But civilians would free them from their prison wagons so as to take their place on the train. Then the Commander-in-Chief was compelled to condemn convicted bandits and rapists to death. Thus, after an interval of almost three centuries, public execution was reinstituted on earth.

In June the lack of essential items became evident. Provisions and medicines were in short supply. The transport of goods by rail began to be curtailed; production in the city came almost to a complete standstill. De Ville organised city bakeries and the distribution of bread and meat to all residents. Public canteens were established in the city on the model of those already existing in the factories. But it was impossible to find sufficient numbers of workers for them. Volunteers worked themselves to exhaustion, but their number was decreasing. The furnaces of city crematoria blazed around the clock, but the number of dead bodies in the mortuaries failed to diminish—on the contrary, it increased. People began to find bodies on the streets and in private homes. The city's public works—the telegraph, telephone, light, waterworks and sanitation—served an ever-decreasing number of people. It is amazing how de Ville coped. He had his eye on everything and kept track of it all. From his communications one might think that he knew no rest. And everyone who was saved from the catastrophe has unanimously testified that his work was beyond the highest praise.

In the middle of June the shortage of rail workers began to make an impact. There weren't enough drivers and conductors to maintain the trains. The first derailment occurred on the Southwest line on June 17th, caused by a driver who had been stricken with "contradiction." In a fit of illness, the driver flung the entire train off a ten-metre embankment onto an icy field. Almost all the passengers were killed or maimed. The news of this, brought by the next train to the city, was like a thunderbolt. A hospital train was sent without delay. It brought back corpses and mutilated, barely breathing bodies. And then, towards evening of that very same day, news spread of an analogous catastrophe on the Number One line. Two railway lines connecting Star City with the world had now been rendered inoperable. Detachments were sent both from the city and from North Port to repair the rails, but during the winter months in those parts work is all but impossible. It became evident that any hopes of restoring the lines in the near future must be relinquished.

These two catastrophes merely set the stage for what was to follow. The more anxiously the drivers went about their work, the more certain it was that, in a morbid fit, they would repeat the tragic mistakes of their predecessors. Because they *feared* somehow destroying the train, that is precisely what they did. In the five days from June 18th to 22nd, seven trains crammed with people were flung off precipices. Thousands of people met their death by injury and starvation on the snowy plains. Only a very few were able to find the strength to get back to the city. With these disasters, all six trunk lines joining Star City with the world were ruined. Balloon transport had come to a halt even before that. One balloon had been smashed by an angry mob, enraged that air routes were being reserved for the very rich. All the other balloons, one by one, were also destroyed, most likely for the same reasons that led to the rail catastrophes. The city's population, reduced by then to 600,000 people, was now cut off from all humanity. For the time being the only remaining connection was the telegraph line.

On June 24th the city's underground transportation was halted due to a shortage of workers. On June 26th telephones went out of service. On June 27th all chemists' except the central one were closed. On July 1st the Commander-in-Chief issued an order to all residents to move into the city centre, completely abandoning the periphery, in order to make it easier to maintain order, distribute provisions and render medical assistance. People abandoned their homes and moved into flats deserted by their owners. The sense of private property vanished. No one minded leaving his things behind, no one found it strange to use someone else's. On the other hand, there were still marauders and bandits, who ought more properly to be considered "psychopaths." They just kept on looting, and now hoards of gold and precious stones are being discovered in the deserted rooms of abandoned homes, and lying nearby the half-decomposed corpse of the robber.

It is remarkable, however, that despite this widespread death and destruction, life continued much as it always had. There were still merchants who opened new shops, selling—for some reason at incredible prices—wares that had escaped destruction: delicacies, flowers, books, weapons . . . Shoppers tossed their useless gold away without regret, while skinflint merchants secreted it away, for what purpose no one knows. There were also secret clubs—for cards, wine and debauchery—where miserable people flocked in order to forget the horrors of reality. There the ill mingled with the well, and no one chronicled the horrible scenes that took place there. Two or three newspapers came out as well, the publishers of which struggled in the general havoc to preserve the meaning of the literary word. Issues of these papers, already being bought and sold today at ten or twenty times their original cost, will surely become the most valuable bibliographic curiosities. A vivid and terrifying picture of everything that unhappy city suffered is reflected in these columns of text, written in the midst of the reigning madness and set by half-mad typesetters. Reporters communicated the "metropolitan news" in these pages, writers hotly debated the state of affairs, and satirists even sought to entertain in those tragic days. Meanwhile, the telegrams that arrived from other countries, telling about real, healthy life, must have filled their readers' hearts with despair, doomed as they were to perish.

Desperate attempts were made to escape death. In the beginning of July an enormous group of men, women and children, led by one John Dieu, set out on a risky journey by foot from the city to the nearest settlement, Londontowne. De Ville understood the madness of their attempt, but was unable to stop them, and he himself supplied them with warm clothing and food rations. That entire group, approximately 2,000 people, lost their way and perished in the snowy plains of that Antarctic country, in the midst of the black, six-month-long night. A fellow called Whiting began to advocate other, more heroic means. He proposed killing *everyone* stricken with the illness, the idea being that this would bring an end to the epidemic. He found more than a few followers, and if truth be told, in those dark days even the most insane, the most inhumane proposal promising relief would have found its supporters. Whiting and his friends ranged all over the city, breaking into all the houses and exterminating the ill. In the hospitals they carried out large-scale massacres. In their frenzy they killed even people who could only be suspected of being not completely well. Madmen and thieves joined in with the ideological killers. The whole city became a battlefield. In those difficult days Horace de Ville gathered together the assistants under his command, rallied their spirits and person-ally led them into battle against Whiting's supporters. The pursuit went on day and night for several days. Hundreds fell on both sides. Finally, Whiting himself was captured. It turned out he was in the last stage of *mania contradicens*, and they were compelled not to execute him, but to take him to hospital, where shortly afterwards he died.

On July 8ᵗʰ the city suffered one of the most terrifying blows of all. In a paroxysm of illness, the managers of the central electric station works wrecked all the machines. Electric light-ing was shut down, and the entire city, every street and every private dwelling was plunged into absolute darkness. Since the city used only electricity for lighting and heat, all residents now found themselves in an utterly hopeless plight. De Ville had foreseen this danger. He had prepared stores of pitch torches and fuel. Bonfires were lit on all the streets. Thousands of torches were distributed to residents. But those meagre lights couldn't possibly illuminate Star City's gargantuan avenues, which stretched out in straight lines for tens of kilometres, nor the menacing height of the thirty-floor buildings. With the onset of darkness, the city's last vestiges of discipline gave way. People were now wholly and irrevocably in the grip of horror and madness. The healthy could no longer be distinguished from the ill. They were now a people bereft of any hope, and a terrifying orgy began.

Moral decline spread with amazing rapidity. Culture that

had taken thousands of years to accumulate was shed by these people like a fragile crust, laying bare the savage within—the man-beast as he had once roved over the virgin earth. All notion of law was lost, and only force was recognised. For women, the only law remaining was the craving for sensual pleasure. The most modest mothers behaved like prostitutes, passing from hand to hand with abandon and speaking in the obscene language of brothels. Young women ran about the streets, calling out to whoever so desired to take advantage of their virginity, and they would lead their chosen one to the nearest doorway and give themselves to him on the closest bed, not even knowing whose it was. Drunkards feasted in plundered cellars, undaunted by the uncollected corpses sprawling in their midst. All this was continually made even more convoluted by paroxysms of the illness that held sway. The plight of children, abandoned by their parents to the mercies of fate, was especially pitiful. Disgusting perverts raped some, while others were subjected to tortures by devotees of sadism, who were suddenly to be found in significant number. Children died of hunger in their nurseries, and of shame and suffering after being raped; some were murdered, and others were killed accidentally. It is rumoured that there were monsters who kidnapped children in order to satisfy newly-awakened cannibal instincts with their flesh.

In that final period of the tragedy Horace de Ville could not, of course, help the entire population. But he arranged a shelter at the Town Hall for all who still possessed their sanity. The entrances to the building were barricaded and guards constantly kept watch. Inside, stores of food and water had been prepared to last 3,000 people 40 days. But there were not more than 1,800 men and women with de Ville. It goes without saying that there were others with unclouded minds still inside the city, but these did not know about the shelter and were hiding in other buildings. Many did not dare to go outside, and at the present time the corpses of people who died alone of starvation are still being discovered in rooms throughout the city. It is remarkable that among those shut up inside the Town Hall there were very few cases of the "contradiction" illness. De Ville managed to maintain discipline in his small community. He kept a journal of everything that took place until the final day, and this journal, together with de Ville's telegrams, serves as the best source for what we know about the catastrophe. The journal was found in a secret cabinet in the Town Hall, where especially valuable documents were kept. The last entry is dated July 20th. There, de Ville reports that a maddened crowd had begun storming the Town Hall, and that he had been forced to repel the attack with volleys of revolver fire. "What I am hoping for," de Ville writes, "I don't know. Help certainly won't come before spring. To last until spring on the stores at my disposal is impossible. But I will carry out my duty until the end." These are de Ville's last words. Noble words!

One can only assume that the crowd took the Town Hall by storm on July 21st, and that its defenders were all slaughtered or dispersed. De Ville's body has not been found. We have no reliable accounts whatsoever of what took place in the city after July 21st. Judging from the traces left behind and now being found during the clean-up, one must suppose that anarchy had reached its final limits. One can imagine the half-dark streets, lit up by blazing bonfires made from furniture and books. Fire was made by striking flint on iron. Around the bonfires throngs of the mad and the inebriated made wild celebration. A communal cup made its way around. Men and women drank. And scenes of animal lust took place right on the spot. Some kind of dark, atavistic feelings were roused in the hearts of those city dwellers, and, half-naked, unwashed, dishevelled, they danced the circle dances of their distant ancestors—the contemporaries of cave bears—and sang the same wild songs as did the hordes when they fell upon a mammoth with their stone axes. Mingling with their songs, incoherent speech and idiotic laughter were the mad shouts of the ill, who had lost the ability to express in words even their delirious hallucinations, and the moans of the dying as they writhed among decaying corpses. At times the dances turned into fights—for a barrel of wine, for a beautiful woman, or simply without any cause whatsoever, in a fit of the madness that spurred them to senseless, contradictory actions. There was no escape: everywhere were the same dreadful scenes, the orgies, battles, bestial merrymaking and bestial rage—or else absolute darkness that seemed even more terrifying, even more unbearable to a deranged mind.

In those days Star City was an enormous black box, where several thousand still-living, human-like creatures were thrown into the stench of hundreds of thousands of rotting bodies, where among the living there was no longer a single one who was conscious of his condition. It was a city of madmen, a gigantic madhouse, the greatest and most disgusting Bedlam the earth had ever seen. And these madmen stabbed each other with daggers and sank their teeth into each other's throats. They died of madness, they died of fright, they died of hunger and of all the diseases reigning in the infected air.

It goes without saying that the government of the Republic did not remain an indifferent witness to the cruel disaster that had befallen the capital. But almost immediately it had to relinquish any hope of rendering aid. Doctors, nurses and military units serving in any capacity whatsoever refused categorically to go to Star City. After all train and balloon services were suspended, direct contact with the city was lost, since the severity of the climate there precludes other modes of communication. Moreover, the government soon turned all its attention to the cases of "contradiction" that had started to crop up in other cities of the Republic. In several of these the disease threatened to take on an epidemic character, and a general panic ensued, reminiscent of the events in Star City. This led to emigration from all the inhabited regions of the Republic. Work in all factories ceased, and the entire industrial life of the country came to a halt. However, thanks to decisive measures taken in a timely fashion, the epidemic was curbed in those other cities, and nowhere did it attain such proportions as in the capital.

Everyone knows how avidly the world followed the misfortunes of the young Republic. In the beginning, when no one could have expected the disaster to grow to such incredible proportions, the dominant feeling was one of curiosity. The leading papers of every country (including our own *Northern European Evening Bulletin*) dispatched special correspondents to Star City to report on the course of the epidemic. Many of those brave knights of the pen fell victim while fulfilling their professional duty. Then, when news of a threatening nature began to arrive, private societies and the governments of various states offered their services to the government of the Republic. Some dispatched regiments, others organised medical units, others raised money, but events transpired with such swiftness that the greater part of those initiatives couldn't be realised. After rail services to Star City were suspended, the Commander-in-Chief's telegrams were the only source of news about life in the city. Those telegrams were immediately relayed to all corners of the earth and were disseminated in millions of copies. After the breakdown of the electric generators, the telegraph functioned for another few days, since the station's batteries were charged. The precise reason telegraph communication came to a final halt is not known: perhaps the equipment was ruined. Horace de Ville's last telegram is dated June 27th. From this day, for almost a month and a half, all mankind was deprived of any news from the Republic's capital.

In July, some attempts were made to reach Star City by air. Several new balloons and flying machines were supplied to the Republic. However, all attempts ended in failure. Finally, aeronaut Thomas Billy was lucky enough to make it all the way to that unfortunate city. He picked up two people from a city roof; they had lost their minds long ago and were half-dead from cold and starvation. Through the propellers, Billy saw that the streets were shrouded in absolute darkness, and he heard wild shouts that proved there were still living beings in the city. But Billy didn't dare to descend into the city itself. At the end of August one electric railway line was successfully reinstated, to Lissis station, a hundred and five kilometres from the city. A detachment of well-armed men, furnished with provisions and first aid supplies, entered the city via the Northwest Gates. This detachment, however, was unable to penetrate further than the first blocks due to the horrible stench that hung in the air. They were compelled to go step by step, clearing the streets of dead bodies and purifying the air by artificial means. Every living person they found was insane. They resembled wild beasts in their savagery, and they had to be overpowered by force. Finally, towards the middle of September, proper communication was established with Star City and its systematic reconstruction began.

As of today the greater part of the city has been cleared of bodies. Electric lighting and heat have been restored. Only the American quarters remain unoccupied, but it is presumed that there are no living creatures there. As many as 10,000 people have been rescued, but the majority of these are incurably deranged. Those who are more or less recovering are very reluctant to speak about what they endured in those disastrous days. In addition, their stories are full of contradictions and quite often are not borne out by the documented facts. In various places copies of newspapers that were put out in the city until the end of July have been found. The most recent of these, dated July 22nd, contains a report of Horace de Ville's death and a call to restore the shelter at the Town Hall. True, one more newspaper dated in August was found, but its content proves most certainly that its author (who was probably setting the text of his own delirium) was decidedly out of his mind. At the Town Hall they discovered Horace de Ville's journal, which chronicles in an orderly fashion the events that took place in the three weeks between June 28th and July 20th. The grisly discoveries made both in the streets and inside homes give us a clear picture of the atrocities committed in the city during those last days. There were horribly mutilated bodies everywhere: people who had died of starvation, who had been strangled and tortured, who had been killed by frenzied madmen, and, finally, half-eaten bodies. Corpses are being discovered in the most unexpected places: in the tunnels of the underground, in sewer pipes, in various storerooms, in boiler rooms—everywhere insane residents had sought escape from the surrounding horror. Virtually every home was completely ransacked, and property that was ultimately of no use to the plunderers was hidden away in secret rooms and underground spaces.

Without a doubt, a few more months will pass before Star City becomes habitable once again. Now it is almost completely deserted. In a city that can house as many as 3,000,000 residents, there are now about 30,000 workers cleaning up the streets and houses. Some of the former inhabitants have shown up as well, to look for the bodies of their friends and relatives and to collect what remains of their ruined and plundered belongings. A few tourists have come, too, attracted by the unique spectacle of a deserted city. Two entrepreneurs have already opened two hotels, which are doing a brisk business. And a small nightclub is opening soon, for which performers have already been booked.

The Northern European Evening Bulletin, for its part, has dispatched a new correspondent, Mr. Andrew Evald, to the city, and plans to acquaint its readers in detail with all the new discoveries to come in the unfortunate capital of the Republic of the Southern Cross.

The Coming Huns

Trample their paradise, Attila.
— *Vyacheslav Ivanov*

Where are you, coming Huns
That threaten the world like a storm!
I hear your cast-iron tread
Over Pamirs as yet unexplored.

Like a frenzied horde fall upon us,
Crashing down from dark camps in a flood;
Revive our decrepit old bodies
With a wave of fiery blood.

Slaves of freedom, set up huts
By our palaces, as of old,
And bring back joyous fields
There, where once stood our throne.

Cast all our books in your fires
And dance by their jubilant blaze,
Desecrate all of the temples,
In all you are blameless as babes.

And we, the sages and poets,
Wardens of mystery and faith,
We will take our burning lights
To catacombs, deserts and caves.

And, of our cherished creations,
What will playful Chance spare

From the tempest of destruction,
From the storm that rages there?

Perhaps all that we alone knew
Will perish in oblivion,
But those who have come to destroy me,
I meet with a welcoming hymn.

Valery Briusov, 1905

We are not used to bright colours,
We wear clothes of earthy shades;
We slowly trudge through dust,
And drop our timid gaze.

We breathe the dust of rooms,
We live among books and pictures,
And dear to our impotence
Are single moments and lines of verse.

But what do I long for? Blood and war.
And what do I dream of? Wild cries.
The northern sovereigns are my brothers,
The age of the Vikings is my time.

Valery Briusov, 1899

Distinct lines of mountain peaks;
The pale, unsteady sea . . .
Extinguished, the rapturous gaze
Drowns in impotent space.

In secret dreams I've created
A world of ideal nature—
What is this dust before it?
Steppes, and rocks, and waters!

Valery Briusov, 1896

The Sting of Death: The Story of Two Boys

Fyodor Sologub

The sting of death is sin.
(1 Cor 15:56)

I

Two boys on holiday in the country had ensconced them-
selves in a remote, wooded nook on the bank of a river and
were fishing. The river was running shallower now, and gur-
gled among the rocks, so the children could easily ford it in a
number of places. The bottom was sandy and clear.

One of these two young holidaymakers was concentrating
on his fishing; the other fished distractedly, as if thinking
about other things. One, Vanya Zelenev, seemed hideous at
first sight, although it was difficult to say what was especially
ugly about him: was it the greenish tint to his face? Or its lack
of symmetry? Or his big, flimsy, protruding ears? Or were his
eyebrows too black and bushy? Or was it that tuft of black hair
above his right eyebrow, about which the other kids some-
times teased him, calling him "Three-brow"? None of this
would have mattered, however, had it not been for something
distorted about that face, something oppressed and malicious.
He was always somewhat hunched-over, and liked to grimace
and contort his body. This had become second nature to him
to such an extent that many people assumed he was a hunch-
back. But his back was perfectly straight, and he was strong,
agile, bold and sometimes even brash. He liked to climb trees
and plunder birds' nests, and if the occasion arose, he was
always ready to give younger boys a thrashing. His clothes
were old and patched.

The other boy, Kolya Glebov, immediately impressed one

as handsome, although again, on closer examination, his fea-
tures displayed neither strict regularity nor any particular
fineness of expression. He was a nice clean boy with a cheerful
disposition. When he laughed, a little lump bulged under his
chin, and this was awfully endearing. His Mama liked to kiss
him exactly on this spot. His outfit was clean and handsome: a
sailor suit, short pantaloons, black stockings and yellow shoes.
He was the son of a naval officer who was abroad at sea. Kolya
was spending the summer here with his Mama.

Not far from the boys stood two tins filled with water. The
boys tossed their catches into these. But today the fish weren't
biting . . .

"Such a pretty place," Kolya said in his gentle, vibrant
voice.

"What's pretty about it?" retorted Vanya in his hoarse,
child's bass, twitching his shoulders strangely.

"The precipice there is so steep, frightfully steep!" Kolya
said, gesturing with his chin across the river at the steep
opposite bank. "And look how the birches cling to it. And
how they can barely hold on!"

"The water will undercut it," Vanya said in his deep voice,
"and the precipice will collapse."

"Come on!" Kolya said distrustfully, and looked at Vanya as
if asking him not to do that.

"Well, it's the truth," said Vanya with a malicious grin.

Kolya looked sadly at the precipice: its thick layers of red
clay were piled up high on top of each other, as if they had
been sheared smooth by a giant shovel. Here and there barely
noticeable cracks separated one layer from the next. In other
places, nearer to the water, there were smallish hollows, seem-
ingly washed out by the water. The water ran as pure and clear
as could be, and splashed ever so gently against the mighty
precipice.

"It's clever," thought Kolya. "It just licks away at it little by
little. To think that this whole enormous wall, with all those
pretty birches on it, could suddenly fall down into the river!"

"Well, it won't be for a while," he said aloud.

The boys were silent for a little. And again Kolya's voice

sounded, soft and sweet, "And in the woods it's really nice! Smells of pine sap."

"Turps," Vanya put in.

"No, it smells good," Kolya went on joyfully. "This morning I saw a squirrel. It was running along the ground, and then it was up a tree in just a whisk of its tail."

"And I saw a dead crow under a bush," Vanya announced. "Over there," he said, gesturing with his head and shoulders, contorting himself completely in the process. "I marked the spot."

"What for?" Kolya asked, amazed.

"To bring it home," Vanya explained, "and put it on Marfa's bed."

"But she'll be frightened," Kolya said cautiously.

"The crow, you mean? Nah, brother, it's dead," Vanya said in the same malicious tone, as if he really liked it that the crow was dead.

"Not the crow—Marfa," Kolya said, smiling a little and narrowing somewhat his happy eyes, which made his gentle face look as though he'd eaten something sour, like barberries.

"A-ah," Vanya drew the word out, "I thought you were saying the crow would be frightened of Marfa. She's as ugly as deadly sin. Mother doesn't keep pretty girls around—she's jealous of Father."

"Oh, jea-ealous!" Kolya drew out the not wholly familiar word, as if trying out the sound.

"Afraid he'll fall in love," Vanya clarified, and he laughed. "As if he can't get any on the side, anyway," he said with malicious pleasure.

Again there was a short silence. And then Kolya spoke again, but no longer in such certain tones. "Look at that beautiful meadow over there, to the right! Lots of flowers, all different from each other—it makes the meadow all colourful. And some of them smell really good."

Vanya looked at him with irritation, and growled, "And cows have crapped in it."

"I guess nothing is good enough for you," Kolya said, and again his face had that sour look.

"I don't like sentimental slop," said Vanya. "I like drinking and smoking."

"Drinking?" asked Kolya, surprised and horrified.

"Yeah, wine or vodka," said Vanya with false tranquillity. He gave a sideways glance at Kolya and grimaced savagely.

"We're not allowed to drink wine," said Kolya, his voice tinged with horror. "Only grown-ups can, and it's bad even for them."

"That's all nonsense," Vanya answered firmly. "Just a bunch of made-up rules they push us around with. Parents think we're their property. They do whatever they want with us."

"But anyway, drinking is bad for you—you could get ill," Kolya said.

Vanya held him in his strange, disturbing gaze. Little amber sparks flashed in his light, almost transparent eyes.

"What?" he asked, smiling and grimacing.

Kolya had lost himself in those eyes, and he forgot what he wanted to say. Vanya's eyes disturbed him, and their transparent gleam seemed to dim his memory. Rousing himself with difficulty, he managed to say, "Mama will get angry."

"Mama!" Vanya said scornfully.

"Well, but you have to mind your Mama, don't you?" Kolya asked uncertainly.

Vanya again looked at Kolya. Those transparently light eyes of Vanya's seemed strange and nasty to Kolya, and Kolya started to feel scared.

Vanya, pronouncing the tender words with disdain, said, "All right, let's say that your Mama loves you—but are you going to be Mama's little precious forever? Me, I like to do things my own way. Freedom, brother—that's another thing entirely! It's not about sniffing flowers and picking a bouquet for Mama. All right, then, for instance—you like it here, right?"

"I really love it, of course!" Kolya said with quiet happiness sounding in his voice.

"All right, then, but how long can you stay here?" Vanya went on animatedly, twitching his skinny shoulders. "Like it or not, you can only fool around here for a little bit, and then it's back to the city to choke on dust."

Kolya was silent, and his thoughts turned to Mama.

Mama loved Kolya; she was tender and light-hearted. But she had her own life. She loved to be with the lively young people who often came to their house, laughed, had spirited, jocular conversations, treated Kolya affectionately, sometimes made gentle fun of him . . . Kolya didn't find them boring, he himself was lively, talkative and trusting—but they were different and distant from him, and seemed to draw Mama away from him.

"Anyhow, the fish aren't biting," said Vanya. "And it's time to go home. Come to the edge of the forest this evening."

"All right," said Kolya.

II

The boys carried their buckets and fishing rods home.

They walked along the road that led right through the village. The cottages pressed against each other and seemed poor and dilapidated. From beyond them came the sound of the river. Peasant children, dishevelled and dirty, were playing near the houses, swearing at one another with crude, horrible words, and crying. Their hands and feet—usually so beautiful in children—were a pathetic and disgusting sight, they were so dirty.

At one of the cottages an inquisitive gentleman, dressed in a dark-blue shirt beneath a frockcoat and high boots, was sitting on a bench. He asked questions of everyone who passed by.

"Catch anything?" he asked Kolya.

Kolya trustingly showed him the little fish in his tin bucket.

"Not much," said the gentleman. "Where do you live, then?"

"Over there on the hill, Yefim Gorbachev's cottage," said Kolya.

"Oh, that's Yefishka Gorbachev!" said the gentleman.

Kolya laughed.

"Do you live with your father?" asked the inquisitive gentleman.

"No, with my Mama," answered Kolya. "My papa is at sea. He's a naval officer."

"And does your Mama miss him?" inquired the man.

Kolya looked at him in surprise, and thought for a moment. "Mama?" he said slowly. "No, she's acting. Soon there's going to be a play here, and she's got a part in it."

Meanwhile Vanya had gone on a little way and then returned. "Come on, then, are we going?" he said to Kolya, darting angry glances at the curious gentleman.

The boys moved off. Gesturing with strange motions of his shoulders and elbows behind them, towards the inquisitive gentleman, Vanya said, "That man asks everyone questions— he's a proper bastard. About your parents, about everything— he probably writes for the papers. I told him a couple of good fibs."

Again the amber sparks blazed in Vanya's transparent, sharp eyes.

"You di-i-id?" Kolya giggled as he drew out the word.

"I told him that my father worked as a detective," Vanya recounted. "Now he's really afraid of me!"

"Why?" asked Kolya.

"I told him that my father is investigating a certain swindler in these parts, and so he's scared."

"But he's not really a swindler, is he?" Kolya asked with a giggle.

"But I told him a description that sounds like him," explained Vanya, "and so now he's scared."

The boys laughed.

They came to Vanya's cottage and began to say good-bye.

Vanya's mother was standing in the garden, hands on her hips, smoking. She was tall, fat and red, and she always wore a dull, pompous expression on her face—the kind that habitual smokers often have. Kolya was afraid of Vanya's mother.

She looked severely at Kolya, and Kolya felt uneasy.

"Tonight, then," said Vanya.

Kolya set off for home at a good clip.

"Friends!" Vanya's mother said angrily. "I'd give it good to both of you . . ."

There was no reason whatsoever to be angry; she was simply in the habit of being angry and scolding.

III

After dinner the boys met up again—on the main road, where it entered the forest.

"Tell you what," said Vanya, "there's a little place I have to show you."

Kolya's trusting eyes suddenly lit up with curiosity. "Show me," he blurted out rapturously, already looking forward to something mysterious and unusual.

"I know this place where no one will find us," said Vanya.

"But we won't get lost, will we?" asked Kolya.

Vanya looked at him contemptuously. "If you're afraid, don't come," he said scornfully.

Kolya flushed. "I'm not afraid," he said in an offended tone. "It's just that if it takes long to get there, we'll get really famished."

"We won't get hungry, it's not very far," Vanya said firmly.

The boys trotted off into the forest thicket.

It quickly became dark and wild around them. It got quiet and frightening . . .

Straight in front of them was the brink of a wide, deep ravine. The gurgling of a stream at the bottom was audible, but from the top the stream couldn't be seen through the thicket, and it seemed impossible to find a way through. But the boys began to climb down towards the stream. They descended, clinging to branches and at times skittering down the steep slope. Branches grazed them and whipped them in the face. Thick, strong bushes had to be pushed aside with some effort. There were a lot of dry, prickly twigs, and as they went down it was hard to keep from scraping their faces and arms. Sometimes a cobweb, thick and extraordinarily sticky, would cling to them.

"Any minute you could fall and break something!" said Kolya fearfully.

"Don't worry!" Vanya shouted. "It's not that bad."

He was far ahead, and Kolya was only barely inching down.

The lower they went, the damper it became. Kolya felt annoyed and unhappy that his yellow shoes were full of wet clay, and that his arms were all smeared with clay as well.

Finally they got all the way down to a narrow, dark hollow at the bottom. The stream splashed against the rocks, purling with a gentle music. It was damp, but nice. It seemed that people, the sky—everything was high, high up, and that no one would come here, no one would see . . .

Kolya, twisting around, looked with chagrin at his trousers. They were torn. Kolya was vexed. "What will Mama say?" he thought worriedly.

"It's not a calamity," said Vanya.

"But they're my new trousers," Kolya mournfully replied.

Vanya laughed. "My clothes are all patched already," he said. "They don't let me wear good things here. It's the forest, brother, not a sitting room. You don't wear new things here."

Kolya sighed and thought, "At least I'll wash my hands." But no matter how much he splashed the cold water on them, they remained red from the clay.

"That clay's really sticky," Vanya remarked carelessly. He took off his shoes, sat on a rock and dabbled his feet in the water. "Tore your clothes, got muddy, scratched your arms and legs," he said. "That's it, brother, it's not so bad. And here you don't have to take orders from anyone—you can do whatever you want."

And then, after a little silence, he suddenly said with a smile, "Flying here, that'd be the way."

"Too bad we're not sparrows," Kolya said with alacrity.

"We will—we'll fly," Vanya said with an odd certainty in his voice.

"But that's impossible!" Kolya protested mistrustfully.

"Lately I've been flying every night," Vanya told him, "almost every night. The moment I lie down, I take off. But

84

I can't do it yet in the daytime. Maybe I'm scared? I'm not sure." He sank into thought.

"We don't have wings," said Kolya.

"What do we need wings for?! It's not a matter of wings," answered Vanya, deep in thought as he gazed unblinkingly at the stream of water at his feet.

"What, then?" asked Kolya.

Vanya fixed Kolya with a long, malicious, transparent gaze, and said quietly, "You won't get it." He gave a ringing laugh like a mermaid, and started grimacing and twitching.

"Why are you making such faces?" Kolya asked shyly.

"What of it? Is there something wrong with it?" Vanya retorted dismissively.

"It scares me a bit," said Kolya with his sour smile.

Vanya stopped making faces, sat down quietly, and looked thoughtfully at the forest, the water and the sky. "There's nothing to be scared of," he said quietly. "People used to believe in devils and demons. But now, brother, there's no such thing. There's nothing to be scared of," he repeated quietly, and then he went on in a barely audible whisper, "except man." He whispered the saying he had often heard from his father: "Man is a wolf to man."

IV

With a chuckle, Vanya took an open pack of cigarettes from his pocket. "Let's have a smoke," he said.

"Oh, no, how can you?" Kolya said in horror.

Vanya sighed and said, "We're all of us—children—too used to being obedient—we got it from our fathers. Grown-ups obey like mad—whatever their boss says, they do. Now, womenfolk, though, they're more headstrong."

And after a silence, he said in a derisive and persuading tone, "Hey, you're a fine one—don't want to smoke. You like pretty flowers, grass and little leaves, don't you?" Vanya asked.

"Yes," Kolya said uncertainly.

"Well, that's all tobacco is—a kind of grass." Vanya looked at Kolya with his transparent mermaid's eyes, and, with a chuckle, held out the cigarette again.

"Take it," he said.

Captivated by the transparent gleam of Vanya's eyes, Kolya indecisively reached out for the cigarette.

"That's it," Vanya said encouragingly. "Just try it. You'll see for yourself how good it is."

He lit up both his own and Kolya's cigarette—the matches came from one of his deep pockets, among all kinds of junk and rubbish. The boys began to smoke—Vanya like a habitual smoker, Kolya with a worried face. And he choked right away, on the first puff. A fiery cloud filled his throat and chest, and in the smoke fiery sparks whirled before his eyes. He threw down the cigarette.

"Hey, what are you doing?" said Vanya.

"It's bitter," said Kolya in a dismayed whisper, "I can't."

"You're such a baby," said Vanya scornfully. "Just smoke one little fag—a little at a time, don't take deep puffs, then you'll get used to it."

Kolya, against his will, almost lifeless, put the cigarette in his mouth. He sat on the ground, his back against a tree, pale, with tears in his eyes, and smoked—and felt dizzy. He barely managed to finish. His head started to hurt, and he felt nauseous. He lay down on the ground, and the trees swayed slowly and gracefully above him, in a circular, tedious motion . . .

Vanya was saying something. His words barely registered in Kolya's dimmed consciousness. "When you're alone now and then, you can make it really nice for yourself," said Vanya.

"What do you mean?" asked Kolya in a weak voice.

"You start by imagining . . . Nah, you won't get it . . . I'll tell you later . . . Just come and visit me here. Really, let's start meeting here," Vanya entreated.

Kolya wanted to decline, but couldn't. "All right," he said weakly.

V

At home, a worried Kolya showed Mama his torn trousers. Mama laughed when she looked at his mournful face. She was feeling happy that day because she had been given the part she dreamt of playing in the amateur play.

"From now on, be more careful," she said to Kolya. "Just look at your new clothes!"

Kolya smiled a guilty smile, and Mama immediately guessed that there was something else on his conscience. Mama took his chin in her hand and tilted his face upwards. "Now why are you so pale?" she asked.

Kolya flushed and lowered his head, freeing himself with difficulty from Mama's grasp.

"Now then, what's this about?" Mama said severely, and bent down to him.

Kolya smelt of tobacco.

"Kolya!" Mama cried angrily. "What is this, you smell like cigarettes! A little early for that, isn't it, sweetheart?"

Kolya started to cry. "It was only one cigarette," he confessed in a guilty, wavering tone.

Mama was amused and at the same time vexed. "What are you carrying on with that awful Vanyushka for? He's a nasty boy, a green frog," she said angrily.

"I won't smoke anymore," Kolya said between sobs, "but his father lets him."

"Well, that's just wonderful," Mama said indignantly.

"He's a good boy, really, and anyway what's wrong with it if they let him?" Kolya persisted.

"Hmph! My young smoker," said Mama. "Don't let it happen again, you hear me?"

VI

That night Kolya dreamt of a crow. A repulsive, frightening one. He woke up. It was still night—a half-lit, northern night.

Then Kolya dreamt of Vanya and his clear eyes. Vanya

stared intently and said something indistinct. Kolya's heart started pounding, and he woke up.

Then Kolya dreamt that he got out of bed and was flying near the ceiling. His heart was quailing. It was terrifying and exhilarating. His body floated effortlessly. He was scared he might crash into the wall above the door. But all went well— Kolya flew down in the right place, and in the next room he again floated up under the dark, twilit ceiling. There were a lot of rooms, each with a higher ceiling than the last, and his flight through them grew faster and faster and more and more terrifying. Finally he flew out of a high, dark window that opened noiselessly before him into the open air, climbed high up into the sky, and circling languidly and delightfully in its deep, sun-filled heights, all of a sudden stopped, fell and woke up.

VII

The next day Kolya, against his better judgment, found himself in the same ravine. He didn't want to go. But he went, as if by habit.

And there, far from people, they talked . . .

"You were saying yesterday . . ." Kolya began uncertainly.

"What?" Vanya asked angrily, and his body jerked all over.

"About what you imagine," Kolya said shyly.

"Oh, so tha–at's it," Vanya drew out the words. He sat down quietly on a rock, clasped his arms about his knees, and gazed fixedly off into the distance. And Kolya asked him again, "What is it you imagine?"

Vanya was silent for a bit, gave a sigh and turned to Kolya, looked him over with a strange smile, and said, "Well, a lot of things. The best is when it's about something shameful. No matter how they offend you," said Vanya, "no matter how angry you are, just wind up your hurdy-gurdy, and you forget all the bad things."

"Your hurdy-gurdy?" Kolya repeated.

"That's what I call it, winding up your hurdy-gurdy,"

explained Vanya. "It's too bad, though, that it doesn't play for long."

"Not long?" Kolya repeated again with sympathetic inquisitiveness.

"It's tiring," said Vanya. He suddenly seemed to deflate, and stared ahead with weary, sleep-filled eyes.

"So anyway, what do you imagine?" insisted Kolya.

Vanya smiled crookedly and twitched his shoulders . . .

And so, far away from people, they talked about strange fantasies, about atrocious and torrid things . . .

And their faces flamed . . .

Vanya was silent for a bit and then began to talk about something else. "One time I didn't eat anything for three whole days," he said. "My father thrashed me for no reason at all, and I got really angry. Just you wait, I thought to myself, I'll give you a good scare. So I stopped eating."

"You really did?" Kolya asked, his trusting eyes wide. "So, and what happened?"

"My guts twisted from hunger," Vanya told him. "At home everyone was scared. They gave me another thrashing."

"And then what?" Kolya asked.

Vanya frowned and tightened his fist. "I didn't hold out," he said sullenly. "Stuffed myself. I'd got so weak from hunger. I went at my food like . . . They say you can live for three weeks without eating, if you only drink water. But without water you turn up your toes in no time. You know what? Let's not eat anything tomorrow," Vanya said quickly.

And he stared fixedly at Kolya with his transparent, bright eyes.

"All right," Kolya said weakly, in a strange-sounding voice.

"And mind, no tricks now."

"Of course not."

It smelt warmly of moss and ferns, and resinous pine needles. Kolya's head was swimming a little, and he was overcome by a languid weakness of will. Mama suddenly came to mind, but she seemed far, far away, and Kolya thought about her with indifference, without that surge of tender feelings that thoughts of Mama had always provoked in him.

"My mother will get angry. She'll get red in the face," Vanya said calmly, "but if it gets really bad, I'll just run off to the forest."

And suddenly, in a completely different, lively and cheerful tone, he said, "Let's ford the stream here. The water's nice and cool."

VIII

Vanya's father, Ivan Petrovich Zelenev, a lawyer by training and a swine by nature, worked in the Ministry, riding to work every day on the morning train and returning towards evening, often a bit tipsy. He was a red-haired, stout, cheerful and worthless man. Both his thought and his words were vulgar in the highest degree—as if he lacked character, as if there were nothing in him that was real and true. In conversation, he would wink at the other person for no apparent reason, often in the most inexpressive places. He would croon fashionable songs from operas out of tune. He wore a ring with a fake stone, and a necktie studded with a paste-jewel tiepin. He gave himself out to be a lover of freedom, and he liked to repeat bold phrases and criticise the government. At work, on the other hand, he was diligent, ingratiating and even rather base.

They were having supper late. Zelenev was drinking beer with his supper. He gave some to Vanya, too. Vanya drank it like an adult.

His father asked, "Now then, Vanka, why have you taken up with that namby-pamby mama's boy?"

"Now what!" Vanya rudely replied. "Not allowed to make friends! That's a new one!"

Neither Vanya's father nor his mother was disturbed in the slightest by Vanya's rudeness. In fact, they did not even notice it. They were used to it. And anyway, they were rude themselves.

"There's going to be no end of complaints," his father explained. "What are you giving him cigarettes for? His mother is complaining. And I'm losing out here, too, brother: I can't buy cigarettes for every boy in the village!"

"And he's not at all namby-pamby," Vanya said. "He's just a little pampered. And he's a good walker. And the main thing I like about him is, he's obedient."

"That's my fighter!" his father said proudly. "That's the way to be, brother, always try to finish on top. People, brother, are just a lot of cattle." Zelenev spoke with strange smugness. "There's no sense standing on ceremony with them. If you're too soft with them, they'll eat you right up."

"Without a doubt," his mother said.

"The stronger man is in the right," his father continued in a didactic tone. "The fight for existence. That, I'm telling you, brother, is the great law."

Zelenev lit up a cigarette and winked at Vanya enigmatically, out of habit as usual. He wasn't thinking anything in particular just then that would have called for winking.

"Give me a fag!" Vanya begged.

His father gave him one. Vanya lit up with the same placidly pompous expression he'd worn when he'd been drinking beer a little while ago.

His mother angrily grumbled, "Now they're both smoking the place up."

"Let's go out to the garden, brother," said his father.

IX

That night Kolya couldn't get to sleep. He was oppressed by strange emotions. He recalled what Vanya had told him about his dreams—and Vanya's dreams tempted him to dream of that, too. How was that possible? . . .

In the morning Kolya asked Mama for permission not to eat anything that day. At first Mama was worried. "Where does it hurt?" she asked.

But then, when she found out that nothing hurt, that Kolya just wanted to fast a little, Mama got angry and didn't allow it. "More of that Vanya's mischief!" she said. "That fiend is always up to no good!"

Kolya admitted that he and Vanya had agreed to eat nothing

that whole day. "How can I eat my fill while he's going hungry?" Kolya said, troubled.

But Mama said firmly, "Don't even think of it."

Kolya was very troubled. He tried not to eat anyway, but Mama was so strict with him that he had to obey in spite of himself. Kolya ate as if he were guilty of something. Mama smiled even as she frowned.

Meanwhile, Vanya really was going hungry all day. His mother said calmly, "If you don't want to stuff yourself, then don't. A little hunger won't kill you, and if it does, it's no great loss."

Towards evening, the boys met in the ravine.

Kolya was struck by the hungry gleam in Vanya's eyes and his sunken face. He looked at Vanya with tender pity and respectful admiration. And from that moment he became like a slave to Vanya.

"You eat?" Vanya asked him.

Kolya made a guilty, sour face. "They made me eat," he said sheepishly.

Vanya shook his head in disgust.

X

If Kolya's Mama hadn't been so busy with rehearsals for the play that was to be performed in a few days, she would surely have noticed and been worried by the strange change in Kolya. Formerly cheerful and affectionate, the boy had changed completely.

More and more often, Kolya was afflicted by depressed moods he had never known before, and Vanya sustained them. It was as if he knew some fatal and irresistible spells. He lured Kolya into the forest and cast his spells there under the dusky forest canopy. His depraved eyes charmed Kolya into oblivion—an oblivion so profound that sometimes Kolya looked around with absolutely unrecognising, uncomprehending eyes. What had once been delightful and alive now seemed new, alien and hostile. And even Mama herself sometimes receded into the murky twilight of distant memories: when Kolya wanted to say something about Mama as he used to, he would feel all of a sudden that he had neither words, nor even thoughts about her.

Nature, too, was strangely, sadly dimmed in Kolya's eyes. It was as if its outlines were fading away. And nature was becoming uninteresting for Kolya, and unnecessary.

Yielding to Vanya's temptations, Kolya occasionally smoked. Not more than one cigarette each time. And each time Vanya gave him mint leaves to cover up the smell of tobacco. Tobacco no longer made Kolya's head spin as it had at the beginning. But its effect was even more harmful: each time after smoking, Kolya could feel an extraordinary emptiness in his soul, and an indifference. It was as if someone were taking his soul out of him with stealthy, thieving hands and putting in its place a cold, free, elemental mermaid's soul—with soulless, eternally calm breath. This made him feel freer and more courageous. And somehow he didn't feel like thinking about anyone or anything.

Dark circles appeared under Kolya's eyes from the smoking and the night-time fantasies. And Mama noticed this, got worried and decided to keep a closer eye on Kolya, but she was soon distracted by her other fun and festive activities.

XI

Even in the ravine it was hot. And quiet. Kolya had got to the forest before Vanya.

The pines and spruces were emitting their resinous scent, and this gave Kolya a momentary, feeble stirring of happiness. Not for long. His soul responded joyfully, as if from habit, to the greeting of nature, so dear and familiar to him and only seemingly indifferent. His soul rejoiced, and just as suddenly forgot its joy, and seemed even to forget that there was such a thing as joy on earth . . .

The stream splashed gently, with a perplexed, questioning

93

murmur. In the forest there was an occasional rustling. Shyly concealing itself and concealing its firm objectives, nature was living its mysterious life, so dear and familiar to us . . .

Kolya continued to wait. A melancholy boredom oppressed him. Around him there were so many things of every kind that had once given him pleasure—trees, grass, sounds and movements—but all this seemed somehow empty. And far away.

There was a rustling sound far off, and Kolya knew immediately that it was Vanya coming. And Kolya felt happy. It was as if he had been lost and alone in a strange and frightening place, where melancholy dwelt, and he had been found and rescued from its dark fascination.

Then the branches stirred, resiliently and stubbornly resisting some violation, then forgetting about it immediately and springing back into place, and Vanya's grimacing face looked out from the green thicket. "Waiting?" he cried. "And have I got something for us!"

He shouldered the branches aside and came out to the stream, happy, sweaty, barefoot. He had a bottle in his hand. Kolya gazed with amazement.

"Madeira," said Vanya, showing the bottle. "Pinched it."

He was full of excitement, and his face was jerking with more than the usual grimaces. He spoke in a breathy whisper. "My old man likes to have a swig now and then. Chances are he won't notice a bottle's gone missing. And if by bad luck he does remember, he'll think he drank it himself. Or the maid did."

The boys squatted on their haunches by the stream, and gazed with dumb excitement at the bottle. Kolya asked, "But how do you open it?"

"How, indeed," Vanya answered with an important air. "And what do you think corkscrews are for?"

Vanya put his hand in his pocket, dug around, and pulled out a penknife with a corkscrew. "See," he said, showing Kolya the knife, "I have this knife. It has two blades, and on the bottom—a corkscrew."

"On the bottom," Kolya repeated with a laugh.

Slowly, with difficulty—and taking pleasure in the difficulty—they uncorked the bottle. Vanya gave the bottle to Kolya and said, "Drink."

Kolya flushed, giggled, made a little grimace, brought the bottle to his lips, and took a tiny sip. Sweet and bitter. And a light thrill of feverishly happy excitement ran through Kolya. With a discomfited laugh he handed the bottle to Vanya. Vanya hurriedly lifted the bottle to his lips and straightaway swigged a big mouthful. His eyes began to shine.

"Why are you taking such tiny sips?" he said, passing Kolya the wine. "Take a bigger swig, you'll see how good it is."

Now Kolya drank more boldly, as much as he could in one gulp. But this was too much for him and made him cough. Suddenly he felt scared and awful. The forest swam smoothly and slowly before his eyes. And then suddenly he was happy.

Passing the bottle between them, they drank in turns, taking big gulps or small ones. And both of them were soon drunk. Vanya's grimaces were more intense than ever. The boys laughed loudly. Kolya began to shout and laugh wildly: "The forest is dancing!"

"It's dancing, it's dancing!" Vanya seconded him.

"Look, what a funny bird!" Kolya yelled.

And everything they saw aroused their gaiety and seemed funny to them. They danced and capered around. Their loud gaiety gave rise to wild, silly games. They knocked down saplings, and clawed at each other, and all of their movements were unexpected and awkward, and everything was hazy, disconnected and funny in their eyes.

They had tossed the bottle away somewhere. Then they remembered it and began to look, but couldn't find it. Vanya said, "There was still wine there. It's rubbish that we lost it."

"So what, we got drunk enough anyway," said Kolya, laughing.

Now Vanya quietened down. His rowdy happiness had subsided. And right away his changed mood communicated itself to Kolya. In a relaxed, drunken, complaining tone,

Vanya said, "I wish we could drink tomorrow. My head's splitting."

Kolya lay down on the grass under a tree. His face had paled. It seemed to him that something inside him was picking him up, turning him, carrying him . . . but where?

"Let's swim," said Vanya. "The water'll cool us off and sober us up."

The boys stripped off, waded into the water, and almost drowned in the stream. The water kept pushing at the backs of their knees. They laughed, fell down on all fours and gulped water. The water got in their noses and throats. It was frightening, and funny. Finally, they somehow scrambled out and plopped down on the grass, laughing uproariously.

They began to put their clothes on. Vanya asked, "You want me to sail two boats?"

"Sure, go ahead," said Kolya. "But where are the two boats?"

"Oh, I'll find them," Vanya replied with a smirk. All of a sudden he grabbed Kolya's yellow shoes and threw them in the stream. "Look at that, two boats!" he shouted, laughing loudly.

The shoes, bouncing between the rocks, were quickly carried off. Kolya cried out and ran after them, but it soon became obvious that he wouldn't be able to catch them—the bushes were getting in his way and his legs were disobeying him. Kolya sat on the ground and burst into tears. "Why did you do that?" he reproached Vanya.

"Well, you yourself said, 'Go ahead,' " Vanya said with a malicious grin.

"How am I going to get home now?" Kolya asked sadly.

"The same way I do," Vanya chortled. His transparently light eyes squinted and laughed. He made a face at Kolya and ran up the slope, quickly, clambering up like a cat. Kolya scrambled along after him, crying and scraping his feet.

"Better get home as quickly as I can," he thought, feeling bitter and humiliated.

But hardly had they reached the road when again he felt

happy and the whole adventure with the wine, the stream and the shoes seemed amusing.

XII

Evening was coming on, and Kolya still wasn't home. Kolya's Mama had begun to worry. She sent the maid over to the neighbours'. The maid came back and said, "And that Vanya isn't back at the Zelenevs' yet, either."

"Loafing together somewhere. Well, I'm definitely going to give it to him," Kolya's Mama said angrily.

But actually she was frightened. Anything might have happened. In her imagination she saw horrible pictures of Kolya's violent death.

She stood at the gate and worriedly looked down the road. From behind her came the sound of someone's quick, quiet footsteps. Mama turned around. It was Kolya: he was hurrying in through the back garden. Mama gasped. "Kolya, what a mess you are! Your coat sleeve is torn! And where are your shoes?"

Kolya laughed gaily, waved his hand and said, "My shoes floated away . . . far away."

And the slurred, raspy sound of his voice horrified Mama. Kolya could barely move the tongue in his mouth; he was pale, but very cheerful, and he quickly began to tell about his adventures in jumbled, confused words. And it was awfully strange to him that Mama didn't laugh at his funny story.

"You smell of wine," Mama exclaimed sadly. Her drunken boy seemed so frightening to her that she just couldn't believe her eyes. But Kolya happily related, "Mummy, we drank Madeira in the ravine, it was tasty as anything! And we sailed two little boats—two boats. So much fun—it was lovely, it really was!"

Mama was horrified, but Kolya chattered on and on.

Finally, Mama somehow managed to get Kolya to bed. He quickly fell asleep. Mama went over to the Zelenevs.

When Alexandra Dmitrievna got to the Zelenevs', the head of the house said to his wife, "You sort it out among yourselves however you want."

And he retreated to the terrace.

"Is your Vanya home?" asked Alexandra Dmitrievna, gasping with emotion. "He got my son plastered."

Mrs. Zelenev flushed, put her hands on her hips, gave a malicious laugh and said, "Oh, he's home alright. Snoring. It seems he and your precious boy got themselves good and drunk—he stinks of wine. And we'll see who got who plastered. He may be a bad boy, but such goings-on as this never happened before he took up with your kid."

Both women began to shower one another with reproaches and insults. Mrs. Glebov said, "Your son is the worst tearaway in the village. A boy oughtn't to be allowed to behave as he does."

"What are you barking about?" Mrs. Zelenev answered rudely. "Your little falcon seems a right fine one, too, for all your talk. He drank away his shoes today; how do you like that? A fine one, that boy."

"What do you mean?!" Mrs. Glebov shrieked with indignation. "Your Vanya threw them in the stream!"

Mrs. Zelenev gave a malicious laugh. "What's all the fuss about," she said. "They got sloshed! It doesn't happen every day, thank God. Your Kolya'll dry out soon enough. He'll sleep it off and come to just fine."

Alexandra Dmitrievna started crying. Mrs. Zelenev gazed at her with disdainful sympathy. "Now don't you be angry," she said peaceably. "We're not teaching him to do it. With kids you never know what's next—you can't keep 'em in cotton wool—and sometimes they get into mischief. Our Vanya's going to get it, that's for sure. But you give that silly little twit of yours plenty of kisses, and tomorrow he'll cry you a river of tears, he'll be so sorry. And you and I have nothing more to talk about."

She turned and walked away.

On the next day, when Vanya had slept it off, his father whipped him. It was early in the morning, but the neighbours listened with pleasure to how Vanya roared in a low, fierce voice.

"I'm going to drown him," Vanya said after the punishment.

But no one was listening anymore. His father was hurrying to catch his train. His mother was seeing his father off . . .

His father left. Vanya lay in the storeroom for a long time, motionless and silent. Then he got up and left the house. His mother shouted after him, "Vanya, don't you dare go anywhere today. You stay home!"

"You think I'm so stupid?" Vanya answered rudely. "As if I'm going to sit at home." He opened the gate and ran down the street. His mother started to chase after him, but it was clear from the start that she wasn't going to catch him.

"Marfa!" she shouted to the maid, who was grinning as she watched from the kitchen. "Run down the lane, get him."

"It's too late, he's already clean away," Marfa answered, and laughed heartily. Her employer's helpless fury amused her.

"You're gonna get it, you little scoundrel!" cried Mrs. Zelenev after her son.

XV

Vanya was sitting on the bank of the forest stream, gloomily staring at the water and thinking cruel, malicious thoughts. From time to time he whispered, "A stone around his neck, into a sack and into the water." All his anger and hatred was concentrated on Kolya. The desire for Kolya's death tormented and gladdened him.

Drown him! But how to get him into the water?

But anyway what for? Better to make it so he drowns on his own. He's obedient. You can make him, convince him, charm him into it.

A vicious smile contorted Vanya's face into a cruel grimace. He ran into the forest and yelled loudly, "Hey, hey!"

No one answered.

"Let it be at night, then," Vanya thought. "He'll drown, and I'll say I was sleeping when it happened."

And this made Vanya feel happy.

"I'll get away from the house on the sly," he thought.

XVI

Kolya, after he woke up from a good night's sleep, recalled yesterday's events with horror and shame. He cried for a long time in Mama's arms, repenting and promising never to do anything like that again. And Mama's fears abated. She was terribly busy with her rehearsals.

But Kolya longed to go back to the forest. As soon as he could, he ran off and made his way to the ravine.

Vanya met Kolya with a malicious, vengeful glance. "Pop you into a sack and into the water with you," he thought again.

But he hid his anger, and started telling Kolya how he had been punished. Kolya listened to him with kind and tremulous sympathy. When he noticed this, Vanya gave a laugh and said, "It doesn't matter to me. Let them do what they want with me; I'm not a bit scared. Anyway they already thrashed me for what I did. They say not to steal. Always guarding their precious stuff. So steal if you want, just don't get caught."

The boys were squatting on their haunches at the riverside, staring thoughtfully into the water. A fish jumped, as if it felt cramped there in the cool, clear water. Midges hovered above the water. Everything was the same as usual: indifferent, pretty on the whole, but monotonous in the details, and not much fun.

Vanya grew quiet. He whispered in a sad tone, "You know, I'll tell you: I don't want to live."

Kolya gave him a surprised look, his eyes wide. "What do you mean?" he asked.

"What I said," answered Vanya calmly and as if mockingly. "I'll die, and that's all there is to it. I'll drown myself."

"But aren't you scared?" Kolya asked, frightened.

"Scared? No, nothing scares me. Except living!" Vanya went on, fixing Kolya with the irresistibly transparent gaze of his spellbinding eyes. "It's nasty living here, on this cursed earth. Man is a wolf to man here, on this hateful earth. What's there to be afraid of? You choke for just a little, and then just like that you're on the other side. And there everything is different."

"Different?" asked Kolya shyly, trustingly.

"Completely different. Just think about it," Vanya went on with conviction. "For instance, if you love travel . . ."

"I do," said Kolya.

"Well, then," Vanya continued, "no matter where you go on earth, it's the same old rivers, trees and grass—everything, everything, brother, is just the same old thing. But there, beyond the grave, it's totally, totally different. What it is, I don't know, nobody knows, but you don't like it here, do you?"

Silently Kolya shook his head.

"Yeah, it's sickening to live here," Vanya continued. "What's frightening about dying? Are you afraid of death? That's just here, death is just here on earth, we all die, but there, there isn't any death. Here if you don't get any grub, you'll die—for lack of some stupid crusts, and you're depending on them—but over there is freedom. Right now you've got a body. So much torment you get from it. You cut yourself and it hurts. But there won't be any of that there. Your body will rot—who needs it? You'll be free—and nobody will take you."

"But what about Mama?" asked Kolya.

"What Mama?" Vanya answered in a compelling tone. "Maybe you dreamt her. You don't have a Mama. All of that only seems to be, but really there isn't anything, it's just a fraud and that's all. Think about it yourself: if all this really existed, would people die? How could it be possible to die? Here everything fades away, disappears like a ghost."

Kolya looked away from Vanya's cold, transparent eyes, and

gazed at his own body in bewilderment. "How can that be?" he said. "It's still a body."

"But what's it good for?" Vanya retorted. "People laugh at it. If you have a tuft of hair growing in the wrong place, or a mole, or you're cross-eyed, everybody laughs at you. And they beat you up—and it hurts. You think: I get beaten up a lot; I'm used to it now. But you never get used to it. The physical pain—that doesn't matter. But you never get used to the injustice of it. But over there, nobody wrongs you. Nobody tells you not to do things, nobody scolds, nobody reproaches you. Whatever you feel like, you do. Everything is possible. It's here on earth that everything is the way it is—take one extra step, move a bottle from one place to another—and you're already a thief and they humiliate you."

Vanya talked on, and Kolya looked at him with trusting, humble eyes. And the wrongs Vanya was talking about pained him very much—more than if they had been his own. And anyway, what did it matter who was wronged!

A black bird flew over the children, and its broad wings moved quickly and noiselessly. Vanya spoke in a mournful and quiet, but irresistibly convincing tone, "You swallow a certain kind of liquid, and it's like you've become a different person. There's nothing of that sort there. You can't hurt anyone and no one can hurt you. It's good there. Here you look at people—you envy one, feel sorry for another—and your heart's all in splinters. There there's nothing of the kind."

And Vanya talked on like this for a long time, and Kolya came more and more under the spell of the sad sound of Vanya's voice and the mournful allure of his incantations.

Vanya fell silent, and the magic of his voice seemed to dissipate like airy smoke from an extinguished censer in the piney aromas of the forest. He gazed off into the distance, weary and silent, and Kolya suddenly wanted to make an objection that would be so strong it would be the last word. An eternally joyful and comforting feeling came over him. He raised his gladdened eyes to Vanya, and said in a gently resonant voice, "What about God?"

Vanya turned to him and grinned, and Kolya again became

frightened. Vanya's transparent eyes blazed with an unchild-like meanness. Quietly and sombrely he said, "There is no God. And if there is—what good does he do you? You accidentally fall in the water—God won't lift a finger to save you."

Kolya, pale, listened with horror.

XVII

The village kids took it into their heads to tease Vanya. They shouted to each other, "Hey, guys, there goes Three-brow—they gave him a proper drubbing today."

"Pulled down his britches, gave him some switches!"

Coarse and insulting words showered down on him. Vanya stopped in his tracks. He looked silently at the kids with his clear, snake-like eyes, round and staring. The children quietened down, and timidly goggled at him with stupid, uncomprehending eyes. A peasant woman popped out from around the corner. She managed to sweep all the children together into one big armful, and angrily muttering something, dragged them off.

"Trying to curse them, the blighter," she grumbled.

"What's the matter, aunty?" her neighbour asked.

"He's got the evil eye," she explained in a whisper.

Vanya heard. He grinned mirthlessly and continued on his way.

It was already evening and his father was having his after-dinner doze by the time Vanya got home. He brought his mother a small basket of wild strawberries.

"I'll give you what for," his mother said savagely. "This morning wasn't enough for you?"

"I didn't eat a single berry, I saved them all for you," Vanya said piteously.

"Where'd you get the basket?" his mother asked angrily, but there was already less ferocity in her voice.

"Am I getting another whipping?" Vanya asked weepily. "I tried so hard."

"How dare you scarper off like that!" his mother shouted.

"But I just wanted to go to the forest," Vanya said plaintively.

"Watch it, or I'm going to tell your father," his mother said, but more complacently. "Sit down, you might as well eat something."

"So Father's sleeping?" Vanya asked with a knowing smile. He sat down at the table and greedily set to his food.

"Starved," his mother thought pityingly.

"He had his dinner; he'll be snoring till teatime," she said. "Came home tipsy. No worse than you were yesterday. Taking after your dad."

She stood there with her hands on her hips, smoking, and looked at her son with a tenderness that seemed funny and out of place on her coarse, red face. She felt sorry for him for having been whipped on account of that "namby-pamby" kid. "And he looks so green," she thought. "Oh, well, he's a fine, strong lad, our boy," she soothed herself. "He'll come 'round in no time in this air."

"Somebody got him plastered?" asked Vanya, and gave a sly wink towards the next room, from where the sleeping man's snores could be heard.

"It was Strekalov of course—dragged him into it," his mother answered. "Those people are just despicable."

She talked completely openly with her son, on equal terms, unabashed.

XVIII

Now every time the boys got together, they would talk about death. Vanya extolled both death and the afterlife. Kolya listened and believed what he heard. And he became gradually more oblivious to nature, and death became more and more desirable and appealing—comforting, calm and assuaging all earthly sorrows and worries. It liberated, and its promises were forever immutable. There is no lover on earth more tender and faithful than death. And if the name of death terrifies people, it's because they don't know that death is true and eternal, forever immutable life. Death promises a different form of being, and it will never betray you. Unlike everything and everyone else, death alone will never betray you.

And it was sweet to dream of it. And whoever said that it is horrible to have such dreams? It's sweet to dream of death as a faithful woman, far off, yet always close by.

And Kolya started to forget about everything. His heart was turning away from everything he was attached to. And Mama, whom he had always held so dear—what did she matter? And did she even exist? Wasn't everything on this earth equally false and dreamlike? Here nothing was really true; this inconstant world, soon to vanish into boundless oblivion, was inhabited only by passing shades.

Vanya's spellbinding gaze, instilling a single obsession deep in Kolya's soul, drew him to the forest every day, into the ravine where the stream murmured the same things Vanya's light, transparent eyes said to him as they led him into oblivion.

Deeper and deeper the oblivion became, and sweeter.

And when Vanya looked at Kolya for a long time with those clear, unmoving eyes—beneath this merciless gaze Kolya forgot everything as completely as people do in the embrace of that most comforting of angels—the angel of death.

But Kolya's angel of death grimaced and concealed his malicious thoughts. Even before, his thoughts had been depraved and cruel, but now they had taken on an especial edge. He dreamt of death—of Kolya's death, and then of his own as well. And he spent anguished nights in mad fantasies, imagining the cruellest mortal agonies.

In tempting Kolya, he had seduced himself with the most fatal temptation of all. The poisoner had been poisoned at his own hands.

In the beginning he had wanted to drown Kolya and walk away. But then he forgot about walking away. He was captivated by his own dreams of death.

And Kolya's fantasies and dreams had become just as mad. They passed back and forth between the boys as if they were the same.

One afternoon they met at the edge of the forest. Vanya's face was pale and swollen.

"Why are you so pale?" Kolya asked.

"I was doing a lot of dreaming," Vanya told him.

The boys were silent for a bit. Vanya looked all around, making sure no one was around, and said, "I know a deep place. As soon as you fall in you drown."

"Where is it?" asked Kolya.

Vanya started laughing, and stuck his tongue out at Kolya. "No," he said, "I'm not showing you ahead of time, or you'll go on your own. And I want to go with you."

Vanya embraced Kolya, and said in a sinister, quiet voice, "Together with you, my dear."

Kolya saw the clear, blank eyes so close, close up, and, as always, those eyes enveloped him in dark oblivion. All was forgotten, he didn't want to think about anything—an abyss in those eyes . . .

The boys agreed to go away that night and die.

"Mama is performing today," Kolya said.

"All the better," answered Vanya.

And the talk of Mama did not arouse any feeling in Kolya.

Vanya laughed and said to Kolya, "But when you leave the house, leave your cross at home—you won't need it."

Vanya left. Kolya remained alone. He didn't think about Vanya's words. Not that he forgot them—the anguish they aroused remained, and the poisonous words kept burning in his soul. There they lived and continued to grow, while Kolya lived, as always, with his usual impressions: Mama, playing, the swing, going to the river, the boys in the village—just as before.

Except that just as before it was terribly monotonous. Boring. The important thing was that Mama didn't see how bored he was.

And Kolya always met Mama with his former, habitual, sour smile.

Night fell. And it was mournful, quiet, dark, and long, like the final night.

Mama was performing that day at the theatre. She had managed to get her favourite part, and today was the premiere. Mama was so happy. She left right after dinner, and would not be back for quite a while: after the performance there would be dancing until four in the morning. Kolya would already be asleep when Mama got back.

The maid gave Kolya his tea, put him to bed, locked the door and went off on her own. Kolya was alone. Not for the first time. He wasn't afraid.

But when the click of the latch, a light metallic click, reached his ear, he was seized by a feeling of cold alienation.

He lay in bed for a little while, on his back, gazing at the dark ceiling with darkened eyes. "What about Mama?" he thought from time to time.

"There is no Mama," someone seemed to say, or perhaps it was someone's words echoing in his head.

With a wry grin, Kolya slipped quietly from the bed and began to get dressed. He was going to take his shoes, but then he remembered that the ground was damp and cool now—it would feel tender and caressing on his feet.

Moist Mother Earth![1]

Kolya threw his shoes under the bed and went to the window. There was a full moon, light green and ugly, in the sky. It seemed to be hiding behind the treetops, spying. Its light was soft and lifeless, and its rays were tremulous and mesmerising as they penetrated through the branches . . .

Vanya cut through the back gardens to the garden behind Kolya's cottage. All the windows were dark. Vanya gently rapped at Kolya's window. It opened. Kolya looked out. He was pale, and smiling his sour smile. The moonlight fell full on Vanya's face.

---

[1] Moist Mother Earth (*Mat' syra zemlya*) is an ancient and powerful pagan Slavic earth goddess.

"You're green," Kolya said.

"That's how I am," Vanya answered. His face was calm and expressionless, almost lifeless. Only his eyes were alive, and glowed with a liquid, transparent gleam. "Right, let's get going then," he said. "It's time."

Kolya, awkwardly grasping the windowsill with his small, white hands, climbed out of the window. Vanya helped, supporting him. "Should have worn shoes, it's cold," said Vanya.

"And what about you?" Kolya retorted.

"I'm fine. I'm not afraid," said Vanya, and smiled cheerlessly.

"Me, neither," Kolya said quietly.

The boys left the garden and went along the narrow edge of the field towards the darkened forest nearby. Vanya whispered, "See, the moon is so bright. There used to be people there, too, but they all died. That was when the earth was a sun. It was warm on the moon, and there was air and water, and day and night followed each other by turn, the grass grew, and happy, barefoot boys ran in the grass, in the dew. Hey, brother, they all died, they cooled down, and who gives a fig for them now?"

Kolya turned to Vanya with a sour, sad smile, and whispered, "And now we're going to die."

"Don't start snivelling," Vanya scowled. "Next you'll be crying. Are you cold?"

"I'm all right," Kolya answered quietly. "Will we be there soon?" he asked.

"We're almost there."

The boys went down to the river. Here it was squeezed between its narrow banks: on the far side was a cliff wall, and the near bank angled steeply down to the water. A few large stones lay on the bank and in the water near the bank. It was quiet. The moon, bright and cold, hung above the precipice, staring and waiting. The water seemed still and dark. The trees and bushes stood in silence. Tiny, ugly flowers, white and ominous, stood out against the grass.

Vanya felt around near one of the stones on the bank and came up with two nets with broken handles. He tied twine to the edges, making them into a pair of sacks, and put a stone in each. "Two bags," he said quietly.

The two boys stood next to each other near the water on a broad, low stone like a gravestone, and both gazed at the dark water in equal fright. Captivated, they stood there, and now there was no going back. And each of them had a sack with a stone in it hanging on his chest, the twine pulling at his neck.

"Go ahead," said Vanya. "First you, then me."

"No, let's go together," answered Kolya in a quietly resonant voice.

"Together? Let's go, then," Vanya said decisively, and grinned.

Vanya's face suddenly changed, growing thin and dark. A cold, final passivity weighed upon him . . .

Kolya wanted to cross himself. Vanya grabbed his hand.

"What are you doing, don't!" he said angrily. "You're still a believer? All right, then, if He wants to save you, let these stones in our sacks turn into bread."

Kolya raised his eyes to the sky. The dead moon looked dully down on him. No prayer stirred in his enfeebled soul. The stone remained a stone. . . .

Kolya noticed a slim branch with little leaves above him. Its very elegant black contours stood out against the dark-blue sky.

"Beautiful!" Kolya thought. Someone called him from behind, as if in Mama's voice: "Kolya!"

But, it was too late. His body was already bending towards the water, falling faster and faster.

Kolya fell. There was a heavy splash. Cold, heavy drops splashed Vanya in the face.

Kolya drowned at once. A cold anguish seized Vanya. It drew him irresistibly forward after Kolya. His face was distorted with pathetic grimaces. Strange shudders ran through his body. He was all bent over, as if trying to pull away from someone who was holding him and pushing him forward. And suddenly he stretched out his hands, gave a plaintive cry, and fell in the water. The water parted with a slap, spray flew up, and dark circles rippled through the water and died away. And again it was quiet.

The dead moon, bright and cold, hung above the dark precipice.

O death! I am yours. Everywhere I see
Only you, and I hate
The charms of the earth.
Human pleasures I disdain—
Battles, festivities and haggling,
The din and dust of the mundane.

The reign of your unjust sister
Life, contemptible and meek,
I rejected long ago. Not I,
Fanned by the mystery
Of your extraordinary beauty,
Not I will fall at her feet!

Not I will go to the brilliant feast
Whose haughty fire sears
My somnolent eyes,
On which has fallen, as clear
And lucid as pure crystal,
Your cold tear.

Fyodor Sologub, 1894

Since I fell in love with you,
All else I hate.
Since I fell in love with you,
Only you I contemplate.

And I often wonder how
I ever could have missed
That you reign everywhere, O death,
And life does not exist.

Fyodor Sologub, 1894

Hymn of the Order of Liberators in the Drama *Earth*

Death, who art eternally pure,
Hearken to our praise,
Your loving lips have set us
    All ablaze!

Naked, you will stand before us,
Each of us, one day.
You won't deceive, you won't betray
    Anybody's faith!

You will come to us in bed,
A goddess, all in flames.
Come to me, O death, and show
    Your fiery face!

With caresses stern and tender,
Come and kiss me!
Wound me mortally,
    And heal me!

Blissful are those who have known
Your lips' sweet blade,
Who are free, who have surrendered
    Their corpse to the flames!

Valery Briusov, 1904

The Poisoned Garden

Fyodor Sologub

> *Nature of the parched plains*
> *Begat it on a day of wrath.*
> A. Pushkin, "Anchar" ("The Upas Tree")[1]

I

"Beautiful Youth, what are you pondering, so lost in thought?" asked the Old Woman, from whom the Youth was renting a room.

She had quietly entered his half-dark room in the evening and, with a barely audible rustle of soft slippers over the uneven, brownish-red painted floor, she drew near the Youth and stopped just behind him. He started in surprise—he had been standing for half an hour at the single window of his cramped sleeping quarters in the upper rooms of the old house and was staring intently at the beautiful Garden lying before him, where a multitude of plants blossomed, giving off their soft, sweet and strange fragrances.

In answer to the Old Woman, the Youth said, "No, Old One, I am not thinking about anything. I'm standing, looking and waiting."

The Old Woman shook her grey head disapprovingly, and the tied ends of her dark kerchief bobbed like two pointed,

---

[1] "It" refers here to the subject of Alexander Pushkin's well-known 1828 poem, the upas tree "Anchar." The Beautiful Lady's account in part VII of her ancestor's journey to gather poison from the tree for his master's arrows, his subsequent death and his master's military victories comes from Pushkin's poem. Sologub's story thus picks up where the narrative of Pushkin's poem leaves off.

pricked-up ears. Her wrinkled face, yellower and drier than the faces of the other old women living on that street at the outskirts of the enormous Old City, now wore an expression of concern and anxiousness. In a soft, sad voice, the Old Woman said, "I pity you, dear Youth."

Her voice, old and hoarse as it was, rang with such sadness, such heartfelt sympathy, and her aged, faded eyes looked so sorrowful, that suddenly, for just a moment, it seemed to the Youth, there in the half-light of his room, that those outward signs of age were only a very cleverly worn disguise, and behind it was concealed a young and beautiful Wife who not so very long ago had suffered the heart-rending grief of a Mother mourning the death of her Son.

But this strange moment passed, and the Youth smiled at his fantastic imaginings. He asked, "Why do you pity me, Old One?"

The Old Woman drew next to him, looked for a while through the window at the Garden, beautiful and blossoming, and all illumined by the rays of the setting sun, and said, "I pity you, dear Youth, because I know where you are looking and what you are waiting for. I pity you and your Mother."

Perhaps because of these words, or perhaps for another reason, something in the Youth's mood changed. The Garden, blossoming and fragrant beyond the high fence below his window, now struck him as somehow strange, and his heart was transfixed by a dark feeling like sudden terror, seemingly born of the heady, languorous fragrances exuding from the brightly-coloured flowers below.

"What is happening?" he thought in bewilderment.

He did not want to yield to the dark enchantment of evening melancholy. He bestirred himself, smiled cheerfully, tossed a black lock of hair off his high forehead with a quick, strong hand, and asked, "What could be bad, Old One, about what I'm looking at and waiting for? And how do you know what I am waiting for?"

And at that moment he was merry, brave and handsome, and his black eyes blazed, and his ruddy cheeks glowed,

115

and his bright scarlet lips now seemed just-kissed, and from behind them his strong, white teeth gleamed, glad and fierce.

The Old Woman said, "Here you are looking at the Garden, dear Youth, and you don't know that it is an evil Garden. Here you are waiting for the Beautiful Lady, and you don't know that her beauty is fatal. Two years you've lived in my room, and never before today have you stared out of the window in this way, lost in thought. Apparently your turn has come. Come away from the window before it is too late, don't breathe in the evil breath of these insidious flowers, and don't wait for the Beautiful Lady to arrive under your window and enchant you. She will come, she will enchant you, and you will follow her whither you'd not want to go."

Speaking thus, the Old Woman lit two candles on the table where his books lay, banged the window closed and pulled the curtain over the window. The rings slid with a light scraping sound along the copper rod, the yellow linen curtain billowed and lay quiet again, and the room brightened up, becoming cosy and tranquil. And it seemed that no Garden lay outside the window, and enchantments didn't exist, and that all was simple, normal and firmly established for all time.

"But it really is true," said the Youth. "Never before have I noticed this Garden, and today was the first time I saw the Beautiful Lady."

"You've seen her already, then," the Old Woman said sadly. "The evil seed of her magic has already been planted in your soul."

But the Youth continued speaking, perhaps to the Old Woman, or perhaps reasoning with himself. "Of course, I had no time before. During the day there were lectures at the university, and in the evenings I studied or went to parties or the theatre with my merry companions and pretty girls, somewhere way up in the balcony, or even in the parterre for the student rate when there weren't enough regular ticket-buyers: entrepreneurs love us—we clap heartily and shout, calling out the actresses again and again until they extinguish all the lights. And when summer comes you go home. That's why I've only just heard that right next door is the magnificent Garden of our professor, the famous Botanist.

"And why is he famous? Because he sold his soul to the devil," the Old Woman said angrily.

The Student laughed gaily.

"But still," he said, "it seems strange that until this very evening I had never laid eyes on his daughter, although I have heard much about her wondrous beauty and about how many distinguished young men, from the Old City and other places both far and near, have tried to win her love, and had high hopes, but their hopes were dashed, and some of them even died, unable to endure her coldness."

"She is guileful," said the Old Woman. "She knows the value of her charms, and doesn't display them to everyone. A poor student will have a hard time making her acquaintance. Her father taught her much that even scientists don't know, but she doesn't go to your meetings. She spends her time with rich men, who are more likely to lavish gifts on her."

"Old One, today I got a good look at her, and it seems to me," protested the Youth, "that a maiden with such a beautiful face, such pure, bright eyes, such graceful ways, and who is dressed so prettily, cannot be guileful and venal and always seeking after gifts. I have firmly resolved to make her acquaintance. This very day I am going to visit the Botanist."

"The Botanist won't let you set foot over his threshold. His servant won't even bother to announce you once he's seen the tattered rags you wear."

"My clothes are not his affair!" the Youth exclaimed in vexation.

"Let me put it this way: if you were to arrive on the back of a winged serpent, then they would admit you without a glance at your patches."

The Youth laughed and cried gaily, "All right then, Old One, I'll saddle up my winged serpent, if there's no other way to get in."

The Old Woman grumbled, "It's all because of those strikes of yours. Had you been tending to your studies, you

117

wouldn't have started caring about that artful Beautiful Lady and her terrible Garden."

"What is so terrible about her Garden?" asked the Youth. "Anyway, we had no choice but to strike: our rights and the university's are being violated. Do you really think we can humbly submit to that?"

"Young people must get their education," the Old Woman muttered, "and not busy themselves with their rights. And you, dear Youth, before you go and make the Beautiful Lady's acquaintance, have a good look at her Garden from your window tomorrow morning at daybreak, when all is clearly and truly visible. You will see that in that Garden there are none of the flowers we are all familiar with here; the flowers there are of a sort no one in our City knows. Give that some good long thought, for it isn't so simple. The Demon is guileful—could not this be his creation, designed to bring men to their ruin?"

"Those are plants from faraway countries," said the Youth. "They were brought from hot countries where everything is different."

But the Old Woman didn't want to discuss it any further. She waved her hand in irritation and left the room, scuffing her slippers and angrily grumbling harsh words under her breath.

The Youth's first impulse was to go to the window, pull aside the yellow linen curtain and look again at that enchanting Garden, and wait. But he was interrupted: his Friend arrived, a loud and ungainly young man, and invited the Youth to a place they often went to talk at length, argue, shout, sing and laugh together. On the way there his Friend, laughing, looking indignant and waving his arms somewhat more than was necessary, told him about something that had happened that morning in the classrooms and hallways of the university, how all the lectures had been cut short, how the opponents of the strike had been put to shame, what beautiful words their favourite, good professors had spoken, and how their least favourite, and therefore bad professors had made fools of themselves.

The Youth spent an interesting evening. He spoke excitedly,

118

like everyone else. He heard sincere, fiery speeches. He looked at his friends, whose faces expressed both the carefree courage of youth and its passionate indignation. He saw young women, pretty, smart and demure, and dreamt of how he would choose himself a sweetheart from their merry midst. And he almost forgot about the Beautiful Lady in the enchanting Garden.

He got home late, and fell soundly asleep.

II

In the morning, when he opened his eyes and his gaze fell upon the yellow linen curtain at the window, it appeared to him that its yellow was tinted with the crimson of dark desire, and that it held within it a kind of strange, horrible tension. It seemed that the sun was insistently and passionately thrusting its burning, bitter rays into the linen, which was shot through with golden light, and it was calling, and demanding, and rousing. And in answer to this amazing outer tension of gold and crimson, the Youth's veins filled with blazing vitality, his muscles flooded with supple strength, and his heart became like a fountain of furious wildfires. Pierced sweetly through and through with millions of live, burning, stimulating needles, he leapt from his bed, and with gay, childlike laughter, without getting dressed, he suddenly began to leap and dance about the room.

Attracted by the unusual sound, the Old One, his landlady, glanced in from the doorway. She shook her head reproachfully, and grumbled, "Dear Youth, you are dancing and joyful and disturbing everyone, but you yourself know not what you are happy about, and you know not who is standing beneath your window and what she is preparing for you."

The Youth was discomfited, and once again became quiet and decorous as he had been before, which was in keeping with his character and the fine upbringing he'd had at home. He washed up more attentively than usual, perhaps because he didn't have to rush off to any lectures that day, or perhaps for an entirely different reason, and he dressed with just as much care, taking a long time to get his rather worn clothing brushed clean; he didn't have any new clothes, since his parents were not rich and couldn't send him much money. Then he went to the window. His heart started beating anxiously as he pulled the yellow linen curtain aside. An enchantingly beautiful sight opened up before him—although today he noticed immediately that there was something strange in the whole aspect of that extensive and perfectly designed Garden. He could not immediately make out what exactly it was that so surprised him, and he began to examine the Garden attentively.

What was it that made its beauty unpleasant? What made the Youth's heart so terribly faint? Was it that everything in the enchanting Garden was too perfect? The pathways were laid out straight, all of the same width and monotonously strewn with a uniform layer of yellow sand; the plants had been placed with painstaking accuracy; the trees were pruned in the form of globes, cones and cylinders; the flowers were chosen by their hue, so that their combination was a feast for the eyes, but also inexplicably wounded the soul.

But, reasoning coldly, what was so unpleasant about a tidiness that bore witness to the fact that the Garden was diligently tended? No, that was not the cause of the strange uneasiness troubling the Youth. It was something else, something the Youth did not yet understand.

One thing was certain: this Garden was unlike any other garden the Youth had ever seen in his life. Here he saw flowers that were enormous and too brightly coloured. Sometimes it seemed that multicoloured flames were burning among the vibrant greenery, with its brown and black stems of creeping vines, thick like tropical snakes, and strangely formed leaves of exorbitant size and unnaturally bright green colour. Airy waves of spicy and languorous fragrances poured in through the open window, puffs of vanilla, and incense, and bitter almond, fragrances sweet and bitter, ceremonial and mournful, as during the triumphant mysteries of a funeral mass.

The Youth felt the soft but arousing touch of a light breeze on his face. But in the Garden, apparently, the wind lost its force, weakly coming to rest on the soothingly green grass and in the shade beneath the strange shrubs. And because that strange Garden's trees and grasses were breathlessly silent, and did not hear the wind blowing softly above them, and did not respond to it in any way, they seemed lifeless. And this in turn made them seem deceitful, sinister and hostile to man.

However, now one of the plants did stir. But the Youth laughed when he had a closer look. What he had taken for the leafless trunk of a strange tree was a rather short, gaunt man dressed all in black. He had been standing in front of a shrub with bright purple flowers, and he now set off slowly along the pathway, leaning on a thick stick and approaching the very window where the Youth stood looking out. It wasn't so much by his face—which, shaded as it was by the broad brim of his black hat, was only partially visible from above—as by his manner and walk that the Youth recognised the Botanist. Not wishing to appear brash, the Youth began to turn away from the window. But just then he caught sight of the Beautiful Lady, the Botanist's youthful daughter, going to meet him.

Her bare arms were raised to the crown of black braids encircling her head, for just at that moment she was pinning a bright vermilion flower to her hair. Her thin, short tunic was fastened at her shoulder with a gold clasp. Her legs, lightly tanned and bare to the knee, were as shapely as the legs of a resurrected goddess. The Youth's heart began to pound, and forgetting all caution and modesty, he rushed back to the window and gazed greedily at the lovely vision. The Beautiful Lady threw a quick, fiery glance in his direction—her eyes flashed a dark blue from beneath black, even brows—and her smile was tender and arch.

If there are happy people, if there are times when the mad sun of joyousness shines on them, carrying them off in a sweet whirl of ecstasy to undreamt-of lands—then where are the words to tell about it? And if there is such a thing as truly bewitching beauty, how can one describe it?

But now the Beautiful Lady paused, gazed intently at the Youth, and then laughed, joyfully and merrily, and in an unutterable whirl of ecstasy, the Youth forgot himself completely, leaned impetuously out the window and cried out in a voice ringing with emotion, "Dear Lady! Fair Lady! Divine Lady! Come to me! Love me!"

The Beautiful Lady came up close, and the Youth heard her gently ringing, clear voice, its every sound wounding his heart with sweet torment. "Dear Youth, do you know the price of my love?"

"Even though it were life itself!" exclaimed the Youth. "Even at the dark gates of Death!"

Like a laughing, blazing dawn, she stood before the Youth and stretched out her shapely, bare arms towards him. And she spoke, and from her words wafted a seductive, languorous fragrance, like puffs of delicate tuberose.

"O, dear Youth, wise and passionate, you who know and see, your patience will be rewarded. Many have loved me, many thirsted to possess me, all handsome, young, strong men, and I have smiled an enchanting smile at many of them, like the smile of she who gives final consolation, but never until you have I said to anyone these sweet and terrible words: I love you. Now I want to, and I am waiting."

Her voice rang with passion and desire. She loosed from around her waist the black silk cord with its bronze key, and had already drawn back her arm to throw the key to the Youth, but she wasn't quick enough. Her father had hurried over as soon as he noticed from afar that she had fallen into conversation with an unknown Youth. He grabbed her roughly by the arm, took away her key and started shouting in a hoarse old man's voice, repellent as the leaden croaking of an old raven at a cemetery, "Are you mad, what are you trying to do? You've no cause to speak with him. This Youth is not born of those for whom we grew our Garden, once we had mixed the juices of these plants with the poisonous resin of Anchar. Not for the likes of this penniless man did our ancestral father perish, having breathed the lethal fragrance of the terrible resin. Go on, go home, and don't dare to speak with him."

Tightly squeezing her hands, both of which he had seized

in one of his own, the old man pulled his daughter towards the house, which was visible in the depths of the Garden. The Beautiful Lady docilely followed her father, laughing. And her laughter was clear, ringing and sweet, and it stung the Youth's ardent heart with thousands of sharp stings.

He remained standing a long time at the window, examining with straining eyes the carefully planned and pruned vistas of the enchanted Garden. But the Beautiful Lady did not show herself again. All was quiet and motionless in the wondrous Garden, and the monstrously bright flowers seemed lifeless, and when their fragrance reached the Youth, it made his head spin and his heart grow faint with terrible languor—a fragrance reminiscent of the dark, urgent, greedy breath of vanilla, cyclamen, datura and tuberose, wicked and unhappy flowers, dying as they destroy, captivating in their fatal mystery.

III

The Youth firmly resolved to find a way into the wondrous Garden, breathe his fill of the mysterious fragrances that the Beautiful Lady breathed, and win her love, even though it might cost him his life, even though the path to her might be a fatal one, a path of no return. But who could help him get inside the house of the old Botanist?

The Youth left the house. For a long time he wandered about the City, asking everyone he knew about the Beautiful Lady, the daughter of the Botanist. Some could not take him inside the old Botanist's house, and others would not, and everyone spoke unkindly of the Beautiful Lady.

His Friend said, "All the young Optimates of our City fall in love with her and praise her elegant and refined beauty. But to us, the Proletarians, her beauty is hateful and unnecessary: her dead smile irritates us, and we find the madness hiding in the depths of her blue eyes repugnant."

A Young Woman, seconding him, said, "Her beauty, about which many idle, rich young men speak, is in our view no real beauty at all. It is merely the dead allure of decay and corruption. I dare say she uses powder and rouge. She smells like a poisonous flower; even her breath is scented, and that is repugnant."

A Popular Professor said, "My colleague the Botanist is a renowned and learned man; but he does not want to subject his science to the higher interests of humanism. His daughter, they say, is enchanting; some talk of the originality of her dress and manner; however, I have not had a chance to engage in any sort of substantial discussion with her, as she is rarely to be met with in our circles. I think, however, that her charms contain something harmful for the health. I've heard strange rumours, the truth of which I obviously cannot vouch for, rumours that the percentage of fatalities among the young aristocrats who visit that house is higher than average."

The Abbot, with a thin smile on his shaved, pale face, said, "When the Beautiful Lady comes to me in church, she prays too earnestly. One might think that she has some heavy sins on her conscience. But I hope we won't ever have to see her standing at the church doors in the woollen shirt of a repentant sinner."

A Mother, after sending all her daughters out of the room, said, "I don't understand what people find attractive about her. Men ruin themselves over her, she's flirtatious, breaks the hearts of young men, takes bridegrooms away from their brides, and meanwhile she herself loves no one. I do not permit my dear daughters, Minochka, Linochka, Dinochka, Ninochka, Rinochka, Tinochka and Zinochka, to socialise with her. My girls are so well-mannered, dear, obliging, cheerful, amiable, diligent, such capable housekeepers, so good at needlework. And even though it will be difficult for me to part with them, that's the way it must be, and I would gladly give my eldest's hand to such a well-mannered young man as you."

The Youth left in a hurry. The seven sisters smiled to him from the window, jostling against one another. It was a dear and pleasant scene to behold, but the Youth's heart was full of sweet and terrible visions of the Beautiful Lady.

The old Botanist led his daughter into the house. His anger had subsided, and although he didn't let her clasped, slender hands out of his own big, bony fingers until he had got the gaily smiling Beautiful Lady past the threshold, he no longer squeezed them so painfully or pushed her so roughly ahead. His face was sad. He let go of his daughter's hands and she followed him docilely into his study—an enormous, sombre room, its walls covered with shelves holding many huge, dusty books.

The Botanist sat down in the dark leather-upholstered armchair at his heavy oak desk. He seemed weary. He shaded his eyes, which still held their youthful gleam, with a parchment-yellow, trembling hand, and peered reproachfully at his daughter. The Beautiful Lady dropped to her knees at his feet, looked up at the old Botanist's face, and smiled tenderly and submissively. She held herself erect, with her arms at her sides; there was a subdued submissiveness in her pose, and affectionate obstinacy in the curve of her alluring smile. Her faced looked pale, and it seemed as if the flames of mad laughter still flickered on her lips, and mad yearnings lurked secretly in the dark blue depths of her eyes. She said nothing, waiting for what her father would say.

And he spoke slowly, as if finding the words with difficulty. "My dear, what did I hear you say? I did not expect this from you. Why did you do it?"

The Beautiful Lady bowed her head, and quietly and sadly said, "Father, sooner or later it is bound to happen."

"Sooner or later?" asked her father, with what sounded like surprise in his voice. And he went on, "Then let it happen later rather than sooner."

"I'm aflame," the Beautiful Lady said softly.

And the smile on her lips was like the reflection of burning flames, and dark blue lightning smouldered in her eyes, and her bared shoulders and arms were like fine alabaster vessels filled with molten metal. Her splendid bosom rose and fell in uneven breaths, and two white waves strained to be free of the tight embrace of her dress, which was of a soft yellowish pink colour, like a peach. From beneath the folds of her rather short dress her shapely legs and feet were visible, resting nervously on the dark-green velvet of the rug.

Her father shook his head quietly, and in a sad and severe voice said, "You, dear daughter, so experienced and so artful in your wondrous ability to enchant while yet remaining chaste, you must know that it is still early for you to be leaving me and abandoning my plan before it has been perfected."

"But will it ever be finished?" the Beautiful Lady protested. "They keep coming and coming."

"No one knows," said the Botanist, "if there will ever be an end to it, and whether we will see our plan come to fruition or hand it down to succeeding generations. But we will do what we can. Remember that now a young Count is coming to see you. You will kiss him and let him choose from a bouquet of poisoned flowers. And he will go away full of sweet hopes and giddy anticipation, and once again the inevitable will happen to him as well."

An expression of submission and boredom settled on the Beautiful Lady's face.

"Go along, then," said her father.

He bent down and kissed her on the forehead. The Beautiful Lady touched her sultry, scarlet lips to his wrinkled, yellow hand, pressed her white, half-bared bosom to his dry knees, sighed and stood up. And her sigh was like a moaning reed.

V

Half an hour later, the Beautiful Lady stood in the same dress before a handsome, arrogant young Count in the midst of the Garden by a round bed of brightly coloured, enormous flowers from which wafted a stupefying fragrance, and with a sweet smile she was saying, "Dear Count, you ask for too much. Your desires are too ardent and too impatient."

Her smile was tender and arch, and her chaste, clear gaze took in with gentle admiration the slim figure of the young

Count and his rich costume, tailored fashionably and handsomely from the most expensive fabrics and decorated with gold and gemstones.

"Dear enchantress," said the Count, "I know that you have been cold towards many others who sought your favour. But you will be more tender towards me. I will be able to earn your love. I swear by my honour that I will make the cold blue of your eyes darken with passion."

"And how will you gain my love?" asked the Beautiful Lady.

The expression on her lovely face was impenetrable, and her voice betrayed none of the excitement that so easily overcomes young ladies when they hear the sultry voice of the passion they have inspired. But the self-assured, arrogant Count was not deterred. He said, "My predecessors left me a not insignificant fortune, and I myself have increased it many times over with my gold and valour. I have many precious gems, rings, necklaces, bracelets, fine fabrics and perfumes from the east, Arabian horses, silk and satin clothing, rare weapons, and much more that I can't begin to list, that I can't even call immediately to mind. I will pile it all at your feet, enchantress; I'll pay with rubies for your smiles, pearls for your tears, gold for your fragrant sighs, diamonds for your kisses, and a blow from my trusty dagger if you betray me."

The Beautiful Lady laughed. She said, "I am not yet yours, and already you fear my betrayal and threaten me. That just might make me angry."

The Count threw himself to his knees before the Beautiful Lady and showered kisses on her hands, so supple and shapely, with soft skin from which rose a light, uncanny fragrance.

"Forgive my madness, enchantingly Beautiful Lady," he prayed, suddenly forgetting all his arrogance. "My love for you has deprived me of my tranquillity and prompts my wild deeds and strange words. But what am I to do! I love you more than my very soul, and to possess you I am ready to pay not only with my fortune, not only with my life, but with something dearer to me than life and the redemption of my soul—my honour!"

The Beautiful Lady said with enchanting tenderness, "Your words have touched me, dear Count. Stand up. I will not exact excessive payment from you for my love. It cannot be bought and is not for sale. But he who loves must also be capable of waiting. True love always finds a way to the heart of the beloved."

The Count got up. With an elegant gesture he adjusted the lace cuffs of his green satin caftan and fastened a long, rapturous gaze on the Beautiful Lady. Their eyes met, and the expression in the Beautiful Lady's blamelessly bright eyes was as impenetrable as ever.

Seized by the dark anxiety that overcomes even the arrogant and self-assured in moments of mortal danger, the Count stepped away from the Beautiful Lady. On a bench nearby lay a prettily carved oak casket. The Count opened it and with a respectful bow brought it to the Beautiful Lady. The sun's rays quivered like merry laughter on the diamonds and rubies of a diadem. And it seemed to the arrogant Count that the radiance and laughter fell on the priceless stones from the glowing lips of the Beautiful Lady. But her smile was just the same as before, and she gazed curiously at the gift as if it were a worthless, but nonetheless pleasing token of his regard. Then for a fleeting moment she was touched lightly by sorrow, her face clouded, and she said, "My forebears were slaves, and you offer me a diadem even a queen would not refuse."

"Enchantress!" the Count exclaimed, "You are worthy of an even more splendid diadem."

The Beautiful Lady smiled at him cordially and again became a little sorrowful, her face troubled, and said gently, "My forebears were fated to spill hot drops of their blood beneath the whips of cruel masters, while to me befall festive rubies of wedded happiness."

And so quietly it was scarcely audible, she whispered, "But I won't forget."

"Why think about days long past?" the Count exclaimed. "Our bright, youthful days are full of joy; let's leave the sorrow of remembrance for old age."

The Beautiful Lady laughed, her laughter chasing away her

sorrow, which was only momentary, like a storm cloud dissipating in the summer sun. She said to the Count, "For your wonderful gift, dear Count, I will give you today one flower of your choice and one kiss. Only one."

The young Count became so ecstatic and expressed this so vehemently and noisily that the Beautiful Lady repeated, sweetly and severely, "Only one, not more."

And she asked the Count, "Which flower, dear Count, do you want to have from me?"

The Count answered, "Lovely temptress, whatever you give me will make me unspeakably grateful to you."

Smiling, the Beautiful Lady said, "All the flowers you see here, dear Count, have been brought here from afar. They have been gathered with great effort and at great risk. My father has improved their form, colour and fragrance through his assiduous care. He has long studied their properties, transplanting, cross-breeding and grafting them until finally he attained his ends, having developed poor, wild, ugly flowers from fields and woods into these enchanting, fragrant blossoms."

"And the most enchanting blossom of all is you, dear Beautiful Lady!" the Count exclaimed.

The Beautiful Lady gave a little sigh and continued, "Many find their fragrance too strong and heady. And I notice that you, dear Count, are growing pale. You and I have spent too long among these sultry fragrances. I'm used to it, I've been breathing them in since childhood, and my very blood is saturated with their sweet vapours. But you had better not stand here too long. Choose quickly which flower you want to take from me."

But the young Count insisted that the Beautiful Lady herself pick him a flower—he was waiting impatiently for her second gift, the promised kiss—the first kiss. The Beautiful Lady looked at the flowers. A fleeting shadow of sadness once again darkened her face. With surprising speed, as if her movements were governed by a will not her own, she extended her arm, so lovely in its bared shapeliness, and plucked a white, double blossom. She slowed her hand, bent her head, and finally, with an expression of timid indecision, she approached the Count and inserted the blossom in the buttonhole of his caftan.

A strong, sharp fragrance rose into the young Count's whitened face, his head began to spin, and he was suffused with languor, the strength drained from him. Indifference and weariness overwhelmed him. He was all but fainting, and hardly felt how the Beautiful Lady took him by the hand and led him to the house, away from the fragrances of the wondrous Garden.

In one of the rooms of the house, where all was well-lit, pink and white, the Count came to. The youthful freshness came back into his face, his black eyes again lit up with passion, and once again he felt the joy of living and the tumult of desires. But his doom was imminent. A white arm, bare and shapely, settled on his neck, and the Beautiful Lady's fragrant kiss was tender, sweet and long. The two deep blue lightning bolts of her eyes flashed right before his own eyes, and then were shrouded by the quiet mystery of her long lashes. Terrible flames of sweet pain whirled in a maelstrom around the young Count's heart. He raised his arms to embrace the Beautiful Lady, but with a little cry she broke away and ran lightly and softly away, leaving him alone. The Count sprang after her. But the old Botanist met him at the doorway of the pink chamber. Caustic was the smile on those thin lips, cutting across the parchment-yellow face in a scarlet line. The Count was dumbfounded. With uncharacteristic confusion, and feeling a strange weakness throughout his body, he said good-bye to the old Botanist and left.

The terrible whirlwinds of sweet pain circled faster and faster about the young Count's heart as he rode home on his black Arabian racehorse, hardly hearing the distinct ringing sound of hooves on stone. His face grew paler and paler. Suddenly his eyes closed, his hand let go of the reins, and he slumped heavily down, sagging from the saddle. The frightened horse reared up on its hind legs, threw off its rider and galloped off. When they raised the Count up from the ground, he was already dead—his head had smashed against

a rock, and no one knew how he had died. They were sur-
prised—he had been such an accomplished horseman!

Night fell. The full moon shone sweetly and tremulously,
conjuring and enchanting with its cold, deathly silent rays.
The Youth's heart was full of dim terror as he went to his
window. Having grasped the edge of the yellow curtain, his
hands delayed and hesitated for a long time before he steeled
himself to unhurriedly pull it aside. Swinging slowly, the yel-
low linen rustled, and its swish was like the barely audible hiss
of a snake in the forest undergrowth; and the light copper
rings gently rang and scraped against the copper rod.

The Beautiful Lady stood beneath the window, and looked
at the window, and waited. And the Youth's heart skipped a
beat, and he couldn't understand whether fear or rapture was
making his heart falter.

The Beautiful Lady's black braids were undone and fell
about her bare shoulders. Her shadow lay sharply outlined on
the ground at her unshod feet. Illuminated from the side by the
moon, she stood there like a sharp, clearly defined vision.
The folds of her white tunic were severe and dark. Dark was
the blue of her eyes, mysterious her immobile smile. The dull,
smooth surface of the broach fastened at her shoulder
gleamed dimly on her strangely motionless body and clothes.

She began to speak softly, and her words were fragrant with
ambergris, musk and tuberose, and they sounded like the fine
silver chains of a lit censer.

"Dear Youth, I love you. By obeying your call, I have gone
against my father's will, and I came to you to say this: be afraid
of me and my charms, run far away from this Old City, and
leave me to my dark fate, leave me, who am steeped in the evil
breath of Anchar."

"O, lovely maiden!" the Youth answered her. "You, whom
I have only just discovered, and who are already dearer to me
than my own life and soul—why do you say these cruel words

131

to me? Or do you not believe in my love, which ignited so suddenly, but will never die?"

"I love you," repeated the Beautiful Lady, "and do not want to destroy you. My breath is saturated with poison, and my lovely Garden is poisoned. You are the first I've told this to, because I love you. Hurry now to leave this City, run from this Garden with its lethal beauty, run far away, and forget about me."

Intoxicated with rapture and sorrow sweeter than any earthly joy, the Youth exclaimed, "My beloved! What is it that I need from you? Does my soul not thirst for but a single moment? To burn up in the blissful flame of rapture and love, and at your sweetest feet—to die!"

A slight shiver ran through the Beautiful Lady's body, and she became as radiant as the clear joy of dawn behind a white fog. With a solemn, expansive gesture she lifted her bare arms, and striving with all her being towards the Youth, she said, "O, my beloved! Let it be as you wish, and sweet it will be to die with you. Come to me, come to my terrible Garden, and I will tell you my dark tale."

Again, as that morning, the bronze key on its pink ribbon flashed in her hand. Then, with a bright laugh like a boy's, she ran back a little way, her shapely legs a dull white on the dim yellow sand of the path, and with a quick, agile swing of her arm, she tossed the key up to the window. The Youth reached out and caught the key in midair.

VII

There they stood, the Youth and the Beautiful Lady, intoxicated with rapture and sorrow in the poisoned Garden, in the shade of those mysterious plants, where the lifeless moon mingled the poison of its melancholy with the toxic breath of earthly, evil flowers. They looked into each other's eyes, and the Beautiful Lady spoke in a voice that sounded like the fragile voice of a harpsichord. "My forebears were slaves—but even slaves thirst for freedom. One of my forebears, obeying his master's will, made the long, arduous journey to the desolate plains where Anchar grows. He gathered the poisonous sap of Anchar and brought it to his master. Not a few of his master's victories can be attributed to his poisoned arrows. But my forebear died after breathing so much of the evil fragrance. His widow began to think how to get revenge on that wicked clan of warriors. She stole the poisoned arrows, soaked them in water, and hid away the solution like a precious wine in a deep cellar. She poured a drop of that solution into a barrel of water, and with that she watered the wasteland at the edge of Old City, where our house and Garden now stand. Then she took a drop of water from the bottom of that barrel, mixed it into bread and fed it to her son. And the soil of this Garden became poisoned, and she inoculated her son with poison. And since that time all of our blood relatives, from generation to generation, were brought up on poison. And now the blood in our veins flows with fiery poison, and our breath is fragrant, but lethal, and whoever kisses us dies. And the strength of our poison doesn't weaken as long as we live in this poisoned Garden, as long as we breathe the fragrances of these monstrous flowers. Their seeds are brought from afar—my grandfather and my father went wherever plants that are evil and harmful to people could be found—and here, in this soil poisoned for so long, those evil, lethal flowers have fully revealed their furious strength. Smelling so sweet, so joyful, those guileful blossoms turn even the dew falling from the sky into deadly poison."

Thus the Beautiful Lady spoke, and her voice rang with joy, and her face burned with great jubilation. She finished her tale and began to laugh, softly and mirthlessly. The Youth bent down before her and silently kissed her hand, breathing in the languorous aroma of myrrh, aloe and musk that wafted from her body and her thin dress. The Beautiful Lady again spoke. "Heirs of our oppressors come to see me, because my evil, poisoned beauty enchants them. I smile at them, at those who are doomed to death, and I pity each of them, and some I even almost loved, but I never yielded to any of them. I gave to each only a single kiss. My kisses were innocent, like the kisses of a loving sister. And whoever received my kiss died."

In horror and rapture, two such incompatible passions, the bewildered Youth's soul languished. But love, which conquers all, overcoming even the anguish of a man's final moments, triumphed now as well. Ecstatically opening his trembling arms to his tender and terrible Beautiful Lady, the Youth cried out, "If death is in your kiss, O my beloved, let me be intoxicated with an uncountable number of deaths! Cling to me, kiss me, love me, breathe upon me the ambrosial fragrance of your poisoned breath, let death after death flow into my body and into my soul, until you utterly destroy all that I once was!"

"Is that what you want?! You're not afraid?!" cried the Beautiful Lady.

Pale in the rays of the lifeless moon, the Beautiful Lady's face became like a dim, white lantern, and tremulous and deep blue were the lightning bolts of her sorrowful and joyful eyes. With a trusting, tender and passionate gesture she clung to the Youth, and her naked arms wound about his neck.

"We'll die together!" she whispered. "We'll die together. All my heart's poison is aflame, and its fiery currents are streaming through my veins, and I am like a bonfire in the all-consuming embrace of a great flame."

"I'm aflame!" whispered the Youth. "I'll burn up in your embrace, and together we are two flaming bonfires, burning with the great rapture of poisoned love."

The sad, lifeless moon grew dim and sank, and black night came and took its turn on watch. It shaded their secret love and kisses, fragrant and poisoned, with darkness and quiet. And it listened as the rhythmic beating of their two hearts died away, and in sympathetic silence it watched over their last, shallow breaths.

It was thus that, having breathed his fill of the fragrances breathed by the Beautiful Lady, and intoxicated by her sweet love, its sting so tender and fatal, the handsome Youth died in the poisoned Garden—and on his breast died the Beautiful Lady, having consigned her poisoned, yet fragrant soul to the sweet enchantment of love and the night.

With a secret joy I would die
      In the hour when the moon rises.
The shadow of a mysterious dream
      Fans me with a strange sweetness.

Devoted to boundless distances,
      Where sound fades and light dims,
I will leave the familiar circle
      Of repeated thoughts and words.

My heart will freely pass
      The limits of knowledge and compassion,
And tirelessly, in the eternal abyss,
      Forward, forward it will swim.

And the phantom of a dream
      Will fan me with an ever new, strange sweetness.
With a secret joy I would die
      In the hour when the moon rises.

Valery Briusov, 1898

Follow Me

The scent of half-wilted lilies
Clouds my light reveries.
The lilies speak to me of death,
The time when I shall no longer be.

Peace to my quieted soul.
Nothing cheers me, nothing hurts me.
Do not forget my last days,
Understand me, when I shall no longer be.

I know, my friend, the road is not long,
And the poor body is quickly fatigued,
But I know: love, like death, is strong.
Love me, when I shall no longer be.

A mysterious vow appears to me . . .
And I know the heart shall not be deceived—
In parting there is no forgetting for you!
Follow me, when I shall no longer be.

Zinaida Gippius, 1895

What makes you beautiful? Not your dress,
Nor your boots, nor your elegant corset;
What's a corset? It's mere deceit;
Without it your figure is naturally sleek.
Can your beautiful legs be seen in boots?
You are lovelier when you go barefoot,
And you shine when you are naked—
Enchanting, young, and animated.
You can save your fancy dress
For the crowd, for strangers, and for friends,
But I, my love, am always glad
To see your body all unclad
When we're alone in bed at night,
Your nakedness gleaming in candlelight.
And, as I lie with you in bed,
I feel trembling and warmth beneath my hand,
And I perceive with arrogance
That I may fondle, and caress,
And, with my love, exhaust you,
And torment you, and beat you.

Fyodor Sologub, 1893

Light and Shadows

Fyodor Sologub

I

Volodya Lovlev, a thin, pale boy of about twelve, had just got home from school and was waiting for dinner. He stood in the living room by the piano, looking at the latest issue of *Field*, which had been delivered that morning from the post office. A newspaper was lying there as well, partially covering a page of *Field*, and from it fell a small booklet printed on thin, grey paper—an advertisement for an illustrated journal. Inside the booklet, the publisher listed the future contributors (a good fifty well-known literary names), lavishly praised the journal as a whole and its numerous individual sections, and gave sample illustrations.

Volodya began to leaf distractedly through the grey booklet, examining the tiny pictures. His big eyes gazed wearily from his pale face.

One page suddenly caught the boy's interest and made his wide eyes open even wider. From the top down, along the whole length of the page, six drawings were printed, portraying hands folded together in various ways. Their shadows, cast against a white wall, formed dark silhouettes: a lady's head in a funny-looking horned headdress, the head of a donkey, a bull, a sitting squirrel, and so on.

Volodya, smiling, became absorbed in his examination of the drawings. He was familiar with this game: he already knew how to place the fingers of one hand to make a rabbit's head appear on the wall. But here were some Volodya had not seen before, and—most importantly—these figures were all fairly complex, for two hands.

Volodya wanted to make these shadows. But now, in the uncertain light of a dying autumn day, of course it wouldn't work well.

"I should take the booklet to my room," he thought. "Nobody else needs it."

Just then he heard approaching steps and his mother's voice from the next room. Suddenly and unaccountably reddening, he quickly shoved the booklet into his pocket and stepped away from the piano, towards his mother. Smiling affectionately, she came up to him. She was remarkably like him, with the same wide eyes in a pale, beautiful face.

Mama asked, as she usually did, "What did you do in school today?"

"Nothing," Volodya said frowningly.

But immediately he felt he was speaking rudely to his mother, and he was ashamed. He gave her an affectionate smile and began to recount how his day at school had gone— but this only made him feel more vexed.

"Pruzhinin distinguished himself again today in our class." He began to tell about a teacher who was disliked by the pupils because of his rudeness. "Our Leontiev gave the wrong answer in a lesson, and he says to him, 'That'll do,' he says, 'sit down—wood may as well sit on wood!' "

"Well, you notice everything now," said Mama, smiling.

"He's always awfully rude."

Volodya was silent for a while, then sighed and said in a complaining tone, "And they're always rushing us."

"Who?" asked Mama.

"The teachers. They all want to get through the course as fast as possible and then review it all thoroughly for the exams. If you ask about something, they probably think you're trying to drag out the time to the bell, so you won't be called on."

"Well then, talk with them after class."

"Yes, but after the lesson they're also in a hurry, to get home or to the girls' school for classes. And it's all so fast— first geometry and then Greek right away."

"Try to keep up!"

139

"Yes, keep up! Like a squirrel in a wheel. Really, it annoys me."

Mama smiled gently.

II

After dinner Volodya went to his room to do his lessons. Mama was careful to make sure Volodya was comfortable, and everything he might need was there in the room. No one disturbed Volodya here—even Mama did not come in while he was studying. She would come in later to help Volodya, if necessary.

Volodya was a diligent lad, and what they call talented. But today he was having trouble studying. No matter which lesson he took up, some unpleasant thing occurred to him—he would recall the teacher of that subject, a biting or rude phrase of his, tossed off in passing and lodging deep in the impressionable boy's heart. Many of the most recent lessons had somehow gone poorly: the teachers seemed dissatisfied, and it was tough going. Their bad mood communicated itself to Volodya, and now a vague uneasiness drifted towards him from the pages of his books and notebooks.

He went hurriedly from one lesson to the next, then to a third—and he was annoyed by these useless and unnecessary trivialities, the frantic pace of all these petty things that had to be done as quickly as possible, so as not to become "wood on the wood" of his bench tomorrow. He even began to yawn from boredom and vexation, and impatiently jiggled his legs as he nervously shifted in his seat.

But he knew without a doubt that it was imperative to learn all these lessons, that it was very important, and that his entire fate depended on it—and he conscientiously did the work that bored him.

Volodya made a small inkblot on his notebook and put down his pen. Taking a close look, he decided it would be possible to remove it with a penknife. He was glad of the diversion. There was no knife on the table. Volodya put his

hand in his pocket and dug around. Amidst all kinds of rub-
bish and junk of the sort boys stuff their pockets with, he felt a
little knife—and as he fished it out, along with it came a little
booklet.

He didn't yet know what the paper in his hand was, but as
he pulled it out he suddenly remembered that it was the book-
let with the shadows, and immediately he livened up and felt
happier.

And that's what it was—the little booklet he had completely
forgotten about as he was doing his lessons.

He nimbly leapt up from his chair, moved the lamp closer
to the wall, gave a cautious, sidelong glance at the door (which
was slightly ajar) to make sure no one was coming—and with
the booklet opened at the familiar page, he began to carefully
examine the first drawing and put his hands together the way
it showed. At first the shadow came out badly, not the way it
was supposed to. Volodya moved the lamp around and bent
and stretched his hands this way and that—and finally he got a
woman's head in a horned headdress on the white wallpaper
of his room.

Volodya was having fun now. He angled his hands and
gently wiggled his fingers—the head bowed, smiled, made
funny faces. Volodya tried another figure, and then another.
All of them were difficult at first, but Volodya eventually
managed to get them.

He spent half an hour or so doing this and forgot all about
his lessons, school and everything in the world.

Suddenly familiar steps sounded outside his room. Volodya
flushed, shoved the booklet into his pocket, quickly put the
lamp back, almost knocking it over in the process, and sat at
his place, bending over his notebook. Mama came in.

"Let's have tea, Volodya dear," she said.

Volodya pretended he was looking at the blot and getting
ready to open his knife. Mama gently laid her hands on his
head . . . Volodya flung the knife aside and clung to Mama, his
face flushed. Evidently, Mama had not noticed anything, and
Volodya was glad about that. But he still felt oddly ashamed, as
if he had been caught playing stupid, childish games.

On the round table in the middle of the dining room the samovar quietly crooned its gentle, cooing song. The hanging lamp drenched the white tablecloth and dark wallpaper in a drowsy atmosphere.

Mama was lost in thought, bending her beautiful, pale face over the table. Volodya laid his hand on the table and stirred the tea in his glass with a spoon. Sweet streaks ran through the tea, and fine bubbles rose to its surface. The silver spoon jingled softly.

Boiling water fell splashing from the tap of the samovar into Mama's cup.

A thin shadow from the spoon fell on the saucer and the tablecloth and dissolved in the tea. Volodya looked closely at it: among the shadows thrown by the sweet streaks and light bubbles of air, this one reminded him of something—what exactly, Volodya couldn't decide. He bent and turned the spoon and ran his fingers along it, but nothing came of it.

"But still," he thought stubbornly, "you can make shadows from more than just your fingers. You can make them from anything, you just have to get the knack of it."

And Volodya started examining the shadows of the samovar, the chairs, Mama's head, the shadows the dishes cast on the table—and in all these shadows he tried to discern some likeness. Mama was saying something. Volodya listened with half an ear.

"How is Lyosha Sitnikov doing at school?" Mama asked.

Just then Volodya was scrutinising the shadow of the milk jug. He gave a start and said, "Like a cat."

"Volodya, you're fast asleep!" his mother said in surprise. "What cat?"

Volodya flushed. "I don't know what made me say that," he said. "Excuse me, Mama, I didn't hear."

The next evening before teatime, Volodya again remembered the shadows and again began to work on them. One shadow kept coming out badly, no matter how he stretched and bent his hands.

Volodya was so caught up in this that he didn't notice Mama's approach. Hearing the creak of the door opening, he shoved the booklet into his pocket and turned from the wall in confusion. But Mama was already looking at his hands, and a look of timorous anxiety flashed in her wide eyes.

"What are you doing, Volodya? What did you hide?"

"It's nothing, really," Volodya mumbled, blushing and awkwardly shifting from one foot to the other.

It somehow seemed to Mama that Volodya had wanted to smoke and had hidden a cigarette.

"Volodya, show me right now what you hid," she said in a frightened voice.

"Mama, really . . ."

Mama grabbed Volodya by the elbow. "Come now, shall I check your pocket myself?"

Volodya blushed even redder than before and fished the booklet out of his pocket.

"Here," he said, holding it out to Mama.

"What's this?"

"Well, look," explained Volodya, "there are drawings here—there, you see, shadows. Well, I was showing them on the wall, and they weren't coming out very well."

"Well, what's all this hiding business, then?" Mama said, more calmly now. "What sort of shadows are they? Show me."

Volodya was acutely embarrassed, but obediently began to show Mama the shadows.

"Here's one—the head of a bald man. And here's a rabbit's head."

"You silly!" said Mama. "So this is how you do your lessons!"

"It was only for a little, Mama."

"Only a little, eh? What made you blush so much, you dear boy? Never mind, then—after all, I know you'll do everything you ought."

Mama ruffled Volodya's short hair, Volodya laughed and hid his burning face under Mama's elbows.

Mama went out—but Volodya still felt awkward and ashamed. Mama had caught him doing something he himself would laugh at if he found a schoolmate doing it.

Volodya knew that he was a smart boy, and considered himself serious, but this was a silly game, the kind no one but a group of little girls would play.

He shoved the booklet with the shadows as far back as possible in a drawer of his desk and didn't take it out again for more than a week, and even hardly remembered the shadows that whole week. Only occasionally in the evening, as he went from one subject to another, would he smile as he remembered the horned headdress of the lady—sometimes he would even go into the drawer after the booklet, but at that moment he would remember how Mama had caught him, and then he would feel ashamed and get back to work.

V

Volodya and his Mama, Evgenia Stepanovna, lived in the outskirts of a regional capital, in a house Mama owned. Evgenia Stepanovna had been widowed nine years ago. Now she was thirty-five. She was still young and beautiful and Volodya loved her dearly. She lived entirely for her son. She studied ancient languages in order to help him and suffered over all his troubles at school. Quiet and affectionate, she looked upon the world a bit fearfully with wide eyes that gently shimmered in her pale face.

They lived with one servant. Praskovya, a morose tradesman's widow, was a strong, tough woman; she was about forty-five, but her stony silence was that of a hundred-year-old hag.

When Volodya looked at her glum, stony face, he often wished he knew what she thought about during the long winter evenings in her kitchen, when her cold knitting needles, clicking against one another, stirred tranquilly in her bony hands and her dry lips kept a silent running account. Was she remembering her drunkard husband? Or her children who had died young? Or did she see the spectre of a lonely and comfortless old age?

Her petrified face was hopelessly despondent and severe.

VI

A long autumn evening. Rain and wind beyond the walls.

How tiresomely, how indifferently the lamp was burning!

Volodya was propped on his elbow, leaning all the way over the table on his left side, and looking at the white wall of his room, and at the white curtain on the window.

He couldn't make out the pale flowers on the wallpaper . . . Boring white . . .

The white lampshade partially screened the lamp's rays. The entire upper half of the room was in half-light.

Volodya stretched up his right hand. On the wall dimmed by the lampshade stretched a long shadow, vague and diffuse at the edges . . .

The shadow of an angel flying away into the heavens from a depraved and sorrowful world, a transparent shadow with broad wings, its head bent in sorrow on its magnificent breast.

Wasn't the angel carrying something significant and neglected away from the world in its tender embrace? . . .

Volodya sighed heavily. His hand sank down listlessly. He bent his yearning eyes over his books.

A long autumn evening . . . Monotonous white light . . . Weeping and babbling beyond the walls . . .

Mama caught Volodya making shadows a second time. This time he was doing a bull's head really well, and he was admiring it and making the bull stick out its neck and bellow.

But Mama was not pleased.

"So this is how you study!" she said reproachfully.

"It was only for a little, Mama," Volodya whispered, abashed.

"That's something you can do in your free time," Mama continued. "After all, you're not a baby—you ought to be ashamed of spending your time on such nonsense!"

"Mummy, I won't do it again."

But it was hard for Volodya to keep his promise. He really liked making shadows, and the desire to do so frequently came to him in the midst of some uninteresting lesson.

Every once in a while his little evening diversion took up a lot of time and prevented him from preparing his lessons properly. He had to make up for lost time then, and didn't get enough sleep. But how could he give up the game?

Volodya successfully invented several new figures, and not just by using his hands alone. And these figures came to life on the wall and, it sometimes seemed to Volodya, carried on fascinating discussions with him.

But he had always had quite an imagination.

VIII

Night. It is dark in Volodya's room. Volodya has gone to bed, but he can't sleep. He lies on his back and looks at the ceiling.

Someone with a lantern is going down the street. There on the ceiling his shadow is flitting by amidst red patches of light from the lantern. Evidently, the lantern is swinging in the hands of the passer-by—the shadow sways, flickering unevenly.

Volodya is inexplicably terrified. He quickly pulls the

blanket over his head, and shivering all over in his haste, turns quickly onto his right side and summons pleasant thoughts.

He starts to feel warm and nice. Lovely, naïve fantasies are forming in his head, the kind he has before falling asleep.

Often when he goes to bed he is seized by terror, and he seems to become smaller and weaker—he hides in his pillow, forgets how a big boy behaves, becomes tender and affectionate, and he wants to hug and kiss Mama.

IX

Grey twilight was thickening. Shadows merged. Volodya was sad.

But here was the lamp. Light poured onto the desk's green felt, and vague, pretty shadows darted along the wall.

Volodya felt a surge of happiness and revived spirits and hastily pulled out the grey booklet.

The bull bellows . . . The young lady laughs loudly . . . What angry round eyes that bald gentleman makes!

Now his own.

The steppe. A pilgrim with a bundle. One can all but hear the sorrowful, drawn-out travelling song . . . Volodya is happy and sad.

X

"Volodya, this is the third time I've seen you with that booklet. So now you're spending whole evenings at a time admiring your hands?"

Volodya stood awkwardly by the desk, like a naughty child caught in the act, and turned the booklet around and around in his hot hands.

"Give it here!" said Mama.

Abashed, Volodya held out the booklet. Mama took it and left without a word—and Volodya sat down to his schoolwork.

He was ashamed that he had upset Mama with his stubbornness, and annoyed that she had taken the booklet away, and ashamed again that he had got himself into this silly fix. He felt terribly awkward, and his annoyance towards his mother distressed him: it was wrong of him to be angry with Mama, but he couldn't *not* be angry. And because it was wrong to be angry, he became even angrier.

"Let her take it, then," he finally concluded. "I can manage without it just as well."

And Volodya really did know the figures by heart and had been using the booklet just to be sure.

XI

Mama brought the booklet with the drawings of shadows to her room, opened it, and fell into thought.

"What is it about them that is so enticing?" she thought. "He's such a good, smart boy—and all of a sudden so keen on this nonsense! . . . But if that's the case, then it can't be just nonsense! . . . So what is it, then?" she asked herself insistently.

A strange dread arose inside her—a sort of hostile, shy feeling towards those black drawings.

She stood up and lit a candle. With the grey booklet in her hands she went up to the wall and hesitated in fearful anguish.

"I've just got to find out what this is all about," she decided, and she began to make the shadows, from the first to the last.

Insistently and attentively, she placed her fingers together and bent her hands until she got the figure she needed. The confused, timid feeling stirred inside her. She tried to overcome it. But the dread grew and enchanted her. Her hands shook, but her thought, intimidated by life's twilight, sped on towards the sorrows that threatened ahead. Suddenly she heard her son's approaching steps. She shuddered, hid the booklet and put out the candle.

Volodya entered and stopped on the threshold, taken aback

by how severely Mama looked at him, and by her awkward, strange position by the wall.

"What do you want?" asked Mama in a harsh, uneven voice.

A dim suspicion flashed through Volodya's mind, but he hurriedly banished it and began to talk with Mama.

XII

Volodya was gone.

Mama paced up and down the room several times. She noticed that her shadow moved behind her along the floor and—how odd!—for the first time in her life her shadow made her feel uncomfortable. The thought that the shadow was there kept recurring to her—but Evgenia Stepanovna was somehow afraid of this thought and even tried not to look at her shadow.

But the shadow crept after her and teased her. Evgenia Stepanovna tried to think about something else—but in vain.

She suddenly stopped, pale and agitated.

"So it's a shadow, a shadow!" she exclaimed aloud, stamping her feet with a strange feeling of annoyance. "So what? What about it?"

And suddenly she realised that it was stupid to shout like that and stamp your feet, and she calmed down.

She went up to the mirror. Her face was paler than usual, and her lips trembled with frightened anger.

"Nerves," she thought. "I must take myself in hand."

XIII

Twilight was falling. Volodya was lost in a daydream.

"Let's go for a walk, Volodya," said Mama.

But shadows were everywhere outside as well, evening shadows, mysterious and elusive, and they whispered something familiar and endlessly sad to Volodya.

Two or three stars peeked out from a hazy sky, seeming very far away and alien to both Volodya and the shadows surrounding him. But Volodya, in an effort to do something nice for Mama, began to think about those stars: they alone were alien to the shadows.

"Mama," he said, not noticing that he had interrupted Mama, who was talking to him, "it's too bad one can't get all the way to those stars."

Mama looked up at the sky and answered, "Whatever for? Earth is the place for us—up there it's different."

"How weakly they shine! But I guess that's for the best."

"Why?"

"Because if they shone brighter, they would have shadows, too."

"Oh, Volodya, why are you always thinking about shadows?"

"I didn't mean to, Mama," said Volodya in a repentant tone.

XIV

Volodya kept trying to prepare his lessons better; he was afraid of upsetting Mama with his laziness. But he concentrated all the powers of his fantasy on piling up the objects on his desk each evening so that they would throw a whimsical new shadow on the wall. He would lay out everything that came to hand this way and that, and was glad when he could make sense of the outlines that appeared on the white wall. These shadowy outlines were becoming near and dear to him. They were not mute—they talked, and Volodya understood their babbling language.

He understood what the poor wretch was grumbling about as he plodded along the high road in the autumn sludge, a walking stick in his trembling hands and a bundle on his bent back.

He understood what the snow-covered forest was complaining of, its frosty branches crackling as it stood miserably in the winter silence, and what the slow raven was croaking about in the grizzled oak, and why the busy squirrel was mourning in its empty hollow.

He understood why the old beggar women were weeping in the mournful autumn wind, decrepit, homeless women shivering in their ancient tatters in the cramped cemetery, among the rickety crosses and hopelessly dark graves.

Oblivion and agonising sorrow!

XV

Mama noticed that Volodya was still frittering away his time. At dinner she said, "At least you might find something else to do."

"Like what?"

"You could read."

"The thing is, you start to read, but you feel like making shadows."

"You might think up some other game—like making soap bubbles."

Volodya smiled sadly. "Yes, the bubbles float up and their shadows float behind them along the wall."

"Volodya, you're going to ruin your nerves in the end! I can see—you've lost weight since you started doing this."

"Mama, you're exaggerating!"

"Please! I know you're not sleeping well at night and sometimes you talk in your sleep. What if you fall ill?!"

"Really now, Mummy!"

"God forbid you should go out of your mind or die—how could I bear it?"

Volodya gave a laugh and threw his arms around Mama's neck. "Mummy, I won't die. I won't do it anymore."

Mama saw that now Volodya was crying.

"All right, that's enough now," she said. "God is merciful. There now—see how nervous you've become? You're laughing and crying all at once."

XVI

Mama fixed her fearful gaze on Volodya. Every little thing now worried her.

She noticed that Volodya's head was slightly asymmetrical: one ear was higher than the other, and his chin jutted a little to one side. Mama looked in the mirror and noticed the same irregularities in her own face.

"Maybe," she thought, "this is one of the signs of bad heredity, of degeneration? And who, then, is the source of this evil? Is it me—I'm so high-strung . . . or his father?"

Evgenia Stepanovna thought about her late husband. He had been the kindest and nicest of men, weak-willed, with senseless, impetuous ideas and ecstatic and mystical tendencies, a man who dreamt of a better social order, who "went to the people,"[1] and who drank heavily in the last years of his life.

He was young when he died—only thirty-five years old.

Mama even took Volodya to the doctor and described his illness. The doctor, a jovial young man, heard her out, chuckling, and gave various recommendations about diet and lifestyle accompanied by funny little witticisms, cheerfully wrote out a prescription and playfully added, clapping Volodya on the back, "But the best cure would be a touch of the strap."

Mama was mortally offended on Volodya's behalf, but she followed all the other instructions to the letter.

XVII

Volodya was sitting in class. He was bored. He was only half-listening.

He lifted his eyes. On the ceiling near the front wall of the classroom a shadow was moving. Volodya noticed that it was

---

[1] In the 1870s, idealistic members of the educated class made trips to the countryside to live among the peasants and to teach them about their downtrodden position and potential to effect revolution. This was known as "going to the people".

falling from the first window. At first it stretched from the window towards the middle of the classroom, but then it quickly flitted away from Volodya to the front—obviously, someone was walking outside beneath the window. When this shadow moved yet again, another shadow fell, from the second window, also first towards the back wall and then heading quickly towards the front. The same thing repeated in the third and fourth windows—shadows fell onto the ceiling of the classroom, and as the passer-by moved forward, they stretched back.

"Yes," thought Volodya, "it's not the same as in an open place, where the shadow stretches behind the person; here, when the person goes forwards, the shadow slides back, and different shadows meet him again further on."

Volodya turns his gaze to the dry figure of his teacher. The teacher's cold, yellow face irritates him. Volodya looks for the teacher's shadow and finds it on the wall, behind his chair. The shadow bends and sways monstrously—but it doesn't have a yellow face and a sarcastic sneer, and Volodya likes looking at it. His thoughts fly off somewhere far away, and he doesn't hear a thing.

"Lovlev!" his teacher calls his name.

Out of habit, Volodya gets up and stands there gazing dully at the teacher. He has such a faraway look that the other schoolboys snicker, and the teacher looks accusingly at him.

Then Volodya hears the teacher making fun of him, in a polite and nasty way. Volodya trembles from the offence and his own weakness. Then the teacher informs him that he is giving him an "F" for not knowing the answer and being inattentive, and invites him to sit down.

Volodya smiles stupidly and tries to work out what has just happened.

XVIII

An "F"—the first of Volodya's life!

How strange this was for Volodya!

"Lovlev!" his school-friends tease, laughing and shoving. "Got a 'fork'! Congratulations!"

Volodya feels uneasy. He does not yet know how one behaves in such a situation.

"What if I did!" he retorts with annoyance. "It's none of your business!"

"Lovlev!" shouts lazy Snegirov. "Our ranks have swelled!"

His first "F"! And he would have to show it to Mama. This was embarrassing and humiliating. Volodya felt a strange, clumsy weight in the knapsack on his back—that "fork" was sticking uncomfortably in his consciousness and could not be connected with anything else in his mind.

An "F"!

He could not get used to the idea of an "F" and couldn't think about anything else. When the corner policeman near the school looked at him with his usual severity, Volodya thought for some reason, "But if you only knew I got an 'F'!"

This was completely awkward and out of the ordinary—Volodya did not know how to hold his head and where to put his hands—his entire body felt awkward.

And on top of this, he had to put on a nonchalant expression in front of his school-friends and talk of something else!

School-friends! Volodya was certain that all of them were terribly glad about his "F."

XIX

Mama looked at the "F," turned her uncomprehending eyes to Volodya, again glanced at the grade and gently exclaimed, "Volodya!"

Volodya stood before her and wished he were dead. He looked at the folds of Mama's dress, at Mama's pale hands, and he felt her frightened glance on his own quivering lashes.

"What is this?" asked Mama.

"But Mama," Volodya suddenly spoke, "it's the first one I ever got!"

"The first!"

"It could happen to anyone. And it happened by accident, really it did."

"Oh, Volodya, Volodya!"

Volodya began to cry, rubbing the tears off his cheeks with his palm like a child.

"Mama, don't be angry," he whispered.

"It's those shadows of yours!" Mama said.

Volodya could hear tears in her voice. His heart sank. He shot a glance at Mama. She was crying. He flung himself into her arms.

"Mama, Mama," he said over and over, kissing her hands, "I won't do it anymore, really and truly, I won't make any more shadows."

XX

Volodya exerted all his willpower—and made no more shadows, no matter how badly he wanted to. He tried to catch up on his unfinished lessons.

But the shadows kept haunting him. Even though he didn't summon them with hand-shapes, even though he didn't heap up object upon object so they would make a shadow on the wall, the shadows themselves clustered around him, importunate and insistent.

Volodya had lost his interest in objects—he almost didn't see them anymore. All his attention went to their shadows.

When he was on his way home and the sun happened to peek out from the autumn storm clouds, even if only through a hazy shroud, he felt happy at how shadows moved everywhere.

Shadows from the lamp stood nearby him when he was at home in the evening.

Shadows all around everywhere—sharply defined ones from lights, dim ones from the dissipated light of day—they all crowded around Volodya, falling across one another, enveloping him in an indissoluble web.

Some of them were incomprehensible and mysterious; others reminded him of something, hinted at something—but there were also the nice shadows, dear and familiar to him—- those were the ones Volodya himself sought out (albeit involuntarily) and tried to catch everywhere amidst the disorderly and fleeting impressions of the other, unfamiliar shadows.

But they were distressing, these nice, familiar shadows. Whenever Volodya noticed that he was seeking these shadows out, his conscience would torment him and he would go to Mama to confess.

Once it happened that Volodya couldn't overcome the temptation, and he went to the wall and began to make himself a shadow bull. Mama caught him doing this.

"Again!" she exclaimed angrily. "That's it, I'm going to ask the director to have you put in lock-up."

Volodya flushed with annoyance and answered sullenly, "There are walls there, too. Walls are everywhere."

"Volodya!" Mama exclaimed sorrowfully. "What are you saying!"

But Volodya was already repenting of his rudeness and was crying. "Mama, I don't know myself what's happening to me!"

XXI

Mama still cannot overcome her superstitious fear of the shadows. The thought occurs to her more and more often that she, like Volodya, will get caught up in shadow-watching, but she tries to reassure herself.

"What stupid thoughts!" she says to herself. "Everything will turn out all right, God willing: he'll eventually get tired of it and stop."

But her heart quails with suppressed fright, and her thoughts run on, fearful of life and its approaching sorrows.

In the dreary moments of morning she searches her soul and thinks back on her life, and she sees that it has been empty, unnecessary, aimless. Nothing more than shadows senselessly flitting by and fading into thickening twilight.

"What have I lived for?" she asks herself. "For my son? But what for? So he, too, could fall prey to the shadows, so he could turn into a maniac with narrow horizons—riveted to illusions, to senseless reflections on a lifeless wall? And he, too, will enter into life and give life to yet more beings, who will be as ghostly and unnecessary as a dream."

She sits down in an armchair by the window and thinks and thinks.

Her thoughts are bitter and dreary.

She wrings her lovely white hands in anguish. Her thoughts are distracted. She looks at her twisted hands and begins to think about what kind of shadow figures they could produce. She catches herself thinking this and jumps up in fright.

"My God!" she exclaims. "But this is. . .madness!"

XXII

At dinner Mama looks at Volodya.

"He's grown so thin and pale since he discovered that wretched booklet. And he's changed completely, in his personality, and in everything. They say your personality changes before death. What if he dies?. . .Oh, no, no, God forbid!"

The spoon trembles in her hands. She lifts her timorous eyes to the icon.

"Volodya, why aren't you eating your soup?" she asks fearfully.

"I don't feel like it, Mama."

"Volodya, now be a good boy, sweetheart—it's not good for you not to have your soup."

Volodya smiles absently and slowly finishes his soup. Mama gave him too much. He leans back in his chair and wants to say with annoyance that the soup wasn't good. But Mama has such a worried face that Volodya doesn't dare to say anything about it and he smiles wanly.

"I'm full now," he says.

"Oh, no, Volodya, but today we're having all your favourites!"

Volodya sighs sadly: he already knows that if Mama is talking about his favourite dishes, it means she's going to stuff him. He suspects that at tea, too, Mama will make him eat meat, as she did yesterday.

XXIII

In the evening Mama says to Volodya, "Volodya, my dear, you're going to get distracted again. You'd better not shut the door!"

Volodya begins to work on his lessons. But he is annoyed that behind his back the door is open and that every once in a while Mama passes by the doorway.

"I can't stand this!" he shouts, pushing his chair back noisily. "I can't do any work at all with the door open."

"Volodya, why are you yelling?" Mama reproaches him affectionately.

Volodya is already sorry and crying. Mama caresses and cajoles him, "Volodya, darling, I'm just looking after you, so I can help you keep from getting distracted."

"Mama, sit here for a while," Volodya says.

Mama takes a book and sits down near Volodya's desk. For a few minutes Volodya works peacefully. But her presence soon begins to irritate him. "As if I were ill!" he thinks with resentment. His thoughts are interrupted; he shifts irritably and bites his lips. Mama finally notices this and leaves the room.

But Volodya feels no relief. Repentance for showing his impatience gnaws at him. He tries to study, but can't. Finally he goes to get Mama.

"Mama, why did you leave?" he asks timidly.

XXIV

The night before a holy day. Lamps flicker before the icons.

It's late and quiet. Mama isn't sleeping. In the mysterious twilight of her bedroom she is on her knees, praying and crying, sobbing like a child.

Her braids fall on her white dress; her shoulders are shaking. She raises her hands to her breast as if pleading and looks at the icon with eyes swollen from crying. The icon lamp on its chain wavers almost imperceptibly from her hot breath. Shadows flutter, crowd in the corners, stir behind the icon case and babble something secret. There is a hopeless longing in their babble, an indescribable sadness in their gently flickering glimmer.

Mother gets up, pale, with wide, strange eyes, and sways on unsteady feet. Quietly, she goes to Volodya's room. Shadows crowd around her, gently rustling behind her back; they crawl at her feet, and fall, lightly, like a cobweb, onto her shoulders; and gazing into her wide eyes, they babble incomprehensibly.

Cautiously, she approaches her son's bed. In the rays of the lamp his face is wan. Odd, sharply defined shadows lie on him. His breath is inaudible; he is sleeping so quietly that it frightens her.

She stands there surrounded by dim shadows and stirred by dim fears.

XXV

The high church vaults are dark and mysterious. The chanting of vespers rises up to these vaults and reverberates there with solemn sadness. Dark icons look on mysteriously and severely, illuminated by the yellow flames of wax candles. The warm breath of wax and incense fills the air with majestic sorrow.

Evgenia Stepanovna has placed a candle before the icon of the Mother of God and is now on her knees. But her prayer is absent-minded. She is looking at her candle. Its flame is wavering. Shadows from the candlelight fall on Evgenia Stepanovna's black dress and onto the floor and they sway negatively.

Shadows hover on the walls of the church and are swallowed

up in the upper reaches, in those dark vaults, where solemn, sad songs are reverberating.

XXVI

Another night.

Volodya has woken up. Darkness surrounds him and soundlessly stirs.

Volodya has freed his hands from under the blanket and lifted them, and is now moving them gently, his gaze fastened on them. In the darkness he does not see his hands, but it seems to him that dark shadows are stirring before his eyes. . .

Black, mysterious shadows, carrying grief within them and a babble of lonely longing. . .

Mama, too, can't sleep—longing oppresses her.

Mama lights a candle and quietly goes to her son's room to look in on him and see how he is sleeping.

Soundlessly, she opens the door a crack and looks at Volodya's bed.

A ray of yellow light shudders on the wall, falling across Volodya's red blanket. The boy is stretching out his hands to the light and watching the shadows with a pounding heart. He doesn't even think to ask where the light is coming from.

He is completely absorbed by the shadows. His eyes, fastened on the wall, are full of impending madness.

The band of light grows wider, the shadows run ahead, sullen and hunchbacked, like wandering vagabond women hurrying to bring their heavy burden of ragged belongings to some unknown destination.

Mama, trembling with horror, goes up to the bed and softly calls out to her son, "Volodya!"

Volodya comes to. For half a minute or so he gazes at Mama wide-eyed, then he starts shaking all over, springs from the bed and falls to her feet, embracing her knees and sobbing.

"What dreams you are having, Volodya!" Mama exclaims sorrowfully.

XXVII

"Volodya," Mama said over their morning tea, "you mustn't do this, sweetheart; you'll wear yourself out completely if you're going to catch shadows in the night as well."

The pale boy sadly hung his head. His lips trembled nervously.

"Know what we'll do?" Mama continued. "Let's try playing shadows together a little each evening, and then later we'll sit down and do lessons. All right?"

Volodya brightened up a bit. "Mummy, you're—so nice!" he said bashfully.

XXVIII

Outside Volodya felt sleepy and a little fearful. A thick fog had set in, and it was cold and dreary. The outlines of houses were odd in the fog. Sombre figures of people moved beneath the foggy haze like sinister, unfriendly shadows. Everything was extraordinarily huge. As it loomed out of the fog, the horse of a cabby dozing at the crossroads seemed like an enormous, fantastic beast.

A policeman looked antagonistically at Volodya. A crow on a low roof prophesied grief for him. But the grief was already in his heart; he was sad to see how hostile everything was towards him.

A little mangy dog yapped at him from under a gate, and Volodya felt strangely insulted.

And the street urchins, too, it seemed, wanted to insult and mock Volodya. In times past he would have dealt with them easily, but now timidity constricted his chest and pulled his weakened arms down.

When Volodya got home, Praskovya opened the door for him and gave him a malicious, sullen look. It made Volodya feel uncomfortable. He went inside as quickly as possible, not daring to raise his eyes to Praskovya's cheerless face.

Mama was sitting by herself in her room. It was dusk—and it was boring.

Somewhere a light flashed.

Volodya ran in, enlivened, cheerful, with wide, slightly wild eyes. "Mama, the lamp is burning, let's play a little."

Mama smiles and follows Volodya.

"Mama, I invented a new figure," Volodya says excitedly, setting the lamp in place. "Look here. . .see? It's the steppe, covered with snow—and it's snowing, a snowstorm."

Volodya lifts his hands and puts them together. "Now, you see, there's an old man going by. The snow is knee-deep. It's hard going. By himself. An empty field. The village is far away. He's tired, and cold, and afraid. He's all bent over because he's so old."

Mama adjusts Volodya's fingers.

"Oh!" Volodya exclaims delightedly. "The wind's blown off his cap, it's blowing his hair about, it's burying him in the snow. The drifts are getting higher and higher. Mama, Mama, do you hear?"

"The blizzard."

"And him?"

"The old man?"

"Do you hear him moaning?"

"Help!"

Both of them pale, they look at the wall. Volodya's hands sway—the old man falls.

Mama is the first to come to.

"It's time to get to work," she says.

XXX

Morning. Mama was at home alone. Deep in disconnected, gloomy thoughts, she was going from room to room.

Her shadow, vague in the dissipated rays of a sun shrouded by fog, was outlined on the white door. Mama stopped at the door and raised her arm in a wide, strange gesture. The shadow on the door swayed and whispered about something familiar and sad. A strange delight spread through Evgenia Stepanovna's soul, and she moved both hands as she stood before the door, smiled a wild smile, and watched how the shadow flitted from place to place.

Praskovya's steps approached, and Evgenia Stepanovna remembered that she was doing something absurd.

Once again she feels frightened and despondent. "We need a change," she thinks, "to go somewhere far away, somewhere new. To get away from here!"

And all of a sudden she recalls Volodya's words: "There are walls there, too. Walls are everywhere."

"There's nowhere to go!"

In despair she wrings her lovely white hands.

XXXI

Evening.

In Volodya's room, on the floor, a lamp is burning. Behind it, on the floor by the wall, Mama and Volodya are sitting. They look at the wall and make strange movements with their hands.

Shadows flit and sway along the wall.

Volodya and Mama understand them. They smile sadly and talk about something oppressive and impossible. Their faces are peaceful, and their reveries are clear; their joy is hopelessly sorrowful, their sorrow wildly joyful.

Madness, blissful madness, shines in their eyes.

Above them night is falling.

My tedious lamp is alight,
Again, as always, it hurts my eyes.

Lord, if I am to be meek,
If I am to be poor and weak,

If I am to languish every night
Over work that is boring and slight,

Just once, grant me my request—
That I may conquer my weakness,

That a perfect work I may create,
And flare up in a pure, immortal flame.

Fyodor Sologub, 1898

Death and sleep, sister and brother,
Are very much alike,
But we all gladly welcome him,
While she inspires fright.

But sometimes the reverse is true—
We drive the sister away
And entreat the brother desperately,
"Please, death, end my pain!"

The brother reminds us of our evil deeds,
And in the silence of the night,
Oppressive, dark and endless,
We moan, "I can't stand life!"

But those fatigued by life
The sister comforts soon:
She saves them from despair
With the silence of the tomb.

Fyodor Sologub, 1889

You raised the veil of night
And drove away sweet sleep,
But my eyes will not stay bright for long,
For daytime wearies me.

I lie, indifferent to your call
To labour and to play.
I refuse to follow you;
You beckon me in vain.

In vain you dress the charm of day
In sundry masks,
The joy and grief you offer me
I cannot grasp.

Soon my saviour will return;
I'll leave you then for sleep,
And drift off to a distant place—
Oblivion, darkness and peace.

Fyodor Sologub, 1898

The Living and the Dead (Among the Dead)

Zinaida Gippius

I

Charlotte was the daughter of the warden of the big Lutheran cemetery outside the city. The respectable Ivan Karlovich Buch had held that position for many years. This was where Charlotte had been born, and where quite recently Buch had given his elder daughter in marriage to a rich young watchmaker. Charlotte did not remember her mother. She knew only that she was not dead: there was no grave for her in the "park," among all the other graves. She didn't dare ask her father about it. When the children spoke of their mother, his blond brows would furrow, and in spite of his gentle, good nature, his entire red, full face would take on an expression of anger, or perhaps sadness.

Ivan Karlovich was quite portly, almost bald, and jovial. He loved his nice white house beyond the cemetery fence, and adorned his front garden and terrace with climbing plants and all sorts of flowers. The canvas curtains on the terrace had prettily embroidered red calico edging. Ivan Karlovich had decided to put stained glass—yellow and red—in the windows of the cool dining room, and although it was darker that way, the light that came through those windows was extraordinarily pleasant, as if it were always sunny in the garden.

Ivan Karlovich's office accounts were always kept in perfect order. All the graves were numbered, and for each it was noted how much money had been left for special upkeep during the summer months. The only furniture in the big, empty front room—the reception room—was a desk and some dark chairs. Large and small wreaths, made of immortelles, wool, scraps of cloth, big beads and the tiniest little coloured beads, hung in

glass cases fixed to the walls. These wreaths were wrought
to perfection by Charlotte and—until she got married—her
sister Caroline. On a table in the corner were a number of
thick albums, containing drawings and models of various
monuments and samples of tombstone inscriptions in German.
When visitors came, Ivan Karlovich bore himself with great
dignity, almost with sorrow, but the rest of the time he moved
with alacrity, despite his girth. He loved to laugh so that his
entire corpulent body shook, and he fed the pigeons himself
and raised a special kind of turkey, and in the evenings he was
wont to play a hand or two of cards with the neighbours from
German Street, and, if no one came over, he himself would go
visiting.

II

Charlotte was sitting in her room upstairs, the little white
room under the eaves that she used to share with her sister
and now occupied by herself. Although she loved her sister,
Charlotte was glad to have the room to herself. Caroline, who
was tall, ruddy and jovial just like her father, sometimes irri-
tated the more reticent Charlotte, who was pale, serious, quite
thin and smaller than average. In the German school she'd
attended for several years, the other girls didn't like her,
although she was pretty. "Your sister isn't at all lively," they
would say to Caroline. "It's like she's made of porcelain and
you're afraid if you touch her, she might break." However,
their family doctor, Finch, Ivan Karlovich's friend, saw no
sign of illness in her, and recommended only that she get
more fresh air. And Charlotte spent many a day amidst the
verdant growth in the cemetery park, where she did her work,
threading big and little beads for her endless wreaths.

Now Charlotte was sitting upstairs in her favourite place,
on the left side of the wide Venetian window. She hadn't been
in the park for a long time; she had hurt her leg and couldn't
walk. Today she was feeling better. The day seemed summery,
warm and clear, although it was only the end of April. The

tops of the birches, pale green and still almost bare, swayed slightly. From here, from the height of the second storey, she had an excellent view of the central avenue and the rows of white and black crosses amidst the greenery, as well as Frau Sommer's chapel and General Friederich's monument. Charlotte knew that if she squinted her eyes she would even be able to see the fence around little Heinrich Wiegen's grave. But from Charlotte's favourite place the whole realm of the cemetery, the sandy avenues, the trees, and the monuments' white stones, seemed different—absolutely extraordinary. When Ivan Karlovich was putting the red and yellow glass into the dining room windows, he was accidentally sent a light-blue one as well. Charlotte asked that the glass be put in her window, on the side where she liked to work. Everything was transformed in Charlotte's eyes: the tiny little forget-me-nots became a darker blue, and the colourless daisy took on soft hues. Light-blue stripes lay on the white tablecloth, burning with a pale, cold light, like a swamp fire. And beyond the window, the world seemed different, translucent, and quiet, as if underwater. The crosses and monuments glowed as if lit up, the painfully bright foliage took on more muted tones, and the sand on the pathways turned greyish. A monotonous, light haze enveloped the park. And the sky became such a soft shade of blue, so azure and clear, such as Charlotte had seen only when she was a small child, in pictures—and also sometimes in dreams.

And when Charlotte would finally tear herself away from her window and from her work, and go downstairs for lunch with her sister and father, everything around her seemed too defined, too red. Blood showed through in her father's fat neck and bald head and through the soft skin of Caroline's ruddy cheeks. And Charlotte would drop her eyes, and she would be quiet and paler than ever, as if the reflection of the light-blue window still remained on her face.

But Charlotte found the park tolerable enough. She had grown accustomed to it and now always saw it the way it looked from her room. She had really missed it in the past few long days. She wanted so much to see if everything was still

169

the way it had been before, and how her dear, quiet friends were doing, and if Frau Tesch's cross had fallen down, because it had been leaning before, and whether the wind had blown the woollen wreath off Lindenbaum's grave. The wreath had been poorly fastened. Charlotte had her favourite graves that she tended to specially. Many of them were not visited even by the deceased's own relatives, who had forgotten them or died themselves, but Charlotte cherished them year after year, and decorated them with turf and flowers. Beginning in spring, all over the park, from every direction, the heavy smell of funerary flowers rose up beneath the ancient trees' vaults.

"The gardener's been to papa three times already," thought Charlotte. "Probably there's been a lot done there. I can't stand it, I simply must go."

She could restrain herself no longer, and although she had not quite recovered yet, she seized her big white kerchief, draped it over her thick flaxen braids, which she had wrapped in a crown around her head, and went out to the park.

III

But at present it did not smell of flowers in the avenues; they had just been put in and hadn't had time to blossom yet. Even the greenish-white and deep purple buds of the lilac that was always so plentiful were still tightly closed. It smelled of sticky new birch leaves, new grass and the innocent yellow stars of dandelions that were scattered along both sides of the avenue and next to and behind the little fences around the graves.

The sand crunching beneath her heels, Charlotte walked on. The new foliage did not yet meet overhead, and Charlotte, raising her eyes, saw the sky. There were hardly any visitors at that hour. Charlotte avoided strangers: they bothered her. She disliked funerals, and disliked and feared the deceased. They should be hidden away in the earth as quickly as possible and covered over with a lovely, even mound and a layer of fresh turf . . . In the mornings, a nightingale sings in the lilac bushes, and dew wets the turf and the large black pansies by the crosses. And there aren't any of those long, cold, yellow people who get brought there in wooden boxes. What remains is a name, perhaps a memory—a trace left in the heart—and a fresh mound of earth. Charlotte never thought about the bones of the people whose graves she cherished and adorned. Ever alive, invisible, incorporeal, like the sounds of their names, they were constantly with her, always young, independent of time. In one little nook at the end of the second lateral pathway, there were two tiny little graves. The inscription on the cross said that here lay Fritz and Minna, twins who had died on the same day. Charlotte especially loved Fritz and Minna. When their decayed cross fell down, she spent her own money to put up a new little white cross. Fritz and Minna had died a long time ago. According to the inscription, they died before Charlotte was even born. But for her they eternally remained two-year-old children, little, sweet and unchanging from year to year. She herself planted flowers for them and indulged them with wreaths skilfully made of big, bright beads.

Now Charlotte turned her steps towards Fritz and Minna. Along the way she had a look into the crypt of the Barons Rhein. It was very nice there. A white chapel with carved windows. Inside—an altar, a few white chairs, an icon lamp. Its flame was barely noticeable, as the bright sun was beating in through the door of the chapel. To the right of the entrance a curved staircase led down into the crypt itself. The steps were broad and white, the stairway so radiant and inviting that it seemed it must be a pleasure to descend. Next door, at the grave of a certain Nordenschild, a half-withered wreath hung unattractively from the arm of an enormous angel in an unnatural pose. Charlotte adjusted the wreath and went on. She didn't like Nordenschild. In general she very much disliked graves with gigantic monuments—always clumsy-looking—accompanied by long inscriptions and verses: what memories or peacefulness they might have held had been destroyed by the vain stupidity of the living.

Charlotte turned to the right, onto a small pathway, quite narrow, that wound among the endless little fences and crosses.

It got more shady and damp: the freshly-thawed earth had not yet had time to dry out. The rows of familiar graves stretched out in front of Charlotte. Mrs. Ein, her husband . . . And there was the broad, but not very large, grave of a general with his portrait on the cross. He was so jovial and nice, that general, that Charlotte always answered him with a smile. She turned to the right—and here, finally, were Fritz and Minna. Her poor children! Charlotte's absence showed clearly now. The last time she had come here before her injury, Fritz and Minna had still been covered by a white blanket of late snow. The snow hadn't been swept off in time, and it had melted right there and left a penetrating dampness. The grass was half-heartedly trying to grow on the little unkempt graves. Dead branches lay all around.

"My poor little ones!" Charlotte whispered. "Just wait a bit, tomorrow I'm going to tidy you up, and I'll plant you some flowers . . . Mark will give me some flowers," she said, thinking of the old gardener who loved her very much.

There was one thing here, near Fritz and Minna, that Charlotte didn't like: in the opposite corner, very close, was a gigantic monument someone had raised over a mechanical engineer. A black cross made of some sort of iron was supported by wheels, some smooth and some cogged, connected by chains. The intricate, tall, heavy monument, all those chains and wheels to which the engineer had once devoted himself and left behind him when he passed away—all this seemed to weigh on the grave. At dusk, the cross, so tall and dark, probably looked like a gallows. Charlotte was angry at the engineer: she was vexed that this stupid, frightening monument had been put right next to her children.

She went a little closer and raised her head. The wheels and chains were unwavering and inviolable. They were only slightly rusted from the snow. A mausoleum like that would stand for a long, long time.

Charlotte decided to walk to the outer pathway, next to the tall, old board fence that faced the still-damp meadows and the distant forest beyond the river. She could see these meadows and the forest through the cracks in the grey fence.

The outer pathway ran parallel to the main avenue, although it was quite a distance away, and it was narrow and very long, running the whole length of the cemetery. Here it wasn't yet so crowded, the graves coming at longer intervals. There was one place Charlotte especially loved: in the summer, she would sit for whole hours at a time with her invariable work on an old bench among white lilac bushes, not far from Fritz and Minna.

Charlotte took a few steps—and then suddenly stopped in surprise. What was this? Her place had been taken. When had this happened? How had she overlooked it? True, she hadn't been by this way, this deep in, since autumn. Somehow she had been certain that everything would be just as it had been before, that no one would take her favourite spot. The lilacs, fresh and glistening, waved their clusters of buds ever so slightly. But now all the lilac bushes were confined behind a very tall, graceful metal railing with spiked tips. Charlotte went closer. There was a door in the fence, which opened right up, easily and silently. Charlotte went inside.

Only one grave occupied that spacious quadrangle. A curved wooden bench stood beneath a lilac tree. Fresh turf embraced the grave. It had been thickly planted with large, dark-purple violets, which gave off a heavy fragrance. At one end of the grave was a simple cross of grey marble on a modest pedestal. Approaching closer still, Charlotte was able to discern a medallion of white marble on the pedestal; it was round, and there was a profile on it, also white and barely noticeable. The relief was so slight that the face's features were almost indistinguishable. Charlotte could discern the straight line of a nose, tossed-back hair that was not very long, and the face of a girl or youth. Still lower a simple inscription faintly gleamed, in Russian:

"Albert Renault.
Died in the twenty-fifth year of his life."

And that was all.

Charlotte sat down on the bench and lapsed into thought. The fragrance of violets clouded her head, and the bluish veins on the transparent skin of her temples began to throb. Who was this mysterious Albert Renault? Was this his portrait—this fine, almost invisible profile on white marble? Charlotte knew that her father charged a high price for rare garden violets. That meant that his relatives were wealthy. However, to Charlotte's experienced eye, it appeared that the grave had not been visited for some time, for the grass around it had not been disturbed.

"If only I dared . . ." Charlotte thought. "That grey cross, it's lovely, but it seems too mournful to me. What a fine wreath I could make! From big and little beads . . . No, that wouldn't be right. It has to be a soft one, from scraps of silk. Forget-me-nots, really big ones and very pale . . . But I don't dare!" she interrupted herself. "The relatives might come and be upset . . . What am I to him?"

Suddenly she felt sad. She got up from the bench and sat down on the turf and sand at the very edge of the grave. The violets, dark and velvety, were right by her face. Now, under a ray of sun that had suddenly penetrated through the branches, the marble profile was completely erased. The tall sharp spikes of the railing shut out the pathway and the other monuments. Only the top edge of the wooden fence and the clear sky above it could be seen. Charlotte, tilting her head back towards the fragrant grave, looked at the sky. It seemed so close and familiar to her, like the blue glass in her window. And it seemed to her that beyond it she could see another world, quiet, hazy and unknown.

IV

When her father went to have his afternoon nap, Charlotte shyly and cautiously stole into the big "reception" room. A difficult task lay ahead of her. She had to find the number of Albert Renault's grave. Charlotte understood that otherwise her questions—who he was, when he was buried, whether his relatives visited often—would all come to nothing. Her father knew only the numbers.

"A railing and a cross," thought Charlotte. "It's hard to put up monuments in the winter, and in the spring—most likely not, the earth would have been dug up, but there's grass there now. It must have been sometime in the autumn."

In September she had still often sat by the outer pathway. Could it have been at the very end? But there was nothing under September. She started into October. The books were enormous and heavy, and Charlotte's slender hand could hardly turn the thick pages with the rows of names and numbers. It was so hard! No, she'd never find it. She was beginning to feel dazed. Aside from that, Charlotte was constantly glancing around, fearing that someone would come in and disturb her. She didn't know what, precisely, she was afraid of; her father, even if he was a little hot-tempered, was a kind man, and anyway, what was so wrong with looking at the books? Still, her heart was in her throat, as if she were furtively doing something forbidden.

Suddenly, at the end of a page, a familiar name caught her eye. In her father's calligraphic hand was written: October 20 Albert Renault No. 17311.

Now her work was easier. Charlotte immediately looked at the receipt-books. Opposite number 17311 was: "30 roubles sent. Violets."

Sent! That meant that the relatives themselves hadn't come. They'd just sent money. Her father knew something after all. Almost certainly they were very wealthy people. But nonetheless they didn't come to visit.

Charlotte, deep in thought, went out onto the terrace and began to make the six-o'clock coffee as usual. The evening was altogether summery, warm and mild. The climbing vines had not yet managed to wrap around the pillars of the terrace, but a cluster of stunted, thick trees behind the flower garden, the gazebo, and the green fence hid even the nearest crosses from view. A little lane between pruned, blossoming acacias ran alongside a low brick wall leading to the main gates, which were of the same red brick, tall, with a bell on top. It was intersected there at right angles by the cemetery's main avenue. But from here on the terrace, you could see neither the gates nor the crosses. The garden seemed to be simply a garden.

Ivan Karlovich emerged sleepily, with screwed-up eyes and crimson stripes on his rumpled face. Unexpectedly, her sister Caroline appeared with her husband and one-and-a-half-year-old son. Her three years of marriage had taken the roses from Caroline's cheeks. She didn't laugh anymore; instead, she moaned and complained. The watchmaker she had married for love turned out to be extremely sickly, gloomy and subject to fits. He sat with his coffee, looking green and defeated. The child he'd fathered looked even greener and sicklier, as though he might die at any moment.

"Believe me, papa," Caroline sometimes said with despair, "I'm not living, it's like I'm stewing in a cauldron. Every day I expect the worst. If he coughs or heaves a sigh, I think: here we go, get ready for the worst. And the child, too, is barely alive: the doctors have found seven things wrong with him. Sometimes it pains your heart so much, you think: ah, then let it happen already! Right now! Perhaps it would be easier."

Their father didn't understand Caroline's complaints and despairing wishes. He put on a severe face and lectured her, but silent Charlotte understood. She looked at the watchmaker and his green son, and felt glad that she wasn't bound to these frail vessels by the chains of love. *Her* friends were eternal, reliable, unchanging. Today the watchmaker felt better and said a few words, and Caroline seemed to cheer up. She even gave her baby two biscuits.

"What's the matter, Lottchen, why are you so silent?" she said, turning to her sister. "Thank God, you're healthy. Young ladies need to have a little fun, they need company."

"Company, hah!" Ivan Karlovich spoke out. When he was home and with his children he always spoke Russian, and he was extremely fond of speaking Russian. "We know what Lottchen needs. Her mature years are approaching, it's only natural! A nice husband, a couple of children . . . She's less pale already. Heh-heh-heh! We know a certain someone who's got his eye on us!"

He gave a wink, trying to look sly.

Charlotte was mortified. She understood her father's hints. Johann Rotte, the eldest son of a very wealthy butcher at the far end of German Street, was asking for her hand. Johann was a sensible, energetic fellow. Her father could not conceive of the possibility of her refusal. But it had been so long since they had talked about it that Charlotte had begun hoping that Johann had his eye on another bride—and now it had come up again!

"I don't want to get married yet," Charlotte said in a barely audible voice. She was a humble and submissive daughter, but the thought of wedding Johann set her trembling.

"Tut-tut, tut-tut!" her father said, raising what little eyebrows he had. "It's for us to know whether you want to get married. Our daughter must take our wishes into consideration. A young lady of your age always wants to settle down."

"Absolutely right," the watchmaker declared hollowly. "Young ladies are special wares. And they must be looked after."

"I can't look after them, I can't look after them!" All of a sudden Ivan Karlovich got agitated and his face flushed crimson. "How am I supposed to look after them? Naturally, young ladies need to get married."

"Don't get excited, papachen," Caroline said, and kissed her father on the head. "Charlotte is a clever girl, she understands. Johann's father is such a rich man. And Johann! Healthy as a horse! What sort of girl would refuse him?"

Charlotte, swallowing silent tears of horror, gave her father his long pipe. The conversation gradually settled into a more tranquil vein.

Charlotte gathered up her courage. "Papa," she asked, "Whose is that grave with the number seventeen thousand three hundred and eleven? I haven't seen it before. There used to be a bench there. And now I go there and there's a fence. And such wonderful violets."

"Hmm . . . Seventeen thousand three hundred . . ." Ivan Karlovich responded, puffing at his pipe. Violets, you say? So the violets are pretty? Let that mam'selle the countess, his fiancée—or was it cousin?—come and have a look at whether

177

Buch the Warden conscientiously fulfils his obligations or not! Thirty roubles sent—and there are your flowers! And if she doesn't come, it's all the same to me. Whether you see for yourself or not, you get the best flowers for your money!"

"But who is it, papa?" asked Caroline.

Charlotte was mute and pale.

"It's . . . It's a certain . . . A young man who had great things ahead of him, they told me. And then suddenly—*ein, zwei, drei*[1]—and he's gone. *Ein Maler*,"[2] he added, not finding the Russian words. "So? The violets are pretty, are they, Lottchen?"

And he laughed his corpulent laugh.

Caroline and her family had long since gone, her father had retired to his room, and all was quiet in the house. Charlotte went upstairs and lit her lamp. Outside the window was the vague gloom of a moonless April night. Charlotte wanted to finish her work, a large wreath of red poppies, but she couldn't. She was tormented by thoughts. Albert, *ein Maler*, a painter . . . He had a cousin, a fiancée . . . Why didn't she come to visit him? Did he love her? What was she like?

And Charlotte smiled at the thought that even though this cousin was a rich woman and a countess, Albert wasn't with her now, but right here, close by, and would be here forever; and not the countess, but Charlotte would sit near him tomorrow and bring a watering can full of water for the violets and weave, if she felt like it, a soft silken wreath of very large, very pale forget-me-nots . . .

Suddenly her heart gave a heavy lurch. She remembered Johann. The unfinished poppies scattered from her lap. She jumped up, undressed in a hurry, extinguished the lamp and flung herself down on the bed. Straight to sleep, so as not to think about anything!

[1] one, two, three.
[2] a painter.

178

The July day was unbearably hot. The sun heated the dry, hazy air through and through. The trees with their broad, fully-grown leaves silently, sleepily, happily took in the sun's rays, like lizards at noon on a hot stone. The smell of dust and every kind of flower hung in the air. The whole cemetery park was now full of flowers. All was immaculately clean and tidy, the graves carefully tended and cheerful-looking. But mingling with the various fine fragrances and the aroma of blossoming lime trees, there was another smell, barely noticeable, but unsettling, elusive and heavy. It is a smell found only in cemeteries during extremely hot spells. Charlotte always thought that it was the breath of dying lime blossoms. They smelled exactly like that when they were falling. Charlotte didn't feel the heat. Her fine face was as pale as always, her hands working away as usual. And here, behind the fence of Albert's grave, where she was now in the habit of spending her days, it was especially shady. The lilac, long past blossoming, was now dense with new growth, and the old birches met in a thick green awning overhead. There were no more violets on Albert's grave. Two big white rose bushes grew there now. Charlotte herself looked after them, and nowhere were the blossoms so fresh and luxuriant as here.

Today Charlotte was wearing a light-coloured dress with short sleeves. She'd felt happy since morning. Her happiness, like Charlotte herself, was quiet and inconspicuous. It was as if an even, gentle flame were glowing in her heart. As she twisted long stems of lavender into a wreath that had been ordered, she suddenly began to sing in a quiet, fine voice, and this made her feel flustered. She so rarely forgot herself like that.

The white medallion beneath the cross was now half-hidden by roses. Charlotte liked to draw her hand along the gentle, scarcely protruding profile of that half-seen face: the marble was cool to the touch, velvety and always caressing.

It seemed to have got muggier. Hazy air crept from the surrounding bogs and from the direction of the distant forest. Charlotte, tearing her eyes away from the lavender for a moment, turned her gaze upward. She shuddered, cried out weakly and blushed: above her, on the old wooden fence, beyond which stretched other peoples' gardens, and further still lay the bog and a coppice, sat a solid, handsome youth in a skilfully embroidered crimson shirt. It was Johann.

"Don't be frightened, Mam'selle Charlotte," he said, very politely, even gallantly, as he tipped his white peaked cap. "Forgive me for . . . coming by the direct route. From my place it's much closer to come like this, although the way is a bit difficult. But I knew that you had chosen this little nook . . . And not wishing to disturb your respected papa by coming through the main gates and the house . . . Will you allow me to join you?"

"Yes," Charlotte whispered, with lowered lashes.

Her happiness had vanished without a trace. A dull anxiety sucked at her heart. Now it seemed more hot and humid than ever to her, and thick fragrances clouded the air.

Johann sprang lightly down onto the path and in another moment was sitting with Charlotte on the comfortable little bench right by Albert's grave.

"What a charming little nook!" Johann said, removing his cap and passing his hand with its somewhat short and thick fingers through his tight black curls. Johann had every right to be called handsome: he wasn't tall, but was broad in the shoulders, agile, with a warm, dark complexion, and on the upper lip of his slightly pouty mouth he sported a shortish, handsome, somewhat bristly moustache. Charlotte was never able to bear the gaze of his big bulging eyes, which were black as olives and ever so slightly bloodshot.

"It's been a long time since I've had the pleasure of seeing you, Mam'selle Charlotte," Johann continued. "I'm busy all day at the shop and there's hardly ever a free moment. Last year, as I recall, you once did us the honour of visiting our little shop . . . For me that day, believe me, made a big impression . . . That was my first year of helping my father, I'd just finished school."

Charlotte shuddered again, and involuntarily moved a little away from him, to the very edge of the bench. She also

180

remembered how she and her father had once chanced to go into Johann's shop. The place was well-lit and clean. There was an acrid smell of blood and freshly-splintered bones. The very freshest, bright red carcasses of bulls, their hides removed and muscles exposed, protruding legs lopped off at the knee, hung empty like sacks by the door and on the walls. Lower down little calves hung, their bodies much paler and plumper, almost grey, empty like the bulls, and like the bulls the bones of their legs extended as far as the knee-joint. On a gleaming table of white marble, a little to the side, lay dark, limp chunks of flesh with streaks of golden fat on the edges. Johann stood there in a white apron, jovial, strong and healthy, and skilfully cut large pieces from the chuck with a knife the size of an axe. Charlotte remembered the short, firm sound of the knife. Spatters of bone flew onto the floor. There were dark splotches on the front of Johann's apron and on the marble table. Charlotte went out into the fresh air, saying timidly that she felt dizzy. She had probably not yet grown accustomed to that spicy, heady aroma that so invigorated Johann.

"We're renovating, have you heard?" asked Johann. "We've built a third floor. Papa's going to move up there himself, and the second storey—the whole thing—above the shop is going to be for me. Not right away, of course . . . But, God willing . . ."

He fell silent.

Charlotte understood. He was talking about her. The floor above the shop—that was for her, when she married Johann. When she was home upstairs, she would hear the firm, cheerful sound of his axe as he began to chop fresh, plump pieces of meat near the marble table.

"The only drawback is that there are a lot of flies in the shop. The place is swarming with them. They'll be flying into the flat as well. But we can put up flypaper."

Charlotte didn't answer.

"It really is nice here," Johann began again. "Shady, cool . . . So many flowers! Whose grave is it, anyway? You're always coming here. Someone you know?"

"No, not really . . ." Charlotte managed to say.

Not for anything in the world would she have begun talking about Albert with Johann. She didn't even want him to see the white medallion with the portrait. It would probably remind him of his marble table.

"Well, it seems to me it must be frightening for you, isn't it, Mam'selle Charlotte? When you take your evening strolls here . . ."

"Why would it be frightening?" asked Charlotte in surprise.

"Come, now! Spending all your time with them . . ."

"What do you mean, 'with them'?"

"You know, corpses."

Charlotte smiled weakly. "Really, now! What corpses? There are no corpses here. They're all underground, deep down. There's nothing but graves and flowers here. Where you live, on the other hand," she dared to add, "you're the one who has corpses . . . I remember it—all those dead bodies, and the blood . . ."

Johann burst into loud laughter. "Oh, Mam'selle Charlotte! What a joker you are! Calling our bulls and calves corpses! Ha, ha, ha!"

Charlotte looked at him with narrowed eyes; a row of strong teeth gleamed in his pink, half-open mouth.

"Why are we talking about such inappropriate things?" Johann began again when he had stopped laughing. "I have something to ask of you, Mam'selle Charlotte: my most heartfelt desire. Don't refuse me!"

He made an imploring face. "You won't refuse me?"

"No . . . If I can . . ."

"Give me a flower you've made with your own skilful little hands. I'll wear it always in my buttonhole, and at night I'll put it under my pillow. Mam'selle Charlotte! You know how I treasure every one of your glances. Your eyes are like the very finest violets. Why are you so severe with me? Am I repulsive to you, Mam'selle Charlotte?"

There was deep sincerity in his voice. Slender, ever pale and reticent, Charlotte very much appealed to Johann.

"Am I repulsive, then?" he repeated, moving a little closer to her.

All around was silence and sultry heat. Even the crickets had fallen silent. An oppressive, stifling, invisible haze rose from the warmed earth. The lifeless aroma was a little dizzying.

"No . . . why . . . that's not it . . ." Charlotte babbled. Her heartbeats came fast and frightened.

She didn't finish her sentence. Just at that moment strong arms pressed her and warm, moist, soft lips greedily clung to her mouth. She remembered those lips: just a moment ago they had been before her eyes, too crimson, like the red calico of his shirt, or a little darker. And his hot, coarse touch felt like a blow to her. Red spots floated before her eyes.

"Let me go!" she cried wildly, in a voice she didn't recognise as her own, and she jumped up and pushed him violently away from her. "Let me go! Don't you dare! You mustn't, you mustn't!"

She shouted, her voice broke, and a horror unlike any she had ever known flooded her heart.

Johann stood there, bewildered and disconsolate.

"Forgive me, Mam'selle Charlotte," he said in a ragged voice. "I didn't know. Perhaps I've frightened you . . . But I had hoped . . . Your papa . . . and my papa . . ."

Charlotte's anger disappeared, leaving only fright and sorrow.

She covered her face with her hands.

"Go away," she whispered helplessly.

"I'll go now," Johann continued, a little encouraged. "If I understand correctly, you forgive me? You are so vulnerable, so delicate . . . You're a highly-strung, impressionable young lady . . . But I adore you, you must know that, I'm worthy of forgiveness precisely because I honestly, sincerely adore you, and as soon as tomorrow my father is going to . . ."

"Go away," Charlotte said again in a pleading whisper, her face still covered. "Oh, God!" she thought. "Here! How offensive, how shameful! Here, in front of him!"

The far-off voices of visitors could be heard around the bend. Johann looked round, sprang agilely up onto the fence and jumped down to the other side. Charlotte stood up, not daring to take her hands away, not daring to glance to the right, where silently and serenely the big roses gave off their fragrance, their heads slightly inclined, and where among their greenery gleamed the faint outline of a dear face.

Not turning around, her head bowed, Charlotte headed slowly for home. Her heart was full of shame and fright.

VI

Charlotte was ill for a long time and didn't leave her room. Her father frowned and suggested calling for Doctor Finch. But Charlotte got better and once again began to go out. It was already August and the autumn flowers were beginning to bloom on the graves.

Once, after dinner, Charlotte was quietly making her way down the familiar pathways to her favourite place. It had rained all morning, but now a yellow, moist sun peeked out and gilded the swaying foliage, already beginning to thin. Charlotte wanted to turn to the right, but then she noticed that the gate to Albert's grave was open. She knew that the gardener had not come, and she herself always closed the gate firmly. That meant that someone was in there.

Quietly, trying not to make noise on the fallen leaves, Charlotte turned back and went the other way around the fence, where the branches were thinner and it was possible to see through the lilac bushes what was happening inside.

Charlotte looked in—and involuntarily seized at the thick, wet trunk of a birch so as not to fall down. On her bench, near Albert's grave, a woman was sitting.

For the entire summer, since the very beginning of spring, no one had ever visited Albert. Charlotte was used to thinking that he was lonely, that no one cared about him, that he belonged only to her. And now an unknown woman, perhaps someone closer to him than Charlotte, had come—with every right to do so—and was sitting beside him.

Charlotte clenched her teeth, and sharp pangs of anger and hatred tore at her heart, which had always been so kind and timid. She stared avidly at the unknown lady.

The lady was shapely, though not tall and not at all thin, and she was dressed very elegantly, even richly, all in black. Her pretty young face expressed great sorrow, but the sorrow didn't go with her pert little nose and round black brows. One so wanted that face to smile. But instead, the lady took out a handkerchief and wiped her eyes with it. Then she sighed, sank to her knees as she gathered up her dress, put her hands together, laid her head down on them and was still for a few moments. Her crepe veil fell in beautiful folds. Charlotte noticed that an enormous, expensive and clumsy porcelain wreath hung on the cross. A broad ribbon with an inscription covered the marble medallion. A few silent, cold tears fell from Charlotte's eyes. She didn't notice them. Yes, yes! This was the one. This was the countess, the cousin, his beloved fiancée, who could take down the modest, light wreath made by Charlotte's hands, pull out the flowers she had planted, and hang her own jangling porcelain garlands, who could touch and kiss the delicate marble face, and lock up the door of the fence—and then Charlotte would never, ever be able to come here . . . Her whole humble soul was outraged and filled for the first time with real anger. Charlotte wanted to throw herself upon the unknown lady, seize her by her clothes, by that long veil, shout, drive her out and lock the gate.

"And him, him!" she said bitterly, as if she knew for certain that Albert was glad about the visit and the porcelain flowers. "How long she waited to come! And I came all the time, my flowers, my wreaths! It was always me, always for him! And now all of a sudden—it's over!"

The lady stood up, brushed the sand from her dress, adjusted the ribbon, stood a little longer, sighed again, crossed herself in the Catholic way, and gathering up her black suede reticule, went back towards the gates. She didn't know the way, and had trouble finding the main avenue. Charlotte followed her quietly, like a cat, from a distance. Finally, the lady found the right path and turned straight towards the warden's house.

Charlotte had already guessed that the lady would go there. Quickly, hardly stopping for breath, and gathering up her long, heavy braids, which she hadn't pinned up, she ran around the other way and woke up her father.

"What lady?" Ivan Karlovich grumbled unhappily as he put on his frockcoat.

"The countess . . . his cousin . . . seventeen thousand three hundred and eleven . . ." Charlotte babbled, trying to catch her breath.

"Ah . . . Good! I'll be right there."

Charlotte slipped after him into the big, dark reception room and, unnoticed, concealed herself in the far corner behind the table with its pile of books.

Ivan Karlovich invited the lady to sit down near the desk, not far from the windows. From her corner, Charlotte could see the lady's fresh face clearly.

"Oh, I'm so grateful to you for my darling's grave . . ." began the lady in Russian with a slight foreign accent. "It's so tidy, such lovely flowers."

"Yes, indeed, madam," Ivan Karlovich said, with reserve, but also with self-satisfaction. "We keep strict order around here. The number of your grave is 17311?"

"I don't really know . . . Albert Renault . . ."

"Yes, that's right, 17311. We've done everything possible. The remaining money . . ."

"Oh, no, no, please! I wanted to give some more . . . Here's fifty roubles for now."

"But what for? It's nearly autumn now, the graves won't be tended."

"Yes, but you see . . . I'm going away. Very far away, abroad. I don't know when I will return . . ."

"In that case, I can promise you that this money will cover the upkeep of the grave for two years, not more."

"But I'll send you more much sooner than that! I'll send a lot . . . I just don't know if I will be able to come myself . . . My name is Countess Lueben. That young man, taken so early from us, was my fiancé . . ."

She lowered her eyes. Ivan Karlovich only grunted indifferently. He hadn't had enough sleep.

"And now," continued the countess, who was evidently

not against chatting a bit, "I revere his memory . . . Circumstances dictated that I . . . that I must marry a . . . a distant relative of the deceased and go away forever to France. I'm French myself by birth," she added spiritedly and smiled, which immediately made her look twice as beautiful.

"I see," Ivan Karlovich said thoughtfully. "So you're going to be married, then? . . . Nonetheless, I must give you a receipt for the money I've received from you for the upkeep of grave No. 17311 for the next two years . . ."

Charlotte was no longer listening. Just as noiselessly as she had entered, she slipped out, crossed the terrace and set off at a run for the park, pressing her hands to her heart, which was beating hard and fast. It was cool, although the wind had died down; a bluish early dusk was coming on. The cemetery was desolate.

Charlotte ran all the way to Albert's gate and threw it open. Now she was entering as a queen. That other woman, so cold-hearted, had lost all her rights. Why had she come here? To mock him? His fiancée, before wedding another! Cursed, cursed woman! Away right now with those crude flowers! They were chilling and hurting him.

And Charlotte tore down the rich porcelain wreath and stamped on it, and crumpled the broad ribbon with the gold inscription "Hélène à son Albert"[3] and tried to rip it with her teeth. How dare she? Her Albert! She was unfaithful, had stopped loving him, and on top of that she had come to mock the defenceless! Never would Charlotte allow even a single flower to be planted here with her money. There was a little in her money-box . . . and she could earn more . . . and substitute her own money without her father noticing . . . it wouldn't be hard.

Flying bits of porcelain had cut Charlotte's hand. She shuddered when she saw a crimson drop on her palm. But now she seized her handkerchief and bound the wound.

Big, pale chrysanthemums with almost no fragrance, the

[3] "From Helen to her Albert."

kind that bloom only in damp autumn soil, were now swaying gently on the grave in place of the summer roses. Charlotte gently pulled aside the stems and pressed her cheek to the velvety, cold marble bas-relief. She barely sensed the unevenness of the profile's outlines. O, my dear, O, my poor dear! And she, she who was herself guilty before him, had dared to reproach him! How had she failed to understand right away that he had to be protected, he who had no words with which to respond, that this Elena had come to mock him, that she couldn't possibly love him! She had found herself another man, one who existed, one who was warm, with red, soft lips, like Johann . . .

Charlotte, on the other hand, loved Albert with all her mind and all her heart. Now she wouldn't give him up to anybody. And he . . . What did he need Elena for—that horrible, foreign, living woman? Charlotte was infinitely closer to him.

And Charlotte remained lying down like that, her face pressed to the marble cross. Her love, all her love, was full of the sweetness of hopelessness, that quiet, sweet bliss of despair that exists in the depths of the heart after the last tears have been wept, at the end of every sorrow—like an autumn day's dusk, with its unclouded, cold, greenish skies above the silent forest.

VII

One day at tea, when Caroline and her sickly watchmaker were present, a scene took place that was inevitable, and yet somehow still took Charlotte by surprise.

Their father was uncharacteristically gloomy. The watchmaker sighed and wrapped himself up in the muffler he unfailingly kept with him. Caroline kept casting meaningful glances at her sister, which she, as it happened, didn't see.

Ivan Karlovich began ceremoniously: "My daughter, do you know that today Mister Rotte was here for the final answer? And in this he is entirely justified. November is already here. The time is absolutely appropriate. Everything got drawn out on account of your illness. But now you are well. Johann is a very, very fine, upstanding young man."

"Papa," Charlotte uttered with difficulty, "I beg of you . . . I can't now."

"What's this: 'I can't'? What is that supposed to mean: 'I can't'?"

"I can't get married . . . I'm still young . . ."

"Young! So we're to wait until we're old to marry? Tut, tut! That's no way for young ladies to answer their fathers. Fathers are experienced, fathers know. They are to be obeyed."

"I can't!" Charlotte almost screamed. "I don't like Johann! I won't do it!"

"What is this? You won't do it? Look at this, my children!" Ivan Karlovich, turning crimson, shouted. "She doesn't like the fine young man chosen by her father! The eldest son of a most wealthy merchant! She won't marry him, when I told his father that as of tomorrow Johann may present himself as my daughter's fiancé! Which means my word counts for nothing!"

Charlotte gave a weak moan and covered her face with her hands.

Caroline broke into the conversation. "Lottchen, what are you thinking! Come to your senses. After all, you must get married. Look at what a dashing fellow Johann is! How many girls are pining for him! Don't worry, papa dear, she'll come around. She's a young girl . . ."

"Yes," the watchmaker, clearing his throat, joined in. "Young girls, they're a strange breed . . . By the way, you've got to keep your eye on them all the time . . . It's right hard to look after them properly!"

"What for . . . I don't need looking after . . ." In a broken voice, Charlotte tried to speak. "Can't I just stay . . . Am I really in the way?"

"What do you mean you don't need looking after?" Ivan Karlovich shouted, beside himself with rage and instantly turning crimson again. "No, you do, my lady, you do! And I'm old, I can't look after you! I can't take the responsibility! I can't, I can't! Everything's decided! I gave my word! Mister Rotte is my best friend! And I can't be looking after you! The apple doesn't fall far from the tree, that's the trouble!"

He was beside himself, waving his arms and gasping for breath. Charlotte sprang from her chair and rushed sobbing from the room. Caroline ran after her.

"What do you want?" Charlotte cried, sounding almost bitter, when she saw her sister coming into the room. "Have you come to preach at me? Why are you all so cruel to me? Why do I have to get married? What about you, you did! And look at you now, are you so happy?"

"We're not the cruel ones, Charlotte—you are," Caroline protested. "I don't understand what's happened to you. You've changed completely. You say I'm unhappy. But if Franz was healthy and I didn't have to worry all the time about losing him, I wouldn't quibble with my fate. And little Wilhelm so ill all the time! But with you it's another matter. Johann is so healthy and strong, you won't worry about him, and you'll have strong children . . . It's papa I would be very, very worried about, if I were in your place."

"Why?" Charlotte asked, frightened. Her outburst had passed, and now she sat on her bed, timid and sorrowful, her arms lowered and head bowed.

"Do you mean to say you really don't know? He may have a stroke; he could die at any moment. You shouldn't upset him. Did you notice how red in the face he gets? He's had apoplectic fits for some time now. You're upsetting him, agitating him with your disobedience, and he'll have a stroke and it will be your fault . . . You ought to be worrying about him constantly . . ."

"Oh, what can I do? What should I do?" Charlotte, crushed, now whispered in despair. "Why are you scaring me, Caroline?"

"I'm not scaring you at all. This is absolutely normal. All of us who have relatives and dear ones must protect them and worry about them, always remembering how fragile people are. You may as well resign yourself to it, Charlotte. Take some advice from your sister."

Charlotte suddenly remembered Johann's full face, smiling, and his slightly bloodshot, bulging eyes. The marble table, the limp, dark flesh with its grainy fat, the fresh bodies of bulls, the smell of blood, the flat above the shop, and all those flies . . . Charlotte gave her sister one last, pleading look, as if she could change everything. Just at that moment the watchmaker's head appeared in the doorway.

"Caroline," he whispered hoarsely, "Come, your papa is calling. Come quickly, something's wrong with him."

"Aha! There, you see!" a triumphant Caroline said to her sister as she got up. "This is the work of your hands."

Charlotte sprang up, too, and in mortal terror grabbed hold of her sister's dress. "Caroline, Caroline! Wait! What's happened to him? Oh God, what am I to do?"

"Let me go, you wicked daughter! Let go of me now."

"Caroline, tell him . . . Oh, it doesn't matter, if he can't forgive me, allow me . . . What am I saying? Tell him that I agree to everything."

She fell back on the bed, burying her head in her pillow. Caroline hurried out of the room.

Ivan Karlovich's bout of illness turned out to be of no consequence. Caroline and the watchmaker stayed for a long time, conferring in self-satisfied whispers. They troubled Charlotte no further. Let her recover from her agitation, now that she has agreed . . .

VIII

It was around three in the morning when Charlotte came to her senses. She didn't know whether she had been sleeping or just lying there oblivious, without tears, without thoughts, without moving, with her face to the pillow, ever since the moment her sister had left the room. She raised herself up a little on the bed. Her body ached, as if from weariness, and there was an empty rushing in her head. She remembered what she had said to Caroline, and knew that there was no going back. Tomorrow Johann would come, her fiancé, her

191

husband. She had to resign herself . . . because she must. Oh, God can see this is not her fault! How can she fight against it, she who has always been so weak and timid? But she didn't want to be unfaithful, and anyway, she wasn't capable of being unfaithful, as she was incapable of falling out of love. Albert, Albert . . .

She got up, slowly and perfectly quietly. From the wide window, its curtain still open, shone the blue light of the moon, seeming even brighter because of the snow's whiteness. There had been an early snowfall and it now lay unmelted, but not deep. From the part of the window where the stained glass had been installed, the moon's rays, passing through it, fell on the floor in fiery, lustrous dark blue patches. Inside her room, as in the quiet graveyard outside the window, all was still and indistinct. Now and then fast-moving snow clouds screened the moon from view, and for a moment everything would grow dim and murky, shadows would run, slip, widen, and then suddenly disappear, and again the thin air would become cold and bluish.

Charlotte quietly slipped off her boots, so as not to make any noise, and changed her wrinkled dress for a white flannel housecoat. She moved noiselessly and hurriedly. One thought, clear and implacable, possessed her now. She had to go. Tomorrow would already be different. Tomorrow she would no longer be herself. Tomorrow Johann would come and kiss her, and she would accept his kiss, because she was to become his bride and then his wife, so she could move into the newly renovated flat over the shop. It had to be now, today, while she was still Charlotte, still herself, still alive. She must go to the man she loved.

"I'll go . . . say good-bye . . ." she whispered disjointedly, occupied only with the task of slipping out of the house without disturbing anyone.

She needed no words to tell Albert that it wasn't her fault. But it dimly seemed to her that he would sense it more quickly if she were there, close to him.

White and insubstantial as a ghost, she slipped down the stairs in her stocking feet. Not a single step creaked. The door leading out to the terrace was locked. They had been meaning to oil it, but hadn't yet had the time. Beneath the black ceilings, night noises that only made the silence seem deeper—the breathing of sleeping people, the creaking of furniture, rustling behind the wallpaper—faded away to nothing. With an effort Charlotte turned the rusty key. It protested weakly, and then the swollen door thumped open. The cold and the smell of snow made Charlotte wince. But in another moment she was already running along the greenish-blue, sparkling avenue, her little, unshod feet leaving a light trail of barely indented prints.

It was very dark beneath the black trees. Charlotte's teeth were chattering, and she hurried to get there, as if there, at Albert's grave, warmth awaited her. Again snow clouds covered the moon and everything grew dim, the gleam disappeared, and the shadows deepened. But the clouds broke apart, and once again the light-blue, quiet, indistinct rows of crosses lay before Charlotte, a world that now looked just like what she had seen through the glass of her window.

Here was the outer path, and here the gate. Charlotte fell upon the snowy rise of the grave, her arms joyously thrown open, the way people fall into an embrace. And really, she wasn't at all cold now. The snow, exactly the same white as her dress and almost the same colour as her blonde, unpinned braids, pressed so tenderly beneath her narrow body. It was gentle and soft. It sparkled beneath the moon's rays on the marble bas-relief. As always, Charlotte touched her cheek to the barely protruding, tender, now frosty contour. Her breath made the snow crystals melt, disappear, fly off, and the features of that elusively beautiful, indifferent face became clearer and clearer. And Charlotte lay like that for a long time, her hands, grown even whiter, clasped around the cross. Albert was with her, and she had never felt so close to him. She was at ease now, not afraid of anything: she was guilty of nothing, and he knew it, because he and she were as one. A sweet languor, unlike anything she had ever known, spread through her, and warmth enveloped her limbs. He, Albert, was with her, caressing, coddling and lulling her weary body to sleep. The hours flew by, or perhaps ceased to exist. Charlotte didn't see how once again the bulging clouds gathered, how in a moment the troubled air grew dark, and without a rustle, without a sound, big flakes, light as foam, began to fall to the ground . . . At first just a few, then faster and faster, they began to dance and spin unsteadily, blending together the moment they touched the ground. Lulled by an unearthly bliss, Charlotte slept. She dreamt of a light-blue world and of a love that exists only there.

And from above, the caressing snow kept on falling and falling, dressing Charlotte and Albert in a single shroud, white, sparkling and ceremonious, like a bridal veil.

O evil life, your gifts
Are naught but illusion and fraud;
They deceptively attract,
But they shift and change like fog.

No sooner has beauty had time
To blossom and entrance,
Already you rush to weave
New fabrics from its threads.

And no sooner has death arrived,
Bringing mortals liberation,
You zealously call forth
Ever new generations.

O death! O tender friend!
I don't understand at all:
Why don't all mortals and gods
Rush at once to your splendid halls?

Fyodor Sologub, 1904

Everything Around Us

Dreadful, rude, sticky, filthy,
Rigidly dull, always ugly,
Pettily devious, rending slowly,
Slippery, shameful, cramped and lowly,
Openly smug, secretly lascivious,
Wretchedly craven and trivially ridiculous,
Slimily stagnant, viscous and miry,
Equally unworthy of death and of life,
Slavish, boorish, purulent, black,
Sometimes grey, in grey obstinate,
Eternally lazing, devilishly sluggish,
Stupid, withered, drowsy, spiteful,
Cold as a corpse, pitifully worthless,
Unbearable, a lie, a lie!

But what's the point of crying? There's no need to complain,
For we know, we know: it will all be different one day.

Zinaida Gippius, 1904

The Earth

A moment of weakness . . .
        A hesitant moment . . .
And the wings of holy madness
        Are broken.

I stand above a grave,
        Where audacity sleeps . . .
Oh, all of it was merely
        Excitement, revelry,

And pure, sacred joy
        In our eyes,
Springtime dawns,
        Eight-leafed lilacs . . .

How deceptive!
        Did it really happen?
With a strange hope
        Above a grave I stand . . .

I seek signs of movement
        Beneath dust and ashes,
I await resurrection
        With a fearful prayer . . .

But I grow more apprehensive . . .
        Defenceless I stand . . .
The open grave, gaping,
        A black abyss, laughs;

My omnipotent soul
Demands a miracle . . .
But from down there comes only
The grave's earthy smell . . .

Zinaida Gippius, 1902

Moon Ants

Zinaida Gippius

November 1, 1909

I was walking along the Izmailovsky Bridge last month, at dusk. It was cold and windy. Not a lot of people about. All of a sudden I see something dark bolting for the railing, tumbling heavily over it and plummeting down into the greasy black slush of the already freezing river.

There's an uproar, whistles blow, a crowd gathers, people run down from the pavement towards the empty pier, near the barracks.

I go, too. As I push my way through the crowd, I hear, "They fished him out. Got him right away with the long hook and fished him out."

And this little fellow is already standing there on the pavement, water dripping off him, hair all plastered over his eyes, and he's snorting and shaking all over. In the grey dusk it's hard to see, but by now I'd got close. A very young chap, small and thin.

The policeman next to him is angry, and keeps shoving him along. "C'mon, you, take that! Let's go, then, move along!"

"But my hat," the fellow mumbles, "my favourite hat . . ."

"So we're to go fish your hat out as well, are we? Sit down and be quiet . . . Hey, driver!"

A disgruntled but acquiescent cabby materialised.

Indignant exclamations sounded among the crowd. All were against the little fellow.

"But my hat," he insisted, shaking. "For pity's sake . . . Your honour . . ."

"What an eyeful! Bored with life, how do you like that!" a workman snorted scornfully. "I'll give you 'for pity's sake'!"

A lady shrilled, "Officer, what are you doing? Take him to hospital! He's swallowed a bellyful of river water, he'll get cholera!"

The policeman, now completely enraged, swore and shoved the little fellow into the cab, got in himself, trying to keep as far away as possible, and thumped the driver on the back.

The suicide was shaking his wet hair and babbling helplessly about something, most likely the same thing as before, and they drove off, jolting into the grey murk.

The crowd dispersed, grumbling.

"Hanging's too good for the likes of them!" said a merchant, and spat. "A worm like that, and he thinks he's a suicide! So much trouble! What sort of new fashion is this?"

A girl in a kerchief protested mildly, "But if living's too much for him . . ."

The merchant just snarled at her and spat again.

"Likely doesn't have a job, or else he lost his master's money," someone said hollowly.

No one paid any attention to this. Indifferently, they went their separate ways. An everyday occurrence.

But the little fellow's face still loomed before me. Wet, snorting, babbling about his hat. And what got into him, anyway, why did he throw himself over the railings like that? He was just walking along, and then suddenly over he goes.

Since that time I've been drawn to suicides. I've begun keeping a record of them from the newspapers, looked into every case. Don't understand it at all. There are whole regiments of them stretching out before me, swarms of them. The reasons are all different—and they're all the same, and all somehow incomprehensible.

What are they going through before they make up their minds? What are they like? Is there any way to know beforehand who they are?

Last spring a student I knew shot himself. I saw him not long before it happened and noticed absolutely nothing. Afterwards his friends said he'd seemed "lost in thought" before he did it. But that's nonsense; he wasn't at all "lost in thought."

November 8

Since I began to keep count, I've simply lost my peace of mind. I can't work. And the strangest thing of all is that there are such a lot of them. More than there has ever been. I know this for a fact, I've checked. And then there are the "reasons." Actually, the absence of any "reason," because what they give as "reasons" are simply the conditions of life. And life has always been the same. Sometimes better, sometimes worse. The same.

It's especially common with simple girls. They're drinking vinegar essence by the bucketful. But it's not just them— they're everywhere, these self-murderers, absolutely every- where, only you hear about the girls more.

For some reason Rocky Katy made an especially deep impression on me. Why she in particular, I myself don't know. I even went to the hospital to find out what happened to her. They saved her. She recovered. She stated that there had been no reason.

November 15

Yesterday evening I finally went to Ligovka Street.[1] It was so cold you could hardly breathe.

Two women of that sort, in thin, shabby coats, started making up to me. Their noses were red.

"Listen, my dears," I say to them. "Don't imagine things, you won't find me of any particular use, but if you want to go somewhere and warm up for a half hour or so, I'll treat you to a cup of tea if you like."

---

[1] Prostitutes plied their trade on St. Petersburg's Ligovka Street, which was populated with a variety of other shady characters and businesses as well .

They shift uneasily, they don't understand. I suddenly catch sight of a pair of eyes gleaming under a streetlamp: it's a *kartuznik*.[2] He stops, takes a look, listens in. An ordinary mug, young and untrustworthy.

"How about it? You know, just for conversation."

They snorted. "Us? Well, we . . ."

"If you like, we can take this young gentleman along with us, seeing as how he looks to be a friend of yours."

The *kartuznik* approached. "What's all this?" he asked in a guttural voice. I repeated my simple proposition, which seemed so extraordinary to all of them. I made ready to move on; I'd had my fill of this.

"There's a little place nearby, the Record, we could go there," one of the girls suddenly said. "I'm freezing. It's got me by the throat. But what kind of conversation were you thinking of?"

"Any kind," I said, waving my hand dismissively.

And I rudely added, "I'm curious to find out, why do you idiots keep poisoning yourselves for nothing?"

The girls laughed. "There's no shortage of silly girls! And we're no better!"

We set off for the Record. The *kartuznik* followed after us. Actually, he oughtn't really to be called a "kartuznik," since on his head he wore a battered, faded student's uniform cap. But I knew what it meant, that peaked cap: "A man in this kind of hat must not be denied entrance into the tavern." One of those types explained this to me a long time ago.

The Record turned out to be the most ordinary sort of tavern—rather dingy, as one would expect, but not wretchedly filthy.

We sat down in the public room. We asked for tea. I purposely did not order beer for them.

[2] A peaked uniform cap, the *kartuz* was typically worn by men involved in illegal businesses such as prostitution. The word *kartuznik* came to mean not so much "a man wearing a *kartuz*" as "a man involved in illicit business".

The girls turned out to be very similar—both skinny, ignorant and young.

"We're two friends: Barb and Darla. But we won't tell you our nicknames, because they're of no use to you."

"Do you by any chance know Rocky Katy?" I asked.

"What do you want her for, sir?" the man in the peaked cap answered with his own question.

"Not much, just conversation. I told you already, there's a certain thing I'm interested in. But never mind. What is your name?"

"Mine? I have plenty of titles. But among others, they call me John Khan. Among others. Because I have a lot of wives. And this is Johnny Convert."

I turned around. I hadn't noticed before that another man had come in after us, wearing the same type of cap; fat jowls, his figure tall, thin and limp; he walked softly, like a cat, slouching along, placing one foot in front of the other along the same floorboard.

"Don't let me interrupt."

"Sit down and join us," I said. "So what are you, originally Jewish?"

"Heavens, no!" Khan answered for him (and really, it didn't seem like it). "Convert, because after the revolution he became a Lutheran, fixing to marry a Jewess. But it didn't pan out."

Convert turned to me with a mysterious look. "You, sir, if you're from a newspaper about the poisonings, these girls won't do for you. But I know Rocky Katy and others like her."

"You're lying!" Barb cried out. "You don't know Rocky Katy. Matara knows her, that's who knows her! Only now Katy's not much good. She's in hospital, and there's a kitty for her when she comes out."

"But do you understand what it's all about? Do you? Matara knows! Why don't I bring this Matara here right this minute? How about it, sir, you want Matara?"

I waved Convert off. "First of all, I'm here not with the newspapers at all. I'm here on my own account. And secondly, please quiet down a little. Don't bother trying to talk me into anything, I won't end up being of any use to you, so you don't have to go making up stories. I'm happy to treat you to a little something, if you don't mind chatting with me, but not more than that. If you know someone who knows Rocky Katy or Matara, tell them. I'll come again tomorrow for half an hour or so, we'll talk, and have a little tea.

They were all pleased with this. Pleased with my frankness.

"I'll bring Matara!" Convert declared.

Barb and Darla, laughing, whinnied, "Oh, tea, just pure tea! It's enough to make you 'tea-spair'!"

They drank, however, with pleasure. I promised that next time they might have a little beer as well.

The girls wriggled happily and senselessly, like young sparrows. Neither they nor John Khan and Johnny Convert seemed anywhere near to "despairing of life." Not in any way!

November 17

I'm deepening our acquaintance. Yesterday I was at the Record again, and I'm just fresh from there now.

Yesterday Convert brought Matara (Martha, surely). Cheerful, thin and not stupid. She began to complain loudly about "life," but clearly, she herself doesn't pay attention to her own nonsense. It's all so trivial.

"You never know what tomorrow may bring, that's for certain. A full belly, that's all I need. I suppose even counts and princes don't have it all sunshine and roses, wouldn't you say?"

"Gentlemen and men in general are more likely to take a bullet, if things aren't going well," said Johnny Khan with a thoughtful air. "But for us, since we're forbidden to carry firearms, we go more for the noose. Women, though, generally take the vinegar essence route. But anyway, it doesn't really matter, as far as the result is concerned."

Convert tittered. "The noose! Fat lot of good that will do,

strangling yourself. If you're in a bad way—begging your pardon, not that you would be—you're better off rummaging through someone's flat for whatever might turn up."[3]

"That's another possibility," Khan responded indifferently. "It's simple. Better or worse, as far as the result is concerned there's no difference."

"What do you mean?" I said, not understanding.

But I got no explanation.

Besides the two silly sparrows—Barb and Darla—there was a third, a very young girl. Darla recommended her with solemnity: "Tina. Her own sister what got poisoned."

"Really? When?"

"A little more than a week ago," Tina responded eagerly. "And she tried to tempt me, too. 'Why not?' she says, 'there's nothing to live for, anyway.' I say, 'All in good time,' and she ups and does it. It was me done took her to hospital."

"And what then?"

"That's all. Later she said, 'Just fine,' she says, 'fine. Only it hurts.' "

"So she recovered?"

"No, no, she kicked it. She said that after the sacrament."

Matara darted a glance at me and said, "Say, is it really true that there's such a thing as a poison that's not painful? And cheap?"

"There is. Potassium cyanide. You can't buy it. But by the way, anyone who does photography can get it easily."

All of a sudden they livened up: Khan, Convert and the girls, all equally so. "You don't say? What is it, exactly? And what about you, are you a photographer?"

I was a bit taken aback. And didn't mention to them that actually this summer I had dabbled a bit in photography.

This time we had beer as well as tea, but not too much. I did not at all want to buy their chitchat by treating them. And besides, the conversations were turning out to be

[3] In the turbulent years immediately after the 1905 revolution, during which this story takes place, military tribunals could sentence anyone convicted of any crime (here, burglary is implied) to hanging.

uninteresting, or at least not what I'd been looking for. Maybe I was talking to the wrong people?

However, I trudged off to see them again today. Again the same people, except for Matara. I was already bored and ready to leave. Suddenly Matara shows up and with her an extraordinarily tall girl wearing a neck scarf.

"Here you go, you wanted to meet her: it's Rocky Katy," said Matara proudly. "I barely convinced her to let me bring her to talk with you. She's ill now. Hardly any of the locals here know her. Only I do."

Everybody else, though, remained indifferent. Only I was . . . touched somehow. I even felt a little shy.

"Hello, Katy. Will you have some tea?"

Rocky Katy sat down. She was heavy-set, pale, unmoving, but not at all sombre.

"How about with a little cognac?" she asked in a husky voice.

"Sure, a little cognac as well."

Matara broke in obsequiously: "The gentleman here has been wanting to know for a long time why you poisoned yourself."

Katy turned her gaze on me. "Why did I? . . . A lot of people have asked me that."

Tina seized on this: "See, now I bet you're a rich girl, they took up a collection for you in the hospital. It'll last a long time, now. But what about Natalya, who kicked it this spring? She threw herself out a window. She had a pretty new jacket, brand new, and someone pinched it. Naturally, she was upset."

"No, it's not that," Rocky Katy said again. "I just . . ."

"Because of life," Matara explained. "Of course, the way our life is . . ."

Convert tittered. "Whatever way it is. Look at 'em, phoo! You Persian princesses. Don't like it, who needs you?"

To me, Rocky Katy seemed just like everyone else. As if she had never tried to kill herself, like Barb, Tina, myself and Khan.

"So, there wasn't any reason?" I asked her. "Just because?"

Unexpectedly, Rocky Katy burst into laughter, so unexpectedly that I even winced. "My head is spinning from that cognac. Not used to it anymore. Why what for? Why'd I take it? Is that what you're asking? Well, I've forgotten already. When they were bringing me round, they kept after me for the reason. My innards are burning up, and they keep going on about the reason. So I tell 'em, 'Get away from me, there's no reason, and that's all there is to it!' "

All the girls had a good laugh, while Johnny Khan and Convert, having finished off the whole bottle of cognac under cover of the general hubbub, set to cursing furiously.

I got tired of it and left. On top of all the rest, Tina had been naïvely coming on to me. Clearly she didn't believe that I was just interested in talking. And the conversation wasn't what I'd hoped for, either.

I'll probably go and see them again, but just not right away. Either there's something I'm not seeing, not understanding, or else people are the same everywhere. And there's no such thing as a suicidal psychology. A stolen jacket—that's one reason. The way life is—another reason. No reason—that's a reason, too.

I definitely don't understand a thing.

November 20

I tried to get to work, went to see my professor, spent time in the university library. Saw some people. Looked at them with curiosity. It could be that some of them have already tried to kill themselves, tomorrow others will—but you can't tell by looking. They behave as normally as I do. And their faces look as boring as mine probably does.

Outside the yellow mud is knee-high, and the smell of warm manure is suffocating: there's been a thaw. It's been dark outside since this morning. Some plasterers who murdered someone in the Old Village—robbed him for a rouble and then drank it up—got tried and sentenced with the speed of lightning and have already been hanged. And by the way, the whole time they behaved with complete indifference. It made me think about John Khan: "There's no difference, as far as the result is concerned."

To be sure, they and Khan and Convert all have one thing in common—the psychology of a plasterer.

And what about my little chap—the one who tried to drown himself?

November 21

Today I was given a letter at half past nine. I was still lying in bed. It was so dark that I had to light a candle.

I read it. Didn't understand right away. Read it through again.

This was really something!

The letter was from Lebedev, the little old secretary of the *Kazan News*. I've known him as long as I've known the Tolmachevs. Mr Tolmachev was an editor, and his wife was his faithful assistant. Hardworking, nice people, getting on in years. In September both of them came to St. Petersburg on newspaper business. I saw them often, helped out where I could . . . They were under a lot of pressure. They complained, of course, about the times and how bad it was in the provinces . . . They complained, as people always do, but . . . I didn't notice anything.

Not a thing! And now Mr. Lebedev writes that last week they both, husband and wife, poisoned themselves. From the same glass. I didn't know, somehow I missed it . . . or perhaps they don't even write about what happens in the provinces?

The letter was surprisingly calm, quietly shocked.

"Things kept getting worse . . . It was just impossible to fight it . . . They couldn't hold out . . ."

Things. So. My older, "honest" friends had poisoned themselves. And what would have happened if instead of going to the Record I had gone to Kazan? Just now, a week ago? No, that's nonsense. They would have been the same as they had been in September. I would have sat with them for an evening, they would have complained, as always—and that very night, perhaps, poisoned themselves. Things were going badly. It was impossible to work.

After managing so long, they had given up.

Somehow this didn't shake me. Strangely, it was even as if I had expected it. Or had I just got used to the unexpected happening?

I think about them, though. I feel melancholy, but this melancholy is also because of the dark November thaw. I can't stand thaws.

I think about myself as well. My life is going relatively well. I'm young, single, not much money, but enough to get by, because I don't demand too much. I've been kept on at the university, getting ready to take my master's examination, I love my work . . . that is, I've always loved it. Those "years of transformation"[4] (which didn't transform anything after all) shook me up, took hold of me then, and I . . . but no, it's no good reminiscing about that. I don't want to, don't like to. It's all past now; everything's changed. I'm content like this. Peacefully doing what I do. And why did these suicides suddenly come to mind? I don't know. Whatever you start looking into starts to get into you. Like now with my old couple in Kazan . . . The reason—things were bad. The reason—they stole my new jacket. The reason . . . what else?

There is no reason. And "as far as the result is concerned"—what's the difference? None whatsoever.

November 24

Today I went to the "psycho-metaphysical" society. I never have liked societies, but I was suddenly drawn to this one. The place was packed. What was it that attracted all these people?

Many familiar faces. Although as a rule I try to avoid people

[4] The revolutionary years of 1905–1907.

I know. Got to talking with just one fellow I've always liked—a young lawyer connected with literature.

We chatted about a recent comic duel between two third-rate poets.

"What did they do it for?" I say. "All they did was amuse people and lose a boot."[5]

"Yes . . . But you know, somehow, I looked into it a bit: they were terribly tired of life. Had it up to here."

This was unexpected and hardly believable. I smiled. "And so they lost a boot?"

"Well, they did their best. But I assure you, you can feel it in them."

I left him. From a distance I took another look at my friend. He was just standing there, and his expression was cheerful. But he looked a little weak, abandoned, as if his legs were buckling slightly. I wanted to go back and ask him, hadn't he "had it up to here" with life? But I didn't. He wouldn't know, anyway. His expression was cheerful. And anyway it's beside the point that one gets tired of life! I went into the salon. Took up my place near the door.

I heard neither the lecture nor the debate. Just kept looking at how everyone sat and listened. They sat there as usual. Quietly. Didn't move around much. And somehow carefully, as if they were made of glass. For the first time I noticed this new, limp calmness in the crowd—a cautious and indifferent quietude. And it wasn't that they were bored—not at all! They were just sitting the way they sit.

There were so many of them. Who among them will finally break down tomorrow, unable to bear that their jacket was stolen, or something else? Who among them broke down yesterday and happened to be saved in time, like my Rocky Katy?

I don't know. And they themselves don't know. Not the

---

[5] The narrator is referring to an event that was well-known at the time as the "Story of a Lost Boot." Two poets (both of them certainly better than the narrator ranks them), Nikolai Gumilev and Maximilian Voloshin, in fact had a duel that ended with no loss of life, but the loss of a boot.

people at the Record, and not these here . . . And even my colleagues from Kazan didn't know until the last minute that they would drink the poison, that they had drunk it.

And when did this all happen? Something so enormous happened, and no one noticed. What kind of people are these? Perhaps they're not people at all!

I felt as if I'd been physically struck. I left immediately, went home on foot, deep in thought the whole time. Yes, yes, now it was completely clear. An example had made everything clear.

What had helped me was a novel by Wells. Suddenly it had come to mind, like a bolt of lightning. Two earth people landed on the moon. There were a bunch of creatures living there already. They were like ants that stood on their hind legs—a little shorter than people. There were only the two people, and whole battalions of hostile giant ants began to move against them, in some kind of subterranean tunnels. It seemed this would be the end. But the people suddenly noticed that these ants were extraordinarily weak and fragile. At the merest touch—of a twig or a finger—they crumpled up and fell down dead. Not only that, but the ants themselves, if they even just brushed up against something, would fall apart; their legs would twist up awkwardly, one after another, and down they'd go with the life knocked out of them. And so their dead bodies ended up rolling all around the cavern.

And now people are quietly turning into something like those ants. When did it happen, how long has it been going on, and why?

It was as if someone had saturated the air with undetectable vapours that had hidden powers of transformation; and everyone was breathing it, from the Record to the Psycho-Metaphysical Society, from St. Peterburg to Kazan and Saratov—everywhere, everyone; and they were growing weak and fragile and dropping dead. Dropping dead, from a human standpoint, for almost no reason at all. The ant itself doesn't think about it, doesn't expect it . . . accidentally tripping over something, he's already down, broken apart, already dead, to his own surprise.

What sort of vapours are these? When did this poison spread over our earth? Who has made people into ants, so vulnerable to death?

November 25

I slept well. No dreams. This morning it was a little lighter, at least you can read, once your eyes grow accustomed, without a lamp.

The following particulars were in the *New Times* (I'm purposely copying out the whole article—it is genuine; documents are boring, but edifying). This one is from yesterday, St. Catherine's day:

". . . Riga Blvd.; worker Alexandra Smirnov, 15, went to her grandmother's house and as they were talking suddenly drank a bottle of vinegar essence. She is in critical condition. Alexandra Sergeyev, 17, was found on the embankment of Obvodny Canal after she poisoned herself with liquid ammonia. Disappointment in life. At 3 Mogilev St., Ivan Filev, 29, a mechanic, drank vinegar essence. In Damm's fabric-dyeing workshop, Ivan Philippov, 23, poisoned himself with sulphuric acid. On Maly Ave., Alexander Maslennikov, after an argument with his wife, took vinegar essence. That same evening an unidentified young man threw himself into the Obvodny Canal. Breaking through the ice, he disappeared beneath the water. His body has not been found. Anna Zakharova, 16, took vinegar essence and died at Obukhovsky Hospital. On the same day St. Petersburg court bailiff V. K. Kosminsky was found in his flat, having hanged himself. He was 65. The reason is unknown. At 20 First-Company-of-the-Izmailovsky-Regiment St., retired colonel V. G. Petrovich, 70, cut his own throat. He had been living on his pension, never married, left no note, in critical condition . . ."

That seems like enough already, doesn't it? But there's more: two unidentified girls hired a driver and drank a bottle of vinegar essence while riding in the cab.

In another paper I came upon an interview with Professor

Przibytek. Oh, these endless interviews! But today's ended very sensibly:

" 'I'm not saying,' " the professor declared firmly, 'that we don't need to fight against the self-poisonings, but that in the end, it is futile. No matter *what* efforts we make, and *who* makes them and *how* they try to help, nothing *at all* will come of it.' "

Well said! How does one combat the possibility that an ant-Natasha will have her jacket stolen, that an ant-Filev will argue with his wife, that student B. will be disappointed in life, and that ants everywhere will inevitably slip and fall?

The problem isn't that they will slip and fall; it's a more serious problem, namely, that everyone on earth is going around on ant legs instead of human legs.

This evening I headed off to the Record. None of my acquaintances were there. I went out on Ligovka Street and walked for a long time, turning into neighbouring lanes as well; I saw some people, but didn't want to talk—I was looking for the people I knew. I did ask one girl about Matara; it seems she is very well-known around here. Didn't find out anything useful.

I stopped by two teahouses. Nothing. It was warm and windy, though not terribly wet. At least this sort of weather is possible to bear.

I was ready to head home, when suddenly I caught sight of a familiar, bobbing figure in the shadows just around the corner.

I caught up and softly called him: "Hey, Convert!"

Convert turned and looked at me with hostility: "Whattaya want?"

"What's wrong? Want to drop in at a teahouse? Where did everybody disappear to?"

Convert kept on looking sullenly at me. "Naw, mister, you'd better go about your own business and not hang around here."

"Don't you go off the wall, then," I raised my voice at him. "If you're so busy, go to the devil, and I'll go looking for Johnny Khan."

The shouting had its effect, as it always does. Convert danced up closer to me, and looking around him, muttered, "Pardon me, the thing is, I've been put on notice for a while now. They even made me turn in my student's cap. And, pardon me, you won't find Johnny Khan."

"Why is that?'

"Because. The state's feeding him these days."

"Really?! Has he been there for long?'

"Long, not so long," Convert whispered, moving even closer, "but now he's done for. He smashed a policeman in the snout, pardon the expression!"

"How about that! He must have been drunk?"

"Not at all! We had a little scandal here, of course, everything would have been all right, but Johnny, it was like he exploded, how he went at it with his fists! And then a knife was found . . . Ah, the hell with him, dammit all," Convert added, suddenly growing angry. "He ought not to get other people mixed up in his affairs, the idiot."

"All right, all right, good-bye then," I said. "You all went mad ages ago, you can all go to the devil for all I care!"

"That's for sure, we're all mad. But I, begging your pardon, as you've always been so gracious . . . At least I appreciate a conversation. You were interested in Rocky Katy so you could make your observations . . . But now those two girls have done themselves in."

"What are you talking about? What two girls? Why don't you go and get yourself a drink, if that's how it is? As for me, I'm heading home."

"Thank you," Convert pronounced with dignity, putting away my rouble. (I wasn't in the habit of lavishing money on them, but why not—I'll never see him again).

"I thank you from the heart. But it's true about the girls. Darla and Barb. They hailed a cab and tossed off a draught. Their driver took them straight to Obukhovsky Hospital."

"To Obukhovsky?"

"Where else would he take them? Not to the Winter Palace, that's for sure!"

He giggled idiotically. I turned sharply away from him. So

that was who the "unidentified girls" in the newspaper were! Barb and Darla, stupid, cheerful little girls, like sparrows! But they were no sparrows at all. They were moon ants. "Suddenly" there's something unpleasant. "Suddenly" a ten-kopeck piece buys the poison and "suddenly" they drink it down. And then . . . "It hurts, but I'm fine!" as Tina's sister said "after the sacrament." She slipped and crushed her wings.

A stale thaw wind took my breath away. I waited until it passed, and went on.

November 27, 3 a.m.

It's finished. Let today be the last day of my journal, the day I went to Obukhovsky to see my cheerful little ants. And when I finally understood what I needed to understand. Close up, little notebook! Lie wherever you like! I just don't need you anymore.

It was not easy to find out anything about those girls in that cursed hospital. But I was persistent. I decided that I wouldn't go away without an answer. The people were busy and soon got tired of me. And when I finally got to see them, I saw that there was nothing particular to find out.

They told me that Darla died yesterday, and Barb had been unconscious for more than a day and would die soon. They offered to let me go in to her, but I didn't go to see Barb lying unconscious.

I went back home and now I'm sitting here in my usual room, with my usual papers and books, with the green lamp that always smells slightly of kerosene.

Moon ants . . . And why didn't it occur to me right away (it just now occurred to me) that I, too, I myself am a moon ant? Because for me this is the most important thing. Only now do I understand. I understand that it could not have been otherwise. Because I'm suffocated by the same asphyxia, poisoned by the same transparent, invisible, evil gas that has spread over my earth and turned people—little by little—into fragile, flimsy, vulnerable ants. None of us thinks about death, we don't see it coming—because it is too close, too—right there.

They kill people, knock them down like ants, hang them—and we kill ourselves, get knocked down, hang ourselves—either way we die, and it's all the same "as far as the result is concerned," as John Khan said. And you yourself might even kill for the sake of one rouble and then drink it up. Again the "result is the same," because it's death—your own, in the end. And that way one worthless corpse will pile on top of another in a heap: just like the ants sprawled one on top of another in the cavern in the moon. And why not let them?

I, too, don't think about death at all; I just live my life. But when I remember the past, I remember how I used to be a man. I even recall precisely when this metamorphosis of mine (of ours) began. Yes, yes, it was when those "years of trans-formation" were ending. They were coming to an end, but the metamorphosis was beginning; it was then, after all, that the first rivulets of poison gas seeped into the air. I never used to like to think about those years, about the time when I was still a man, but now that I've understood and submitted to my ant-hood, there's no harm in remembering.

I'm too indifferent to believe in the possibility of being saved—of change. After all, what force of breath is needed to blow away those heavy vapours saturated with poison; for they've penetrated right to this earth of ours—they're close in and clinging tight. It would take God's breath to blow them away, sweep them away, rid the lifeless, silenced earth of them . . . God's breath.

I'm not thinking about killing myself. After all, there's nothing wrong with my life. However, just in case, so as not to go to a lot of trouble later, I got my dusty box of photographic equipment out from under the bed and found my jar of almond-white crystals.

I have a little box full of capsules of pyramidon: I take it when I have a headache. So this is what I decided to do: open up one capsule, dump out the pyramidon, and fill it with that . . . with the white stuff, once I'd prepared the crystals by grinding them up in a mortar. Then I put the capsule back together. I inked a cross on it and put it aside, so that I couldn't possibly take it by accident. God preserve me. I'm not about to poison myself, much less by accident.

Outside the house, by the way, it's getting close to freezing . . . I just don't know how I am going to survive the next thaw. It's too much for my ant strength. It would be good if we didn't have another thaw. But what if there is one? In December? In January?

Well, if there is, then it's the capsule with the black cross. "Just fine . . ." and it doesn't even hurt.

My dear sisters Katy, Darla, Barb and the others, cooks, prostitutes, students, brides, lovers, mothers and old maids— and dear brothers, colonels, mechanics, workers, bailiffs, students, revolutionaries, jurists, editors, schoolboys, and you, plasterers with your rouble, and rebels, and expropriators, and governors—all you who have been killed and who have killed yourselves, all you hanged, drowned, poisoned, knifed and blown up brothers of mine, dead shades—wait for me! I'm yours, I'm like you. A rotten wind will blow from the rotten sea, brown St. Petersburg mud will start squelching under my weak ant legs, and they will get twisted together, and I will fall and crumple up, just like you.

Good-bye, my dears . . . until the next thaw.

To the window of my cell
At the end of evil day
Exultant birds came
And looked in on me.

But the gloom of my cell
Frightened them away,
And the exultant birds took flight
Back to the azure heights.

Fyodor Sologub, 1887

Song

Above the earth my window is so high,
     So high.
I see only the sunset in the sky,
     In the sky.

And the sky seems so vacant and so dull,
     So vacant and dull . . .
My poor heart it pities not at all,
     Not at all.

Alas, I am dying of desperate grief,
     Desperate grief,
I do not know what it is that I seek,
     What I seek . . .

And I do not know from whence this yearning came,
     From whence it came,
But my heart longs to be miraculously saved,
     Miraculously saved!

Oh, may something great happen, something new come to be,
     Come to be:
Something wondrous the pale sky promises me,
     Promises me,

But I weep without tears: I don't trust its word,
     Don't trust its word . . .
What I long for so deeply is not of this world,
     Not of this world.

Zinaida Gippius, 1893

The Last

Happy about everything, like children, at times
People easily live their merry lives.
Oh, let them laugh! There is no joy
In looking into my weary soul's night.

I will not disturb their momentary joy.
I will not open the gates of consciousness for them,
And now, in my resigned pride,
I will take the vow of great silence.

Wordlessly I pass by, I pass by,
Covering my face, into unknown distances,
Towards which I am led inexorably
By cruel and audacious sadnesses.

Zinaida Gippius, 1900

The Abyss

Leonid Andreyev

I

The day was already ending, but the two of them just kept walking and talking, not noticing either the time or the way they were going. On the gentle rise ahead a small grove stood dark against the sky, and through the branches of the trees the sun glowed like red-hot coals, lighting up the air and turning it all into fiery golden dust. So close and bright was the sun that everything else seemed to disappear, and it alone remained, colouring the road and levelling it. It hurt their eyes; they turned back and immediately before them everything dimmed, becoming calm and clear, small and distinct. Somewhere far off, a mile or more away, the red sunset caught the tall trunk of a pine, and the pine flamed amidst the foliage like a candle in a dark room; ahead a crimson patina lay over the road, where each stone cast a long, black shadow, while the girl's hair, permeated with the sun's rays, shone like a golden-red halo. One fine curly hair separated from the rest and curled and waved in the air like golden gossamer.

Though it had become dark ahead of them, their conversation didn't break off or change. Just as serene, intimate and quiet as before, it kept flowing gently along, about one thing only: the power, beauty and immortality of love. They were both very young—the girl barely seventeen years old, Nemovetsky four years older—and both wore school uniforms—she, the modest brown dress of a high school girl; he, the handsome uniform of a technical school student. And like their speech, everything about them was young, beautiful and pure: their slender, lithe figures, airily light, their sprightly step and their fresh voices, conveying thoughtful tenderness even in the simplest words, like the splashing of a brook on a quiet spring night when all the snow has not yet melted off the dark fields.

On they went, turning where the unfamiliar road turned, and two long, gradually tapering shadows, odd-looking with their tiny heads, would at times move ahead separately from one another, at others blend together on one side into a single long, narrow band, like the shadow of a poplar. But they talked on, unaware of the shadows, and as they talked he never took his eyes off her lovely face, upon which it seemed the rosy sunset had left some of its tender colours, while she looked down at the path, flicking little pebbles away with her parasol and watching how, from beneath her dark dress, first one, then the other pointed toe of each little shoe regularly appeared.

Cutting across the road was a ditch, its sides dusty and caving in where people had crossed, and they stopped for a moment. Zinochka lifted her head, gazed around in bemusement, and asked, "Do you know where we are? I have never been here."

He gave a cursory glance around. "Yes, I do. The town is there, behind that hillock. Give me your hand, I'll help you."

He held out his hand—not a rough worker's hand, but slender and white like a woman's. Zinochka felt happy; she wanted to jump the ditch by herself and run ahead, shouting, "Catch me!"—but she restrained herself, and with solemn gratitude she bowed her head slightly and somewhat timidly extended her hand, which was still soft and plump, like a child's. And he ached to press that sweet, timid hand, but he, too, restrained himself, and with a half-bow he took it courteously and turned away modestly when, as she crossed, her ankle was slightly revealed.

And once again they walked and talked, but they were still full of the feeling of how their two hands had briefly touched. She still felt the dry heat of his palm and strong fingers; it made her feel good and a bit guilty; and he sensed the submissive softness of her tiny little hand and saw the black silhouette of her foot in the naïve and tender embrace of its dear shoe. And there was something poignant and troubling in this persistent image of a narrow band of white skirts and her slim foot, and with an unconscious effort of will he put it out of his mind. And then he felt happy and his heart was so expansive and free in his breast that he wanted to sing, reaching his arms to the sky and shouting, "Run, and I'll catch up with you!"—that ancient formula of first love amidst forests and roaring waterfalls.

And because of all these desires, a lump rose in his throat.

The long, odd-looking shadows were disappearing, and the dust on the road was now grey and cold, but they didn't notice and kept on talking. Both of them had read a number of good books, and the wonderful images of people who had loved, suffered and perished for pure love floated before their eyes. They began to recollect snatches of poetry they had read ages ago, poetry that cloaked love in garments of resonant harmony and sweet sadness.

"Do you remember where this is from?" asked Nemovetsky, quoting from memory: ". . . and with me again is the one I love, from whom I hid, wordlessly, all my anguish, all my tenderness, all my love . . ."

"No," answered Zinochka and repeated pensively, "all my anguish, all my tenderness, all my love . . ."

"All my love," echoed Nemovetsky involuntarily.

And then they reminisced some more. They remembered girls pure as white lilies who donned the black garb of the cloisters, girls languishing by themselves in a park sprinkled with autumn leaves, girls happy in their unhappiness; and they recalled men—proud, energetic, but suffering and in need of love and a woman's sympathetic compassion. The images they summoned were sad, but in their sadness the love was all the more bright and pure. Before their eyes it grew enormous like the world, bright like the sun and extraordinarily beautiful, and there was nothing more powerful, or more splendid.

"Could you die for the one you love?" asked Zinochka, looking down at her own childlike hand.

"Yes, I could," answered Nemovetsky decisively, gazing at her frankly and sincerely. "And you?"

"Yes, I could, too." She thought a bit. "Wouldn't it be such happiness, to die for your beloved? I really would want to."

Their eyes met, bright and calm, and something good passed between them, and their lips smiled. Zinochka stopped walking.

"Wait a minute," she said. "You have a thread on your jacket."

And trustingly she lifted her hand to his shoulder and carefully, with two fingers, removed the thread.

"There!" she said, and becoming serious, asked, "Why are you so pale and thin? Is it from all that studying? You mustn't wear yourself out, really you mustn't."

"Your eyes are blue, with light flecks in them, like little sparks," he answered, looking searchingly into her eyes.

"And yours are black. No, brown, and warm. And there are . . ."

Zinochka didn't finish her sentence about what was there, and turned away. Her face slowly flushed, her eyes became embarrassed and shy, but her lips smiled involuntarily. And not waiting for the smiling Nemovetsky, who looked delighted, she started ahead, but soon came to a halt.

"Look, the sun has set!" she cried with sorrowful surprise.

"Yes, it's set," he responded with sudden, sharp grief.

The light was gone, the shadows had died, and everything around was now pale, mute and lifeless. From the place where the incandescent sun had glittered, now, without a sound, dark heaps of clouds had begun to climb, and little by little they were devouring the light-blue space. Heavy storm clouds swirled and bumped into each other; slowly and gravely the contours of wakened monsters changed and reluctantly moved ahead, as if they were being driven against their will by some inexorable, terrible force. Tearing itself away from the others, a light, fluffy little cloud rushed on alone, weak and frightened.

II

Zinochka's cheeks paled, her lips turned red, almost bloody, her pupils enlarged imperceptibly, darkening her eyes, and she

224

whispered quietly, "I'm frightened. It's so quiet here. Are we lost?"

Nemovetsky knit his thick brows and looked searchingly around.

Without the sun, in the cool breath of approaching night, the place seemed unwelcoming and cold; grey fields stretched out in all directions, with stubbly, trampled-looking grass, clay gullies, hillocks and pits. There were a lot of pits, deep and sheer ones as well as small ones, overgrown with creeping weeds; a taciturn fog had already settled noiselessly for the night; and the fact that people had once been here, that they had done something or other and were now gone, made the place seem even more uninhabited and sad. Here and there, like clots of cold, lilac fog, stood groves and scattered bushes, as if waiting for some kind of word from the abandoned pits.

Nemovetsky suppressed a heavy, troubling feeling of anxiety and said, "No, we're not lost. I know the way. First across the field and then through that little wood. Are you afraid?"

She smiled bravely and answered, "No. Now I'm not. But we'd better get home soon—for tea."

Quickly and resolutely they moved forward, but soon slowed their steps. They did not look around, but felt an enormous enmity from the pockmarked field that surrounded them with a thousand dull, unmoving eyes, and this feeling brought them closer to one another and roused memories of childhood. And the memories were wonderful, lit by the sun, by green leaves, by love and laughter. As if this were not life, but an expansive, gentle song, and they themselves were its sounds, two small, sweet notes—one resonant and pure, like vibrating crystal, the other a little deeper, but clearer, like a sleigh-bell.

People appeared: two women sitting on the edge of a deep clay pit. One sat cross-legged, staring fixedly into the pit. Her kerchief had lifted up a bit, revealing dishevelled tangles of hair, and her back was hunched, pulling up her dirty, frayed sweater patterned with flowers as big as apples. She didn't even glance at the passers-by. The other woman reclined alongside, her head thrown back. Her face was coarse and broad, with masculine features, and under her eyes on her jutting cheekbones two brick-red spots burned, looking like fresh grazes. She was even dirtier than the first woman, and looked openly at them as they went by. When they had passed, she began to sing in a thick, masculine voice:

> For you alone, my dear,
> Like a fragrant flower I bloomed . . .

"Varka, d'ya hear?" she turned to her taciturn friend, and receiving no answer, burst into loud, coarse laughter.

Nemovetsky knew this kind of woman, dirty even when wearing rich, beautiful dresses; he was used to them, and now they passed in and out of his view without leaving a trace. But Zinochka, who had almost brushed against them with her modest brown dress, felt something hostile, pathetic and angry momentarily entering her heart. But a few moments later the impression softened, like a cloud's shadow quickly scudding across a golden meadow, and when two more people caught up and passed them—a man in a cap and jacket, but barefoot, and one of those dirty women—she saw them, but felt nothing. Unthinkingly, she watched the woman for quite a while, and was a bit surprised that she had on such a thin dress, and at the way it clung to her legs as if wet, and at the hem with its broad band of greasy dirt that had eaten into the material. There was something disquieting, painful and terrifyingly hopeless in the fluttering of that thin and filthy hem.

And once again they walked and talked; behind them, reluctantly, a dark storm cloud moved and cast a transparent shadow that cautiously fitted itself to the landscape. Yellowish-bronze stains shone dully through the cloud's bursting sides, and then hid behind its heavy mass, leaving bright, noiselessly swirling tracks behind. And the darkness was thickening so stealthily and imperceptibly that it was difficult to believe it was there, and it seemed that it was still day, but a day that was gravely ill and quietly dying. Now they were talking about the unsettling feelings and thoughts that visit a person at night when he lies awake, and neither sounds nor speech disturb him, and the broad and many-eyed darkness that is life presses hard up to his face.

"Do you have any idea what infinity is like?" asked Zinochka, pressing her plump hand to her forehead and squeezing her eyes tight shut.

"No. Infinity . . . No," answered Nemovetsky, closing his eyes too.

"I can sometimes see it. The first time I saw it was when I was still little. It's something like a cart. There's one cart, then another, a third and so on, into the distance, forever, just carts and carts . . . Terrifying." She shuddered.

"But why carts?" Nemovetsky smiled, although he felt uncomfortable.

"I don't know. Carts. One, then another . . . forever."

The darkness stealthily thickened, and the storm cloud had already passed over their heads and seemed to be glancing back into their now pale, lowered faces. And with increasing frequency the dark figures of ragged, dirty women appeared, as though the deep pits—dug who knows why—were casting them to the surface, and their wet hems fluttered uneasily. They appeared singly or in twos and threes, and their voices sounded loud and strangely lonely in the frozen air.

"Who are those women? Where did they all come from?" asked Zinochka timorously and softly.

Nemovetsky knew who the women were, and he was frightened that they had happened upon such a bad and dangerous place, but he calmly answered, "I don't know. They're just there. Don't talk about them. Look, now we just go through this little wood, and then we'll see the gates and the town. It's a pity we came out so late."

It seemed funny to her that he said "late," because they had gone out at four o'clock, and she glanced at him and smiled. But his brow remained furrowed, and she suggested, comforting and reassuring him, "Let's go. I'd like some tea. And anyway, the forest is already near."

"Yes, let's go."

When they entered the forest and the treetops silently

closed over their heads, it got very dark, but seemed cosy and peaceful.

"Give me your hand," Nemovetsky suggested. She hesitatingly gave her hand, and the light contact seemed to chase away the dark. Their hands were motionless and they didn't press one another at all, and Zinochka even moved a little away from her companion, but all their consciousness was concentrated on how it felt at that tiny little place on their bodies where their hands were touching. And again they wanted to speak about beauty and the mysterious power of love, but to speak in a way that wouldn't destroy the silence, to speak not with words, but with looks. And they thought they should look at each other, and they wanted to, but they couldn't bring themselves to do it.

"Oh, look! More people!" Zinochka said gaily.

III

In a clearing, where it was lighter, three people were sitting near an emptied bottle and silently, expectantly watching them approach. One, clean-shaven like an actor, gave a laugh and an appreciative whistle.

Nemovetsky's heart sank and nearly stopped beating, his alarm was so great, but as if propelled from behind, he kept walking straight towards the men, who were sitting alongside the path. They continued to wait, and their three motionless pairs of eyes were dark and frightening. And, vaguely hoping that these sombre, ragged men with their threatening silence would be kindly disposed towards him, to indicate his helplessness and arouse their compassion, Nemovetsky asked, "Where can we get through to the gates? Here?"

But they didn't answer. The clean-shaven one whistled something indistinct and mocking while the other two remained silent and stared with solemn and ominous intensity. They were drunk and malicious, and they wanted love and destruction. One of them, red-cheeked and bloated, half-rose onto his elbows, then without haste, like a bear, leaned his weight on his paws and stood up, sighing heavily. His companions gave him a passing glance, and again stared fixedly at Zinochka.

"I'm frightened," she mouthed, moving only her lips.

Without hearing the words, Nemovetsky understood her from the weight of her hand in his. And, trying to maintain a calm appearance, but feeling the fateful inevitability of whatever was about to happen, he passed on with firm, even steps. And the three pairs of eyes grew closer, flashed by, and then were behind them. "We'd better run," thought Nemovetsky, and he answered himself, "No, better not to run."

"Right sickly, that fellow, more's the pity," said the third one, a bald man with a skimpy reddish beard. "But the girl is pretty. Every man should be so lucky."

All three laughed in a somewhat forced way.

"Sir, just two words!" said the tall one in a thick, bass voice, and he looked at his companions.

They began to get up.

Nemovetsky continued walking without looking back.

"Better stop when you're being asked to," said the red-bearded one. "Or else you might get . . ."

"We're talking to you!" croaked the tall one, and in two leaps he caught up with them.

A massive hand came down on Nemovetsky's shoulder and shook him. Turning around, he found a pair of round, bulging and terrifying eyes staring him in the face. They were so close, it was as if he were looking through a magnifying glass, and he could clearly make out their bloodshot veins and a yellowish pus on the lashes. And letting go of Zinochka's mute hand, he dug around in his pocket and mumbled, "Money! Here you go. A pleasure."

The bulging eyes got even rounder and brightened. And when Nemovetsky turned his own eyes away from them, the tall one stepped back a little and, without swinging, gave Nemovetsky a hook to the jaw. Nemovetsky's head jerked back, his teeth clicked, his cap tipped down over his forehead and fell off, and waving his arms, he fell backward. Silently, without crying out, Zinochka turned and ran for all she was worth. The clean-shaven one gave a long, strange cry: "A–a–a!.."

And shouting, he sped after her.

Nemovetsky jumped unsteadily to his feet, but before he could even straighten up a blow to the back of the head knocked him down again. There were two of them, and he was alone, weak and unaccustomed to fighting, but he struggled for a long time, scratching with his nails like a woman, sobbing with unconscious despair and gnashing. When he finally went limp, they picked him up and carried him; he resisted, but there was a roaring in his ears and he couldn't understand what was happening to him, and he sagged helplessly in their arms. The last thing he saw was a piece of red beard going almost into his mouth, and behind it the darkness of the forest and the light sweater of the running girl. She ran silently and quickly, as she had just the other day while playing tag—and the clean-shaven one sped after her, catching up with his short strides. And then Nemovetsky sensed emptiness around him, and terrified, he flew downward, hit the ground with a force that exploded through his whole body, and lost consciousness.

The tall one and the one with the red beard, having thrown Nemovetsky into a gully, stood there for a while, listening for sounds from the bottom. But their faces and eyes were seeking out Zinochka. From the forest a high, half-smothered woman's scream was heard and immediately died out.

"Son of a bitch!" exclaimed the tall one angrily, and set off at a run, breaking through the brush like a bear.

"Me too! Me too!" yelled the red-bearded one in his thin little voice, setting off after him. He was feeble and out of breath; in the fight he had hurt his knee, and he was annoyed that even though he was the one who had had the idea about the girl, he would be the last to get her. He stopped to take a breath, gave his knee a rub, put a finger up to his nose, blew it, and again set off at a run, plaintively yelling, "Me too! Me too!"

A dark storm cloud had already spread over the whole sky, and the dark, quiet night had begun. In the darkness the rather short figure of the red-bearded one soon disappeared, but the uneven patter of his feet could be heard for a long time, as could the rustle of parting leaves and the shattering, plaintive cry, "Me too! Hey, lads, me too!"

Dirt had got into Nemovetsky's mouth and grated against his teeth. And the first and strongest thing he sensed as he came to was the dense and tranquil smell of earth. His head felt heavy, as if filled with dull lead, so that it was hard to turn; his whole body ached, and his shoulder hurt badly, but nothing was broken. Nemovetsky sat for some time looking upwards, without any thoughts or recollections. Above him dangled a bush with broad, black leaves, through which the now clear sky could be seen. The storm cloud had passed without a single drop of rain, and it had made the air dry and light, and high up in the middle of the sky rose a thin crescent moon, its edge transparent and melting. It was living out its last nights and shone in a cold, sad and lonely way. Small wisps of clouds were skimming fast in the heights, where a strong wind evidently continued to blow. They did not, however, cover up the moon, but cautiously skirted it. The mysterious depth of the night soaring over the earth was palpable in the loneliness of the moon, the timidity of the high, bright clouds and the blowing of wind not felt below.

Nemovetsky remembered everything that had happened, and he didn't believe it. Everything that had taken place was so terrifying and unlike the truth, which couldn't possibly be so awful, and he himself, sitting in the middle of the night and looking from somewhere below at an upside-down crescent moon and rushing clouds—he was just as strange and unlike his real self. And he thought that this was an ordinary bad dream, very bad and vile. And all those many women they had met were likewise part of the dream.

"It can't be true," he affirmed, shaking his heavy head weakly. "It can't be."

He stretched out his hand, groping for his cap so he could go, but his cap wasn't there. And the fact that it wasn't there suddenly made everything clear, and he realised that what he had gone through had not been a bad dream, but the awful truth. In the next minute, faint with horror, he had already clambered upwards, fallen back along with the crumbling earth, and clambered up again, grabbing onto the bush's supple branches.

After climbing out, he set off straight ahead at a run, without thinking and without choosing a direction, and for a long time he ran in circles among the trees. Just as suddenly, for no reason, he ran in the other direction, and again the branches scraped his face, and again everything seemed like a dream. And it seemed to Nemovetsky that there had been a time when something like this had happened to him before: the darkness, the unseen branches, the scraped face, and him running with his eyes closed and thinking that it was all a dream. Nemovetsky stopped, then sat down in the uncomfortable and unusual posture of a man sitting on the bare ground, with nothing to raise him. And again he thought about his cap and said, "This is me. I should kill myself. I should kill myself, even if it is a dream."

He jumped up and started running again, but collected himself and instead began to walk slowly, dimly picturing the place where they had been attacked. It was totally dark in the forest, but sometimes a pale ray from the moon broke through and played tricks, illuminating the white tree trunks, and the forest would seem full of immobile and strangely silent people. And this had happened before, and it seemed like a dream.

"Zinaida Nikolaevna!" Nemovetsky called, pronouncing the first word loudly, but the second quietly, as if between the sounds he were losing hope that someone would respond.

And no one responded.

Then he happened upon the path, recognised it and reached the clearing. And once again, this time fully, he understood that it was all true, and in horror he began to run aimlessly, crying, "Zinaida Nikolaevna! It's me! Me!"

No one called back, and turning his face to where the town ought to be, Nemovetsky distinctly shouted out, "He-lp me-ee! . . ."

And again he started running about, whispering something, rummaging through the bushes, when before his very feet something dull and white showed, looking like a still patch of weak light. It was Zinochka lying there.

"Lord! What is this?!" Nemovetsky said with dry eyes, but in the voice of a man who is crying, and, dropping to his knees, he touched the woman lying there.

His hand lit on a naked body, smooth, supple, cold, but not dead, and with a shudder Nemovetsky jerked his hand back.

"My dear, my darling, it's me," he whispered, seeking her face in the darkness.

And he reached out his hand once more, this time in the other direction, and again he felt her naked body, and no matter where he put his hand, he met everywhere with that naked woman's body, smooth, supple, and seeming to warm beneath his touching hand. Sometimes he quickly jerked his hand back, but sometimes he lingered, and just as he, tattered and missing his cap, had seemed unreal to himself, in the same way he could not connect his image of Zinochka with this naked body. And he imagined with sickening clarity what had taken place here, what people had done to this mute female body—and a strange kind of buzzing response surged through his limbs. Stretching so far over that all his joints cracked, he stared dully at the patch of white and knit his brows like a man thinking. The horror of what had happened cooled inside him, hardened into a ball, and lay in his soul like something unrelated to him and powerless.

"Lord, what is this?" he repeated, but the words sounded false and hollow.

He felt for her heart: her heartbeat was faint, but even, and when he bent down to her face he detected weak breathing, as if Zinochka weren't in a deep faint, but simply sleeping. And he quietly called her: "Zinochka, it's me."

And suddenly it seemed to him for some reason that it would be better if she didn't wake up for a while. Holding his breath and furtively glancing around, he cautiously stroked her cheek and kissed first her closed eyes, then her lips, which gently parted under the firm kiss. Frightened that she would wake up, he pulled back and froze. But the body was mute and immobile, and in its helplessness and accessibility there was something pitiful and irritating, and irresistibly attractive. With profound tenderness and stealthy, hesitant caution, Nemovetsky tried to toss the remains of her dress onto her, and the dual sensation of the material and the naked body was as piercing as a knife, and as incomprehensible as madness. He was both her defender and her attacker, and he looked to the surrounding forest and darkness for help, but the forest and darkness gave none. There had been a banquet of beasts here, and, suddenly cast out of his comprehensible, simple, human life, he caught the scent of hot lust flooding the air, and his nostrils flared.

"It's me! Me!" he senselessly repeated without comprehending, brimming with memories of how he had once seen a white band of skirt and the black silhouette of a foot tenderly embraced by its little shoe. And listening intently to Zinochka's breathing, never glancing away from the place where her face was, he moved his hand. He listened again and moved it further.

"What is this?" he cried out loudly and despairingly, and he sprang up, horrified at himself.

Zinochka's face flashed before his eyes for just a second and disappeared. He tried to understand that this body was Zinochka, with whom he had been walking today, and who had talked about infinity, but he couldn't. He tried to feel the horror of what had happened, but the horror was too great if one were to think that it was really true, and he was unable to feel it.

"Zinaida Nikolaevna!" he shouted, pleading. "Why? Zinaida Nikolaevna?"

But the ravaged body remained mute, and Nemovetsky fell to his knees, babbling nonsense. He pleaded, threatened, said he would kill himself, shook the woman lying there, lifting, turning and pressing her to him and all but sinking his nails into her flesh. The slightly warmed body gently yielded to his efforts, obediently complying with his movements, and all this was so frightening, incomprehensible and bestial that Nemovetsky once again sprang to his feet and cried in a broken voice, "Help!" But the sound was forced and false.

And again he threw himself upon the unprotesting body, kissing, crying, feeling a kind of abyss before him—dark, frightening, and drawing him in. Nemovetsky was gone, Nemovetsky had been left behind somewhere, and that other one now kneaded her hot, pliant body with passionate cruelty, and said with the wily grin of a madman, "Answer me! Or don't you want to? I love you, I love you."

With the same wily grin he brought his bulging eyes right up to Zinochka's face and whispered, "I love you. You don't want to speak, but you're smiling, I see. I love you, I do, I do."

He tightly embraced the soft, limp body, which had roused a wild passion in him by its lifeless submissiveness; he wrung his hands and soundlessly whispered, having retained only one human capability—to lie.

"I love you. We won't tell anyone, and no one will find out. And I'll marry you—tomorrow, whenever you want. I love you. I'm going to kiss you, and you answer me back, all right? Zinochka . . ."

And forcefully he pressed his lips to hers, feeling how his teeth pressed into her flesh, and in the pain and force of the kiss he lost the last glimmer of thought. It seemed to him that the girl's lips quivered. For a single moment a flashing fiery horror lit up his mind, revealing before him a black abyss.

And the black abyss swallowed him up.

I am evil and weak. With my mind
I have crossed the earthly sea . . .
Just as sorrow once reigned,
Now in my soul rules defeat . . .

For the young spring of good
And passion long past I long,
I await another unearthly power,
Another summer morn . . .

I am evil and weak. I seek in vain . . .
I flag in my faith—I spitefully resist,
But it's hard to resist . . . I grow feeble and sway,
And quickly towards death I slip . . .

Alexander Blok, 1899

Children of Night

Fixing our gaze
On the glimmering east,
Children of sorrow, children of night,
Will our prophet come? We wait to see.
We sense the unknown,
In our hearts we believe,
Dying, we yearn
For worlds unconceived.
Our words are defiant,
But doomed, we all know,
Too early precursors
Of a spring that's too slow.
We are the resurrection,
And, in the dark of night,
The crow of a cock,
And the cold morning light.
For a novel beauty
We transgress all limits;
We break all laws,
And our moans are our hymns.
We are the temptation of the thirsting,
We are a laughing-stock,
At a desecrated altar
We are the dying sparks.
We are steps above the void,
Children of darkness, we wait for the sun—
We will glimpse its rays, and then, like shadows,
We will die when it comes.

Dmitry Merezhkovsky, 1894

Captive Beasts

We are captive beasts,
We wail as best we can.
The doors are shut tight,
And we dare not open them.

Our hearts true to tradition,
Finding solace in howling, we howl,
We forgot long ago, we don't notice
That the zoo is fetid and foul.

Monotonously and tediously we cuckoo,
Our hearts accustomed to repeat;
The zoo is impersonal and boring,
But we no longer wish to be freed.

We are captive beasts,
We wail as best we can.
The doors are shut tight,
And we dare not open them.

Fyodor Sologub, 1906

In the Fog

Leonid Andreyev

From the first rays of dawn on that day, a strange, motionless fog hung over the streets. It was thin and translucent, not a blanketing fog, but whatever went through it took on an anxious, dark-yellow colour, and the fresh rosiness of women's cheeks and the bright splotches of their dresses peeped out from it as through a black veil, darkly and distinctly. Towards the south, where the low November sun was hidden behind a bank of storm clouds, the sky was light, lighter than the earth, but to the north it descended in a broad, evenly darkening curtain, becoming yellowish-black and opaque as night where it met the earth. Against this oppressive background the dark buildings looked light grey, and the two white columns at the entrance to a desolate, autumnal garden were like two yellow candles over the deceased. And the flowerbeds in that garden had been dug up and trampled over by rude feet, and the late flowers, painfully bright in the fog, were gently dying on their broken stems.

And no matter how many people were out on the streets, everyone was in a hurry, and everyone was gloomy and taciturn. That eerie day, choking in the yellow fog, was dismal and terribly disquieting.

In the dining room, twelve o'clock had already struck, and then the short chime of half-past twelve, but it seemed like dusk in Pavel Rybakov's room, and a blackish-yellow reflected gleam lay over everything. In this light the notebooks and papers scattered over the table looked yellowed, like old ivory, and on one of the papers an unsolved algebra problem, with its clear figures and mysterious letters, looked ancient, abandoned and useless, as if many dull years had passed it by; and Pavel's face, too, was yellow in the light, as he lay on the bed. His strong young arms were folded behind his head and were bare almost to the elbows; an open book lay face down on his chest, and his dark eyes stared fixedly at the painted stucco ceiling. There was something monotonous, tiresome and tasteless in the motley, dirty shades of paint that recalled the dozens of people who had lived in that flat before the Rybakovs, where they had slept, talked, thought, done whatever they did, and left everywhere their alien imprint. And these people made Pavel think of hundreds of other people, of teachers and companions, of noisy and crowded streets where women walked, and (this was for him the most oppressive and frightening of all) of what he would prefer to forget and not to think about at all.

"Boring . . . bo-or-r-ing!" Pavel drew out the syllables, closed his eyes and stretched out so that the toes of his boots touched the iron springs of the bed. The corners of his thick brows contorted, and his face twisted in a grimace of pain and revulsion, strangely distorting and deforming his features; when the wrinkles smoothed out, it became evident that his face was young and handsome. And especially lovely were the bold outlines of his full lips, and the youthful absence of a moustache above them made them look pure and sweet, like a young girl's.

But lying with closed eyes and seeing in the darkness of his closed lids the same, horrible thing again and again, the thing he wanted to forget forever, was even more tormenting, and Pavel's eyes started open. Their bewildered gleam lent his face an aged and anxious air.

"What a poor fellow I am! What a poor fellow!" he pitied himself aloud, and turned his eyes to the window, greedily seeking light. But there wasn't any, and yellow semi-darkness insistently crept through the window and spread over the room, and it was so palpable that it seemed one could touch it with one's fingers. And once again before his eyes the ceiling unfolded above him.

The stucco moulding on the ceiling depicted a Russian village: a peasant's hut stood at a diagonal, as is never the case in reality. Next to it stood a peasant frozen in mid-stride, and he held a stick that was taller than he was, and he himself was taller than the hut. Further on was a tiny, crooked church, and near it a huge cart bulged out, with a horse so small it resembled not a horse, but a hunting dog. And it had a sharp muzzle like a dog's. Then everything repeated in the same order: the hut, the big peasant, the church and the huge cart, and so on around the room. And all this was yellow against a dirty pink background; it was ugly and boring and recalled not a village, but someone's dreary and senseless life. The craftsman who had sculpted the village without giving it a single tree was detestable.

"Why isn't it breakfast-time yet?" Pavel whispered, although he didn't feel at all like eating, and he turned impatiently on his side. The movement dislodged the book, which fell to the floor, its pages flapping randomly, but Pavel didn't reach out to pick it up. On the cover, in gold on black, were the words: *Buckle. The History of Civilisation*, and this made him think about something old, about the multitude of people who for untold centuries have wanted to make something of their lives but couldn't; and about life, in which everything is incomprehensible and happens with cruel inevitability; and about that sad and oppressive thing, something like a crime that had been committed, that Pavel didn't want to think about. And suddenly he felt such a yearning for light, broad and clear light, that his eyes ached. Pavel jumped up, avoiding the book lying on the floor, and began to tug at the drapes by the window, trying to open them as wide as possible.

"Ah, dammit!" he swore, and threw aside the material, but it was heavy and fell dully back into its orderly, indifferent folds. Suddenly tired and spent, Pavel flipped it idly aside and sat down on the cold windowsill.

Outside was the fog, and the sky beyond the grey rooftops was yellowish-black, and its shade fell over the houses and the lane. A week ago the first, insubstantial snow had fallen and melted, and since then a sticky, greyish scum coated the lane. Here and there, wet stones reflected the black sky and gave off an oblique, dark gleam, and carriages rolled over them, jolting

241

and swaying along. The rumbling was not audible from higher up; it died out in the fog, helpless to rise above the earth, and this senseless movement beneath the black sky, among the dark, sodden houses, seemed pointless and boring. But there were women among the pedestrians and riders, and their presence gave the picture a cryptic, anxious meaning. They were going about their errands and to all appearances were absolutely ordinary and unremarkable; but Pavel saw their strange and terrifying particularity: they were different, alien from the rest of the crowd, and did not blend into it, but were like sparks in the midst of darkness. And everything was for them: the streets, houses and people, everything gravitated towards them, thirsted for them—without understanding them. The word "woman" was burnt in fiery letters into Pavel's brain; it was the first thing he saw on every turned page; people spoke quietly, but when the word "woman" came up, it seemed as if they were shouting it out—and for Pavel, it was the most incomprehensible, most fantastic and terrifying word. His sharp and suspicious glance followed every woman, as if she were just about to come up to his house and blow it up with everyone in it, or do something even more horrifying. But when his glance happened on a pretty, feminine face, he drew himself up to his full height, tried to look handsome and attractive, and commanded with his eyes that she should turn around and look at him. But she never did turn around, and again his heart would feel empty, dark and frightened, like a desolate house through which a sombre plague had passed, killing all the living and boarding up the windows.

"Bo-or-ring!" Pavel drawled, and he turned from the street.

For some time now there had been movement, talking and the clanking of dishes in the dining room, next to his room. Then it grew quiet except for the voice of the man of the house, Pavel's father Sergey Andreyevich—a throaty, fatherly bass. From its very first rounded, pleasant sounds it seemed redolent of fine cigarettes, clever books and clean linen. But now there was something cracked and distorted in it, as if the dirty-yellow, monotonous fog had penetrated even Sergey Andreyevich's larynx.

"And what about our young man, does he please to sleep in?"

Pavel couldn't hear his mother's answer.

"And at the institute, of course, he didn't please to go to mass?"

Again the answer couldn't be heard.

"Well, naturally," his father continued mockingly, "the custom is antiquated and . . ."

Pavel didn't catch the end of the sentence, because Sergey Andreyevich had turned away; but no doubt it was something funny, and Lily laughed loudly. When Pavel's father was secretly displeased with him for something, he always scolded him for getting up late on holidays and skipping mass, although he himself was completely indifferent to religion and hadn't set foot in church for twenty years or so—since his marriage. And since the beginning of summer at their cottage, he had been holding something against Pavel, and Pavel thought he probably suspected. But now he decided sullenly, "Let him!"

Taking a notebook from the table, he pretended to read. But his eyes remained directed with belligerence and caution towards the dining room, like a man accustomed to hiding and prepared for an attack at any moment.

"Call Pavel!" said Sergey Andreyevich.

"Pavel! Pavel darling!" his mother called.

Pavel quickly got up from the bed and evidently hurt himself badly in doing so: he doubled over, his face contorted in a grimace of suffering, and his hands convulsively clutched at his stomach. Slowly he straightened up, clenched his teeth, which made the corners of his mouth pull downward towards his chin, and smoothed his jacket with trembling hands. Then his face grew pale and lost all expression, like a blind man's, and he went out into the dining room with unfaltering steps that nonetheless betrayed traces of the cruel pain he had just experienced.

"What were you doing?" Sergey Andreyevich asked abruptly; they were not in the habit of saying good morning.

"Reading," answered Pavel just as abruptly.

"What?"

"Buckle."

"Oh-ho, Buckle!" Sergey Andreyevich said, gazing threateningly through his pince-nez at his son.

"What about it?" replied Pavel unhesitatingly and defiantly, and he looked his father straight in the eye.

After a brief silence, his father retorted, with heavy significance, "Nothing."

Here Lily intervened, feeling sorry for her brother, "Pavel, are you going to be home tonight?"

Pavel remained silent.

"He who doesn't answer when he is asked a question is usually deemed a boor. What is your opinion on this matter, Pavel Sergeyevich?" asked his father.

"Drop it, Sergey Andreyevich!" his mother intervened. "Eat, the cutlets are getting cold. What awful weather, even with the lamps lit! And how will I manage this trip? I just don't know."

"I'll be home . . ." Pavel answered Lily, whereupon Sergey Andreyevich adjusted his pince-nez and said, "I can't bear this melancholy, this world-weariness . . . A proper boy must be bright and cheery."

"You can't be cheery all the time," said Lily, who always was.

"I'm not forcing anyone to enjoy himself. Why aren't you eating anything? I'm talking to you, Pavel!"

"I don't feel like it."

"Why not?"

"I'm not hungry."

"And where were you last night? Gadding about?"

"I was home."

"Home, were you?"

"And where do you think I was?" Pavel asked insolently.

Sergey Andreyevich answered with killing politeness, "How would I know where Pavel Sergeyevich deigns to *amuse* himself?" he said, stressing the word "amuse." "Pavel Sergeyevich is an adult. Pavel Sergeyevich will soon grow a

244

moustache. Pavel Sergeyevich, perhaps, even drinks vodka . . . How would I know?"

Breakfast continued in silence, and everything touched by the light falling through the window seemed yellow and strangely gloomy. Sergey Andreyevich gazed attentively and curiously into Pavel's face and thought, "And bags under his eyes . . . But surely it can't be true, that he's intimate with women—a boy of his age?"

That frightening and tormenting question, which Sergey Andreyevich didn't have the strength to think through to the end, had arisen recently, this summer, and he remembered vividly how it had happened—he would never forget. Behind their little shed, where the grass was thick and a white birch cast its cool, dark-blue shadow, he had happened to spot a torn and crumpled sheet of paper. There was something peculiar and disquieting about it. That was the way people tear and crumple notes that provoke hatred and anger, and Sergey Andreyevich had picked it up, smoothed it out and taken a look. It was a drawing. At first he didn't recognise what it was; he smiled and thought, "It's one of Pavel's drawings! How well he draws!" Then he turned the paper sideways and clearly discerned the monstrously cynical and dirty picture.

"Disgusting!" he said angrily and threw the paper down.

In about ten minutes he came back for it, took it to his study and examined it for quite a while, trying to solve the tormenting, gnawing riddle: did Pavel draw this, or someone else? He could not imagine that Pavel could have drawn such a dirty, vulgar thing, and that as he drew it, he knew all about the lewdness and filth it contained. In the boldness of the lines an experienced and depraved hand was evident, unwaveringly approaching the most secret of secrets, which unspoiled people were ashamed to think about; the naïvety of a profound and unconscious fall was clear in the studiousness with which the lines had been rubbed out, redrawn and emphasised with red pencil. As Sergey Andreyevich looked, he could not believe that his Pavel, his intelligent and cultivated boy, whose every thought was known to him, could draw with his own hand— the tanned hand of a strong, pure young man—such a disgusting thing, and know and understand everything he was drawing. And since it was very frightening to think that it was Pavel who had done this, he decided that it was someone else; but he folded the paper away. And when he saw Pavel jumping down off his bicycle, cheerful, lively, still full of the clean scents of the fields he had been riding through, he decided again that it wasn't Pavel who had done it, and he was glad.

But the gladness quickly passed, and just half an hour later Sergey Andreyevich looked at Pavel and thought: who is this alien and unknown youth, strangely tall and like a man? He talks in a coarse and manly voice, eats a lot and greedily, calmly and independently pours wine into his glass and jokes patronisingly with Lily. He calls himself Pavel, and his face is Pavel's and he laughs like Pavel, and when he just now bit off the top crust of bread, he did it in the way Pavel does—but Pavel isn't there inside him.

"Pavel, how old are you?" Sergey Andreyevich asked. Pavel laughed.

"I'm an old man already, dad! Almost eighteen."

"It's a long way yet to eighteen," his mother corrected him. "You won't be eighteen until December sixth."

"And you don't even have a moustache!" Lily said. And they all started joking that Pavel didn't have a moustache, and he made as if he were crying; and after dinner he stuck some cotton above his lip and said in an old man's voice, "Where's my old woman?"

And he went around seeming happy and relaxed. And then Lily remarked that Pavel seemed especially cheerful; after which Pavel frowned, took off the moustache and went to his room. And ever since then, whenever Sergey Andreyevich looked for that dear and familiar boy he once knew, he found something new and mysterious, and he was sorely perplexed.

And then he discovered something else new in Pavel: his son was having mood swings. One day he would be cheerful and full of mischief, and then he would frown for whole hours at a time, become irritable and exasperating, and even if he kept it under control, it was clear that something was causing him to suffer. And it was very distressing and hard to see that a loved one was sad, and not to know any reason for it, but that it was causing this loved one to become a distant stranger. Simply from the way he would come in, drink his tea without relish and crumble his bread in his hands, all the while staring off in another direction, towards the neighbouring forest—his father could sense his bad mood, and he fumed. He wanted Pavel to notice this and to understand how uncomfortable he was making his father with his bad moods; but Pavel never noticed, and he was always in a hurry to leave as soon as he finished his tea.

"Where are you going?" his father would ask.

"To the forest."

"Again to the forest!" his father would angrily remark.

Pavel, a note of surprise in his voice, would reply, "So what? I go to the forest every day."

His father would turn away in silence, and Pavel would leave, and it was always obvious from his broad, calmly swaying back that he hadn't even given a thought as to why his father was angry, and had completely forgotten his existence.

And for a long time already Sergey Andreyevich had wanted to have a forthright and open talk with Pavel, but the impending conversation was too distressing, and day after day he put it off. And since they had moved back to the city, Pavel had become especially gloomy and nervous, and Sergey Andreyevich was afraid he wouldn't be able to speak with enough calm and conviction. But on that day, at that lengthy and monotonous breakfast, he decided that today they had to talk. "It could be that he's just in love, as happens with all young boys and girls," he reassured himself. "Look how Lily's in love with that Avdeyev fellow; and I can't even remember which one he is—a high school student, I think."

"Lily! Is Avdeyev coming today?" asked Sergey Andreyevich with forced, exaggerated indifference.

Lily fluttered her long lashes in fright, dropped a pear she had been holding and let out a whispered "Ahh!" Then she crawled under the table after the pear, and when she got back up she was bright red, and even her voice sounded red.

"Tinov is coming, Pospelov is coming . . . and Avdeyev is coming, too."

It had got a little lighter in Pavel's room, and the stucco village on the ceiling stood out more sharply, gloating with dull and naïve self-satisfaction. Pavel turned away angrily and took up a book, but soon put it down on his chest and started thinking about what Lily had said: the high school girls were coming over. That meant that Katya Reimer was coming, too—ever-serious, ever-pensive, ever-sincere Katya Reimer. This thought was like a fire his heart had fallen into, and with a groan he quickly turned over and buried his face in the pillow. Then, just as quickly assuming his former position, he brushed two burning tears from his eyes and stared up at the ceiling, but now he saw neither the big peasant with the big stick, nor the huge cart. His thoughts returned to the summer cottage and a dark July night.

That night was dark, and the stars trembled in the dark-blue abyss of the sky, and a black storm cloud, climbing up from beyond the horizon, was snuffing them out from below. And in the forest, where he lay behind the bushes, it was so dark he couldn't see his own hand, and sometimes he imagined that he himself wasn't even there, and there was only silent, deep darkness. The world spread out far away in all directions, and it was endless and dark, and with all his lonely and sorrowful heart Pavel felt its immeasurable and alien enormity. He lay there and waited for Katya Reimer to come down the path with Lily and the other happy, carefree people who lived in a world alien to him and who were themselves alien to him. He hadn't gone with them, since he loved Katya Reimer with a pure, beautiful, languishing love, and she didn't know about this love and could not possibly ever share it. And he felt like being alone and near to Katya, so as to feel more deeply her inaccessible allure and the full gamut of his own grief and loneliness. And he lay there in the bushes, on the ground, alien to all people and outside of life, which was passing him by in all its beauty, songs and joyousness—passing by in that dark July night.

He had been lying there a long time, and the darkness had become even thicker and darker, when from far ahead came the sound of voices, laughter and the snapping of twigs under-foot, and it became clear that a throng of happy young people was heading his way. And all this drew closer in a swarm of happy sounds, and then it was right next to him.

"Oh, my goodness," Katya Reimer was saying in a thick, resonant contralto, "you could bang your head here! Tinov, let's have a light!"

From the darkness the strange, funny voice of a punchinello squeaked out, "I've lost my matches, Katerina Eduardovna!"

Amidst general laughter, another voice sounded, a youthful and reserved bass, "Allow me, Katerina Eduardovna, I'll strike a light!"

Katya Reimer answered, and her voice was serious and changed, "Please do, Nikolai Petrovich!"

A match flared and burnt for a second with a bright, white light, illuminating in the dark only the hand that held it, as if it were hanging in the air. Then it was darker than ever, and everyone, with laughter and jokes, went on.

"Give me your hand, Katerina Eduardovna!" the same young, reserved bass rang out.

There was a moment of quiet, as Katya Reimer gave him her hand, then the sound of firm masculine steps and along-side them the modest rustle of a dress. And that same voice asked gently and tenderly, "Why are you so sad, Katerina Eduardovna?"

Pavel didn't hear an answer. They now had their backs to him as they walked; immediately their voices became more muffled, flared up again like the dying flame of a bonfire, and were extinguished. And when it seemed that there was noth-ing left but the muffled darkness and silence, a woman's laugh resounded with surprising sonority, such a clear, innocent and strangely coy laugh that it seemed it wasn't a person who had laughed, but a young, dark birch or someone hiding in its branches. And a ricocheting whisper seemed to whisk around the forest, and everything quietened down in anticipation, when a man's voice, golden, soft, burnished and sonorous, sang out high and passionate: "You told me: 'Yes—I love you!' . . ."

So blindingly bright, so full of life force was that voice, that the very forest seemed to stir, and something sparkling, like fireflies dancing, flashed in Pavel's eyes. And again the same words, and they ran together as they rang, like a groan, like a shout, like a deep, indivisible sigh: "You told me: 'Yes—I love you!' . . ."

And again, and again, with mad insistence the singer repeated the same short and long phrase, as if he were thrusting it into the darkness. It seemed he couldn't stop; and with each repetition the burning appeal became stronger and more uncontainable; there was now something merciless in the sound—someone's face grew pale—and happiness became almost indistinguishable from mortal anguish.

A minute of black silence—far away, quietly sparkling, mysterious as summer lightning, a woman's laugh—and then all was still, and the heavy blackness seemed to swallow them up. It became deathly quiet and empty, as in empty space a thousand miles above the earth. Life had passed by with all its songs, love and beauty—passed by in the dark July night.

Pavel came out from behind the bushes and quietly whispered, "Why are you so sad, Katerina Eduardovna?" and quiet tears came to his eyes.

"Why are you so sad, Katerina Eduardovna?" he repeated and walked aimlessly ahead, into the blackness of the darkest night. Once he brushed against a tree next to him, and halted in confusion. Then he put his arms around its rough trunk, pressed his face against it as if it were a friend, and froze in a quiet despair unrelieved by tears and frenzied cries. Then, quietly, he staggered back, away from the tree that had been his refuge, and went on.

"Why are you so sad, Katerina Eduardovna?" he repeated like a lament, like a quiet prayer of despair, and his entire soul was concentrated there, beating and weeping in those sounds. Enveloped there in ominous dusk, and full of great love, it prayed for something pure and radiant, something of which it had no knowledge, and it was this that made its prayer so fervent.

Now the tranquillity and quiet of the forest was gone: the breath of a storm stirred the air, the treetops set up a distant murmur, and the wind snickered dryly through the leaves. When Pavel came out to the edge of the woods, the wind all but blew off his hat and hit him powerfully in the face with its cold freshness and the scent of rye. It was grand and threatening. Behind him the forest billowed in a black and dully groaning mass, and ahead a heavy, black thundercloud, like darkness that had taken form, bore down on him. And beneath the cloud the field of rye spread out, and it was completely white, and because it was so white amidst the darkness, when no light fell from anywhere, an incomprehensible and mystical terror began to stir. And when lightning erupted and the clouds were etched as a gauzy, uneasy mass of shades, a broad golden-red fire fell across the field from one end to the other, and the ears of grain ran with their heads down, like a startled herd—ran into that thundering July night.

Pavel climbed up on a high embankment, stretched out his open arms as if calling down upon his breast the wind, the black storm cloud and the entire sky, so marvellously beautiful in its fiery wrath. And the wind circled about his face as if feeling it all over, and with a whistle it tore into a thicket of pliant leaves, while the thundercloud flashed and rumbled, and the ears of rye, bending low, ran on.

"Come on then, come on!" shouted Pavel, but the wind caught his words and savagely crammed them back down his throat, and the rebellious and prayerful words, addressed by one small man to the great unknown, were lost in the rumbling of the heavens.

That had been in the summer, on a dark July night.

Pavel gazed at the ceiling, smiling a sweet and proud smile, and tears brimmed in his eyes. "What a cry-baby I've become!" he whispered, shaking his head, and naïvely, like a child, he wiped his eyes with his fingers.

He turned hopefully to the windows, but only dirty city fog, gloomy and monotonous, looked back, turning everything yellow: the ceiling, the walls and the creased pillow. And the pure images of the past that he had flushed out into the open wavered, grew dim and collapsed, shoving and moaning, somewhere into a black pit.

"Why are you so sad?" Pavel said like an incantation, like a prayer for mercy; but it was powerless in the face of new, yet unclear but already familiar and terrible images. Like rotten fog over a rusty swamp, they rose from that black pit, and his aroused memory powerfully called up more and more pictures.

"Not that, not that!" Pavel whispered, and he writhed and twisted in pain.

Once again he saw the summer cottage, but now it was day—a strange, ominous day. It was sweltering and the sun shone, and a disquieting burning smell hung in the air; and he was hiding in the bushes near the riverbank and trembling with fright as he looked through binoculars at some women bathing. And he saw the bright pink spots of their bodies, and the blue sky that seemed red, and himself, pale, with shaking hands and dirt stains on his knees. Then he saw the stone city, and again women, indifferent, tired, with insolent, cold eyes.

Their made-up and pale faces streamed by and receded into the depths of the past, and among them flashed moustached male physiognomies, bottles of beer and half-finished drinks, and in a smoky haze half-lit shadows circled in a dance, and a piano clanged away relentlessly, belching out the dolorous, relentless sounds of a polka.

"Not that!" whispered Pavel, gently, already giving in.

And the memories cut into his soul like a sharp knife cutting into living flesh. And they were all of women, of their soulless bodies, as repulsive as the sticky muck of backyards, and yet strangely alluring in their brazen dirtiness and availability. And they were absolutely everywhere. They were in the cynical, vitriolic conversations and idiotic jokes he heard from others and could himself tell so masterfully; they were in the drawings he drew and showed with a laugh to his friends and in his lonely thoughts and fantasies, which were as oppressive as nightmares and as alluring as dreams.

And a certain night arose before him, as lifelike as only that which can never be forgotten: an acrid, smoky night. That night, two years ago, he had given his pure body and his first pure kisses to a debauched and shameless woman. Her name was Luiza; she had been dressed in a hussar's uniform and complained incessantly that her stockings were tearing. Pavel could only barely remember how he had been with her. The only thing he remembered well was his house, to which he had returned late—shortly before dawn. The house was dark and quiet; in the dining room his dinner was waiting, the thick cutlet covered in a layer of white, congealed fat. He was feeling nauseous from the beer, and when he lay down the stucco ceiling, poorly illuminated in the candlelight, swayed, spun and swam. He went out several times, staggering, trying not to make noise and clinging to chairs. Because he was not used to being barefoot, the floor seemed terribly cold and slippery, and this extraordinary cold made it especially clear that it had been night for quite a while now, and everyone was quietly sleeping, while he alone was up and suffering from a pain that was alien to everything in this pure, good house.

Pavel looked around with hatred at his room with its revolting stucco ceiling and, submissive before this surge of memories, yielded to their terrible power.

He recalled Petrov, a handsome and confident young man, who spoke absolutely calmly and dispassionately about bought women, and taught his companions, "I never permit myself to kiss a streetwalker. You should only kiss someone you love and respect, not those bitches."

"But what if she kisses you?" asked Pavel.

"Let her! . . . I turn away."

Pavel gave a bitter, sad smile. He wasn't capable of doing as Petrov did, and he kissed those women. His lips touched their cold bodies, and once there was a time when—and this was frightening to remember—in a strange challenge to himself he had kissed a limp hand that smelled of perfume and beer. He kissed it as if punishing himself; he kissed it as if his lips might work a miracle and turn a bought woman into a pure, beautiful one, worthy of great love—the thirst for which consumed his heart. And she said, "What a licker you are!"

And he had caught something from her. He had caught a

shameful and dirty disease, which people talked about in secret, in a mocking whisper, behind closed doors—a disease impossible to think of without horror and self-loathing.

Pavel jumped up from the bed and went to the table. There he shuffled through papers and notebooks, uncovering things and covering them back up, and his hands trembled. And from the corners of his eyes he nervously sought out that place on the table where, locked up and carefully hidden by papers, the necessaries for medical treatment lay.

"If I had a revolver, I would shoot myself right now. Right here . . ." he thought and brought his finger to his left side, where his heart was beating.

And looking fixedly ahead, thinking about which one of his friends could get hold of a gun, he walked over to his rumpled bed and lay down. Then he fell to thinking about whether he would manage to hit his heart, and after unbuttoning his jacket and shirt, he began to examine with interest his young, as yet undeveloped chest.

"Pavel, open up!" came Lily's voice at the door.

Giving a startled shudder, as he now always did at the least unexpected sound or cry, Pavel hastily collected himself and unwillingly undid the bolt.

"What is it?" he asked with a frown.

"Just wanted to give you a kiss. Why do you lock yourself in all the time? Are you afraid of being robbed?"

Pavel lay down on the bed, and Lily, after an unsuccessful attempt to sit down by him, said, "Move over! You're such a grump! Can't you even make room for your little sister?"

Pavel silently moved over.

"I'm bored today," Lily said. "I don't know. Something's not right. It's probably because of the weather; I love sunshine, and this is so disgusting. I'm feeling so grumpy I could bite."

And cautiously stroking his short-cropped, prickly head, she looked tenderly in his eyes and asked, "Pavel darling! What's made you so sad?"

Pavel looked away and answered curtly, "I wasn't happy before."

"No, Pavel, I know better. You've been like this ever since

we came back from holiday. You hide yourself away from everyone, you never laugh. You don't dance anymore."

"Dancing is stupid . . ."

"But you didn't used to think so. You dance the mazurka better than anyone, and the other dances, too. Pavel, come on, tell me what's wrong? Tell me, darling, you nice, good old fellow!

And she kissed him on the cheek, above his flushed ear.

"Don't touch me! Go away!" And twitching his shoulders, he added quietly, "I'm dirty . . ."

Lily laughed aloud and tickled him behind the ear, saying, "You're clean as clean, Pavel! Remember how we used to take a bath together? You were so white, like a dear little piglet, clean as can be, absolutely squeaky clean!"

"Go away, Lily! Please! For God's sake!"

"I'm not going until you cheer up. You have little sideburns by your ears. I just noticed. Let me kiss them!"

"Lily, go away! Don't touch me! I'm telling you," Pavel said hollowly, hiding his face, "I'm dir . . . dirty . . . Dirty!" With a heavy sigh he breathed out the torturing word and his whole body, from head to toe, shook in a fit of instantly loosed and suppressed sobs.

"What's wrong, Pavel, dear heart?" Lily was frightened. "Shall I call dad?"

Pavel hollowly, but calmly replied, "No, don't. Nothing's wrong. My head hurts a little."

Lily stroked the cropped, angled back of his head with a wary tenderness and looked at him thoughtfully. Then she said in a neutral tone, "Katya Reimer asked about you yesterday."

After a silence Pavel, without turning, asked, "What did she ask?"

"Just, you know, generally: how you are, what you are doing, why you never visit. I guess they invited you over?"

"Not likely! . . ."

"No, Pavel, don't say such things! You don't know her. She's very intelligent and cultured, and she's interested in you. You think she only likes dancing, but she reads a lot and wants to start a reading club. She always says to me, 'How intelligent your brother is!' "

"She's a flirt . . . and a bitch."

Lily flushed scarlet, furiously pushed Pavel away and got up.

"You're vile yourself if you talk that way."

"Vile? Yes. So what?" Pavel retorted challengingly, looking with angry, welling eyes at his sister.

"Don't you dare talk that way! Don't you dare!" shouted Lily, completely red, her eyes just as angry and glistening.

"But I'm vile!" Pavel insisted.

"You're rude, unbearable, you're spoiling everyone's life . . . Egoist!"

"And she's a bitch, your Kat . . . Katya. And you're all bitches, you're rubbish!"

Lily's eyes flashed. Grasping the door handle, she stifled the trembling in her voice and said, "I was sorry for you and that's why I came to see you. But you're not worth it. And I'm never coming to see you again. You hear me, Pavel?"

The angled back of his head remained immobile. Lily gave an angry nod and left the room.

With an expression of total scorn, as if something impure had just gone out of the door, Pavel painstakingly fastened the lock and began to pace about the room. He felt better, now that he had heaped invective on both Katya and Lily, and called them what they were: bitches and rubbish. And pacing cautiously, he began to think about how all women were bad, egoists and limited beings. Lily, for instance. She could not understand that he was unhappy, and that's why she talked that way and gave him such a dressing-down, like a trades-woman. She was in love with Avdeyev, but the day before yesterday Petrov came over, and she had yelled at the maid and then at their mother because they couldn't find her red ribbon. And Katya Reimer was just the same: she was pensive, serious, interested in him, in Pavel, and said that he was intelli-gent; but as soon as that Petrov comes to her house, she puts on a sky-blue ribbon for him, and she primps in front of the mirror and makes a pretty face. And that's all for Petrov; and

Petrov is a cocky, vulgar dimwit, and everyone in the entire school knows it.

She was a sweet young thing, and was only dimly aware—but did not permit herself to think about it—that there were such things as debauched women and diseases—horrible, shameful diseases that could make a man unhappy and revolting in his own eyes, and make him shoot himself with a revolver, for all his youth and promise! And she herself had walked on the promenade in a *décolleté* dress this summer, and when she held hands, she pressed close as she walked. She may even have kissed someone already . . .

Pavel clenched his fists and whispered through gritted teeth, "Disgusting!"

She probably had kissed someone . . . Pavel didn't even dare look her way, and here she was already kissing, most likely with Petrov—he was cocky and insolent. And eventually she would give him her body, too, and she would do with him what people do with streetwalkers. How hideous! How base life was, containing nothing that brightened the eyes, shrouded in grief and despondency! Who knows, maybe now, even now Katya might have—a lover.

"It can't be!" Pavel cried out, but someone inside him calmly and maliciously continued, and his words were terrible: "Yes, she does, probably some carriage driver or stable-boy. There have been cases where pure girls like her had servants for lovers, and no one knew about it, and everyone thought they were pure; but in the night they hurried off to meet their lovers, running in bare feet over freezing cold floors. Then they would get married and cheat on their husbands. It happens—he had read about this sort of thing. The Reimers have a stable-boy, a common, handsome lad . . ."

Pavel turned sharply and began to walk the other way.

Or maybe Petrov . . . She went out to meet him somewhere, and Petrov—he was insolent and daring—said to her, "It's cold here; let's go someplace warm! . . ." And she went.

Pavel could no longer think. He stood by the window, and it was as if he were being suffocated by the yellow, revolting fog, which was seeping sullenly and imperiously into the room, like a formless yellow-bellied viper. Fury and despair were choking him, but nonetheless he felt better knowing that he was not the only one who was vile, but everyone was vile, the whole world. And his disease didn't seem so frightening and shameful. "It's nothing," he thought, "Petrov had it twice, Samoilov got it three times, Schmidt and Pomerantsev are already better, and I'll get better, too."

"I'll be the same as they are, and everything will be fine," he decided.

Pavel tested the lock, went to the table and took hold of the drawer handle; but suddenly he thought of all those well-hidden instruments, the vials of muddy liquid with their yellow, revolting labels, how he had bought them at the chemist's, burning with embarrassment, and how the chemist had turned away from him as if he, too, were embarrassed; and how he had gone to see the doctor, who was a man with a noble and extraordinarily wholesome face, and it had even seemed strange that such a pure man was compelled constantly to deal with such dirty and disgusting diseases. And Pavel's stretched-out hand dropped, and he thought, "Leave it, then! . . . I won't take the treatment. Better to die . . ."

He lay down, and before his eyes stood the vials with the yellow labels, and they made it clear that everything bad that he thought about Katya Reimer was a wretched, abominable lie, as disgusting and dirty as his disease. And he was ashamed and frightened that he could think those things about a girl he loved and before whom he wasn't fit to kneel; that he could think his dirty thoughts and wallow in them, and find them justified and gather out of their filth a strange and horrible hubris. And he became frightened of himself.

"Is this really me, and are these hands—mine?" he thought, and he examined his hand, still tanned from the summer sun and stained with ink at the fingertips.

And everything became incomprehensible and terrible, like a dream. He saw his room, the stucco ceiling and his boots shoved up against the bars of the bedstead as if for the first time. They were fashionable boots, with long, narrow toes, and Pavel wiggled his big toe to make sure that it was his own foot inside, not someone else's. And then he was sure it was he, Pavel Rybakov, and he realised that it was too late for him—he had no hope. It was he who thought such filthy things about Katya Reimer; it was he who had a shameful disease; it was he who would die in no time at all, and people would cry over him when he was dead.

"Forgive me, Katya!" he whispered through pale, parched lips.

And he could feel the filth that enveloped and permeated him. He had been feeling it ever since he had been infected. Every Friday Pavel went to the bathhouse, twice a week he changed his underclothes, and everything he wore was new, fresh and expensive; but it seemed as if he were completely immersed in some kind of foul-smelling swill, and wherever he went he left a foul-smelling trace in the air. He examined any tiny little spot on his jacket with fright and strange interest, and quite often his shoulders or head would start itching, and his underclothes felt like they were sticking to his body. And sometimes this happened at dinner, in front of people, and then he would become acutely aware of how terrifyingly alone he was, like a leper on his own rubbish heap.

His thoughts were equally dirty, and it seemed that if you opened his skull and took out his brains, they would be as dirty as rags, as the brains of animals splayed out in the slaughterhouse among the filth and manure. And women and more women, tired, made up, with cold and insolent eyes! They followed him on the street, and he was afraid to go out, especially in the evening, when the city was seething with such women like decaying flesh seething with worms; they came into his head as if it were their own dirty room, and he couldn't drive them away. When he was asleep and powerless to regulate his feelings and desires, they arose like flaming ghosts from the depths of his being; when he stayed awake, a strange, terrifying force took him in its iron hands and threw him—blinded, changed, unrecognisable as himself—into the filthy embraces of filthy women.

"It's all because I'm debauched," thought Pavel with calm despair. "But not for long—I'll shoot myself soon. I'll see

Katya Reimer today, and then shoot myself. Or no—I'll just listen to her voice from my room, and when they call me, I won't go."

Moving his legs with difficulty, like an invalid, Pavel approached the window. Something dark, terrifying and hopeless, like the autumn sky, gazed in, and it seemed that there was no end to it, that it had always been, and there was no joy anywhere on earth, no pure, unclouded tranquillity.

"If there were light at least!" Pavel said with longing and, as a last resort, he remembered his journal. It was also well-hidden and hadn't been opened since Pavel got infected: when one's thoughts are filthy, and one has no love for one-self, for one's own joys and sorrows, there's nothing to write in a journal. Pavel took the journal, carefully and tenderly, as if it were an ailing child, and lay down with it on his bed. The notebook was beautifully bound and had gilt-edged paper; it was white and clean, and on the pages already covered with writing there was not a single dirty blot. Pavel carefully and deferentially leafed through it, and its gleaming, stiffly bending pages smelled of spring, the forest, sunlight and love.

There were so many thoughts about life here, such serious and resolute ideas, with such a multitude of clever foreign words, that it seemed to Pavel as if it were not he who had written them, but some elderly and terribly clever man; here was the first quiver of sceptical thought, the first pure doubts and questions addressed to God: where are You, O Lord? Here was the sweet sorrow of unfulfilled and unrequited love and the decision to be proud and noble and to love Katya Reimer all his long life, to the very grave. Here was the ominous, frightening question about the purpose and meaning of life and the open-hearted answer, from which wafted the scent of spring and bright sunlight: one must live in order to love people, who are so terribly unhappy. And not a word about those women. Only very sporadically, like the reflection of a black storm cloud on the green and laughing earth, there were short, underlined and terse notations: *feeling bad*. Pavel knew their secret and sorrowful meaning, cursed them with his eyes and quickly turned the page that was tainted by them.

And all the while it seemed to Pavel that it was not he who had been writing, but some other person, a good, clever one; he was dead now, this person, and that was why everything he had written was so meaningful and so sad to read.

And a quiet pity for that dead person filled his heart; and for the first time in many days Pavel felt at home here, on his own bed, all by himself, and not out there, among thousands of hostile and alien lives.

It was already getting dark, and the strange, yellowish gleam faded away; shrouded in fog, the long autumn night came on noiselessly, and the houses and people drew closer together, as if frightened. The streetlamps had begun to burn with a pale, indifferent light, and the light they shed was cold and mournful; here and there, house windows began to blaze with the light of a warm fire, and each such house where even just one window was lit seemed to be glowing with a tender, affectionate smile and became big, black and affectionate like an old friend. Carriages rolled by, swaying, just as before, and pedestrians hurried along; but now it seemed that each one of them had a goal: to arrive as soon as possible at a warm place full of friendly light and friendly people. Pavel closed his eyes and vividly recalled what he had seen before they had left the countryside, when he had been out by himself for a walk one evening: silent autumnal twilight, a velvety rain falling from the sky and a long, straight highway. At either end it receded into an even mist, suggesting an endlessness like life itself; and coming down the road at a brisk pace towards Pavel were two tinkers, yoked to a small cart. The cart rumbled faintly as it went; the tinkers threw their weight against the traces and moved along quickly, their heads bobbing in rhythm; while far away ahead of them, almost on the horizon, a little spark glittered like a bright, vivid point. For a minute, they were alongside Pavel; and when he turned around to look at them, the highway was deserted and dark, as if the people harnessed to the cart had never been there.

Pavel saw the highway and the twilight, and this was all that filled his thoughts. It was a momentary lull, when his rebellious, overwrought soul, worn out from its efforts to break out of an iron circle of contradictions, lightly and soundlessly slipped out of him and rose high up. This was peace and quiet, and a renunciation of life, something so good and sad that it was impossible to convey in human speech. For more than half an hour Pavel sat in his armchair almost motionlessly; it grew dark in the room, and bright spots from lamps and something else as well began to play over the ceiling; and he kept on sitting there, and his face seemed pale in the darkness and not like it usually was.

"Pavel, open up!" came his father's voice.

Pavel jumped up, and at his sudden movement the same sharp, knife-like pain took his breath away. Bent over, clutching at his sunken belly with his cold hands, he gritted his teeth and mentally answered, "Coming," since he wasn't able to speak aloud.

"Pavel, are you asleep?"

Pavel opened the door. Sergey Andreyevich came in, somewhat perplexed, somewhat tentatively, but at the same time commandingly, the way fathers come in when they are aware of their right to enter their son's room whenever they like, while at the same time wishing to appear gentlemanly and strictly respecting the inviolability of other people's living space.

"So, old boy, been sleeping, have you?" Sergey Andreyevich asked gently, awkwardly patting Pavel on the shoulder in the dark.

"No, not really . . . dozing," answered Pavel unwillingly, but also gently, still full of quiet tranquillity and inchoate thoughts. He understood that his father had come in to make up with him, and thought, "What good will it do?"

"Please light the lamp," his father requested. "It's the only escape from the fog, lighting lamps. I've been nervous all day long today."

"He's apologising . . ." thought Pavel, removing the glass and striking a match.

Sergey Andreyevich sat down in the chair by the table, adjusted the lampshade, and having noticed the notebook entitled "Journal," tactfully put it aside and even covered it up with papers. Pavel silently observed his father's actions and waited.

"Have you got a match?" Sergey Andreyevich asked as he got out a cigarette. He had matches in his pocket, but he wanted to allow his son the pleasure of doing him a service.

He lit his cigarette, glanced at the black cover of Buckle, and began, "I disagree radically with Tolstoy and others who pursue the 'simple life,' fruitlessly waging war against civilisation and demanding that we start going around on all fours again. But it is impossible not to agree that civilisation's darker side fills one with extremely"—he raised his hand and let it fall—"extremely serious reservations. For instance, if we look at what's going on now even in, say, that wonderful country of France . . ."

Sergey Andreyevich was an intelligent and good man, and he thought all the things that intelligent and good people of his country and time thought, having all gone to the same schools and read the same good books, newspapers and journals. He was an inspector for the Phoenix insurance company and often left the capital city on business; and when he was home, he hardly had time to catch up with his numerous acquaintances, go to the theatres and exhibitions, and browse through the latest publications. Despite all this he set aside time to be with his children, especially with Pavel, as he attributed special importance to the process of a boy's development. Besides, he never knew what to talk about with Lily, so instead he lavished more affection on her. He didn't cosset Pavel, inasmuch as he was a boy, but he did talk with him, the way he would talk to a grown-up or even a friend, the only difference being that he never discussed trivial matters, trying instead always to direct the conversation towards serious topics. Because of this, he considered himself a good father, and whenever he began to speak with Pavel, he felt like a professor at his podium. And both he and Pavel liked this very much. He even hesitated to probe too deeply into Pavel's progress at the institute, fearing it might destroy the harmony of their relationship with shouting, scolding and reprimands. He was always acutely ashamed of his rare outbursts and justified them by his fiery temperament. He knew all Pavel's thoughts, his views and his newly forming convictions, and he had always thought he knew Pavel inside and out. And he was very surprised and upset when it suddenly turned out that Pavel was not to be found in these convictions and views, but was somewhere outside of them, in some sort of mysterious moods and sickening drawings, about whose origins it was imperative that he should demand an account. Sooner or later—but absolutely imperative.

And now he spoke very well and intelligently about how culture improves particular aspects of life, but that on the whole it leaves a sort of dissonance, a sort of empty, dark place everyone feels, but no one can name—but there was an uncertainty and unevenness in his speech, like that of a professor who is not sure of his listeners' attention and feels their anxious and distracted mood. And there was something else in his speech: something sneaky, slippery and probing. More frequently than usual he turned to Pavel: "What do you think, Pavel? Do you agree, Pavel?"

And he was extraordinarily glad when Pavel expressed his agreement. His white, puffy fingers, which moved in rhythm to his speech and threateningly stretched towards Pavel, seemed to be feeling for something; he was cautiously, cunningly stealing up on something, and the words he was saying were like a voluminous masquerade costume, behind which could be felt the outline of other, as yet unknown, terrible words. Pavel understood this and gazed with inchoate fear at the coldly gleaming pince-nez, at the wedding ring on his father's fat finger, at the slight back-and-forth movement of his leg in its gleaming boot. His fear increased, and Pavel already felt, already knew what his father would talk about next, and his heart, though beating quietly, seemed to echo in his chest. The voluminous costume was quivering and slipping lower, and cruel words strained convulsively to get out into the open. Now his father had finished speaking about alcoholics and lit a cigarette with a slightly trembling hand.

"Here it comes!" thought Pavel, and he shrank back, the way a black crow with a broken wing shrinks back in its cage when someone's enormous outstretched hand reaches towards it through the cage door.

Sergey Andreyevich gave a heavy sigh and began, "But there is something, Pavel, that is even more terrible than alcoholism . . ."

"Here it comes!" thought Pavel.

"More terrible even than the ravages of war, more devastating even than the plague or cholera . . ."

"Now! Now!" thought Pavel, shrivelling up, and his entire body felt as if it were in icy water.

". . . Debauchery! Have you, Pavel, chanced to read any books on this interesting problem?"

"I'm going to shoot myself!" Pavel thought immediately, but aloud he said calmly, and with polite interest, "Not particularly on that subject, but more generally, yes, I've run across it. That problem, dad, interests me very much."

"Really? . . ." Sergey Andreyevich's pince-nez flashed. "Yes, it is a terrible problem, and I am convinced, Pavel, that the fate of all civilised humanity depends on how it is resolved. Really . . . the degeneration of whole generations, even whole countries; psychological disturbances with all the horrors of insanity and enervation . . . So there you are . . . And finally, innumerable diseases that destroy the body and even the soul. You, Pavel, cannot even imagine what a nasty thing such an illness is. One of my university friends—later he entered the military law academy, a certain Skvortsov, Alexander Petrovich—caught something in his second year, and he wasn't even seriously ill, but he got so frightened that he poured a bottle of kerosene over himself and ignited it. They were barely able to save him."

"Is he alive now, dad?"

"Of course he's alive, but monstrously deformed. So there you are . . . Professor Berg cites some striking statistical facts in his capital work . . ."

They sat and conversed tranquilly, like two friends who have struck on an especially interesting topic. Pavel's face expressed horror and amazement, and he interjected questions, occasionally exclaiming, "The Devil only knows what

265

it is! But surely those statistics of yours can't be right?!" And inside he was deathly calm, as if a live heart were not beating in his chest, as if blood did not run in his veins, but instead he was hewn from one huge block of cold, unresponsive iron. What he himself had thought of the dire significance of his disease and his fall was direly confirmed by books, which he believed in—intelligent foreign words and numbers, implacable and incontrovertible as death. Some important, intelligent and omniscient person was speaking objectively about his imminent death, and in the calm neutrality of his words there was something fatal that didn't leave a pitiful man a shred of hope.

And Sergey Andreyevich, too, was of good cheer: he laughed, rounded off his words and gestures, waved his hand complacently, and felt with dismay that in the truth of his words a terrible and elusive lie was concealed. He glanced with suppressed anger at Pavel lounging before him, and he wanted terribly for him to be not his friend, with whom it was so easy to chat, but his son; for there to be tears, shouting, reproaches—but not this calm, false discussion. His son was slipping away from him again, and there was nothing he could find fault with, so that he could shout at him, stamp his feet— even, possibly, hit him—anything to find that vital something, without which life is not possible. "It's helpful, what I'm saying: I'm forewarning him," Sergey Andreyevich reassured himself; but his hand stretched with greedy impatience towards his pocket, where in his wallet next to a fifty-rouble note lay the drawing that had been crumpled and was now smoothed out. "I'll ask now, and that will be the end of it," he thought.

But just then Pavel's mother came in, a stout, pretty woman with a powdered face and eyes like Lily's: grey and naïve. She had just got home, and her cheeks and nose were reddened from the cold.

"Terrible weather!" she said. "It's foggy again, you can't see a thing. Yefim was driving too fast, he almost ran someone down on the corner."

"So you said 70 percent?" Pavel asked his father.

"Yes, 72 percent. Well, how are the Sokolovs?" Sergey Andreyevich asked his wife.

"The same as always. They're bored. Anechka is a bit ill. They want to come over tomorrow evening. Anatoly Ivanovich has arrived, he sends his greetings."

She looked with contentment at their cheerful faces and friendly poses, and gave her son a little pat on the cheek; and as always, he grasped her hand as she drew it back and gave it a kiss. Whenever he saw his mother, he loved her; and when she was gone, he forgot about her very existence. And everyone felt that way about her, family and friends, and if she were to die, everybody would have a good cry over her and forget her the next minute—forget her completely, from her pretty face to her name. And no one ever wrote her letters.

"Having a chat?" She looked at father and son cheerily. "Well, I'm very glad. It's not nice when father and son aren't getting along. Like *Fathers and Sons*. And you forgave him morning mass?

"The fog was to blame . . ." Sergey Andreyevich and Pavel both smiled.

"Yes, terrible weather! As if all the clouds had fallen to earth. I kept telling Yefim, 'Please, slow down!' and he says, 'Yes, madam!' and whips them harder. Where did Lily go? Lily! Call her to dinner! Gentlemen, fathers and sons, come to the table!"

"Just a moment," Sergey Andreyevich requested. "We'll be right there."

"Yes, all right, but it's already seven . . ."

"Yes, yes. Go ahead and serve! We'll be right there."

Yulia Petrovna went out, and Sergey Andreyevich came a step closer to his son. Pavel also stepped forward automatically and sullenly asked, "What?"

Now they were standing opposite each other, openly and directly, and everything that had been said earlier disappeared, never to return—Professor Berg, the statistics and the 72 percent.

"Pavel! Dear boy! Lily told me that you are upset about

something. And in general I've noticed that you've changed lately. It's not trouble at school, is it?"

"No. There's nothing wrong."

Sergey Andreyevich wished he could say, "My son!"—but this seemed awkward and artificial, and he said, "My friend! . . ."

Pavel remained silent, and shoving his hands in his pockets, looked off to the side. Sergey Andreyevich flushed, adjusted his pince-nez with a trembling hand, and took out his wallet. Squeamishly, with two fingers he fished out the drawing with the smoothed-out creases and silently held it out to Pavel.

"What is it?" asked Pavel.

"Look!"

Without removing his hands from his pockets, Pavel glanced back over his shoulder. The paper danced in Sergey Andreyevich's puffy, white hand, but Pavel recognised it, and in the space of a moment he was burning with a terrible feeling of shame. Something rumbled in his ears, like thousands of rocks falling down a mountain; it was as if his eyes had been scorched with flame, and he could neither look away from Sergey Andreyevich's face nor close his eyes.

"Did you do this?" his father asked from somewhere far, far away.

And with a sudden rush of anger Pavel answered proudly and openly, "Yes, I did it."

Sergey Andreyevich let go of the paper, and fluttering at the corners, it quietly sank to the floor. Then his father turned and quickly left the room, and in the dining room his loud and rapidly receding voice could be heard saying, "Have dinner without me! I have pressing business to attend to." Pavel, meanwhile, went over to the washbasin and began to pour water on his hands and face, feeling neither the cold nor the water.

"Plaguing the life out of me!" he whispered, gasping and choking in the stream that spattered against his eyes and mouth.

After dinner, around eight, Lily's girlfriends from school came over, and from his room Pavel heard them having tea in the dining room. There were a lot of them; they were laughing, and their ringing, young voices chimed against one another, like the wings of dragonflies at play, and it didn't seem like a room on a gloomy autumn evening, but a green meadow, where the sun was shining on him from a July, midday sky. And the schoolgirls buzzed low, like May beetles. Pavel listened carefully to the voices, but Katya Reimer's resonant, honest voice wasn't among them, and he waited and waited, and gave a start whenever a fresh arrival spoke up. He prayed for her to come, and once he heard her voice absolutely clearly: "Here I am! . . ." and he all but wept with joy; but that voice blended in with the other voices, and no matter how hard he listened, he didn't hear it again. Then the dining room became quiet, and the housemaid said something in her hollow voice, and from the salon came the sounds of the piano. Mellifluous and light, like a dance, but strangely sad and sorrowful, the music circled round Pavel's head, like quiet voices from some alien, wonderful and forever lost world.

Lily ran in, flushed from dancing. Her untroubled forehead was damp, and her eyes shone, and it seemed as if the folds of her brown school dress still bore traces of rhythmic swaying.

"Pavel! I'm not mad at you!" she said, and kissed him quickly with hot lips, at the same time giving off a wave of the same hot and innocent breath. "Let's go and dance! Come on!"

"I don't feel like it."

"It's a pity not everyone came. Katya's not here, Lida's not here, and Pospelov went off to the theatre. Let's go, Pavel, come on!"

"I'll never dance again."

"Silly! Come on, let's go! Please come; I'll be waiting for you."

At the door she felt sorry for her brother; she came back, gave him another kiss and, her mind eased, ran off. "Hurry up, Pavel! Hurry up!"

Pavel closed the door and began to pace the room with giant steps.

"She didn't come!" he said loudly. "She didn't come!" he

repeated, making a circuit around the room. "She didn't come!"

Someone knocked at the door and Petrov's self-assured, insolent voice said, "Pavel! Open up!"

Pavel stopped in his tracks and held his breath.

"Pavel! What a fool! Open up! Elizaveta Sergeyevna sent me!"

Pavel remained silent. Petrov knocked again, and then calmly said, "Well, you're a swine, brother! And young—and green . . . sweet Katya's not here and he's sulking. Idiot!"

Even Petrov dared to say "sweet Katya" with his impure lips!

After waiting a minute for the music to start again in the salon, Pavel cautiously glanced into the empty dining room, passed through it and picked up his old summer coat from outside the bathroom door, where unneeded clothes were hanging in a jumble. Then he quickly passed through the kitchen and down the back stairs to the yard, and from there to the street.

Right away it was as damp, cold and uncomfortable as if Pavel had gone down into the depths of a vast cellar, where the air was still and oppressive and woodlice crept along the high, slippery walls. And it seemed surprising that in the leaden, rotten-smelling fog some sort of indefatigable, animated life was nonetheless flowing along; it was in the rumbling of unseen carriages and in the enormous, blurry, bright globes, in the centres of which the streetlamps burned with a dull, even glow; it was in the hurried, formless contours resembling smeared ink blots on grey paper, growing out of the fog and disappearing back into it again, often felt only as a strange sensation that unerringly testified to the nearby presence of a human being. An unseen person bumped hard into Pavel and did not apologise; a woman elbowed Pavel and walked past him, looking closely into his face as she went. Pavel gave a shudder and angrily stepped away.

He stopped in a deserted alley opposite Katya Reimer's house. He often came here, and this time he came to show how unhappy and lonely he was, and how cruelly Katya

Reimer had acted in not coming in his moment of mortal yearning and horror. The windows glowed faintly through the fog, and there was a savage and evil mockery in their lacklustre gaze, like that of a man sitting at a banquet table, stuffed to the gills, who looks at a hungry man and lazily smiles. And choking on the rotting fog, trembling from cold in his tattered old coat, Pavel drank in that look with hungry hatred. He saw Katya Reimer clearly: how she sat pure and innocent among pure people and smiled, and read a good book, with no thought for the street, in the dirt and cold of which stood a dying man. She was pure, and cruel in her purity; she was, perhaps, dreaming even now of some noble hero, and if Pavel were to go in to her and say, "I'm filthy, I'm ill, I'm debauched, and because of this I'm dying—help me!" she would turn away fastidiously and say, "Go away! I'm sorry for you, but you disgust me. Go away!" And she would cry; she was pure and kind, and she would cry . . . as she drove him out. And by the charity of her pure tears and proud compassion she would murder the one who had asked her for the humane love that doesn't look back and doesn't fear filth.

"I hate you!" whispered a strange, shapeless blur of a man, gripped by the fog that had snatched him away from the living world. "I hate you!"

Someone passed by Pavel without noticing him. Pavel pressed himself fearfully to the wet wall and moved only after the footsteps had died away.

"I hate . . ."

His voice was smothered in the fog as in cotton wool. The shapeless blur of a man slowly receded; near the streetlamp a metal button flashed, and everything dissolved, as if it had never been, as if only the sombre, cold fog had ever been there.

The Neva River was freezing hopelessly beneath the heavy fog, and it was deathly silent; neither steamboat's whistle nor the lapping of water carried from its broad, dark surface. Pavel sat down on one of the semicircular benches and pressed his back to its damp, tranquil, cold granite. His whole body began to tremble, and his chilled fingers could barely bend, and his

271

wrists and elbows felt numb; but he hated the thought of going home: there was something in the music and festivities of the others that reminded him of Katya Reimer; it was awkward and offensive, like the smile of a chance passer-by at a stranger's funeral. A few steps away from Pavel, dim figures floated by in the fog; one had a small, fiery spot by its head, obviously a cigarette; another one, barely visible, was wearing what were probably hard leather boots, and with every step they went *click-click*. And for a long time the sound of his footsteps could still be heard.

One shade had halted indecisively. It had an enormous head, disproportionate to its height; its outlines were ugly and fantastic, and when it moved towards Pavel, he felt frightened. Close up, it turned out to be a large hat with white, curved feathers of the sort that often adorn funeral wreaths, while the shade itself was just an ordinary woman. Like Pavel, she was shivering from the cold, and she hid her big hands in the little pockets of her short woollen coat to no avail; standing, she was of medium height, but when she sat down next to Pavel, she became almost a head taller.

"Do you have a cigarette, handsome young fellow?" she asked.

"Pardon me, lovely young lady, I don't smoke," Pavel replied, familiarity and excitement in his tone.

The woman giggled shrilly, her teeth chattered from the cold, and the smell of beer wafted over Pavel.

"Let's go to my place," said the woman, and her voice was shrill like her laugh. "Let's go! You'll treat me to a little vodka!"

Something fast, broad and swirling now opened up before Pavel, as if he were falling off a mountain—yellow flames in the midst of the wavering darkness, and a promise of strange celebration, madness and tears. But on the outside he was chilled to the bone by the raw fog, and his elbows were growing numb. And with a politeness in which there was defiance, scorn and tears of hopeless despair, he said, "O, divine one! Do you so desire my passionate caresses?"

The woman seemed to be offended; angrily, she turned

away, her teeth chattered and she said no more, irately pressing her thin lips together. She had been tossed out of the pub because she wouldn't drink sour beer and had splashed it into the barman's face; her boots had holes in the toes and they leaked, and all this made her feel like sulking and giving someone a good scolding. Out of the corners of his eyes, Pavel saw the profile of her face, with its short nose and broad, fleshy chin, and he smiled. She was exactly like the women who haunted him, and he thought it was funny, and a strange sort of feeling made him feel close to her. And he liked it that she was angry.

The woman turned around and exclaimed sharply, "Well? Are we going or not? Why the hell don't you make up your mind!"

And Pavel answered with a laugh, "Right you are, miss: why the hell! Why the hell not, why not go, you and I, and drink vodka and succumb to refined pleasures?"

The woman freed her hand from her little pocket and gave him a half-angry, half-friendly clap on the shoulder. "Whatever you say, mate. Well then, I'll go ahead and you behind."

"Why?" Pavel asked, surprised. "Why behind, and not next to you, divine . . ." he faltered for a moment—"Katya?"

"My name is Manechka. Because you would be ashamed to be beside me."

Pavel grabbed her hand and drew her towards him, and the woman's shoulder awkwardly hit him in the chest. She laughed and walked unsteadily, and now it was evident that she was a little tipsy. At the gates of one building she disengaged her hand, and taking a rouble from Pavel, went to get some vodka from the gatekeeper.

"Hurry up, Katya darling!" Pavel entreated, losing sight of her in the black and murky opening of the gates.

From the distance came back, "Manechka, not Katya!"

A streetlamp burned, and Pavel pressed his cheek to its cold, moist post and closed his eyes. His face was immobile, like a blind man's, and inside him all was as peaceful and quiet as a cemetery. Such a moment occurs in men condemned to death, when their eyes are already bound and the sound of busy steps echoing on the scaffold has fallen silent, and in the threatening silence the great mystery of death is already half-revealed. And, like the ominous beat of drums, a voice rang out hollowly in the distance: "Where did you get to? I was looking and looking for you . . . I couldn't find you any-where. I thought you'd gone, and I was going to take myself off as well."

Pavel took himself in hand, shrugged something off and asked in a cheerful, loud voice, "And what about the vodka? That's the main thing, the vodka! For what are we, you and me, dear Katya, without a little vodka?"

"And what do I call you? I wanted to call you by name, but you didn't tell me what it was."

"Katya darling, my name is a bit strange: they call me Percent, Percent. You can call me Percenty. That way it comes out more affectionate, and our intimate relations admit of that," Pavel said, leading the woman on.

"There's no such name. Only dogs have names like that."

"What do you mean, Katya darling! Even my father calls me that: Percenty, Percenty! I swear to you by Professor Berg and the holy statistic!"

The fog and the lights moved, and again the woman's shoulders banged against Pavel's chest, and before his eyes dangled a large, curved feather, the kind that adorns hearses; then something black, decaying and foul-smelling surrounded them, and then some steps teetered up and then down again. Pavel almost fell in one place, and the woman supported him. Then there was a stuffy room, smelling strongly of cobblers' wares and sour cabbage; a lamp was burning, and the sound of uneven, angry snoring was coming from behind a chintz curtain.

"Shh!" whispered the woman, leading Pavel by the hand. "The master's sleeping, the devil, the cobbler, the lost soul!"

And Pavel was afraid of this cobbler, who was snoring there somewhere behind the curtain so unevenly and angrily, and he stepped cautiously in his heavy, wet boots. Then all of a sudden there was deep darkness and the sound of glass being moved and immediately the room was illuminated by the clear, blinding light of a little lantern hanging on the wall. Beneath the lamp was a little table and on it lay a small comb with fine hairs tangled in the teeth, dried pieces of bread, a large, dirty bread-knife, and a bowl in which lay pieces of potato and chopped onion coated in a layer of yellow sunflower oil. And all Pavel's attention was riveted on the table.

"This is home!" said Manechka. "Take off your coat!"

They sat there, laughing and drinking, and Pavel had his arm around the half-naked woman; her fat, white shoulder with its dingy blouse strap and broken button was right up near his eyes, and he greedily kissed it, sucking in with his moist, hot lips. Then he kissed her face and, strangely, could neither examine it properly nor keep it in his memory. When he looked at it, it seemed already long familiar and known, to the last detail, to the little blemish on her temple; but when he turned away he immediately and completely forgot everything, as if his soul did not want to take in that image and was vigorously pushing it away.

"I'll say one thing," the woman was saying, trying to remove from a piece of potato a long hair that was stuck to it and from time to time indifferently kissing Pavel on the cheek with her greasy lips, "one thing: I'm not drinking any sour beer. Give it to whoever you want, but I for one won't take it. I'm a nasty bit of work, it's true, but I'm not lapping up any sour beer. And I'll say it straight out to anyone, even at the scaffold: I'll not do it!"

"Let's have a song, Katya darling!" Pavel asked.

"And if you don't like it, that I threw it in your ugly mug, you can take me to the police, but you have no right to beat me. I'm proud by nature, and I've seen the likes of you a thousand times, maybe, and I've never once been scared," the woman continued, addressing the barman who had offended her.

"Stop it, Katya darling, forget about it!" Pavel entreated. "I believe you, you're as proud as a Spanish queen, and magnificent. Let's have a song! Good songs, good songs!"

"And I'm not Katya darling, I'm Manechka darling. And

no singing: my master the devil, the cobbler, the lost soul doesn't allow it."

"It's all the same—Katya or Manechka. For God's sake, it's all the same—I'm telling you, I, Pavel Rybakov, the drunkard and reprobate. You love me, don't you, my proud queen?"

"I love you. Only I don't permit you to call me Katya," the woman stubbornly insisted.

"So there you are!" Pavel nodded his head. "We'll sing! We'll sing good songs, the sort they sing. Oh, I know a good song! But it can't be sung like that. Close your eyes, Katya dear, you close your eyes, close them, and imagine you are in the forest, and it's a dark, dark night . . ."

"I don't like the forest. What forest? Go ahead and talk, but not about the forest! The devil take it! Let's better have a drink, and don't upset me. I don't like that . . ." Manechka spoke sullenly, pouring and splashing the vodka.

Evidently she was not well. Her breathing was laboured, as if she were swimming in deep water. And her lips were stretched tight and had a bluish hue.

"A dark, dark night!" Pavel continued with closed eyes. "And it seems people are walking along, and you are, too, and someone is singing beautifully . . . Wait a moment, how does it go? 'You said to me: *Yes—I love you!*' . . . No, I can't, I'm not a good singer."

"Stop shouting, you'll wake the master. What the hell!"

"No, I can't sing at all. I can't!" Pavel said despairingly and clutched at his head. Fiery ribbons wound and unwound before his closed eyes, billowing in fantastic and horrible patterns, and the room seemed as broad as a field and as stuffy as the bottom of a narrow, deep pit. Manechka looked scornfully at him over her shoulder and said, "Sing! What the hell!"

"Yes—I love you . . . Yes—I love you . . . No, I can't!"

He opened his eyes wide and their hidden fire seared the woman's face.

"You must have a heart, don't you? Don't you, Katya darling? Then give me your hand! Give it to me!" He smiled through brimming tears and lowered his burning lips to her hostile, resisting hand.

"Stop this foolishness!" the woman said angrily and jerked back her hand. "He's all weepy now, the slobber-face! Either come to bed or get out!"

"Katya darling! Katya!" he whispered pleadingly, and his tears made it hard for him to see the sleepy, malicious face that stared at him with revulsion. "Katya darling, my sweetheart, my dear darling, have pity on me, I beg you! I'm so unhappy, and I have absolutely nothing, nothing. Lord, if you could only have pity on me, Katya!"

The woman pushed him away forcefully, and, swaying, stood up. "The devil take you!" she shouted, gasping. "I hate you! . . . Drunk as a cobbler, and cracking up . . . Katya darling! Katya!" she mocked him, pressing her thin, bluish lips together. "I know what sort of Katya you need. Go on, take yourself off to her, then! Smooching, and he goes, 'Katya, Katya!' Ugh, stupid boy, you puppy, you with your pretty little mug! It's useless letting you near women, you just go, 'Katya darling, Katya darling!' "

Pavel, hanging his head low and shaking it, whispered something, and the short-cropped back of his head quivered quietly.

"You hear me? Do you?" the woman shouted.

Pavel glanced at her with wet, unseeing eyes and, like a man with a toothache, began to rock steadily back and forth. Scornfully harrumphing, the woman went over to the bed and started turning down the covers. As she went, her striped fustian skirt dropped off, and she kicked it away with her feet.

"Katya darling! Katya darling!" she said as she angrily crushed her pillow. "Go off then to your Katya darling! But I was baptised Manechka, and I've seen about a thousand puppies like you, and I was never once scared. Ugh! He thinks he gave me a rouble and I'm going to show him all kinds of tricks. But maybe I myself have three roubles in my box. Well, go on and come to bed, why don't you?

She lay down on top of the blanket and glared with hatred at Pavel, at the short-cropped and angled back of his head, shaking from his sobs.

"Ugh! You're all so tiresome, you filthy devils! You've

worn me out! What are you carrying on about? Afraid of your mummy?" she said with lazy and malicious scorn. "Afraid of getting a whipping? You're scared, but you do love sweets. You certainly do, don't you? I know you Percents, you devils. Ashamed to say his name, so he thinks one up. Percent! A dog's name, through and through. And when he goes off to his snivelling Katya darling, then he'll tell her to call him Vasya: 'Vasya, my love!' And he'll say, 'Katya, my sweet angel!' Oh, I know, he's a fine boy, that one! Permit me to kiss your hand, and I'll give your dirty face a good slap with that hand. Don't you laugh, you pup, don't laugh!"

Pavel said nothing and went on quietly shaking.

"Well, are you coming to bed or not? I'm talking to you! Or else I'll drive you out, God almighty, I'll drive you out! I don't mind losing the two roubles, but I'll not allow anyone to make fun of me. You hear me, get undressed! He thinks two roubles got him a whole woman! Ugh, a fine prince this one is!"

Pavel slowly unbuttoned his jacket and started taking it off. "You don't understand . . ." he quietly interjected, not looking at her.

"So that's how it is!" the woman shouted angrily. "Such a fool, I don't even understand anything! And what if I come over and punch you right in your mug?"

From behind the partition a hoarse and irritated bass gave a threatening shout: "Manka! You up to your tricks again, you Satan? Keep it down, or you'll get it lively! . . ."

"Be quiet, you bitch!" Pavel whispered, paling.

"A bitch, am I?" she answered hoarsely, starting up.

"All right, all right! Lie down!" Pavel said placatingly, keeping his eyes on her naked body. "I'm coming, I'm coming . . ."

"A bitch, am I?" the woman repeated, gasping and spraying spit.

"Take it easy," Pavel entreated. His fingers were trembling and he had trouble finding the buttons; he saw only her body—the terrible and incomprehensibly powerful body of a woman, a vision from his most torrid nightmares, so repulsive he wanted to trample it beneath his feet, and as enchanting as

278

a puddle of water to a man dying of thirst. "Take it easy, there," he repeated. "I was joking . . ."

"Get out of here!" the woman energetically rapped out, waving him off with her arms. "Go on! Go on! You pup!"

Their eyes met, and their glare burned with open enmity, so scorching, profound and so fully draining their sick souls, that it was as if they were not passing strangers who had chanced to meet, but had been enemies all their lives, had sought each other out all their lives, and finally—with wild, joyful disbelief—had met face to face. And Pavel became frightened. He lowered his eyes and mumbled, "Listen, Manechka! You've got to understand . . ."

"Aha!" the woman gloated, baring her broad, white teeth. "Aha! So it's Manechka now! Get out! Get out!"

She jumped up from the bed, and swaying, showing Pavel the thick, hairy back of her head, started to pick up his jacket. "Get out! Get out!"

"You hear me, devil!" Pavel shouted in a frenzy.

And all of a sudden a wild and surprising thing happened: the drunk, half-naked woman, red with rage, threw the jacket down, swung her arm and hit Pavel in the face. Pavel grabbed her by her blouse and tore it, and both of them began to roll all over the floor in a tangle. They rolled around, knocking over chairs and dragging the blanket off the bed after them, and they appeared to be a strange, fused being with four arms and four legs, frenziedly grappling and choking one another. Sharp nails scratched Pavel's face and dug into his eyes; for one second he saw above him an enraged face with wild eyes, and it was as red as blood; and with all his might he squeezed someone's throat. In the next second he broke away from the woman and scrambled to his feet.

"You dog!" he shouted, wiping his bloody face.

And people were already pounding on the door, and someone cried out, "Open up! You devils, you fiends!"

But again the woman threw herself at Pavel, knocking him down from behind, and once again they thrashed and circled all over the floor, silently, gasping, emitting weak cries of frenzied rage. They got up, fell down, and got up again. Pavel toppled the woman onto the table, and the bowl shattered beneath her heavy body, and near Pavel's hand clattered the long, dirty bread-knife. Pavel seized it in his left hand, barely managing to keep his grip on it, and thrust it somewhere into her side. And the fine sharp blade bent. A second time he thrust the knife in, and the woman's arms gave a shudder and suddenly went limp as rags. Her eyeballs nearly rolled out of their sockets, and she gave a hoarse, penetrating cry, right into Pavel's face, all on one note, the way animals cry when they are butchered: "A-a-ah!"

"Be quiet!" Pavel rasped hoarsely, and again he thrust the knife in somewhere, and again. With each blow the woman jerked like a wooden clown on a string, and she opened her mouth even wider, with its broad, white teeth now awash in bubbles of bloody foam. She was silent now, but Pavel still heard her piercing, horrible howl, and he rasped, "Be quiet!"

And shifting the knife from his wet, slippery left hand to his right, he struck from above once, and then a second time.

"Be quiet!"

The body slid heavily off the table and the hairy head struck the floor with a hollow thud. Pavel bent down and looked at it: the naked, protruding belly still rose and fell, and Pavel poked it with the knife the way one pokes a bubble to let the air out. Then Pavel stood back up, and with the knife in his hand, covered in blood like a butcher, his lip bloodied from the fight, he turned towards the door.

He dimly anticipated shouting, noise, frenzied cries, rage and revenge—and the strange stillness surprised him. There was not a sound, not a breath, not a rustle. The pendulum swung in the clock, and its motion was soundless; thick drops of blood slid off the blade of the knife onto the floor, and they ought to have made a sound but didn't. It was as if suddenly all the sounds in the world and all its living voices had suddenly broken off and died. And something mysterious and terrible was happening to the closed door. It soundlessly swelled out like the stomach that had just been pierced, trembled in soundless agony, and then sank back. And again it swelled out and sank back with a fading tremor, and each time this happened the dark crack at the top got wider and more ominous.

There was an ineffable horror in that mute and threatening onslaught—horror and a terrifying force, as if an entire alien, incomprehensible and evil world were silently and frenziedly forcing its way through the flimsy door.

With haste and concentration, Pavel threw off the sticky rags of his shirt and stabbed himself with the knife in the side, opposite his heart. For a few seconds he remained on his feet and looked with big, shining eyes at the convulsively swelling door. Then he bent over, dropped to all fours as if for a game of leapfrog, and collapsed . . .

That night, until dawn came, the cold city choked in the leaden fog. Its deep streets were unpeopled and silent, and in the garden, deserted now in the autumn, the lonely, doleful flowers were gently dying on their broken stems.

What will take place in your heart and mind,
When, loving mysteriously and tenderly,
You see a vampire in the twilight
With eyes as full as the boundless sea?
I see a woman. Her magical, terrible eyes
Hurled passion, like a flame, into my soul.
It seemed they concealed all the power
Of earth and heaven—but her heart was a stone.
She laughed the laugh of Satan,
And that laugh stung and repelled.
Her eyes flashed, full of joy;
In them some of each man's soul was left.
Oh, if I could throw myself upon her, greedily embrace her,
Drink up the vampire's passion, smother her with kisses,
Then kill her, tear her to pieces, and timidly lay the remains of
    her heart
At the feet of my idol, forgotten for an instant!

Alexander Blok, 1898

Her

She is as grey as dust, as earthly ashes
In her baseness, unscrupulous and pitiable,
And I am dying from this intimacy,
From her indivisibility from me.

She is rough, she is prickly,
She's as cold as a snake.   ·
Her repulsive, burning, coiled scales
Have branded me with pain.

Oh, if only I felt her sharp sting!
Sluggish, dull, silent.
So heavy, so flaccid,
And there's no reaching her—she is deaf!

Stubborn, she caresses me in her coils,
And strangles me in her hold.
And this dead thing, this black thing,
This dreadful thing—is my soul!

Zinaida Gippius, 1905

Calm

We are near the eternal end,
But we don't protest to the Creator . . .
No longer in the seer's mirror
Do we see death—but face to face.

All our lives, hopelessly,
Like moles blind from birth, in the dark,
Through narrow, bottomless fissures,
Groping, towards the grave we crawl,

Towards that black pit, towards that snare,
Where the unknown awaits.
We press on, as in a fevered dream,
Through life's cramped underground caves,

And we whisper: will the end come soon?
We submit to the Supreme Will,
And we do not clutch at life,
Like a drowning swimmer . . .

The brand of death on our foreheads,
We sought good in evil,
We sought truth in lawlessness,
We sought in chaos harmony.

Because God abandoned us,
Spurning the guardian angel,
We called on the spirit of temptation,
But the Devil too refused us aid.

Now we no longer summon anyone,
Before prohibited doors we skulk
Like pallid phantoms, lost,
We do not wait, and we do not knock.

We calmed down long ago:
There is no hope and no repentance,
And, full of silent despair,
We sink into the depths.

Dmitry Merezhkovsky, 1896

The Story of Sergey Petrovich

Leonid Andreyev

I

What Sergey Petrovich found most striking in the teachings of Nietzsche was the idea of the superman and everything Nietzsche said about the strong, free and bold of spirit. Sergey Petrovich didn't know German very well—only what he'd learnt in school—and he had a lot of difficulty with the translation. The work was facilitated considerably by Sergey Petrovich's fellow student Novikov, who had been his room-mate at school for a year and a half, and who had a perfect command of German and was well-read in philosophy. But in October of 189–, with only a few chapters of *Thus Spoke Zarathustra* left to translate, Novikov had been exiled from Moscow for scandalous behaviour, and Sergey Petrovich, now on his own, made very little progress. He didn't mind this in the least, however, for he was fully content with what he had already read, having learnt whole pages by heart—and in German at that. For in translation, however good it might be, the aphorisms lost much of their impact, becoming too simple and easy to grasp, so that it seemed possible to glimpse the very bottom of their mysterious depths; but when Sergey Petrovich gazed at the Gothic outlines of the German letters, he saw in every phrase not only its literal meaning, but also something words could not express, and their transparent depths would then darken and become bottomless. Sometimes he fancied that if a new prophet were to appear on earth, he would have to speak in a foreign language in order to be fully understood. He never did finish translating the end of the book—the only one of Nietzsche's works Novikov had left behind.

Sergey Petrovich was a third-year student in the faculty of natural sciences. He had parents, brothers and sisters (some older, some younger) in Smolensk. One of his brothers, the eldest, was already a doctor and earned a good salary, but he was unable to help support the family, as he had already started his own. Sergey Petrovich was thus obliged to live on fifteen roubles a month, and this sufficed, since he ate for free in the students' dining hall, didn't smoke and drank only a little vodka. Before Novikov had left, they drank an awful lot, but that didn't cost Sergey Petrovich anything, because Novikov covered the costs of their drinking bouts; he always had students who paid well for language lessons. Once, a local judge sentenced both companions to a fine of ten roubles—it was Novikov's fault, as he was fond of sitting, drunk, in the branches of the trees lining the boulevard, and Sergey Petrovich would scramble up after him—and it was Novikov who paid the fine. Given their unaffected friendship, this was completely natural and no one thought twice about it, except for Sergey Petrovich himself. But the absence of money was a fact he had to accept.

There were other facts that he had to accept as well, and when Sergey Petrovich examined his own life more closely, he reckoned that it, too, belonged in that category. He was ordinary-looking—not ugly, but plain, like hundreds and thousands of other people. His flat nose, thick lips and low forehead made him look like other people and blurred the individuality of his face. He hardly ever went near a mirror and even combed his hair without looking; and when he did look in a mirror, he would gaze deeply into his own eyes, which he thought looked murky, like pea soup through which a knife could easily penetrate to the very bottom without hitting anything solid. In that respect, as in many others, he differed from his friend Novikov, who had sharp-sighted, bold eyes, a high forehead and a fine-featured, handsome oval face. Sergey Petrovich's own tall body seemed to him not an asset, but a flaw, if it had to carry a head like his, and perhaps that was why he hunched over when he walked. But the hardest fact of all for Sergey Petrovich was that he was not smart. In school his teachers considered him downright stupid and in the first few years they had said so straight out. Once, an inarticulate response provoked the priest to call him a "Smolensk-and-Mogilev muddlehead," and even though the nickname didn't stick to him personally, but became a common noun applying to any dull student, Sergey Petrovich never forgot its origin. And it seemed he was the only one in the whole class who never did get a nickname, if you don't count the name "Sergey Petrovich," which everyone—teachers, pupils and custodians—called him. There just wasn't anything special about him that could lend itself to a clever sobriquet. At the university his peers, who very much liked to divide their fellow students into groups according to intelligence, put Sergey Petrovich in the ranks of the "shallow," although they never said so straight to his face; but he figured it out on his own, because no one ever approached him with a serious question or conversation, but only with jokes. But as soon as Novikov showed up, the conversation would turn immediately to serious topics. At first Sergey Petrovich tacitly protested against the general view of him as shallow, and tried to do, say or write something intelligent, but nothing except laughter ever came of it.

Then he himself became convinced of his shallowness. He was so firmly convinced of it that, had the whole world hailed him as a genius, he wouldn't have believed it. For the world did not and could not know what Sergey Petrovich knew about himself. The world might possibly hear an intelligent thought from him, but it might not know that Sergey Petrovich had stolen that thought, or else acquired it through inordinate effort, which rendered the thought totally worthless. What others learnt without even trying cost him excruciating effort and even at that, even when it was pounded into his memory for good, it remained alien and extraneous, as though it were not a living idea, but a book that had ended up in his head, banging its corners painfully into his brain. The especial likeness to a book was accentuated by the fact that the page on which he had read the idea always stood clearly and distinctly beside it. Meanwhile, the ideas that didn't have pages beside them, and which therefore Sergey Petrovich considered his own, were the most simple, ordinary and unintelligent ones, and they were exactly like thousands of other ideas on earth, just as his face resembled thousands of other faces. It was hard to accept this fact, but Sergey Petrovich finally did. In comparison with that, the other disturbing facts—his lack of talent, weak chest, clumsiness and pennilessness—seemed trivial.

So gradually that he himself didn't notice, Sergey Petrovich became a dreamer, a naïve and rather shallow one. He might fantasise about winning 200,000 roubles and taking a trip around Europe, but he couldn't picture anything beyond boarding the train, because he had no imagination. Or he would think about some kind of miracle that would suddenly make him handsome, intelligent and irresistibly attractive. After an opera he would imagine that he was a singer; after a book, a scholar; after leaving the Tretyakov Gallery, an artist; and in each scenario there was always a crowd: "them"— Novikov and the others—and they would all bow down before his beauty or talent, and he would make them happy. Whenever Sergey Petrovich entered the dining hall with his long, uncertain steps, hanging his head in his faded cap, it never occurred to anyone that at that very minute this insignificant student with the flat, ordinary face possessed all the world's treasures. In the dining hall he would sit hunched over and hastily swallow his modest meal, and whenever a student he knew walked by, looking for an unoccupied spot, he tried to look in some other direction. He was afraid of those sorts of meetings, since he never knew what to say, and he would sit in silence, feeling awkward. The daydreams that recurred so often began to take on a shade of reality, but the more clearly Sergey Petrovich saw what he might become, what he wanted to become, the more difficult it became to accept the harsh fact of his life.

His detachment from the world of living people was happening just as imperceptibly, and Sergey Petrovich suspected it least of all. With the social habit ingrained in him from his schooldays, he took part in all student organisations and dutifully attended meetings. There he would listen to speakers, joke when he was joked with, and then put his "aye" or "nay" on a scrap of paper, or more often decline to vote, since he couldn't decide in such a short time which side was in the right. But as a rule his decisions were always based on the opinion of the majority, and blended in with it. Sergey Petrovich made social calls as well, and he would always drink with his hosts and the other guests. Then he would sing along with them in his hollow, booming voice, kiss them and be kissed, and go to the brothels. These were the only women he knew, and at that only when he was drunk. When he was sober, they aroused only loathing and fear in him. He never sought out other women, the pure and good kind, since he was certain that not one of them would like him. He knew some of the women students, and he blushed, bowing, when he met them in the street, but they never spoke to this limited and plain-looking student, although they knew, as everyone did, that his name was Sergey Petrovich. Thus, to all appearances he was not one of those isolated students who lived their solitary, secluded lives and appeared only at exams with dismayed expressions and a mass of written summaries, but in reality he utterly lacked the vital connection with people that makes their society desirable and necessary. And he did not love a single one of those with whom he joked, drank vodka and exchanged kisses.

When Sergey Petrovich was not daydreaming or busy, he read a lot and indiscriminately, for the sole purpose of banishing boredom. He did not enjoy reading; serious books had too much in them he did not understand, and novels were either too lifelike and sad as life itself is, or else they were false and not true to life, like his daydreams. He might dream about winning millions, but when he read about such an event in a book, it made him feel laughable and pathetic for having such dreams. Russian novels seemed like true stories to him, but it was painful to read them if he thought about how he himself was one of those small people, ground down by life, about whom those thick, depressing books were written. But there were two novels—both translations—that he loved to read and reread. One of them he liked to read on sad, dreary days, when autumn, dolefully weeping and sighing heavily, looked through the windows and into his soul, and he was ashamed to mention this book. It was *20,000 Leagues under the Sea* by Jules Verne. What attracted him to it was the mighty and elementally free character of Captain Nemo, who had turned his back on people for the unfathomable depths of the ocean, from whence he arrogantly scorned the earth. The other book was Spielhagen's *In Rank and File*, and he liked to talk about it with his fellow students and was glad when they, too, ecstatically yielded to the noble despot, Leo. Subsequently, on the advice of Novikov, who had noticed Sergey Petrovich's love for great men, he began to read their biographies; and he read with interest, but nonetheless invariably thought to himself: he was not like me. And the more he learnt about great men, the smaller he himself became.

And so Sergey Petrovich reached the age of twenty-three. In his first year at university he failed physics, and from then on he began to work in earnest. And since in the faculty of natural sciences there is plenty of work to do, time passed swiftly in labour's iron embrace. The acute pain occasioned by sad thoughts about his failed life gradually eased, and Sergey Petrovich became accustomed to being an ordinary, unintelligent and unoriginal man. Sergey Petrovich's mind was on the borderline of stupidity and intelligence, and from there it was equally easy to see in both directions: to contemplate the supreme nobility of a mighty intellect, understanding what happiness it gives its possessor, and to see the pathetic vulgarity of self-satisfied stupidity, happy behind the walls of its thick skull and as invulnerable as in a fortress. And now he looked more often to that side, and saw that there were many people worse than he, and the sight of those people made him feel glad and at peace. Sergey Petrovich began to read less and drink more vodka, but he drank not a lot all at once, as he used to, but just a glass with lunch and dinner, and it was better that way, being merely pleasant and enjoyable, without the painful effects of a hangover. In the summer, in Smolensk, he had his first love affair, which was highly amusing for everyone else, but for him it was pleasant, poetic and new. His heroine was the girl who came regularly to weed the garden beds, and she was plain-looking, stupid and kind. Sergey Petrovich did not know why she liked him and he felt slightly disdainful towards her for her love, but he liked the secret meetings in the dark garden, the whispering, and the fear. As he was leaving that autumn for Moscow, she wept, and he felt like a new man, proud and pleased with himself, since he, too, had turned out to be no worse than others: he, too, had a real woman who loved him for free and wept at their parting. Like many other people, Sergey Petrovich gave no thought to the fact that he was alive, and he stopped noticing life, and it flowed along and was trivial, shallow and dull, like a marsh stream. But there were moments when he would wake up as if from a deep sleep and realise with horror that he was still the same old shallow, insignificant man; then he would have suicidal fantasies for whole nights at a time, until his angry and demanding hatred towards himself and his fate gave way to peaceful, meek compassion. And then life would again take over, and once again he would remind himself that he had to accept the facts of life.

Just as it seemed both possible and probable that he would resign himself fully to the facts, Sergey Petrovich became friends with Novikov. Their fellow students did not understand this strange intimacy, since Novikov was considered the smartest, and Sergey Petrovich the dullest of the students from Smolensk. Eventually they decided that the arrogant and vain Novikov wanted a convenient mirror to reflect his brilliant mind, and they laughed at his choice of such a cheap, crooked one. They considered Novikov's protestations that Sergey Petrovich was not at all as stupid as he seemed to be an expression of that very arrogance. Perhaps it was indeed so, but Novikov was so very reserved and tactful about showing his superiority that Sergey Petrovich came to love him. And this was the first person he had ever loved and the first friend life had given him. He was proud of Novikov, and he read whatever books he was reading, humbly followed him to various restaurants, climbed up trees, and thought about the good luck that had allowed him to be the friend of a man who was destined by fate for great things. With respectful amazement he followed the feverish activity of Novikov's mind, which left philosophical, historical and economic theories behind it like milestones and boldly surged ahead, always ahead. Sergey Petrovich pathetically trotted along after him, until he realised that with each passing day he was falling further and further behind. And it was a hard day when Sergey Petrovich, who had wanted to drown his own "I" in someone else's deep, strong "I," realised that this was impossible, and that intellectually he was just as far from the friend with whom he lived as from those great men he had read about. It was Nietzsche who helped him realise this—and it was Novikov who introduced him to Nietzsche.

II

When Sergey Petrovich had read through part of *Thus Spoke Zarathustra*, he felt as if the sun had finally risen in the night of his life. But it was a dreary, midnight sun, and it shone not on a joyful scene, but on the cold, deathly and dreary wilderness that was Sergey Petrovich's soul and life. But it was light nonetheless, and he rejoiced in the light as he had never in his life rejoiced about anything. At that time in Russia, not so very long ago, only a few people knew of Nietzsche, and neither newspapers nor journals had a word to say about him. And the profound silence surrounding Zarathustra made his words meaningful, forceful and pure, as if they had fallen straight out of the sky and onto Sergey Petrovich. He did not know who Nietzsche was and did not think about whether he was old or young, alive or dead. He saw before him only thoughts shrouded in the severe and mystical form of Gothic letters, and this detachment of the thoughts from the mind that had created them, from everything on earth that had accompanied their birth, made them seem divine and eternal. And like an ardent believer, a youthful pagan priest upon whom a long-awaited deity had descended, he tried to keep his deity safe from the eyes of outsiders and was pained when it was touched by rude, bold hands—like Novikov's.

Sometimes in the evening, after they had translated several chapters together, Novikov would begin to talk about what they had read. He sat at his table as if it were a rostrum and spoke in ringing tones, clearly and distinctly, articulating each word separately, making logical emphases and observing punctuation marks with short pauses. His large, short-cropped head, resembling a chiselled sphere except for the prominent protuberances on the forehead, sat firm and unmoving on his short neck. His face was always pale, and even when he got extremely agitated only his protruding ears would flame red, like two scraps of red calico stuck to a yellow billiard ball. He spoke of Nietzsche's predecessors in philosophy, of the connections of his teachings to the century's economic and social trends, and he maintained that Nietzsche had leapt a thousand years ahead with his basic thesis of individualism: "I will." Sometimes he scoffed at the book's obscure language, which seemed mannered to him, and Sergey Petrovich would protest feebly. What Novikov was saying seemed very intelligent to him—he himself would never have been able to think it up—but it wasn't the real truth. And Sergey Petrovich felt that he had a better and more intimate understanding of Zarathustra's words, but when he began to try and explain them, it came out flat and pathetic and not at all like what he meant. And he would fall silent, angry at his tongue and head. But sometimes it happened that Novikov got carried away by the beauty of Zarathustra's rhythmical speech and fell under the influence of what was left unsaid. Then he would recite in his clear, strong voice, and Sergey Petrovich would listen enraptured, with his plain, flat head lowered, and every word would burn itself into his sleepy, dull brain.

Sergey Petrovich did not notice the moment when the tranquil contemplation of the facts and the dull melancholy of accepting them came to an end within him. It was as if someone had lit the fuse to a powder keg, and he did not know how long the fuse had been burning. But he knew who had lit it. It was the vision of the superman, that incomprehensible but nonetheless human being who had fully realised his inherent potential and attained his rightful strength, happiness and freedom. It was a strange vision. Bright to the point of pain in the eyes and heart, it was murky and uncertain in its outlines; wonderful and inscrutable, it was simple and real. And by its bright light Sergey Petrovich examined his life, and it appeared totally new and interesting, like a familiar face in the glow of a fire. He looked at what lay ahead and behind him, and what he saw was like a long, narrow, grey corridor, devoid of air and light. Behind him the corridor disappeared into the grey memories of a joyless childhood; ahead it was lost in the twilight of a comparable future. And along the whole length of the corridor not a single sharp, sudden turn could be seen, not a single door to the outside, where the sun shone and living people laughed and cried. All around Sergey Petrovich, grey shadows of people floated down the corridor, devoid of laughter and tears and soundlessly nodding the dull heads that cruel nature mocked so pitilessly.

Until Novikov left Moscow, Sergey Petrovich did the same work day after day and compared himself with his companion, in whom he seemed to catch a glint of the superman. He observed his face, movements and thoughts and blushed when Novikov caught his dull but attentive glances. Late in the night, when Novikov was already asleep, Sergey Petrovich listened to his quiet, even breathing and thought that Novikov even breathed differently from him. And that sleeping man, whom he used to love, now seemed to him alien and mysterious, and everything about him was a riddle: his deep breathing, and his thoughts, hidden beneath the bulge of his skull, and his birth and death. And it was incomprehensible that two men were lying there under one roof, but that for each of them everything was different, separate and unlike the other's; each had his own thoughts and life.

Sergey Petrovich felt no grief when Novikov was sent away from Moscow. Those twenty-four hours Novikov spent with him, packing his things and cursing, passed by unnoticed, and then the two of them were at the train station. They were sober, since there was only enough money for the journey.

"I shouldn't have given you Nietzsche, Sergey Petrovich," said Novikov with that stiff politeness that was one of the oddities of their life together and never left them even in their drunken moments in the trees lining the boulevard.

"Why, Nikolai Grigorevich?"

Novikov was silent, and Sergey Petrovich added, "It's not likely that I'll be reading him. I've had enough already."

The third bell rang.

"Well, good-bye."

"Will you write?" Sergey Petrovich asked.

"No. I don't like to write letters. But you write to me."

After a moment of indecision, they embraced each other awkwardly, not knowing how many kisses were necessary, and Novikov departed. And, now alone, Sergey Petrovich realised that he had long wished for and anticipated this day, when he would be alone with Nietzsche, and no one would disturb them. And indeed, from that moment on no one did.

III

To all outward appearances, Sergey Petrovich's life changed drastically. He stopped going to his lectures and his laboratory altogether and put to one side the thesis he had started writing, "Comparative Characteristics of Fatty and Aromatic Hydrocarbons." He also stopped visiting his fellow students and showed up only for student meetings, and then only briefly. On one occasion a large group of students went to the brothel and found Sergey Petrovich there, and the amazing thing was that he was completely sober. As in the past, he blushed when they started to make fun of him, and when he got drunk he started singing and babbling in his tongue-tied way about some Zarathustra. In the end he started to cry, and then wanted to fight, and he called them all idiots and himself a superman. After that episode, which fuelled a lot of laughter, Sergey Petrovich was for some time completely lost from view.

Since the day of his birth, Sergey Petrovich's head had

never worked so much and so hard as during those short days and long nights. His bloodless brain refused to obey him, and instead of the truth he sought, it produced standard formulas, concepts and phrases. Worn out and exhausted, he was like a workhorse carrying a heavy load up a hill, unable to catch its breath and falling to its knees until the cruel whip urged it on. And the whip was his vision, the mirage of the superman who had attained his rightful strength, happiness and freedom. For minutes at a time a dense fog would enshroud his thoughts, but then the superman's rays would dispel it, and Sergey Petrovich would see his life as clearly and distinctly as if it had been sketched or described by another person. These were not thoughts, strictly logical and expressed in words—these were visions.

He saw a man called Sergey Petrovich, who was barred from everything that makes life happy or bitter, yet profound and human. Religion and morality, science and art all existed—but not for him. Instead of a passionate and active faith, the kind that moves mountains, he sensed in himself a shapeless lump, where ritual habit entwined with banal superstitions. He was not so bold as to renounce God, and not so strong as to believe in Him, and he didn't have the sense of morality and the emotions that go with faith. He didn't like people and could not experience that great bliss, the equal of which the earth has never yet created: to work for people's sake and to die for them. But he could not hate them, either, and he was fated never to experience the searing pleasure of battling against others like himself and the demonic joy of victory over principles sacrosanct to all people. He could neither raise himself up so high, nor fall so low as to rule over life and people—in the first case standing above their laws and himself creating them, in the second being beyond all that people found so necessary and terrifying. Sergey Petrovich read in the newspapers about people who murdered, stole and raped, and each time his reading ended with the same recurring thought: but I couldn't do that. On the street he met people who had sunk to the very bottom of the sea of human existence, and here, too, he would say: but I couldn't do that.

Occasionally he would hear and read about heroic people who met their death in the name of an idea or of love, and he would think: but I couldn't do that. And he envied them all, both the sinners and the saints, and his ears would echo with the pitiless, true words of Zarathustra, "If you are failing in life, if a venomous worm is devouring your heart, know this: in death you shall succeed."

Sergey Petrovich felt no need to commit evil, but he did want to be good. Books and people had instilled in him this desire, which was strong, but fruitless and agonising, like the agonising thirst for light felt by a man blind from birth. He thought about his future, and there was no place in it for good. When he graduated from the university, Sergey Petrovich planned to work in the Customs Service, but no matter how hard he thought, he could not figure out what good he would accomplish as a customs clerk. He could already imagine what he would be like: honest, thorough, hardworking. He saw how he would slowly and steadily climb the ladder of promotions, and having achieved a middling rank, there he would stay, beaten down by the passing years, his scarce means and illness. He realised that his merits in the face of life's cruelties would be appreciated, and that he would celebrate his thirtieth anniversary of civil service, as his father had not long ago. At the celebration speeches would be given, and he would listen to them and weep with emotion, as his father had wept, and kiss and be kissed by little old grey-haired men just like him, who themselves had been or would be similarly honoured, men chewed up and spat out by life. Then he would die with the thought that he was leaving behind a dozen children who were just like him, and the *Smolensk News* would print a short obituary, which would say at the end that a useful and honest worker had died. And this eulogy already seemed bitter and painful to Sergey Petrovich, like the lash of a whip on living, naked flesh. And it was painful because people, wanting to tell a pleasant fib, told the offensive and indisputable truth. And Sergey Petrovich thought that if people always understood what their tongues pronounced, they wouldn't dare talk about other people's usefulness and thus insult the already insulted.

Sergey Petrovich did not immediately understand what made him useful, and for a long time his brain thrashed and shuddered under the pressure of a labour beyond its strength. But then the fog was dispersed beneath the bright rays of the superman, and what had been an insoluble riddle became simple and clear. He *was* useful, useful by virtue of his many qualities. He was useful for the marketplace as that nameless "someone" who buys boots, sugar and kerosene, and as part of the masses that build palaces for the strong of the earth; he was useful for statistics and history as that nameless unit that is born and dies, and on the basis of which the laws of population movement are studied; he was useful for progress, too, since he had a stomach and a body sensitive to cold, thus sending thousands of wheels and machines into humming activity. And the more Sergey Petrovich walked the streets and looked around and behind himself, the more obvious his usefulness became. And at first he found it an interesting discovery, and with new curiosity he gazed at the homes of the wealthy and their luxurious carriages, and he took the omnibus an extra time on purpose so as to provide someone with the usefulness of his five-kopeck piece, but it soon began to bother him that he couldn't take a step without being useful to someone, since his usefulness was beyond his control.

And then he discovered in himself another kind of usefulness, and this was the most bitter and insulting of all, and it caused him to blush with shame and pain. It was the usefulness of a corpse, with which the laws of life and death could be studied, or the usefulness of a helot, made drunk so that others would see how bad it is to drink. Sometimes at night, during this period of spiritual rebellion, Sergey Petrovich imagined the books that would be written about him or men like him. He clearly saw the printed page, many printed pages, and on them his own name. He saw the people who wrote these books, who founded their fortunes, happiness and fame on him, on Sergey Petrovich. Some would tell about how pathetic he was, no good for anyone or anything; they weren't laughing at or making fun of him—no, they were trying to depict his sorrow so pitifully so that people would weep, and his joy so they would laugh. With the naïve egoism of sated, strong people who conversed with other strong people, they would try to show that there was something human even in such beings as Sergey Petrovich; they would argue passionately that such as he felt pain when they were beaten and pleasure when caressed. And if these writers were talented and succeeded in showing what they wanted to show, monuments would be raised to them, the pedestals of which would seem to be granite, but would actually be made of innumerable Sergey Petroviches. Other people would also feel sorry for Sergey Petrovich, but their discussions about him would be based on what the first group had said, and they would assiduously argue about the origins of such people and what to do with them, and what steps were necessary to prevent this type of thing in the future.

He was useful to the capitalist as the source of his wealth, to the writer as a step to his monument, to the scientist as a unit of measure that would bring him closer to the discovery of the truth, to the reader as an object for the exercise of charitable feelings—this was the usefulness Sergey Petrovich found in himself. And his whole soul was overcome by shame and the blind rage of a man who, long unaware that people were making fun of him, turns around and sees their bared teeth and pointing fingers for the first time. Life, which he had long ago accepted as a fact, looked him straight in the face with her deep eyes, and they were cold, serious and horrifyingly inscrutable in their severe simplicity. All that had until now haunted him dimly and manifested itself in indistinct daydreams and dull longing, suddenly spoke loudly and imperiously. His "I"—the one thing he had considered uniquely true and independent from both his weak brain and his dull heart, rose in indignation within him and demanded everything to which it had a right.

"I don't want to be mute material for the happiness of others: I want to be happy, strong and free myself, and that is my right," uttered Sergey Petrovich, articulating the secret thought that haunts the minds of many people and makes them unhappy, but is spoken aloud so rarely and with so much difficulty.

And at that moment, when he pronounced that clear and exact phrase for the first time, he realised that he was pronouncing judgment on what people called "Sergey Petrovich," and that he could never be either strong or free. And he rebelled against nature, which had so depersonalised him, revolted like a slave whose chains had chafed his body to bloody sores, but who had long been unaware of the humiliation of his abject servitude as he submissively bowed his back beneath the overseer's whip. He felt like a horse that had miraculously been given human consciousness and intelligence at the very moment when the whip scourged its back, but possessed neither the voice nor the strength to protest. And the longer, heavier and more pitiless the oppression became, the more furious was the rebel's rage.

It was during this period that Novikov received his first letter from Sergey Petrovich, very long and barely comprehensible, since Sergey Petrovich was in absolutely no condition to couch all that he saw so clearly and plainly in the form of thoughts and words. And Novikov did not answer the letter, since he did not like to write letters and was much too busy with drinking, books and language lessons. However, he did tell a friend of his, whom he was taking around with him to various pubs, about Sergey Petrovich, about the letter and about Nietzsche, and he laughed at how Nietzsche, who loved the strong so much, was being turned into a proselytiser for the poor in spirit and the weak.

The first consequence of his outrage was that Sergey Petrovich turned back to his half-forgotten and naïve dreaming. But he no longer recognised his dreams, so altered were they by the consciousness of his right to happiness. And despairing of himself as a human being, Sergey Petrovich began to wonder whether happiness might nonetheless be possible for him even under the given circumstances. After all, happiness is so vast and multifaceted; a man denied the possibility of being happy in one thing will find his happiness elsewhere. And the answer Sergey Petrovich found for himself persuaded him to revolt against people as he had already rebelled against nature.

IV

Sergey Petrovich lived not far from the Smolensk students' dining hall in a big, four-storey building, populated from top to bottom by women who let rooms of their flats and the students who rented them. He had a small but clean room, and his flatmates turned out to be quiet people, not drinkers, so the atmosphere was equally conducive to studying and thinking. If there was anything unpleasant about it, it was the constant smoke from the kitchen in the mornings. But Sergey Petrovich had quit studying, and for most of the day his room remained empty and dark.

He walked an awful lot, untiringly, and his tall, thin figure in its faded cap could be met with on all the streets of Moscow. One freezing cold, but sunny day he made it all the way to Sparrow Hills, and from there looked a long time at Moscow, blanketed in rosy fog and smoke and the sparkling veil of its river and gardens. It was easier to think while walking, and moreover what he saw eased the work of thought, just as an illustration in a text helps weak minds grasp what is written. Like a landowner who has realised that he is ruined and takes one last tour around his estate, summing up the sad losses, Sergey Petrovich did his summing up, and his totals were equally sad. Everything he saw conveyed that relative happiness was a possibility for him, too, but at the same time he would never be truly happy—never.

There was only one thing that could make Sergey Petrovich happy: possession of what he loved in life and deliverance from what he hated. He did not believe Hartmann—who was always sated and insisted that possession of what one desired could only result in disappointment—and he thought, as did Novikov, that the philosophy of pessimism was created to console and deceive people who were deprived of everything other people had. And he was sure that he could achieve happiness, if only someone would give him money—that freedom that wanders the world and is minted by slaves for their masters.

Sergey Petrovich was industrious by nature, but he did not like work and suffered beneath its weight, since his work was never the kind that can be pleasurable. In school he had had to study things that were uninteresting and alien to him, and sometimes even contrary to his reason and conscience—and then the work became torture. At university the work was easier, less hectic and more reasonable, but gave just as little pleasure to the intellect, and any lessons Sergey Petrovich now gave were just the flipside of those he'd had in school and just as much torture. And his future work as a customs clerk boded the very same joylessness and dutiful tedium. Only in the summertime, at home in Smolensk, did Sergey Petrovich find relief in simple, rude work: he did carpentry, made wooden rifles and arrows for his little brothers, fixed the garden fences and benches and dug the garden beds, turning up the spongy, lustrous earth with his burnished trowel. And this was a pleasure and a joy to do, but it wasn't the kind of work that was intended for the son of a civil servant with a good education. Other people who were miserable because their abilities were not suited for their work sometimes broke out of their moulds and did whatever they wanted, becoming workers, farmers or beggars. But those were strong and courageous people, of whom there are not many on earth, and Sergey Petrovich felt weak, diffident and controlled by some extraneous will, like a locomotive that only a catastrophe can wrench from the rails laid down by unknown hands. Moreover, he could not even imagine how he could possibly rid himself of his proper attire, his flat and his classes, and stagger down roads as a ragged beggar or walk behind the plough. And the first thing that could bring him closer to happiness would be freedom from his alienating and unpleasant labour. And he had the right to this freedom, since he had seen men like himself—born of woman the same as he, with nerves and a brain—who did no work at all and devoted themselves only to things that brought them joy.

"And what others have, I have the right to have," thought Sergey Petrovich in this period of rebellion against nature and people.

Why couldn't pleasurable occupations be found for him as well? The greatest joy for him would be coming to know nature. Not penetration into her deepest secrets—that would demand intellect—but unmediated knowledge by sight, smell and all the senses. He loved living nature with a tender and even passionate, but deeply hidden love, which no one but Novikov suspected. The smallest blade of grass in the spring, the white trunk of a birch emerging from the soft, fragrant earth, with black, thin little twigs clinging to its soft breast— these things riveted his attention and made his heart rejoice. He did not understand why he so loved this black earth, though she had caused him so much sorrow, but when he caught sight of the first patch of earth freed from the cold, dead snow in the springtime, and seeming to breathe beneath the sun, he felt like giving it a long, tender kiss, as one would kiss a beloved woman. And, fated to spend his entire life in a narrow, four-cornered box, on dusty, noisy streets, beneath the dirty urban sky, he envied the beggars whose sleep was guarded by the stars, and who knew and saw so much. But in his own life he had never seen and would never see anything but a birch tree, a little grass, shallow streams and small hummocks. Sometimes he would read beautiful and in all likelihood accurate descriptions of the sea and mountains, but his weak imagination would not be able to produce living images of them. And he wanted to see for himself if it was true that the sea is so deep and endless, whether it was blue or green or even red, whether tall waves travelled over it, while above them fluffy white clouds or black, terrifying storm clouds flew across a dark blue sky. And whether it was true that mountains are so high, sheer and forested, with blue, foggy cliffs, and glittering snowy peaks jutting into the green skies.

Was it true?

A deep, whistling breath from the depths of his dusty lungs lifted Sergey Petrovich's breast and drove the timid, yet rapturous smile from his flat face. And he envied even more than beggars those who possessed the sea and the mountains.

Once, as he was meandering about the city and picking out from the crowd those who were free and powerful and those who were forever deprived of freedom, Sergey Petrovich saw a shop sign showing a stereoscopic panorama, and he went over to have a closer look. It depicted the mountains, lakes and castles of Ludwig of Bavaria. The colour photographs passed one after the other before his eyes and were so alive and clear that he could sense the air and the high, blue sky, and the water sparkled like real water, and the forests and castles were reflected in it. A white steamship, festively decked out and sparkling clean, was raising foamy furrows with its bow, and men, women and children, dressed in their Sunday best, were standing or sitting on the deck, and it seemed one could even make out the joyous smiles on their faces. Then he saw a castle with gleaming white towers and notched terraces above the green forests that cascaded down into the valley, and he could see the inside of the castle as well: majestic halls, an endless number of paintings, the regal splendour of heavy brocade and velvet, and light pouring in through the high Gothic windows and slipping along the parquet floors. And in one of the windows, someone was sitting with his back to Sergey Petrovich, someone calm and indifferent, who was gazing down to where mountain peaks were all that could be seen against the bright sky. For some time Sergey Petrovich scrutinised the seated, motionless figure, and it seemed to him he could see everything the other man saw: forests, valleys and steely dark blue lakes, and he felt how clean and fresh the air that man was breathing must be. And it seemed to him that there, within those majestic halls with ceilings that receded into the distance like the sky, and windows from which half the world could be seen, there couldn't possibly be such a thing as melancholy and sorrowful thoughts. And the most important and most surprising thing Sergey Petrovich saw was this: he saw how the man sat with his leg oddly tucked up under himself with the sole of his boot sticking out in just the way Sergey Petrovich would have tucked up his own leg if it had been he, and that man was breathing mountain air and could wander through the majestic halls. With a sudden flood of rage and anguish, Sergey Petrovich ground his teeth and started forward, as if he were going to fling the motionless, seated fellow into the abyss below, and he banged his forehead and nose painfully against the frame that held the glass. And then he was ashamed at the thought that his rage was a pretence and predicated on the existence of the frame, and that if he had seen that fellow in reality, he would not have dared to lay a hand on him. Shy and humble, a man who shuddered at the sight of a butchered chicken, he was not even capable of rage.

When Sergey Petrovich stepped out of the panorama room onto the crooked, hunchbacked Moscow lane, from which yardmen were sweeping snow while drivers cut through on their sledge runners, the thought occurred to him that there were no facts a man was obliged to accept.

After nature came music and art in all the forms that Sergey Petrovich's limited understanding could grasp, and that could fill his life and make it interesting and varied. After these came romantic love, which his heart craved. At concerts, in theatres and on the street he saw beautiful, well-bred ladies, full of elegance and nobility, and he wanted their love. He remembered one of them, having passed her several times, and he dreamt of her, but she had never once even looked at him and did not even know he existed. He was disgusted when he remembered his love for the girl who weeded the garden beds and stank of manure and sweat, and it was disgusting to think of other women, just as coarse, who would love him and talk to him about roubles and their odious work. He painfully desired the love of that one woman, the one whose name he did not know, and who did not understand all that tormented him and people like him. And as a man who had never had money, he thought that it could give him love, and as a man who had never known romantic love, he thought that it could give him happiness.

It was just during this period that Sergey Petrovich paid a visit to the brothel, where he ran into his fellow students, and he purposely decided not to drink, so as to understand more clearly what falls to the lot of men like him in the world.

The more deeply Sergey Petrovich examined life, the more impotent and worthless nature came to seem in his eyes, so senselessly did she distribute her gifts. And in the place of debased nature another terrible and mighty power arose before his glazed eyes—money. Blinded, lost, he began to think that money had power even over nature. And his weak brain gave in to the deceit, and in his heart a new hope was kindled. He took a silver rouble out of his pocket and turned it in his hands with a feeling of strange curiosity and disbelief, as if he were seeing that glittering coin for the first time. They didn't fall out of the sky, these coins, and he had earned this one and could earn many more, and then he would have in his hands a mighty force with power over nature itself. And like every man who has had a flicker of hope, he began to think not about how to realise it, but about what he would do once it had been fulfilled. And these several days were a respite for Sergey Petrovich, and he climbed as high as possible, so as later to crash down to the ground all the more spectacularly, never to rise again. He took it as a given that he already had a million, and dreamt of the sea, of mountains and of the woman whose name he didn't know, and who hadn't the slightest inkling of his existence.

But it was impossible to stop the thought once it had begun working, urged on as it was by a whip as stinging as the vision of the superman—he who had attained his rightful strength, happiness and freedom. And once the thought had flashed in front of Sergey Petrovich's weary eyes, he discovered with amazement that, just as before, he was yielding to impossible, childish dreams. There were many paths to money, but in front of each was a stumbling block barring Sergey Petrovich's way. He could not steal any more than he could kill, since his actions were being directed not by his own mind, but by an alien, unknown will. The work he was capable of doing could not yield riches, and anything else—playing the stock markets, a factory, a job with a huge salary, art, marriage to a rich woman, anything that was permitted by the law and his conscience and would make him wealthy in a day or a year—none of this could ever be his, any more than intelligence could be. And when Sergey Petrovich realised that money would not rectify nature's injustices, but would only make them worse, and that people always finish off those already wounded by nature—despair crushed his hope, and darkness seized his soul. Life seemed to him to be a narrow cage, and her iron bars were many and dense, and there was only one way out.

And then a new period began in Sergey Petrovich's life. He stayed home all the time and went only to the dining hall, where he appeared only just before it closed so as not to meet any students he knew. Day and night he lay on his bed or paced back and forth, and his neighbours and landlady quickly got used to the monotonous sound of footsteps, such as is sometimes heard from prison cells: one-two-three forward, one-two-three back. A book lay on the table, and although it was closed and covered with dust, from inside it a calm, firm and merciless voice rumbled, "If you are failing in life, if a venomous worm is devouring your heart, know this: in death you shall succeed."

V

Since it was impossible to be the victor, the only answer was death. And Sergey Petrovich decided to die and thought that death would be his victory.

The thought of death was not new: it had occurred to him before, as it occurs to everyone whose path is strewn with stones, but it had been just as fruitless and unproductive as the dreams of having millions. Now, though, Sergey Petrovich saw it as a solution, and death became not merely desirable and possible—it was inevitable and imminent. A way out of the cage had opened, and although it led to darkness and the unknown, Sergey Petrovich didn't care. He dimly believed in a new life and was not afraid of it, since he would take with him only his free "I," dependent on neither a weak brain nor a dull heart, while his body would be spoils for the earth, and let the earth make a new heart and brain of it. And when he sensed in himself a calm readiness for death, for the first time in his life he experienced a profound, proud joyfulness, the joy of a slave breaking his chains.

"I am not a coward," said Sergey Petrovich, and this was the first praise he had ever heard from himself, and he accepted it proudly.

The thought of death ought to have dispelled all concerns for life and for his body, which no longer served any purpose. But the opposite was true for Sergey Petrovich: in the final days of his life he once again became the scrupulously neat and tidy man he had been before. He was amazed that he had allowed his room and desk to lie in disarray for so long, and he tidied up, putting his books back in order, the way they had always been in the past. He put the thesis he had started on the very top—subsequently it would go to Novikov—and in pride of place, *Thus Spoke Zarathustra*. He did not even open Nietzsche and was completely indifferent to the book, which, apparently, he had not finished, judging by the pencilled notes in the margins that went only as far as the middle of the third part. Perhaps he was afraid that he would find something new and unexpected there, and that this would destroy all his long and exhausting work, which had left the impression of a vivid and terrifying dream.

Then Sergey Petrovich went to the city bathhouse, swam in the cold pool with pleasure, and having run into a fellow student on the street, went with him to a pub, "Bavaria," where he drank a bottle of beer. At home, rosy from the baths, clean, in a white linen shirt, he sat for a long time over his tea with raspberry jam, then asked his landlady for a needle and began to mend the jacket of his uniform. It was an old one, tight and forever ripping at the armpits, and Sergey Petrovich had already had to mend it several times. His thick, awkward fingers had trouble gripping the small needle, which lost itself in the rotten grey material. Sergey Petrovich devoted several days to the preparation of potassium cyanide, and when the poison was ready, he gazed with pleasure at the little vial, thinking not about the death contained within it, but about how well he had done the work. The landlady, a little, dark woman who used to be someone's mistress, apparently suspected something, because she was very glad when Sergey Petrovich displayed signs of returning to his usual working life. She came into his room and nattered on at length about how bad it was for young people to be by themselves all the time, and she told him about a certain acquaintance of hers who had been a police officer with a good income, but took to drinking vodka to lift his black moods, and ended up at Khitrov Market, where he now writes petitions and letters for a glass of vodka. She subsequently retold the story about the police officer to all the students who came there, adding that even then she had noticed the similarity between her acquaintance's fate and Sergey Petrovich's.

"Stop by for some tea," she would invite Sergey Petrovich, without, however, any ulterior motive. "Or better yet, you ought to get out and see your mates. It isn't right how no one comes to see you, and you never go anywhere, either."

Sergey Petrovich followed her advice and made the rounds of almost all his fellow students, but did not stay anywhere for long.

Later the students maintained that Sergey Petrovich's descent into madness was already clearly evident, and they were amazed they had not noticed it at the time. Sergey Petrovich, usually reticent and shy even with his closest friends, now chatted about the most trivial things, and reminisced about Novikov as if he were his equal, even reproaching him for being superficial. Moreover, he was cheerful and laughed often. One rather young student had it that Sergey Petrovich even sang, but everyone said that this was an exaggeration. But they unanimously agreed that there was definitely something strange about Sergey Petrovich, and they didn't notice it at the time only because nobody ever paid much attention to him. And certain people, condemning the indifference and egotism of their fellow students especially harshly, raised an interesting question about that lack of attention: would it have been possible to save Sergey Petrovich at that decisive moment in his life? And they concluded that it certainly would have been possible—not by the force of someone's strong reason, but by the influence of someone close to him—his mother or a woman who might have loved him. They supposed that during that whole period Sergey Petrovich was in a state of mental torpor, like a hypnotic trance in which one's own or someone else's idea holds complete sway over one's will. Reason would not have relieved his state of mind, but love might have brought Sergey Petrovich to his senses. His mother's cry from the heart, the look on her face, so dear and beloved with all the little wrinkles he had known since childhood, her tears, which even a coarsened lout would have found unbearable to behold—all of this could have brought Sergey Petrovich back to reality. A kind and honest fellow, he would never have dared to bring death into his mother's heart and he would have gone on living, if not for himself, then for those who loved him. Many faint-hearted souls bent on suicide have been kept on earth by the knowledge that they are needed by those who love them, and they have gone on living after that, strengthened by the thought that it takes more courage to live than to die. And there have been even more who have forgotten why they wanted to commit suicide, and have even come to regret that life is so short.

And with renewed bitterness some of the students attacked others and angrily reproached them for their disgraceful indifference. A ten-word telegram sent to Sergey Petrovich's mother might have saved a human life. For those of the students who were always the first to see the social significance of any event, this case led to thoughts and discussions about the lack of connection among the students, the absence of shared interests and intellectual isolation. For a while self-improvement circles became popular, where books on social questions were read and reports written.

Sergey Petrovich had decided to kill himself on Friday, the 11th of December, when many of the students were planning to leave for the Christmas holidays. On the morning of that day he went to the post office, where he sent a hefty registered letter to Novikov in Smolensk, tucking the receipt away in his wallet. In the letter he reported his death and the reasons for it, the latter laid out in outline form, and the whole letter produced the impression that he was writing not about himself, but about some other fellow, whom he found rather boring. In the afternoon Sergey Petrovich had lunch at the students' dining hall, where he lingered a long time and talked with people he knew, and after lunch he slept, also for quite a long time and very soundly, so it was already after ten o'clock when he got up. The samovar was brought in, and the students on the other side of the wall heard the monotonous sound of pacing: one-two-three forward, one-two-three back. When the sleepy housemaid came late that night to take away the samovar and dishes, Sergey Petrovich kept talking with her, as if wishing she would stay a little longer, and—as she later said—he was very pale.

Sergey Petrovich in no way anticipated what would happen to him on this evening, which he thought would be the last of his life. He was completely calm and cheerful and he didn't think about death, just as on the other days. He started thinking about it only an hour or so before the moment he was to take the poison. And his thoughts came from somewhere far away, and they were fragmented and confused. First he thought about his landlady, and then about how he would be lying there and what he would look like. For a minute his thoughts got sidetracked to memories of childhood, and particularly the death of his uncle. He had died at their house, and they sent Sergey Petrovich—at that time seven-year-old Seryozha—to the home of family friends. As he crossed the entrance hall, already dressed for the journey, he glanced into the main room and saw the table where they always dined, and on it, facing him, the motionless soles of a pair of feet in white cotton socks. He saw them for only a second, but remembered them his whole life, and for a long time he imagined death itself exclusively in the form of the motionless soles of a pair of feet in white cotton socks. Then he remembered a relatively recent episode, when he had seen a very poor and very strange funeral. It was strange because not a single person on the whole street, neither passers-by nor drivers, paid it any attention at all, and it seemed that they did not even see it, since no one removed his hat. Four pallbearers carried the coffin, which was covered with something dark, and they marched in step and so quickly that the coffin was rocking as if on waves, and the edge of the cover lifted with the breeze each time the coffin sank down. And neither clergy nor bereaved were to be seen.

When Sergey Petrovich's mind returned from these memories, it became amazingly sharp, precise and bright, like a knife that had been honed. For another moment it hesitated indecisively, taking note of the surrounding quiet, the extinguished samovar, the ticking of the pocket watch on the table, and suddenly, as if it had found what it needed, it fashioned a picture of Sergey Petrovich's funeral that was so real, vivid and horrifying that he shuddered, and his hands got cold. With the same merciless, terrifying veracity it sketched the ensuing moments one after another: the black, crooked maw of the grave, the hard, cramped coffin, the greenish patina on his uniform buttons, and the process of his body's decomposition. And it seemed that it was not Sergey Petrovich himself doing the thinking, but rather as if before his eyes a gigantic hand was displaying in quick succession all the indescribable hues of his life and death.

And Sergey Petrovich woke up. He was so terrified he wanted to scream, and he stared with horror at the little vial and backed away from it, as if afraid that someone would pour the lethal poison into his mouth by force. And more than anything in the world he was afraid of his own self at this moment—of the horrifying disobedience of his own legs and hands. He backed away, but at the same time his whole body convulsively lunged forward, towards the vial. His feet, hands and mouth were filled—to their very blood and bones, it seemed—with the passionate, insanely powerful desire to snatch up the vial and rapturously, greedily swallow the poison.

"I won't! I won't!" Sergey Petrovich whispered, and he pushed himself away with his hands and backed up, but it seemed to him that he was approaching the vial, which was growing before his eyes. And when the door stopped him, he could no longer see in front of him, and he cried out and took a step forward.

At that moment the housemaid came in for the samovar, and took a long time gathering up the dishes, with which she had some trouble, as her eyes were closing from lack of sleep.

"What time shall I wake you?" she asked as she was going out.

Sergey Petrovich stopped her and started talking, but heard neither his own questions nor her answers. But when he found himself alone again, the phrase, "What time shall I wake you?" stuck in his mind, and continued to sound long and loud until Sergey Petrovich realised what it meant.

He realised that, like anyone else, he could undress and lie down to sleep, and he would be woken up tomorrow when the new day began, and Sergey Petrovich would live, as all people do, because he did not want to die, he would not die, and no one could force him to take the vial and swallow the poison. Still trembling, he grasped the vial, opened it purposefully, caught the scent of bitter almond, and carefully, his hand slightly trembling, placed it on the shelf where it was out of sight behind the books. Now that the vial had been in his hands and he had not died, he no longer feared either it or himself.

When Sergey Petrovich lay down in his bed, it seemed to him that the life that had been saved was rejoicing in every particle of his body, warm under the blanket. He stretched out the legs and hands that had all but committed the crime, and something seemed to be sweetly singing within them in a thin, joyous voice, as if his blood were rejoicing and singing that it had not become a slimy, rotting mass, but was streaming a happy red along its broad and free pathways. And as happy as could be, it filled his heart to the brim, and his heart sang together with it and beat out its own exultant hymn of life.

"Alive! Alive!" thought Sergey Petrovich, bending and unbending his obedient, flexible fingers. Let him be unhappy, persecuted, deprived of his rightful share; let everyone scorn him and mock him; let him be the lowest of the low, a

314

nothing, the dust people shake from their feet—but he would be alive, alive! He would see the sun, he would breathe, he would bend and unbend his fingers, he would be alive . . . alive! And this was such happiness, such joy, and no one would take it away, and it would continue for a long, long time . . . forever! An unending multitude of days ahead would light up at dawn, and every time he would be alive, alive! And suddenly for the first time in many days Sergey Petrovich remembered his father and mother and was horrified, and moved. In his mind he kissed the wrinkles where the tears would most certainly have run, and his heart was bursting with the triumphant victory cry: I'm alive, alive! And when he fell into a light, joyous sleep, the last thing he felt was the salty taste of a tear wetting his lips.

It was a cold, frosty day and the sun was shining when Sergey Petrovich awoke. For some time he didn't understand why his bed was made up as usual, and why he was alive beneath the sheets, when yesterday he was supposed to have died. His head was hurting a little, and his whole body ached as if it had been badly beaten. Gradually, thought by thought, he remembered all that had gone through his head yesterday, and he couldn't understand why he had been so terrified, and what had been so frightening about what he had always known and had pictured dozens of times in his head. Death, the funeral, the grave . . . well, and how else could it be when a fellow dies? Of course he would be buried and for that a grave would have to be dug, and the corpse would rot in the grave. And with wary attention he again went over all of yesterday's horrifying visions, but they were all faded and dim and fading more every moment, as happens with dreams that are terribly vivid at the first moment of awakening but then are quite quickly and completely effaced by the living impressions of reality and daytime. And there was nothing terrifying in the pictures of death, and the joy of living seemed incomprehensible and ridiculous.

And then a thought flashed through his mind, as if in answer to all his questions: he, Sergey Petrovich, was a coward and a braggart.

He remembered the letter he had sent to Novikov, in which he had informed him of his own death as a done deed, and he flushed with shame, and felt that the decision to die remained just as immutable, unwavering and irreversible as it had been yesterday, before he had given in to his faint-hearted, incomprehensible terror. The terror had disappeared, but burning shame lingered on, and with all the strength of his ravaged soul, Sergey Petrovich rose in revolt against the vanished terror, that most humiliating link in the long and heavy chain of the slave. The indifferent, blind force that had summoned Sergey Petrovich from the darkest depths of non-being had made a final effort to chain him to the stocks like a captured runaway, and had managed—even if only for a few hours— to do it.

The burning shame burst forth with renewed force, and its flame burnt the very memory of his momentary fit of terror to ashes. And when its glow dimmed, the dull, aching pain in his body also disappeared, and his whole body felt light, almost insubstantial. His head, too, had stopped hurting, and his mind began to work with incredible speed, force and clarity, as though feverish. His lips trembled from the desire to speak, and words Sergey Petrovich had never used and didn't know were springing to his tongue. And he was saying that if he remained alive now, he would despise himself, and he would be forced to drink such a full cup of self-hatred that in comparison the poison would taste like nectar. His "I," that independent and noble "I," which for a split second had felt itself the victor and experienced the unencompassable joy of a brave spirit's triumph over blind and despotic matter, would kill him if the poison did not do it. And it seemed to Sergey Petrovich that he felt in himself the powerful growth of his "I," he felt that it was rising high up, and the thundering peals of his voice deafened the pathetic squeaks of his body, which had been strong only in the night. Let whoever wants to bow down, but he was breaking his iron cage. And, pathetic, dull and unhappy man that he was, in that minute he was rising higher than any genius, king or mountain, higher than whatever on earth is high, because within him the most pure and beautiful thing in the world was victorious—the bold, free and immortal human "I"! The dark forces of nature could not defeat it; it reigned over life and death—the bold, free and immortal "I"!

What Sergey Petrovich was experiencing was like the proud and chaotic delirium of a megalomaniac, as some thought upon reading his third letter to Novikov, from which we just gave excerpts. He wrote it without getting dressed, on a scrap of paper—a laundry bill, as it turned out—and it reached Novikov only after passing through the hands of the police and the justice of the peace. Right there and then, without leaving the table, he swallowed the poison as well, and when the housemaid arrived with the samovar, Sergey Petrovich was already unconscious. The poison solution turned out to have been inexpertly made and was weak, and they managed to get Sergey Petrovich to Ekaterininsky Hospital, where his life ended only towards evening.

The telegram to Sergey Petrovich's mother got held up, and arrived after the funeral had already taken place. The students who had sent it to her reckoned this was just as well, since Sergey Petrovich, with his hollow, emptied skull and spots on his face, looked very ugly and even downright frightening in his coffin, and the sight of him might have been hard to bear. And all that was left of her son were his books and his second-hand clothes, among which was his worn suit jacket, torn at the armpits and freshly mended.

On the Eve of the Twentieth Century

Distant from others' concerns,
We despondently drag out our lives;
We are indifferent to what, hidden from us,
Always brings others delight . . .
Fate is tired of punishing us,
Without faith we drag out our lives . . .
It is so difficult for us to live,
It will be hard for us to die . . .
Thus, meeting a new line of centuries,
The old century, mercilessly rushing forward,
Hurls at them the cold enigma
Of mad, living corpses . . .

Alexander Blok, 1899

We are weary. Enough. Ever forwards
Nature has tirelessly drawn us . . .
We have returned: it seems we just left the dawn,
But again we stand beneath the rising sun . . .
We have trod the path of life to the end,
And the end is where we began . . .
But the Creator no longer sends us the support
That once adorned our path . . .
There it is—the sunrise we once knew!
But its cold fire no longer moves our souls . . .
We are weary. In vain we await our repose;
We no longer believe in hope . . .

Alexander Blok, 1899

The moon may shine, but the night is dark.
Life may bring happiness to some,
But the stormy weather in my soul
Will not be followed by the spring of love.
With a dead gaze, night,
Spread out above me, meets
The dull stare of a sick soul
Bathed in poison, acrid and sweet.
And vainly, suppressing passions,
In the cold, pre-dawn mist,
I wander through the crowd,
And a sole, secret thought persists:
The moon may shine, but the night is dark.
Life may bring happiness to some,
But the stormy weather in my soul
Will not be followed by the spring of love.

Alexander Blok, 1898

Orpheus

Alexander Kondratiev

"Teacher, I saw Mirrinia crying in the neighbouring grove today. She was beating her breast and swearing that there was no man on earth more unbending than you . . . She even threatened to commit suicide, like Teleboia . . . Why do you drive them away?"

"You desire to know, Haemonian, why I rejected the love of blue-eyed Mirrinia, why I chased away white-handed Teleboia when she came to me in a black cloak? My dear, can you really not have noticed that all women in the world are as nothing for me?"

"O thrice-great Orpheus, O my teacher, so many years have passed since you lost Eurydice. Can it be that even now your inconsolable heart still yearns for her?"

"No, my boy, I do not long for the wife I left behind in Tartarus. And if the god who rules the underworld were to release her once again to the surface of the earth and she were to come to me in Haemonia—believe me—I would only turn away from her in silence."

"Teacher, but didn't you love her? Or is the talk of how you descended to the depths of Hades for the sake of your wife just idle gossip? I have heard that terrible Pluto himself was touched by the music of your lyre and your sad song. I have heard that he allowed you to take Eurydice away, to the bright expanse under the curve of the azure sky. And only because you failed to heed his injunction not to look at her until you were completely out of Tartarus did the winged god Hermes draw her back down to black Hades . . . Isn't this true, son of the sweet-sounding Muse? . . . But forgive me, you are frowning, no doubt I've touched on an unhealed wound in your anguished heart."

For a time there was silence on the crown of the cypress-covered hill. Orpheus sat on the gentle slope. A large black panther lay near him amongst the motley flowers; purring, she arched her back against the singer's caressing hand. The twitching end of the bloodthirsty animal's tail beat playfully on the green grass. On the lower branches of a cypress hung the lyre of glorious renown. Hushed birds sat in the trees all around. They had come from afar to listen to Orpheus.

The Thracian now stopped caressing the animal, and fixing his gaze in the direction of the distant ravines, he spoke in a thoughtful tone, "You have been told the truth, O Antimachus, but not the whole truth. I repeat, if the woman I once called my Eurydice were to return from the dark realm, my heart would not ache with sweet pain. Women and girls no longer exist for me on this earth, washed with blue-green waves. They are all deceivers, and behind the contrived clarity of their gaze shines a dog-like, slavish baseness and a fear of the strong; at the bottom of their hearts lurks eternal lust, and they are forever seeking new embraces, new conquests! . . ."

"But surely, teacher, not your Eurydice?!"

"Yes, even she. I can never forget what happened in the land of the dead . . . When gloomy Pluto, giving in to Persephone's pleas, agreed to give Eurydice back and two nymphs from the dark waters of Lethe led her to me, I cast my attentive gaze over the face of the woman who had been my wife.

"She stood naked, pale, shyly lowering her lashes as if concealing the joy of the meeting with her husband.

" 'Here is your Eurydice! Hermes will escort you to the gates of the kingdom of oblivion. Your wife will follow behind you. But woe unto you if you glance back before you are out! . . . And you, son of Maia, approach so you may hear my commission to my aegis-bearing brother.'

"Hermes approached the king of the underworld, and the immortal gods whispered together for a long time, laughing and glancing now and then at Eurydice and me.

" 'You may go!' said the sovereign of Tartarus finally, and to the amazement of the mournful shades, we started on our way.

"With firm steps I made for the gates. My heart was bursting with the pride of victory. My fingers strummed the strings of my lyre, and our procession was accompanied by celebratory tones . . . Shades of the deceased silently made way for us. Their sad faces gazed apathetically at us from all sides. The gates were close now. An azure and lilac shaft of daylight cut into the gloom.

"I slowed my steps. Behind me it seemed to me I could hear whispers and kissing. I thought at first that it was only a test to make me turn around, and I drove off my suspicions. After another dozen steps I found myself at a turning, from beyond which a current of warm, fragrant air wafted against my face, and a piece of azure sky and flowery slopes and hills covered with forests met my gaze . . . Behind me all was quiet. But then from behind me I again caught the sound of quiet, smothered laughter and someone's drawn-out sigh . . . There could be no doubt. Only she sighed that way, my Eurydice, in the hours of our blissful embraces.

"Forgetting myself in my rage, forgetting Pluto's admonition, like an anthropophagous beast from faraway India, I threw myself back into the jaws of the gate to hell.

"Gods, what I saw there! Around the bend in the path, she, my Eurydice, my tender beloved with all her demure melancholy—like a wild satyress, in ardent ecstasy, was yielding to the caresses of perfidious Hermes . . .

"I stood as if carved in marble, frozen in horror. And only my eyes followed as the son of Maia, with insolent laughter, took the woman who had been my wife back into dark Hades.

" 'You defied the prohibition, son of Calliope, and therefore you'll never see your Eurydice again!' he cried, disappearing into the gloom.

"Clinging to the treacherous god, the white shade of my depraved wife obediently vanished with him.

"Not a single curse did I hurl after them.

"Without a word I lifted my lyre and quietly set off away from Tartarus among green hills and shady hollows. My path led me here, to thickly-wooded Thessaly . . . Here my heart is

not so heavy. Here I can only barely hear that deceitful femi-
nine laughter. Here the wind murmurs in the ravines; dark-
green pines nod their heads at me, and wild beasts follow at
my heels and rub their soft fur lovingly against my bare
knees . . ."

And as if wishing to show that she understood the poet's
speech, the black panther yawned and started tenderly licking
Orpheus's dust-covered feet with her long, pink tongue.

When she finished, she gave a stretch, arching her supple
back like a wave, and then settled back down, assuming a
tranquil pose and attentively fastening her yellow-green eyes
on the face of the Muse's son.

Orpheus and his disciple sat without moving. Around them
silence reigned. Only a single small bird timidly twittered
something in the branches of a cypress.

The Doomed

Secretly my heart prays for death.
Light heart, glide . . .
There, through snowy silver,
Paths have led me out of life . . .

As over that distant hole in the ice
Water sheds silent steam,
So with your silent step
Here you have guided me.

You led me, your arm around me.
Your eyes were my fetters.
Surveying me coldly,
You surrendered me to white death . . .

Where am I fated to languish,
Where is my soul to dwell,
If my heart desires death,
If it secretly prays for the depths?

Alexander Blok, 1907

God's moon is high,
        And I grieve.
The silence tonight
        Disheartens me.

Not a howl
        And not a bark;
All around
        It's still and dark.

The desolate streets
        Are mute and dead;
Not a whisper,
        Not a step.

Anxiously I sniff the ground
        In distress.
In the street I faintly catch
        A stranger's scent.

Footsteps waken no one,
        Yet I expect
A wanderer will come—
        Foe or friend?

Beneath the cold moon
        I am alone.
I cannot bear it, and I howl
        At the moon.

High is God's moon,
    So high.
Sadness, yearning overwhelm me
    Tonight.

Break the silence,
    Sisters, soon!
Howl and bark, I beg you,
    At the moon!

Fyodor Sologub, 1905

Pensive September luxuriously arrays
With crimson foliage the fading forests,
As a weeping mother would adorn
With flowers and brocades her dead daughter.
I contemplate the pale azure vault
Of the lifeless heavens, and I sense in their repose
The harmony of dying nature
And the mysterious, exhausted soul.

Dmitry Merezhkovsky, 1887

In Fog's Embrace

Alexander Kondratiev

A Myth

I, Epigenes of the island of Samos, will now relate to you, O people, what your fathers knew not: how Aphrodite, jealous of the sea goddess and spying on Leto's flowing-haired son, found herself in the embraces of Aerius, god of night fog.

The goddess's eyes flashed ominously as she flew low over the darkened waves to the place where the god Apollo had stolen away to be with cold-bodied, lithe Ostis. Dismal envy tormented the Cyprian goddess's heart, and as she silently descended she could hear her goddess-rival's sighs, full of sweet languor. The deep-blue eyes of the foam-born goddess of Paphos keenly penetrated into the evening twilight.

The golden-haired god was nowhere to be seen; he was ensconced beneath a cool canopy of underwater caverns and there, forgetting heavens and earth, he yielded to the capricious sea nymph's caresses.

It was quiet all around. A grey haze drew across the pale sky. The waves hissed and beat incessantly against the cliffs.

"I'm all alone," whispered the daughter of blood and foam. "I, who give an abundance of all-consuming passion to gods, animals and men! . . . The entire world is filled with my bliss-ful breath, while I, who give love to the world, have none myself!"

And the goddess stood mournfully above the sea on the crags of the desolate Troad, which was wrapped in joyless slumber.

"Once gentle Dardanian Anchises loved me here. I gave him a son, who then founded a mighty kingdom in place of ruined Troy! . . . Yes, that city is no more, and no more are the peoples who honoured my all-victorious name! No more do they burn incense for me among the colourful columns of my once-glorious temples. Neither do the youths spill for me the warm, wine-dark blood of white golden-horned heifers, and the joyous, resonant hymns in my honour no longer sound. The people who inhabit this country have forgotten the ancient, bright gods, and there is no one left for me to give the joy of mutual love!"

It was at that time that Aerius, the son of Darkness and Amphitrite, who had once deceived the sea god, crawled out of his seaside cavern in a pall of night fog and dived into his native element.

From his father he had inherited his sinuous legs, and from his divine mother his dark body's deep blue tint.

Full of dim longings, he swam to a seaside cliff, clambered up its sharp incline and sat down there in the darkness, his legs wound serpent-like around the slippery outcroppings of rock.

Then he caught sight of the goddess once honoured on the shores of Cyprus and at Paphos. With a flick of his long, dark, forked tongue, he licked his bloodless lips, and the naiads dozing in the hollow caves by the sea heard his thin, song-like whistle.

There were no words, only longing, only desire to wind his body about the whole earth and remain there unmoving . . .

Night was coming on. The goddess of dark and sleep spread her black, star-covered wings over the shores and sea.

In the distance sirens sang.

"Which god will give peace and oblivion to the world? Who will grant forgiveness to the fallen titans? Who, laying his hand upon the breast of Oceanus, will say to him, 'Enough, Old Man, you have wearied yourself with your endless sighs; leave off! . . .'? Who, O Mighty One, seeing Mother Gaia shrouded in melancholy, will gently whisper to her that blissful word, 'Sleep!'?"

From her place on the black crag at the edge of the sea, Aphrodite hearkened to the sirens as green and white foam caressed her shapely legs.

Those legs captivated Aerius.

The Son of Darkness, swimming like a snake among the crags, silently approached the goddess of Paphos.

Gathering up all his strength, he wrapped himself in an instant about the rock where the foam-born goddess sat, firmly gripping the goddess's white legs in his mighty coils.

Aphrodite was captured.

Dark and powerful, never loosening his tight embrace, the son of Darkness sat down beside his captive, the wrathful Cyprian goddess.

"Who are you, who dares to wrap his vile, wet tail about my splendid legs?" asked the queen of Paphos.

"He who in just a little while will wrap his arms around you as well, goddess," Aerius responded, suppressing his rising excitement.

The feel of her immortal body aroused a powerful trembling in his limbs.

"Who is the lamia or other daughter of sordid Tartarus, to whom the goddess of fate sent such a magnificent son?"

"My mother's name is Amphitrite, goddess . . ."

"Go away then, vile creature, back to your ocean deep and there fondle freely some walrus cow, but do not dare to cross the will of immortal goddesses!"

"What is the will of the goddesses to me! . . . And anyway, there is no time to argue! Ananke and Fate have granted me your luscious body for this day! Yield to me now, for I am sent by destiny!"

The son of Darkness wrapped his strong coils around the divine waist, firm white bosom and heavenly arms of the Cyprian goddess. She tried to resist, but to no avail. Lithe Aerius had already managed to press his cold, moist mouth to her hot lips.

She lay stretched out on the cliff top, helpless, trying not to see the snake-like visage of the god of fog . . . Suddenly a gleam of hope flashed in the goddess's eyes . . . Sparkling with gentle silver light, the chariot of Apollo's sister drifted lightly across the dark sky.

Artemis reined in her horses and glanced scornfully at the shame of the goddess she little loved.

331

The divine virgin's gaze was fixed on the dark tip of the fog god's tail as it beat playfully against the thighs of the powerless Cyprian goddess.

"Help me, daughter of gentle Latona," moaned the goddess of love. "The monster desires to gain my kisses by force!"

Without a word Artemis took her brightly shining spear and cast it at Aerius's body ... The sharp bronze pierced the coils, and dark liquid sprayed the weary white limbs of the captive goddess. The fog god's embrace immediately loosened.

With a hiss of pain, the son of Darkness flung himself from the crag into the salty waves and vanished without a trace among the rocks and caves lining the shore.

The daughter of blood and foam, her shapely limbs unsteady, stood up and blew the daughter of Leto a kiss.

"I thank you, dark-haired daughter of the Thunder God. Your aim is as sure as in the days when we smote the giants. Tell me, how can I repay you for your service?"

But without uttering a word, merely nodding her head in answer, Artemis, proud in her new glory, urged her fleet-footed black steeds onwards. Her chariot shone brightly. The fine spokes of the bright silver wheels spun easily, and soon a fluffy white cloud hid the goddess from view.

Aphrodite was alone once again. Around her the waves hissed hollowly and beat loudly against the rocks. To stay any longer by these sombre, empty shores would be unsafe, and dreary.

With a sigh, the Cyprian goddess vanished without a trace from the dark sky. The pure white walls of her airy temple and the lonely couch in her pink bedchamber were waiting.

* * *

The next morning she never left her palace, and with anxious hearts men gazed longingly at the foggy, grey veil that spread over the entire sky, seeking there the radiant dawn of her visage.

And it was only towards evening that she once again

appeared over the shores of the Troad. The waves sounded the same as ever as they broke with white, angry foam against the dark cliffs. The hills, covered with sleepy oak forests, were as desolate as ever, and the mute stretches of shoreline remained deserted.

As sorrowfully as ever, the virgin sirens sang their harmonious song.

Her bright gaze alighting on the cliff upon which she had so recently been violently threatened, the mother of Cupid paused and fell into mournful thought.

Downcast, the Cyprian goddess whispered to herself, "In the entire world, only one answered my call of immortal yearning, and he was a loathsome monster!"

Rain

O joyful autumn rain,
Ever falling—tomorrow and yesterday!
Always more carefree, always more perfect,
Monotonously playing.

Stout, dirty, and tearful
The heavens sink.
The voices of the rain
Are joyful, whispering.

Never tiring, they speak endlessly
Of decay and decomposition,
They sing of dying
And universal destruction.

Of shame and grief,
Of sickness in solitude,
Of our dark-eyed life,
Where Fear alone rules.

And, harkening to the prophecies,
Slowly, dully I live,
Indifferently waiting
For them to be fulfilled.

I remember, there was a word: wings . . .
Or am I raving? It's all the same!
Now I'm sinking to the bottom
Without a struggle, and without complaint.

Zinaida Gippius, 1904

The Unknown Woman

In the evenings above the restaurants
The hot air is wild and thick,
And a vernal and putrid spirit
Reigns over a drunken din.

Far off above the narrow, dusty streets,
Above the boredom of country houses,
A pretzel glints gold on a baker's sign,
And a child's crying resounds.

And every evening, beyond the railway
Barrier, experienced wits,
Cocking bowler hats, with ladies,
Stroll among the ditches.

Above the lake the rowlocks squeak,
And a woman's squeal resounds,
And in the sky, inured to all,
A disc senselessly frowns.

And every evening my only friend
Is reflected in my glass,
Like me, subdued and stupefied
By a tart and mysterious draught.

And near us, at adjacent tables,
Sleepy lackeys hang out,
And "In vino veritas!"
Drunks with eyes like rabbits' shout.

And every evening at the appointed hour
(Or do I just imagine it?)
Behind the misty windowpane
Moves a maiden figure swathed in silks.

And slowly, passing through the drunks,
Breathing perfumes and faraway mists,
Without an escort, always alone,
Close to the window she sits.

And her feathered mourning hat,
And her resilient silks,
And her delicate hand in rings
Respire ancient myths.

Entranced by her strange proximity,
I peer beyond her veil,
And see enchanted distances,
And enchanted lands.

Obscure secrets are entrusted to me,
Someone's sun to me alone is bestowed,
And the tart wine has penetrated
The deepest furrows of my soul.

And the bowed ostrich feathers
Sway gently in my brain,
And fathomless blue eyes
Blossom on a distant plain.

In my soul lies a treasure,
And the key is mine alone!
You are right, you drunken monster!
In wine is truth, I know.

Alexander Blok, 1906

Starting Anew

We want to create—and to destroy.
We will start everything anew, from the beginning.
Is the stubborn soul really tired
Of dying and resurrecting?

We will start everything anew. Stop,
Cheerlessly humming distaff,
Long decayed thread, break!
I will miss nothing from the past.

And if you do not break, we will cut you.
Pure is my wrathful blow.
We will divide our being with a sword:
The glimmering blade has been honed.

Zinaida Gippius, 1907

The White Goat

Alexander Kondratiev

Artemis lay in the shade of a branching elm tree and longed with all her heart for sleep. The hunt, two days long without a break, had tired the virgin goddess. The big, white-legged moose had raced tirelessly through the wooded ravines, struggling furiously to free himself from the pack of dogs that clung to him. The bloodthirsty dogs kept after him, barking incessantly.

Twice he shook free of them, leaving a few whimpering where they lay, and ran off with the rest in pursuit. But as he was about to throw them off a third time, Artemis herself approached, far ahead of her retinue.

The spear that never misses its mark whistled through the air, and the beast fell to its knees. The hounds brought him down, and the crimson blood flowing from his wounds stained their savage muzzles.

The drawn-out modulations of the goddess's hunting horn carried merrily through the green forest and shady ravines. But her companions didn't respond, as they usually did, with their own merry signals. Exhausted from their labours, the huntresses had fallen far behind and did not hear the summons. Scattered about the forest, they were resting in the undergrowth and in grottos.

The goddess blew the horn again, but, hearing no answer, guessed that her companions had lagged behind and would be some time in gathering again. Then Artemis concluded that she had better rest as well.

She lay down on the soft grass beneath the spreading elm; her faithful hounds, panting wearily, settled down around her. Placing her quiver beneath her head, the goddess closed her eyes.

The excitement still coursing through Artemis and the strong scent of the flowers made it difficult to fall asleep. Unease about the companions she had left behind roused troubled thoughts. More than a few shaggy satyrs were doubtlessly roaming the dense, untamed forest. Several times during the chase the goddesses had run close to frightening precipices, from the depths of which rose choking fumes. Monsters could be nesting there, or even worse, the terrible divinities that had ruled the earth before the Olympians . . .

Artemis sighed and worried, but little by little fatigue overcame her. The flowers' aromas were dizzying; the leaves on the trees whispered; all around the grass rustled, and it seemed to the goddess that the flowers and trees were singing her a quiet lullaby:

> Sleep, O beautiful goddess,
> Worn out from the hunt, go to sleep.
> Let your eyes as bright as stars
> No longer watchful keep.
>
> Fuzzy bees buzz lazily
> Flowers spill sweet aroma,
> Embraced by dreams so languorously
> Sleep, daughter of Latona!
>
> Through the sedge wind whispers,
> Maples murmur in chorus,
> Zeus's bright-eyed daughter
> Wanders the deep oak forest.
>
> In the densest forest's glades,
> Her arrow ready to loose,
> The virgin of bold gaze
> Tracks the mighty moose.
>
> Whose lance flies unerring?
> Who is swift as the wind?
> Who is fearless and daring,
> Most dazzling of her friends?

You, O daughter of Latona,
You, Zeus's beloved daughter!
Flowers spill their aroma.
Sleep, your dreams untroubled! . . .

Before she knew it, the goddess was asleep.

She dreamt she was hunting at night that same indefatigable moose. He was running as fast as ever, leaping now and then from the crags, swimming across swift currents on which the white foam gleamed under the silvery full moon. The shouts of her friends, the sound of horns and the baying of hounds mingled with the sound of waterfalls. And the white-legged moose ran on and on until it finally leapt off a precipice. Artemis, having far outdistanced both dogs and companions once again, leaned down to see what had become of the beast, and she trembled with horror. At the bottom of the precipice a frightening hulk was stirring, like a mass of snakes, a bull and a man all in one. Now and then it raised its tentacle-like arms and let out nasty, panting breaths. Artemis seized her bow, but her quiver was empty—all the arrows had spilled out during the chase; instead of a heavy lance, she found Dionysus's thyrsus in her hand . . .

The monster raised itself up on its coils, and its horrible, bull-like head panted out, "Mother Earth has heard my prayers and sent me a bride garbed in a short tunic. Come into my fond embrace!"

The long, hellish tentacles snaked round the goddess's bare knees. After the tentacles came the rest of the loathsome body, now crawling out of the ravine . . . Artemis had already despaired of rescue, but suddenly a large white goat appeared at the top of a nearby cliff. The animal's long fleece gleamed silver in the moonlight. His dark eyes attentively took in the scene. He lowered his head and sprang onto the meadow, from which the monster was already drawing the goddess down into its deep chasm . . .

The charging goat's sharp horns struck the abductor's soft flesh with terrible force.

The monster moaned, let go of its prey and dropped

heavily to the bottom of the chasm. Artemis shuddered . . . and awoke.

The sun was already quite low, illuminating the surrounding cliffs, which were grown over with wild forest. Long shadows spread over the meadow. The dogs were chasing a hare somewhere not too far away. Now and then their insistent, frenzied barking carried from the groves.

Her companions had still not arrived. The dead moose's dark carcass lay motionless nearby.

The goddess looked around, and an uneasy feeling came over her. She was all by herself at the centre of a small meadow. The surroundings were very much like what she had seen in her dream. And then, as if to crown the resemblance, a big white goat emerged from the forest grove and proceeded directly towards Artemis.

He approached the goddess calmly, and when he was but a few steps away, he knelt and bowed his horned head. The goddess was so touched by his submissiveness that she allowed the beast to lick her hands.

"If the dream comes true," she thought to herself, "then this goat is to save me from the monster born of Gaia; whoever he is, I'll not let him leave me."

Artemis's magnificent hand lay upon the white, fluffy fleece and sank pleasantly into the warm wool. The goddess put her arms around the beast, who nuzzled her trustingly. Love and devotion shone in his brown, slightly cunning eyes.

The goddess thought she remembered seeing eyes like these somewhere before. "Where could I have seen them?" she thought, as her arms twined round the beast's neck.

The goat merely lay down alongside her, gently and submissively, as if fearing to disturb the tranquillity of the virgin sister of Apollo.

Artemis's fright dissolved. Cold night drew on. One by one the stars came out in the sky . . .

"How nice it is when you have a devoted creature close by, and you can warm yourself in his soft fleece. He'll protect me from the monsters better than my own dogs, wherever they've disappeared to . . ." thought the daughter of Latona to herself as she drifted off . . .

Strange dreams visited Artemis before morning. She dreamt she was marrying a shaggy satyr, as the song of hideous forest folk rang out. Instead of her dear companions, she was constantly surrounded by repulsive swamp nymphs. Large frogs, smeared from head to foot in slimy mud, made up the wedding chorus; their loud croaking resounded ominously in Artemis's ear. Now her betrothed was giving her his shaggy paw, and the goddess, not daring to resist, followed him into the mouth of a dark grotto. There she suffered his caresses, which made her cheeks flame, and her heart alternately pounded and sank.

And this torture lasted a long, long time.

Inquisitive nymphs, little goat-footed satyrs and various forest folk shoved against one another near the entrance, whispering back and forth, clapping their hands, hopping up and down, squeaking and laughing shrilly.

But now someone's laughter rang out louder and louder, drowning out every other voice, filling the forest with its booming peals; the green hills and ravines answered in a victorious, joyous echo.

Artemis sighed deeply and woke up. In a cold sweat, pale, her hair loosed, she sprang to her feet and looked around.

There was no one next to her.

The goat that had come to her in the night had vanished.

Had she perhaps dreamt him? No, the prints of his sharp hooves were there in the earth.

Nearby the body of the dead moose lay motionless. Already swarms of golden flies hummed over it, basking in the sun's bright rays.

The dogs, who had returned towards morning, were settled down close by her. The goat had probably taken cover as they approached . . .

But far, far away in the mountains, peals of someone's merry laughter rang out.

"Only Pan laughs like that," the goddess thought, and her dreams from the night before suddenly and unaccountably stirred in her head, bringing a flush to her pale cheeks.

342

She listened again.

"No, that's not laughter," decided the goddess in a moment. "Now it sounds like the echo of hunting horns . . . It's my companions."

And truly, on the narrow path from beyond the neighbouring hill, one by one, nymphs armed with bows appeared. Some led fierce dogs on leashes; others held short, sharp lances in their hands.

Artemis, immobile as a statue, gazed sternly at them . . .

Meanwhile, surrounded by his devoted nymphs, a satisfied, triumphant Pan was laughing merrily.

"How did you manage it?" his astonished, slightly frowning hamadryads asked.

"Oh, it was quite a feat. I bid the flowers and grasses to whisper dreams full of horrors to her as she slept—horrors from which a white goat would rescue her. Then, just as she awoke, I approached Artemis in the form of that very goat, and I began to nuzzle her. It worked well. She was even unwilling to let me go, and she fell asleep with her arms around my neck. At that point, I could not resist, and I gave her a kiss or two.

"In the morning the returning dogs disturbed me. I had lured them away the evening before with a quick-footed hare, who led them a merry chase before they finally caught him . . . When they appeared, I made haste to leave.

"But please, don't tell anyone!"

It is a foolish man who trusts a woman. In no time Hellas and Phrygia, Thrace, Crete and Cyprus all learnt what had happened to Apollo's sister. The merry nereids spread the news to even the very smallest islands.

Pallas gloated. Hermes laughed loudly. Demeter shook her head sadly, and for three days scowling Phoebus went around looking glum.

From the gods, people learnt about it as well. They told one another in whispers about Pan's bold cunning, and secretly laughed at how poor Artemis had been deceived . . .

And that is why every year a curly-horned, white goat is brought to her for sacrifice.

343

About the Authors

Leonid Andreyev (1871–1919) was a popular writer who was deeply influenced by decadent tendencies at the beginning of the twentieth century. He grew up in poverty, lost his father when he was a child, became an alcoholic and tried to commit suicide three times. He declared that he hoped his work would influence readers to kill themselves and reportedly collected suicide notes they sent to him. In the first years of the century he was associated with the Realist circle around Maxim Gorky. His most famous works are the novella *The Red Laugh* and the short story "The Abyss," included here.

Alexander Blok (1880–1921), poet, playwright and critic, is the most famous poet of the so-called "second generation" of Symbolists, those who began to publish after the turn of the twentieth century. He was born into a family of the cultured elite: his father was a professor; his mother, a writer. Influenced by the cult of Sophia promoted by the philosopher Vladimir Solovyov, he began his poetic career with verses to a "beautiful lady," the mystical "eternal feminine" capable of transfiguring the world. "The Unknown Woman," included here, is one of his most renowned poems. His other famous poems include "The Twelve" and "The Scythians."

Valery Briusov (1873–1924), writer, critic and editor of the Symbolist journal *The Balance*, was the leader of the Symbolist movement. He was, perhaps, the most important representative of the so-called "first generation" of Symbolists, those who began to publish before the turn of the century. He posed as a Satanist, dabbled in the occult and promoted suicide. He contemplated suicide himself on several occasions, including joint suicide with his mistress Nina Petrovskaya in a moment of ecstasy. He also championed extreme individualism and knowledge gained through non-rational means, including sexual passion and creative intuition. His lifelong interest in Roman history, which he studied at Moscow University, is reflected in his work, as is his profound erudition and his interest in modern French literature. Briusov is best known for his poetry, his novel *The Fiery Angel* and the short story "The Republic of the Southern Cross," included here.

Zinaida Gippius (also known as Hippius, 1869–1945), writer and critic, was a first-generation Symbolist. She and her husband Dmitry Merezhkovsky, with whom she had a chaste marriage, advocated an idiosyncratic brand of Christianity they hoped would transfigure the world. To this end they organised the Religious-Philosophical Meetings in St. Petersburg and founded the journal *The New Way*. She dressed to shock, wearing men's clothes or eccentric dresses and smoking cigarettes in a cigarette holder. She and her husband entered into a number of Platonic love triangles with both men and women, and while married she exchanged erotic correspondence with two women, as well as with several men. She was rumoured to be a hermaphrodite. Although her writings evince decadent tendencies, she vociferously denounced decadence.

Alexander Kondratiev (1876–1967) is all but unknown to English readers and unjustly forgotten even in Russia. While working as a secretary in the Ministry of Transportation and subsequently in the Office of the State Duma, in the early twentieth century he hosted readings at his St. Petersburg home and frequented Symbolist literary evenings, although he did not consider himself a Symbolist. He did not consider himself a decadent either; nevertheless, his erotic reworkings of classical myths deserve to be read within the context of Russian decadence.

Dmitry Merezhkovsky (1866–1941), writer and religious philosopher, was a first-generation Symbolist like his wife, Zinaida Gippius (see above). Merezhkovsky is best known for his historical novels, including *Leonardo da Vinci*. His poem "Children of the Night," included here, is canonical.

Fyodor Sologub (1863–1927), a second-generation Symbolist, is considered by some commentators to be the arch-decadent of Russian literature. He is known chiefly for his poetry and his scandalous novel *The Petty Demon*. His favourite themes include suicide and sadomasochism, and these were not just literary obsessions for him: he attempted suicide several times and well into adulthood he apparently enjoyed being whipped by his mother and possibly, after her death, his sister. The son of recently liberated serfs, Sologub started out as a provincial schoolteacher, and his mother made him walk to school and teach barefoot to set an example of humility. In 1892 he moved to St. Petersburg, where he worked first as a teacher and later as a school inspector.